Mauled, Maimed, Mangled, Mutilated Mythology

Mauled, Maimed, Mangled, Mutilated Mythology

by

Jay Dubya

www.bookstandpublishing.com

Published by
Bookstand Publishing
Pasadena, CA 91101
1892_8

ISBN 978-1-58909-217-4

Other Books by Jay Dubya

Adult Fiction

Black Leather and Blue Denim, A '50s Novel
The Great Teen Fruit War, A 1960' Novel
Frat' Brats, A '60s Novel
Ron Coyote, Man of La Mangia
Pieces of Eight
Pieces of Eight, Part II
Pieces of Eight, Part III
Pieces of Eight, Part IV
The Wholly Book of Genesis
The Wholly Book of Exodus
The Wholly Book of Doo-Doo-Rot-on-Me
Thirteen Sick Tasteless Classics
Thirteen Sick Tasteless Classics, Part II
Thirteen Sick Tasteless Classics, Part III
Thirteen Sick Tasteless Classics, Part IV
Thirteen Sick Tasteless Classics, Part V
So Ya' Wanna' Be A Teacher
RAM: Random Articles and Manuscripts
Fractured Frazzled Folk Fables and Fairy Farces
FFFF&FF, Part II
Nine New Novellas
Nine New Novellas, Part II
Nine New Novellas, Part III
Nine New Novellas, Part IV
One Baker's Dozen
Two Baker's Dozen
Shakespeare: Slammed, Smeared, Savaged & Slaughtered
Shakespeare: Slammed, Smeared, Savaged & Slaughtered, Part II
Suite 16
Time Travel Tales
Snake Eyes and Boxcars
Snake Eyes and Boxcars, Part II
UFO: Utterly Fantastic Occurrences
The Psychic Dimension
The Psychic Dimension, Part II

Contents

Gods of Mt. Olympus

<u>Greek Name</u>	<u>Roman Name</u>
Zeus	Jupiter
Poseidon	Neptune
Hades	Pluto
Athena	Minerva
Hera	Juno
Aphrodite	Venus
Apollo	Apollo
Hermes	Mercury
Ares	Mars
Cronus	Saturn
Hephaestus	Vulcan
Artemis	Diana

"Pandora"

Many people erroneously believe that money makes the world go around. That is an absolutely false assumption. Actually, pussy makes the world go around, so this is the story of the first pussy ever created (according to the ancient Greeks), *Pandora's Box.*

The tale starts with the minor Greek god Prometheus, who in addition to liking pornography and engaging in voyeurism watching animals perform sodomy, had an empathetic soft spot in his heart for humans. The *Olympians* had overthrown the *Titans* in a great revolution, and Zeus, the new ruler, trusted Prometheus, so the minor deity was the only *Titan* allowed to live on *Mt. Olympus.* The remaining *Titans* were either given punishments to endure, or provided a task to perform like *Atlas* "holding up the sky", and thus *he* became the first official bandit in Greek mythology.

Prometheus sat on a tiny purple-clothed toilet seat in his marble. windowless apartment inside the basement of *Mt. Olympus,* thinking about how men could successfully use fire to cremate bodies, to practice arson, to become perverted, or to behave like wild and crazy pyromaniacs.

Meanwhile, Almighty Zeus was considering how he could limit man's use of fire, even though Prometheus had never mentioned it directly to the King-god that *he* had planned to give man "the gift". 'Prometheus might be planning a counter-revolution against me and the *Olympians,*' Zeus conjectured. 'These jerk-off' Titans must really be dumb, or stupid, or both! If Prometheus gives man fire, then that will really burn me up and sizzle my testicles!'

Then, Zeus pondered some more upon his platinum throne. 'Men must be doomed to suffer without fire, for if the race is ever given that secret gift by Prometheus, the maniac fools could forge metals, make weapons, and threaten the gods with *their* new-found technology. We might even need a damned fire department up here on *Mt. Olympus!* What in 'blazes' is wrong with *that* fucked-up asshole!'

It was an unwritten law of *Mt. Olympus* that once mankind acquired a gift such as fire, or immortality, the gods could not take it away. Why such a shitty divine law was ever created is beyond human understanding or reasoning. Perhaps the *Olympians* couldn't really prevent men from discovering dangerous ideas, and were afraid of human intelligence and its great potential. At any rate, the gods were authoring their own self-destruction by being too liberal with men and by honoring dumb laws that would eventually leave every temple in ancient Greece just about empty and in ruin. "The *Olympic* torch belongs up here on *Mt. Olympus* and nowhere else!" Zeus pontificated to his apathetic council of gods.

"What could we do?" Hera asked her aggravated husband. "This crisis seems quite urgent!"

"I'll give man a gift that is bound to trick *his* demented species into being subordinate to *Olympus* fiat forever," Zeus hypothesized and stated to his totally-bored spouse. "I'll get even with Prometheus for giving man fire without my consent, and independently going against *my* indomitable will. This new gift will have two round firm tits, and a nice hairy, delicious, pink honey-well that will distract men from inventing and discovering anything for the balance of history. In fact," Zeus elaborated, "history will never begin because mankind will never learn how to write, since his little mind will be preoccupied with stupid tits and ass all the time. Hera, I'm getting half a hard-on just thinking about it. And so," the king-god continued. "We'll have mythology forever without any history interfering, as long as man keeps thinking about idiotic distractions like tits and ass! Long live beaver, that's what the *Hades* I have to say! Yes; long live beaver!"

"Keep it hard dear husband and let's roll in the sack!" Hera suggested. "Zeus; I believe it's now time for you to pop your wonderful weasel!"

After putting the salami to Hera three times, Zeus summoned Hephaestus, the lame blacksmith god, to his throne room and said, "I have put together a new schematic that is unlike anything else down there on Earth. I'll give you the formula to create the female specimen, but make sure it has big breasts like Hera, and a nice sweet, luscious, pink pussy like Aphrodite has. But Hephaestus," Zeus lectured. "I want you to make sure you also mingle in deceit to balance beauty; curiosity to counterweight cunning, and wickedness to go with all the confectionary bullshit. And finally," the king-god declared, "throw in a little sugar and spice and everything nice, and let's see what the fuck your asshole experiments come-up with!"

"I don't know," Hephaestus honestly answered, "but I'm getting a firm erection just thinking about it! Wow! I'm going to pop a load that's gonna' fly off the top of *Olympus* and destroy a whole damned male homo' village down on Earth!"

"Those gay bastards down on Earth are a bunch of queer bait faggots," Zeus concluded. "So, the creation of females will make those homosexual fairies go *straight,* just like their diminutive erections!"

Hephaestus shuffled down the long marble corridor to his cluttered laboratory, which was actually a dirty old, scummy furnace room where the lame blacksmith god forged metals and counterfeit gold coins, and frequently screwed Zeus's horny wife Hera on the various work benches. The metalworking craftsman took gold, silver, dross, nail polish, and lipstick (among other secret unknown ingredients) and mixed them with rain, snow, sleet, hail, mud, honey, gallstones. and kidney stones. The crippled blacksmith god then removed the flowers from a dozen roses, and blended them with snake venom; and with the voice of a babbling brook, and the squall of a female peacock in heat in need of a stiff peacock's cock to shut it up from squawking and begging to get laid over and over again.

Hephaestus next took the ocean's majesty, and the sea's stormy nature, and mixed those elements with a female bitch's (dog's) fury and faithfulness. Aphrodite's ugly husband mixed into the recipe the lion's ferocity, and the mother robin's love for her fledglings. All of those factors Hephaestus swished-together into one concoction, and then molded the new creation into the shape that Zeus had prescribed.

"What the fuck am I doing?" Hephaestus questioned as the notorious bronze craftsman felt the tits and the pussy of the still inanimate specimen. "Am I turning into a pervert or what? The next thing I know, I'll be sleeping with a fuckin' inflatable doll and screwing the shit out of it, too!"

When the new combination of atoms and molecules was finally formed, Hephaestus admired his handiwork and said aloud, "This is no new object. I have merely created a new goddess's image, but I still feel extremely horny just looking at its naked beauty." So, Hephaestus hollered-down to the nearest village on Earth, "Watch out you assholes, and immediately run for cover! You're going to be deluged with a swift savage sperm storm!" right before a thousand-pound ejaculation was ejected from the summit of *Mt. Olympus,* and the gooey mess swiftly hurtled-down into the gay village's main hut like a tremendous wet meteor.

After destroying the main "Public Affairs" hut of the gay village down on Earth with his massive ejaculation, Hephaestus approached Zeus with the model of his latest creation. "Lord Zeus; I followed your directions to the letter," the industrious blacksmith god acknowledged. "But all we've done is made a statue of a goddess with Hera's bust, and Aphrodite's blonde bush. Gee, do I feel like shooting more sperm meteors into the stratosphere!"

"No, Hephaestus," Zeus laughed and corrected. "You've successfully manufactured the first woman." Then the king-god breathed upon the sexy statue, and it suddenly lived, batting her eyelashes; licking her lips; wondering whom she was, and exactly what the fuck was happening.

Then, Zeus summoned all of the other *Olympians* to gaze-upon the first mortal woman, who immediately wanted to hop into the sack with all of them, regardless whether the gods were male or female, or whether the goddesses were male or female.

"She is as lovely as any goddess," Hera observed with a trace of jealousy. "And her tits are as round and as firm as mine are!"

"Zeus; your' screwing-around making this lovely female has made me want to screw around also," Apollo *apolo*gized as a serious bulge appeared in the center of his royal purple tunic. "Down boy! Down boy!"

"Her breasts are as big as Hera's are!" Athena verbally marveled, "while mine are as small as they had been before I entered puberty! What a nasty bummer! Where the *Hades* are my fuckin' sleeping, latent hormones?"

"Now it's time to invent the bikini!" Poseidon, god of the sea chimed-in. "I'd surrender my trident and my left nut right now just for a piece of *that* action!"

The *Olympian* gods and goddesses all agreed that the deities would each provide the first woman with a gift on *her* first birthday, which had amazingly eluded infancy, juvenile delinquency, and adolescent puberty. Hephaetus's secret formula and Zeus's breath had more than done the dual work of a vagina and a functional womb.

Athena, Hera, Artemis, and Aphrodite clad the first woman in splendid apparel, and also provided her with a year's supply of sanitary napkins and aspirin-like tablets to take for her menstrual mood shifts and their' accompanying *periodic* personality disorders.

Hephaestus adorned the "First Lady" (who incidentally was never married to any U.S. President) with sapphires, emeralds, rubies, diamonds, rhinestone bracelets, and gaudy tawdry artificial jewelry. Apollo gave the first woman a girdle, pink panties, and a bra, so that the men's imaginations (of naked ladies) would make the curves of women appear very seductive and desirable. In that way, man's thought processes would be geared to having sex, and not aimed toward creating weapons and inventions that would rival the gods.

Poseidon gave the first woman a huge dildo to use when no men were around to service her alluring snatcheroo. And lastly, Hermes offered the first woman a bouquet of flowers he had obtained by flying to the distant future and stealing the gift from an *FTD* florist delivery store.

Zeus then presented the voluptuous new female with a trunk of glimmering amber that had a lid adorned with flowers, pomegranates, and prickly porcupine quills. The amber chest had two polished semi-circular golden snakes that served as handles.

"Check her out," Zeus commanded to his illustrious colleagues. "This new woman we have created is really the cat's meow that can make any impotent man have an instant erection and blast messy, sticky ejaculations all over the damned place! She is indeed endowed with heaven's most magnificent treasures," Zeus imperially indicated. "And I can't wait to take away her virginity and pump the poop out of her, so to speak! Of course, I'll have to swallow some pride and shrink-down from fifty-foot-tall to six-foot-tall, and my famed penis will have to contract from three-foot-long to a mere twelve inches in length, but I can live with that compromise for at least a half-hour of sublime pleasure!"

"What shall we name the beautiful bitch?" Apollo asked.

"Her name will be Pandora," Zeus attested, "which means 'All-Gifted', including anything from exotic couch dancing to administering good professional blow-jobs. But Pandora is mortal and not fit to be a permanent mate for an *Olympian* stud like you or me. She is to be used to trick the men down on Earth to not make weapons to challenge us Olympus residents."

"Then, why have you tempted and teased us with her abundant charms?" Hermes challenged. "Why do you make me want and lust for what I can't have?"

"Because Shit-head!" Zeus thundered, "I intend to send her down to Earth and wed Epimetheus, Prometheus's moronic brother, who can only see and understand things *after* they have happened, and then it is too late to do anything about them," Zeus maintained. "In this way, *we* can get even with Prometheus by cursing Epimetheus and all mankind with the first woman. *Olympus* and the *Olympians* will now be safe from the potential threat of human intelligence!"

"Way to go, Zeus Baby!" Apollo exclaimed. "You're so shrewd and sly that you could even sell ancient grease to ancient Greece!"

Zeus commanded Hermes (the official messenger god having wings on his sandals and on *his* bronze helmet) to conduct Pandora to Epimetheus's gay village residence, which somehow had been spared being demolished by Hephaestus's most recent violent sperm storm. "Tell the asshole," Zeus instructed Hermes, "that the king of the gods extends *his* goodwill in the form of this enchanting bride, who is also an ultra-fine screwing machine, in addition to being a woman possessing a fantastic dowry from *Olympus*."

So, Hermes delivered the first woman and dowry via *Olympus Express* to Arcadia, a pleasant northern region of ancient Greece, where the inhabitants fun-loving and carefree descendants would eventually learn how to invent sophisticated video and pinball machine games.

When the giant Epimetheus perceived what a knockout Pandora was, and learned that matrimony was her special assignment, the dumb-ass fool had three premature ejaculations during the day, and four white dreams that night, completely obliterating seven innocent gay men's villages clear across the *Aegean Sea* over in Asia Minor.

Prometheus's brother accepted his new bride with her extensive dowry into his house (which was actually a cave because Epimetheus's dwelling had been destroyed by one of Hephaestus's catastrophic sperm storms originating from atop *Mt. Olympus*). Epimetheus wedded Pandora that day without the services of any temple priest, and couldn't wait to get his noodle wet, so the absolute moron completely ignored Prometheus's prior warning about not receiving any gift from Zeus.

According to geeky Greek mythology, Prometheus was clairvoyant and had the power of prophecy; whereas, Epimetheus was a stubborn blockhead that couldn't see events until *after* they had happened. The following morning, the totally dense Earth inhabitant remembered *his* brother's statement, but it was too late to repent for accepting the Pandora, and for receiving the magnificent trunk.

Epimetheus finally realized that the dowry Zeus had conferred upon Pandora had been designed to effectively break *his* balls and to sever *his* aching hemorrhoids. "Pandora, have you opened your box yet?" Epimetheus asked.

"Of course, my dear husband," Pandora answered. "I opened my box eight times, and you screwed the crap out of me eight times last night like a young stud in heat! I think you should change your name from Epimetheus to Dick!"

"Pandora, I meant the amber casket Zeus had given you!" Epimetheus blushed and replied. "Did you open *that* box?"

"Oh no, my dear beloved spouse," Pandora answered. "However, I know right where it is, and am also eager to know precisely what the unscrupulous *Olympians* had placed inside it! I trust it's a wide array of new sex toys and pornographic drawings to actively stimulate *our* docile libidos!"

"Pandora, please listen carefully to what the *Hades* I have to say!" Epimetheus emphatically indicated. "I have a suspicion that your chest

6

contains some dangerous evil secret that will haunt us and our accursed descendants throughout the decadent decades to come."

"I assure you, dear husband," Pandora declared. "*My chest* simply contains hard flesh and erect nipples for you to suck on and fondle, and nothing else!"

"Damn it, Pandora! I meant *the chest* that Zeus had given you as a devious gift! Another word for a box is a chest! Learn the freakin' language, will ya'!" Epimetheus shouted at his beautiful, naïve and very gullible wife.

"Well, dear husband," Pandora responded. "If *you* think that my box is my chest, and that my chest is my box, then that's okay with me, as long as you keep licking and munching away at either! But when you decide to insert your erection inside my box," Pandora clarified, "make sure you don't try and shove it inside my sensitive chest!"

"Pandora," Epimetheus worriedly stated. "As long as we keep that amber casket, or trunk, or whatever you want to call it that Zeus gave you shut, and don't open the lid," the husband insisted, "then the actual difference between a box and a chest really doesn't matter one fuckin' bit. Anyway Pandora," the cretin husband continued, "the hole in that amber trunk Zeus gave you is too big to screw. Not even *Atlas's* enormous dick could fill up that gargantuan cavity!"

"I promise you, dear husband, that I will never be overwhelmed by curiosity to open that amber trunk," Pandora pledged. "All I desire to do is to admire its magnificent external beauty!"

The wife was elated that her after-the-fact, dim-witty husband had permitted her to keep the amber chest, and the spouse viewed the container with pride the entire day long, for no soap operas, B-movies, gardeners, butlers, male heterosexual neighbors, horny milkmen, or sex-minded newspaper delivery boys were around to distract her attention from the marvelous box.

But after several centuries of staring at the dumb amber chest, Pandora wondered what its contents might be. The temptation to look inside the three-dimensional, rectangular object was always present, but Pandora was afraid that Epimetheus would become livid and *flip his lid* if she were to flip hers.

When Epimetheus was out of the house inspecting the heavens for the next possible nasty sperm storm raining down from *Mt. Olympus,* the tantalizing amber box again inspired temptation to reign supreme inside Pandora's curious mind. The first woman laid her avaricious hands upon the delicate surface, lifted the latch, and slowly and apprehensively raised the lid.

A swarm of teeming, winged spirits immediately ascended, and then flew-out of the accursed amber trunk, swirling-around the cave, and then vanishing outside into the atmosphere to plague mankind for the remainder of *his* tenure upon this despicable planet.

Pandora swiftly closed the box with a loud jolt, but her futile effort was far too late to attain any satisfactory results. Tears of guilt and disappointment filled her eyes, for Pandora had released upon the world all of the grief, diseases, woes, and miseries that have afflicted the human race from womb to tomb since the mythological beginnings of antiquity.

Epimetheus entered the nondescript cave all covered with sticky *Olympian* sperm juice from another Hephaestus semen storm that had recently destroyed a neighboring gay village five-miles away. "Pandora, what have you done? I told you not to play with your box while I'm not around!" the brother of sagacious Prometheus strenuously interrogated.

"I'm sorry for opening *my box,*" the penitent wife cried. "But you got me so confused that I thought I was really opening *my chest* instead. At any rate, our unfortunate, doomed descendants are going to be royally screwed by Zeus and the *Olympians* for at least the next ten-thousand-years!"

"It's all partially my fault," Epimetheus reluctantly confessed as the stupid asshole wiped some excess sperm from his scalp and hair. "If only I could be like my brother Prometheus," the dolt reckoned. "Then, I could avoid divine orgasms, and also avoid evil surprises *before* they ever happen!"

And Epimetheus knew exactly what those unleashed evil spirits represented: death, famine, pestilence, disease, work, sickness, murder, theft, jealousy, envy, pride, war, constipation, diarrhea, and venereal warts. Thinking that all of the spirits had escaped the amber dowry box's interior, the sympathetic husband asked his upset-yet-obedient wife to cautiously lift the lid to examine the chest's mammoth compartment.

One timid, weaker spirit still occupied the interior, and it seemed afraid to escape its confinement. As the last sprite finally flapped its wings and fluttered upward, it then lamely ascended out of the chest. Pandora and Epimetheus instinctively knew that the last spirit was 'Hope', the only decent quality given by the gods for man to cope with all of the maladies and curses that had been surreptitiously packed within the evil container.

When Pandora saw that Hope could not easily fly around the room and leave the cave like the numerous malicious spirits had done, she pitied the orphaned sprite, held it to her firm breasts, and nursed it to good health. Hope felt so content that *it* managed to eat right through Pandora's enviable tits, and entered her warm heart, where inside women *it* has resided until this very day.

Ever since that historical, hysterical day, men intuitively know that their lips are sucking their way into a woman's heart when they wean on their wives, or their girlfriends' warm, receptive, erect nipples.

"Ceres Goes Against the Grain"

In Greek mythology, Ceres was the goddess of grain, who had a nasty reputation of tormenting all humans that deliberately or accidentally went against the grain. Since the ancient humans didn't have any police departments, or private dicks around (although men had dicks that were privates), Ceres became known as the world's first maniacal "cereal killer".

Ceres had only one daughter, Persephone, although the notorious goddess of grain couldn't remember ever having sex with anyone, male or female, including her elderly mentor, Celeus. Persephone was known as "the spring maiden" until she mysteriously died near a mountain spring in the spring, so Ceres became so distraught, and so pissed-off that she converted much of the Earth into a frozen wasteland, ten times worse than today's Tundra. Glaciers, snowdrifts, avalanches, and icebergs were all over the damned place, and the only happy creatures on the entire planet were polar bears, Eskimos, huskies, ptarmigans, and frigid women.

Hades, Zeus's screwed-up deadly brother and Lord of the Underworld, carried Persephone off to his subterranean domain in his black chariot, which was pulled by six dark-colored stallions. Ceres's daughter was swiftly transported to the Kingdom of the Dead, where she would help Hades govern over the souls of countless underworld figures, mythological racketeers, and their nefarious henchmen. Ceres rushed to the reported scene of her daughter's demise, but alas, everyone in the spring's vicinity was unaware of Persephone's death, and was casually eating ancient versions of *Rice Krispies, Wheaties, Corn Flakes* and oat-meal.

'Cheerio to this shit!' Ceres lamented. 'Why has Zeus caused me such fuckin' aggravation! Good grief! What am I saying? There isn't anything at all fuckin' good about grief!'

And so, for nine laborious, heart-wrenching days, Ceres wandered all over the frozen desert that was now devoid of nectar and ambrosia, the fertile fruits that ensured the gods' immortality. Soon, a mental transmission from Phoebus Apollo informed Ceres that her daughter had been escorted to Hades, and that Persephone now had become the Death god's wife and queen. The grain goddess immediately left the safety of *Mt. Olympus* and dwelled on the cold Earth, wearing a disguise to keep her unique identity secret from men and gods alike.

Soon thereafter, Ceres arrived in the frozen village of Eleusis, where all of the men were livid because all of their wives and girlfriends had suddenly become frigid, having large ice cubes filling their vaginas. Four frigid sisters came to the village well to draw-up ice chunks to be melted over a fire into drinking water.

"What are you doing here in our remote village?" the oldest cold sister asked Ceres. "Are you left over from the last *Ice Age?*"

"I had been captured by pirates, who all looked like penguins from a distant future city called Pittsburgh," Ceres imaginatively lied. "I've come to this peculiar place seeking shelter and political asylum, although your hamlet looks like a fuckin' insane mental asylum to me. Could you possibly afford me a safe haven? I'm a refugee seeking refuge, if ya' four stupid ugly shits know what the fuck I mean!"

After the four giddy imbeciles filled their wooden pitchers with ice chunks, the quartet anxiously rushed home to inform their mother Metaneira of the strange stranger, looking for an igloo apartment, who had just entered Eleusis. The four adolescent dunces quickly returned to the well where the veiled goddess still sat, sucking on three long icicles, thinking that each was a cold carrot-shaped erection.

"Come home to our ice-house!" the eldest sister requested. "I'll introduce you to our mother and to our Aunt Arctica."

Ceres followed the mentally-challenged girls to their newly-built, three-storied igloo, and the goddess of grain was introduced to Metaneira, who was holding her infant son over her shoulder to burp the little asshole. Everyone in the doltish family suspected that the lady guest was not any random, ordinary personage wandering around the village well, looking for well-wishers during the harsh winter weather. The concerned mother felt obligated to initiate a friendly conversation.

"Won't you have a seat?" Metaneira asked her disguised visitor, pointing to a block of ice. "Please sample the last of our honey-sweet wine. Ever since the most recent *Ice Age,* everything including our wine, has been sour-grapes around here."

"I would prefer some barley-flavored water mixed with mint," Ceres answered in a polite tone of voice. "I need to fuckin' get ripped, because I too am suffering from a bitchin' freakin' cold heart, just like the rest of you shit-head featherbrains."

Now Metaneria had very tiny tits that could not produce sufficient milk for her newborn son, so Ceres lifted little Demophoon to her healthy chest, popped her left boob out of her robe, and expertly nursed the irritated litter wiener into a happy little weaner. And over the course of the next several months, the child grew into a strong specimen, because when everyone else in the igloo was sleeping, Ceres smeared the baby's body with her remaining nectar and ambrosia, and roasted his little ass over the fire in order to provide Demophoon with the wonderful gifts of immortality, and of possessing very large impressive genitals.

One night, Metaneira became restless and awoke from her slumber. The neurotic woman entered the igloo's main chamber and witnessed her toddler strapped to a rotisserie over the fireplace's open flames. The shocked mother screamed in horror at what she considered a satanic ritual being enacted before her very eyes.

"Your unwarranted curiosity has angered and infuriated me!" Ceres yelled at startled Metaneira. "Just for you being overly nosy, your asshole son will now be deprived of immortality, and will experience human hardship and mortal death. But the little sucker shall still be weaned on my succulent hard breasts, and Demophoon will be destined to earn and gain a degree of prestigious honor, despite his mother's tiny tits and her damned diabolical, overwhelming curiosity."

And then, much to Metaneira's astonishment, a radiant light glowed around the house-guest's total being, and the homeowner at once recognized her visitor as being Ceres, the volatile, corny, flakey goddess of grain.

"You and your villagers must construct a temple and dedicate it to me!" the goddess austerely commanded the still-astounded mother. "You and your fellow residents must win back my heart's favor, or else I'll beat the living shit out of all of you, and change all of the ice into freezing water, making the whole lot of you' vulnerable fuck-heads drown while experiencing extreme hypothermia. So now, because of your intolerable insolence," Ceres vehemently squawked, "I must bid you and your fucked-up igloo Cheerio!"

Ceres abruptly dropped the child into his wooden cradle without even covering him with a sheet of ice or a blanket of snow. Celeus, the village's eight-hundred-year-old elder, and also Demophoon's biological father, organized his people and commanded the other men to build a spectacular temple to Ceres so that *he* could go around Eleusis, house to house, and systematically screw all of their frigid wives, aunts, nieces and daughters while the other males were laboring, building the sensational temple. And when the monumental 'temple task' had been completed, Celeus died of dehydration, and was buried without ceremony or sympathy in a cemetery ice hole.

Then, Ceres returned to Eleusis and sat inside her newly constructed, desolate temple, mourning, grieving and longing for her lost Persephone. But Ceres could not be comforted, even with the glory of her mere impeccable, recently-fabricated ice temple, so the grain goddess invented the weather pattern known as "a blizzard", and condemned the *ice*olated village of Eleusis to continuously feel the terrible winter storm's brunt.

"This winter bull-shit weather really sucks!" Metaneira balked to her mentally deficient daughters. "The blizzard really sucks, and the wind really blows! I don't know which wicked devastation is fuckin' worse! How could that devastating wind possibly ever be a howling success?"

That ninety-day winter period had been the most dreadful calamity in Eleusis's unrecorded history. Nothing grew; not even pubic hairs, or penises, or vaginal warts. Seeds were so barren that they couldn't even be planted under five-foot of frozen terrain. The only satisfied creatures on the Earth were oxen that did not have to drag plows forming long farm furrows in the permafrost. Everyone seemed fated to die from famine, and from an apparent lack of sex.

Zeus looked-down upon the frozen Earth, and became incensed that no one was worshipping his magnificence. He sent the other Olympians, one at a time, down to confer with Ceres, in order to end the ongoing winter, but each envoy returned unsuccessfully from his or her appointed mission. Human apathy towards the gods was rapidly spreading like sexually transmitted diseases.

"Ceres will not stop this new phenomenon known as winter until she gets to see her daughter, Persephone!" Hermes announced to the king-god. "Until then, we'll all have to pretend that we're rabbits that only have iceberg lettuce to eat."

"My brother Hades must relinquish his grip on Persephone, or else it'll be eternal salads instead of delicious nectar and ambrosia," Zeus protested to Hermes. "And without nectar and ambrosia growing upon the Earth, both you and I are fuckin' destined to first become obsolete, and next become distinctly extinct!"

"What should we do?" Hermes inquisitively asked. "It's no longer necessary for humans to invent ice-boxes or refrigerators, because there's no longer any foods worthy of preserving!"

"Hermes, I want you to journey-down to the Underworld, but you ought to be very sure you stay away from the Greek Mafia!" Zeus commanded his dependable messenger. "Tell my incorrigible brother Hades to allow Persephone to temporarily return to her mother Ceres, or else one of my frozen thunderbolts will penetrate yours and his sensitive assholes all the way up to your fuckin' esophagus! And then, both of you' assholes will be fuckin' dramatically electrocuted from the inside-out!"

Hermes *bolted* out of Zeus's white marble *Mt. Olympus* temple, and proceeded with dispatch down the dark tunnel that led to Hades' dismal subterranean realm. When Persephone saw the handsome courier god, she eagerly rose from her morbid ebony throne to hear his promising message. And after Hermes delivered the edict from Zeus, Hades reluctantly gave *his* consent to honor the chief god's proclamation.

"Persephone; you must accompany Hermes back to Earth to appease my crazy, unpredictable brother's wrath," Hades suggested to his pallid-faced wife. "If you don't follow Zeus's instructions, my Kingdom of the Dead will soon be overpopulated with corpses, and I'll then have to work my ass off reorganizing the whole fuckin' ghostly operation. And once a god of my stature becomes lazy as I have become," the lethargic Hades emphasized, "then the damned idea of work becomes rather repugnant to me, and its nasty implementation absolutely contrary to my present damned, easygoing, indolent nature!"

"I will do as My Lords direct!" Persephone amiably stated and consented. "Is there anything else I need to know before Hermes leads me out of this foul, despicable hellhole?"

"Why yes," Hades answered with a grim expression upon his countenance. "I insist that you swallow this pomegranate seed, so that you'll be required by fate to return to me in the near future."

Hades reluctantly harnessed his dark horses, and adroitly attached the mighty steeds to his black metal chariot. The death god then handed the reins over to Hermes, and soon the messenger god and Persephone entered the stellar *heavy metal* chariot that featured music sung by the ancient rock group *Styx Flags*. The horses rushed upward, and rapidly ascended the steep tunnel leading to the now-sterile frozen Earth. Soon, Persephone was delivered outside the newly-constructed ice temple in Eleusis, where Ceres persisted in grieving for her lost daughter.

Persephone ran up the cold, snow-laden steps; tripped on a sheet of ice, and after sliding on her ass a full hundred-feet, soon found herself in her mother's waiting arms. The mother and daughter were overjoyed at being reunited.

"Hades made me swallow a pomegranate seed," Persephone revealed to her mom, "so I had to take it with a *grain* of salt, if ya' know what the Hades I mean."

"Yes, my dear daughter," Ceres admitted as the grain goddess embraced her offspring in consolation. "But I must honor King Zeus's mandate, while fully recognizing that your macabre husband Hades is indeed a very *seedy* character."

Then, Zeus sent his mother *Rhea* as a messenger to Ceres's ice temple, without *her* new husband *Dia*, mostly because the king-god didn't want smelly liquid feces laying all over the already-frozen Earth. Rhea, the oldest of the Olympians, hurried-down to what she now described as "terra-frozen-firma", and made her extraordinary announcement in the form of a poem, which was didactically addressed to Persephone.

"It is Zeus's command that you' return to Hades,
To unhappily rejoin all of the other dead stiff ladies.
You'll have great honor in the Underworld halls,
Where all the men and boys, no longer have dicks and balls.
You must for nine months endure your bad luck,
And then in three months' time, you'll be allowed to fuck.
And in that three-month interval, you will discover,
You'll be permitted to live with your fucked-up mother.
And you'll feel like a perpetual mummer,
Awarding the mortals with spring, fall and summer,
But after every nine months, you must prove your worth,
By bringing the season of winter to Earth!
So, it's now off to Hades, and you must be keenly aware,
"That it's now time to get the fuck out of here!"

And so, a workable truce had been satisfactorily enacted to comply with Zeus's new "three months of winter law". Ceres agreed to having Persephone stay inside the ice temple with *her* during the three miserable winter months, and having the other three seasons available to satisfy the fickle humans down on Earth, who were all about ready to rebel against *Olympus,* abandon the tyrannical gods, and systematically exterminate themselves in a monstrous worldwide suicide pact.

"You'll live with Lord Hades below the Earth for nine months, and then live with your detestable mother in her temple for the cold winter," Ceres consoled her pallid-looking, dead as a doornail daughter. "And when fall

16

ends, you can again return to me here in elusive Eleusis, and you may drink some Shirley Synagogues in my temple, while I enjoy chugging-down rye whiskey, vodka and lots of delicious saki."

"And dip-shit humans here on Earth will once again become cheerful and pleasant, and again resume worshipping Zeus and the other despotic Olympians," Queen Persephone reasoned and acknowledged. "And people all over the globe will again revel in eating *Corn Flakes, Rice Krispies* and *Wheaties* for breakfast treats. Cheerio mother!"

"Cherrio, my dear Persephone! See you in nine short months. But please don't return to me pregnant, for I have no more milk in my tits after competently nursing that little dumb bastard Demophoon through infancy," Ceres sadly replied with a lugubrious expression upon her face. "Cheerio, my dear Persephone!"

"Echo's Cursing Curse"

Echo was a fair Nymph who cavorted and frolicked around Helicon's flowered fields with her six sexually addicted lesbian nymphomaniac sisters. The seven lewd Nymphs would perpetually masturbate and perform cunnilingus at every area daffodil and petunia meadow, and also at every familiar mountain-stream. Echo's heart was most blithe, and the Nymph was the envy of her siblings, because she was the greatest storyteller and the biggest ovary-buster among them, and for that matter, in all of Helicon.

"Echo, why the Hades don't you visit our mother Hera with one of your spellbinding tales so that she doesn't journey to Helicon and bust our vaginas all the fuckin' time as is her nasty habit?" an elder sister suggested. "Our mediocre lives are going down the proverbial Fallopian tubes, real quick like. If you can con the Queen of the Goddesses, then we'll collaborate and make you a splendid twined garland for your silky-smooth hair, and we'll also manufacture a nice, especially-smooth dildo out of maple-wood that you could tinker and toy with all friggin' day, and all friggin' night long."

Echo laughed with a gay roar as if she were experiencing a series of multiple orgasms. Her guffawing, in fact, echoed all over Helicon, and her loud laughter even disturbed and interrupted *straight* forest creatures, who were following their instincts and diligently trying to reproduce their fucked-up species.

"What will Hera do when she tires of my illustrious tales?" Echo asked her dastardly eldest sister. "Will she have a crocodile eat my blonde, honey-sweet muffin? Will she dry-up all of the sex hormones in my body, thus destroying my ample libido? Will my vile mother maliciously amputate my luscious brown nipples and feed them to starving, carnivorous insects?"

"When that time arrives, your fuckin' guess is as good as ours," another contemptuous jealous sister chimed-in. "Now please Echo; get the fuck outa' here so that your sisters can have a giant roll in the grass and enjoy some sportive lesbian activity. My damned clit' has already swollen-up to the size of a strawberry, just contemplating such a wild *tit*illating romp!"

The unwanted, young, gorgeous-but-irritating Nymph left her licentious sisters and meandered through the nearby enchanted forest until she located vain Hera massaging the breasts of a white marble statue of herself. The anxious girl got-down on her knees out of respect and reverence for the unpredictable wife of Zeus. Hera looked-down, and the grim frown upon her usually doubting face instantly converted into a rarely seen warm smile. The surprised goddess stroked Echo's golden blonde hair, pretending that it was her husband Zeus's fluffy thick bush that surrounded the king-god's impressive three-foot-long pussy stuffer.

"Oh, beautiful Nymph, and most un-favorite daughter; what has brought you to me?" Hera inquired. "Are you accidentally growing a third tit, or a second clit', or something else abnormal like that? Do you need a new asshole installed?"

"I have an overwhelming urge to address thee, dear mother, goddess of Heaven and Earth," Echo slyly declared. "I have a most fantastic tale to relate to you that'll make you desire to hear more of my stupid, erratic, nonsensical bull-shit! Are you fully ready to listen to my fucked-up lunacy?"

"Your tales are indeed as interesting as the wondrous pornography of yesteryear that abundantly appears on the walls of local caves," Hera acknowledged. "And each one of your tomes I've ever heard is longer than my husband's fabulous humungous vagina-clogger. Do you now have another bizarre story to tell me? Your whoppers are better than even the best charcoal-broiled hamburgers barbecued and sold in ancient grease!"

"My latest story will make you hornier than a toad's head!" Echo genuinely promised her wicked, deceitful mother. "You'll be so aroused that you'll want to screw your whole eternal existence away, and not think about anything else but sex with young mortal males with rock hard bodies, and short-but-firm six-inch-long erections!"

"Okay dear daughter; spin your fabulous story for what it is worth," Hera finally commanded. "But if I'm not pleased with your plot and characters, I might feel compelled to make you into a garland of flowers; or into a splintery wooden dildo; or maybe even sentence you to a more regrettable fate, if I really get extremely pissed-off and offended!"

And so, Echo contemplated earning her twined hair garland, and her forthcoming especially-smooth maple-wood dildo, and then commenced with her graphic and captivating narrative. The girl mingled several tantalizing lies into her melodramatic presentation, and Hera was enthralled with her offspring's lengthy oration until the imaginative Nymph got to the culminating climax, where her mother was having sex with the powerful-but-hideous Minotaur, while simultaneously giving the gigantic grotesque Chimera a heavy-duty blowjob.

"Cease your fuckin' asshole insulting story right this second!" Hera snapped at Echo in wild admonishment. "Your playful gift of gab has both denigrated and deceived me! As a curse, and also a punishment, you'll remain dumb and inarticulate until someone in your vicinity has spoken, and then you, Echo, will be forced to repeat the last words that had been uttered while inadvertently cursing and swearing. In other words, my dear Echo; your terrible curse will definitely involve major, terrible, repetitious cursing!"

The punished and afflicted girl immediately and shamefully departed Hera's excellence, and Echo soon approached her naughty sisters, who were having a significant sex orgy in the familiar daffodil meadow. 'Listen to me, dumb fucks! Listen to me, dumb fucks!' the attractive Nymph thought and attempted to communicate with her naked preoccupied sisters, who were rolling around like marbles in an earthquake, inside the legendary Helicon flower field. But Echo's promiscuous and hedonistic siblings completely ignored the accursed young lady's very real presence, and her innocent intentions.

'Oh shit!' Echo realized. 'I can only repeat what others have said while utilizing obnoxious obscene language. What a fuckin' bummer Hera's cruel whammy has turned into. I'm destined to be fuckin' X-rated for the rest of my doomed, miserable, worthless life!'

One fine morning, a young idiot named Narcissus was aimlessly wandering through the forests of Helicon, and the self-centered moron was desperately looking for a fallen log to rest his ass over, in order to take a fairly comfortable shit. Narcissus grew an immense hard-on as the wanderer labored, and finally discarded, several hard turds from his constipated digestive tract. All the horny women the young, stout jerk-off ever came into contact with always adored and desired him, but the conceited, handsome fellow persisted in loving only himself and his magnificent Olympian-sized genitalia. In fact, right after Narcissus had been born, the blind soothsayer Teresias had boldly prophesied a prediction without ever even seeing the little bastard: "This newly-born, unscrupulous asshole will remain happy, shitting and jerking-off in the forest all day long, only as long as he does not see himself acting like a full-of-shit asshole."

And the augur's prophetic-pathetic words eventually came true, for egocentric Narcissus cared for no one but himself; and his huge pecker; and his accompanying gargantuan testicles; and the egomaniac spurned all women that adored him, regardless of how splendid their enticing physical appearances were.

But Narcissus knew not grief or sorrow, for the knucklehead never encountered rejection from the opposite sex, because the itinerant fool cared only for himself, and the airhead only experienced minor pain when taking constant craps in the forest, since he never knew about laxatives, rich milk chocolate, baked beans, and the like.

The local Nymphs, including Echo, were shy of Narcissus because the wanderer was a mere mortal, and so the horny bitches individually and furtively hid behind rocks and trees to conceal their scrutiny from his surveillance. And after industriously wiping his ass with dried leaves and pinecones, Narcissus thought he had heard a nearby rustle and hollered-out, "Over there! Who art thou spying on me? Where art thou? Is your name Juliet?"

And Echo inappropriately answered, "Who the fuck art thou? And where the fuck are you'? And I'm not this fuckin' Juliet that you've just fuckin' alluded to!"

Upon hearing no further distant words, the slightly-embarrassed Narcissus courageously articulated, "I am clueless Narcissus. I am here clueless in the deep-deep woods!"

"In the mother fuckin' deep-deep woods! In the fuckin' deep-deep woods!" the accursed Echo repeated. "In the son-of-a-bitchin' mother-fuckin' deep-deep woods!"

"Well then, kindly come to me!" impressed Narcissus implored. "Come to me, oh fair forest maiden, so that I may crush and shatter your maidenhead!"

"Go fuck yourself!" Echo's voice rudely cursed. "And before you pop your healthy load, come *in me,* instead of *to me,* you moronic asshole! I said come in me instead of to me, you stupid, fucked-up dip-shit!"

Confused Narcissus looked and searched all about, but could not determine the remarkable, mysterious voice's origin. And every time the curious young stupid-shit investigated in her direction, Echo' cunningly retreated to a more remote section of the forest. And for two solid days, the cursing Nymph followed Narcissus all over the forest, and the accursed maiden incessantly and mercilessly broke his humungous balls with her persistent chattering and predictable cursing, each and every time the dumb-fuck made a sincere interrogative.

'I can't take that bitch's gross voice persistently driveling in my direction any longer!' the egocentric young trekker considered. 'I'm so damned nervous and jittery that I can't even jerk-off to relieve my great tension, and I can't even dare take a healthy shit, fearing that I'll be humiliated and caught off-guard while the risqué maiden's busting my sensitive, ever-expanding hemorrhoids. What the fuck should I do? Maybe I'll just forget about this latest bull-shit misadventure, and find my way out of this fucked-up, Olympus-forsaken-forest!'

The bewildered forest visitor carefully descended down a slope until the befuddled young man arrived on wet turf situated near a pond in the hollow's center. As Narcissus seriously reflected and worshipped his reflection in the reflecting pond, the mischievous Echo approached his presence from behind, and several salty tears dripped-down from her countenance, and plopped into the already contaminated water, with the teardrops rippling the water beneath the kneeling young man.

'Thanks to Hera's mean punishment, I can't even speak normal, courteous language to him!' Echo sighed and recollected. 'I can only curse and elaborate upon what the mortal inadvertently utters to himself! Why does my despicable mother have to be so fucked-up and vindictive?'

"Are you the fair maiden that seeks my handsome body?" the arrogant, self-centered asshole asked as Narcissus stared at his reflection in the polluted pond that every god and forest creature has pissed-in at least ten times each day. "Who seeks me?"

"Who the fuck seeks me?" Echo deviously-but-involuntarily replied. "Who in this fuckin' perverted world fuckin' seeks me? That's what the fuck I wanna' fuckin' know!"

"I have told you, asshole woman, countless times, that it is I Narcissus, that honestly seeks to know your true identity!" the distraught and unnerved lost traveler complained in an infuriated tone of voice. "Please be more cooperative if you desire getting licked and laid."

"You are a totally fucked-up asshole, Narcissus!" the charming-but-haunting voice echoed. "Yes; you are indeed that totally fucked-up nincompoop that can't even fuckin' poop a wet fart!"

"Yes, I am indeed Narcissus!" the young shit confessed as the dim-wit stared at his handsome-but-perplexed features being reflected in the murky water. "But who are you?"

"Well then, who the fuck are you?" the female voice insisted on knowing. "Exactly, who the fuck are you, you insane, inquisitive fucked-up, obsessed, psycho bastard?"

"Are you simply dense, or severely mentally retarded beyond help?" Narcissus impatiently and angrily replied to his tormentor. "I am the incomparable Narcissus in the flesh!"

"Fuckin' Narcissus!" Echo imaginatively echoed with obvious obscenity. "Fuckin' moronic, imbecilc, idiotic Narcissus!" the gorgeous Nymph reiterated as the damsel held-out her hands, imploring the self-infatuated fanatic to notice her alluring physical beckoning.

"Then, tell me, oh magical voice," the kneeling, self-centered, lost ignoramus proceeded as Narcissus again marveled at his wonderful reflection. "Identify yourself and tell me why you're following me? Are you a disoriented shadow?"

"Why the fuck are you' so freakin' dense and egocentric?" Echo vehemently reprimanded the traveler from afar. "And why the fuck are you searching around for your' long-lost insignificant farts, and for your inconsequential dingle-berries in this forbidden, obscure fucked-up forest?"

"Maiden, why must you continuously mock and humiliate me with inane, vulgar language?" Narcissus responded. "Why must you insist on perpetually busting my most excellent testicles, and then pulverizing them into tiny minuscule fragmented gonads?"

"Because if I had *your* balls, I would certainly challenge Almighty Zeus himself to a totally outlandish supreme sperm-shooting contest!" the female voice indulgently laughed. "Balls! If Hera had them, she'd be the fuckin' undisputed *Ruler of Olympus,* and then royally govern over the entire fucked-up planet!"

"You're really pissing me off, big time!" Narcissus yelled at his tranquil reflection in the stagnant water. "Your annoying cursing is most undeniably-and-effectively pissing me off!"

"Look Fuck-head! It's much better to be pissed-off than to be pissed-on!" Echo cutely cursed back. "Let's not get into a childish pissing contest here, because there's no fuckin' wind blowing in the forest to piss into!"

The haughty Narcissus plopped-down upon the tall grass, rolled-over, and the lost slow-learner refused to speak to his tormenting nemesis again. In the meantime, poor accursed Echo' stood by her newly-discovered sex symbol, and incessantly wept, while wanting to explain to the disconsolate nimrod what the hell was actually going on. Soon, the addled maiden drifted-off into the woods to fanatically rub her quivering clit' button, while Narcissus wished that he had the stamina and the pride to grow a decent erection to slap-around, yank, and toy with.

'I need to replenish my liquid supply so that I can pop an abundant load that will destroy this entire forest,' the self-indulgent fool mentally exaggerated. 'Then, I could easily see my way out of here!' the frustrated fellow neurotically thought. 'I'll drink some of this pond-scum water, even if it's horribly infected with every malignant disease and degenerate microorganism imaginable. I just don't give a shit anymore about anything, including death!'

As the conceited itinerant bent-over to cup a mouthful of water, Narcissus observed and *pond*ered a lovely face being reflected from the scummy pond. His heart fiercely raced with a strange new emotion, as the lost visitor perceived a woman's countenance that was nearly as perfect as his own. And Narcissus immediately was smitten with love, passion, and unrelenting desire. The handsome Adonis stretched-out his arms to the slimy water, and the lovely female image being reflected duplicated his aggressive, amorous advance. And then, the affected young asshole sighed and romantically articulated, "I truly love thee!"

"I fuckin' love thee just like I love twined garlands of flowers for my tresses, and just as much as I love smooth shiny maple-wood dildos to shove into various orifices, including my own crotch and asshole!" the female reflection confidently and arrogantly answered. "Do ya' want me to fuckin' repeat that lengthy enunciation or what, you mortal dumb-fuck?"

And then, aroused Narcissus reached his hands into the polluted pond to grab the damsel's firm solid breasts, and the equally aroused Echo lunged for her newly-discovered boyfriend's expanding penis, and both numbskulls simultaneously plunged forward and splashed-around inside the algae-covered, stagnant pond. And when the callow fellow surfaced and grasped for Echo's arms, the gorgeous Nymph suddenly disappeared under the surface, and successfully eluded his avaricious embrace. And after repeating the same futile maneuver two-dozen times, the haughty forest traveler gave-up his vain pursuit in sheer frustration, and the young jerk-off's head quickly sank beneath the deep water.

The prediction of Teresias clattered about inside Narcissus's mind, as the drowning idiot gradually sank to the bottom of the deep pond: "This unscrupulous asshole will be happy shitting-around and jerking-off inside the forest until he does not see himself."

Echo was completely drenched and exhausted from her unexpected contact with the dirty, scummy pond water. The impulsive Nymph crawled-out of the pond to the base of a hill, and then peeked-out from behind a boulder.

Soon, the beautiful Nymph realized what was happening to her unfortunate human lover, and then in sheer desperation, Echo leaped into the water in a frantic effort to rescue the drowning asshole. But her futile attempts were to no avail, for Narcissus had drowned at not being able to possess anything outside of his spoiled, conceited, over-esteemed, egocentric self-concept.

And over the ensuing centuries, and to this very day, Echo's haunting voice remains in every valley, cave, well, cavern, corridor, and big city sewer system. Unfortunate, Narcissus was the last human to ever witness Echo's alluring beauty and charm. But consistent with Hera's brutal curse, the forest Nymph still obediently repeats whatever is yelled or yodeled; however, over the years, the illustrious girl's speech has become more refined and sophisticated, and Echo no longer uses scandalous adjectives, nasty nouns, and vile action verbs, and she no longer egregiously engages in denigrating, offensive, obscene cursing.

Finally, besides the brown scummy pond located somewhere in Helicon, a stubborn flower called a "Narcissus" has sprung-up where the melancholy Nymph had wept and wept, and to this very moment, Narcissus himself has proven, over and over again to the world, that the ingrate indeed was a veritable "blooming idiot", all because of his selfish and all-too-proud, arrogant lifestyle.

"Prometheus and Fire"

Before men became civilized and developed laws, writing, culture, rigatoni, lasagna, and spaghetti, humans were hunters, scavengers, and basically crude savage barbarians, just like we still are today. Then, something rather significant occurred. Men learned how to create and make fire, and with that discovery came warmth, weapons, leisure time, invention, thinking, hot fireside sex, and tropical nudist camp vacations.

According to Greek mythology, which every educated person knows is infallible bull-shit, the gregarious Titan Prometheus gave the first cavemen the gift of fire. But it ultimately was up to clueless primitive savages to learn how to manufacture matches to start flames and master how to construct safe fireplaces and chimneys. Civilized men also had to figure-out how to eliminate toxic fumes from a confined area. Millions of prehistoric people had accidentally died from odorless carbon monoxide poisoning before early men finally realized that the mentally-deficient fools needed chimneys to eliminate something invisible that was incidentally killing them.

Prometheus was not around during the first generation of cavemen that had perished when the Earth's primeval, mortal population was devastated by natural disasters and carbon monoxide poisoning. When cavemen weren't killing each other, and acting like a bunch of insane *Neanderthals,* humans were being eliminated in vast numbers by volcanic eruptions, earthquakes, floods, and cataclysmic tidal waves. When *Mother Nature* finally civilized herself, then men became more settled and less nomadic. Tribes ceased being itinerant, and not wasting precious time searching for food to hunt. The survivors only had to think about seeking asylum from horrendous, inexplicable worldwide catastrophes.

The Titans, under the rule of Cronus, ruled the universe (well, maybe only the Earth and Sky) in the very early prehistoric days. A violent revolution occurred, led by Zeus, son of Cronus, and the extremely tyrannical *Olympians* overthrew the extremely tyrannical Titans. Some of the Titans like Atlas were given specific punishments like separating the Earth from the Sky. Prometheus was a Titan who had conspired against Cronus and assisted Zeus in the successful rebellion, so as a reward for his allegiance, *he* was permitted to live with the new rulers and yardsticks on *Mt. Olympus.*

Zeus became the chief ruler of Heaven and Earth, and was notorious for sending shocking lightning bolts up yahoos' yazoos if *the* mortal violators didn't do exactly what Zeus wanted them to do, which was never clearly defined or outlined by the fickle ball-busting *Olympians*. That's why early humans both hated and despised their gods, and that's why hospitals were eventually instituted so that men could have their inhospitable assholes operated on after getting zapped up the anus by serious volts of electricity, as arbitrary retribution for alleged transgressions and offenses against the whimsical, fickle gods.

Prometheus was Zeus's chief adviser, but the Titan still was uncertain whether he should have participated in the turbulent insurrection of the *Olympians* against Cronus. Zeus had always been suspicious of Prometheus's motivations, and quite dubious of *his* loyalty, so *their* shaky relationship was often fraught with mistrust and doubt.

The *Olympians* knew all about making rain, starting fire, and causing chaos, but the divine-and-bored omnipotents selfishly schemed to keep those special secrets away from man's knowledge to avoid an uprising against the gods, similar to the one that *they* had masterminded against Cronus and the Titans. Hence, metalworking, immortality, spaghetti, lasagna and rigatoni were gifts that only the gods could enjoy, utilize, and treasure, and early men were doomed to a wandering life as meager hunters and scavengers, their existence filled with apprehension, uncertainty, itchy crotches, and myriad venereal diseases.

Zeus had created the first woman, because the first men were all homosexuals that actually thought assholes were vaginas. The chief god ball-buster feared man's potential, and viewed mortals as a threat to *his* supreme dominion over the Earth and Sky. That's why the chief Greek god visited men with plagues, tornadoes, diseases, pestilence, corruption, and war. The king-god wanted to keep men's egos and dicks down, and Almighty Zeus attempted to frustrate mortals, so that science and technology would not evolve to rival the god's supreme authority.

When Cronus was the main ruler, summer had been the only season down on Earth. Men were content just roaming the hills, woods, and mountains searching for food, killing one another in the sunshine, and spending eons trying to invent suntan lotion, bathing suits, and swimming pools. Icy winds, glaciers, and polar bears were banned from man's rather comfortable summer existence, so males didn't need a lot of clothes to protect themselves from freezing their balls off, and the cave inhabitants didn't require emergency shelters, motels, lovers' lanes, or fleabag hotels to shack-up with other men. Men were generally happy and gay, sodomizing one another, and living in sunshine under the auspices of Cronus and the Titans.

Ancient Greek chronicles and manuscripts reveal that after the first great devastating flood, the existing land mass had separated into many fragments. And when Zeus relieved Cronus of *his* dominion over the world, winter winds, ice, snow, sleet, polar bears, Eskimos, and horny women suddenly appeared in order to make life more difficult for "the merries and the happies", for that is what homosexual men were called before *they* were later described as "gays, fruits, and faggots".

The gods knew how to weave clothes, how to start and maintain fires, and how to build magnificent marble edifices and temples up on glorious *Mt. Olympus*. The deities were insulated from winter's harsh distress, even without the aid of earmuffs, overcoats, leg-ins, marshmallows, *Southern Comfort, Jack Daniels,* and anti-freeze. Zeus and his family, however, did not suffer from winter's nasty, bitter blizzards, but the gods derived ample pleasure from observing half-naked, gay men anguishing through the frigid, sub-zero temperatures.

But unfortunately for the victimized men and women down on Earth, winter was a time of crisis, and a desperate struggle for survival. Humans began blaming Zeus and his aristocratic colleagues for *their* innumerable travails, and the pissed-off humans incessantly complained about how 'frigid' everyone had become in the winter, and the disenchanted assholes threatened to return to an exclusive virgin, homosexual existence, thus sending the entire human race on a collision course with certain extinction.

The colossal Titan Prometheus often conferred with Zeus about men and *their* perplexing environ*mental* and mental problems down on Earth.

"Prometheus," Zeus conceitedly began his discourse. "Those wimpy men have become disenchanted rebels who continuously quarrel among themselves when the dunderheads aren't in the act of openly accusing the gods of betraying *their* selfish interests. What the fuck's wrong with those asinine, asshole Arcadians down there?"

"Well, Your Excellency," Prometheus diplomatically responded. "When the Arcadians finally invent pinball machines and video games three or four millennia from now, the dimwits will be completely fascinated and occupied by those wonderful amusement diversions. And after the ludicrous fucks invent pornography and Triple-X movies and videos," the Titan added, "they'll be so busy watching the graphic films, and masturbating, and suckin' and fuckin' all day long, that we'll never again have to regard those silly shit-heads as a direct challenge to *our* supremacy!"

"But until then," Zeus growled and sneered, "I should destroy those despicable Arcadians and replace the simpletons with a new race of men that show more reverence to the gods. I can't quite understand how men with such tiny dicks could have the balls to defy the almighty *Olympians*."

Prometheus sat-down, so as not to intimidate *his* already-irritated Lord. The ruler, Almighty Zeus, was fifty-foot-tall, but the Titan was a mighty seventy-five-foot in height, and often made the mercurial Zeus feel inferior when standing next to him. Still, Zeus could not conceal his extreme animosity for bothersome mankind, and Prometheus had to indulgently listen to the king-god's litany of relentless tirades.

"The whole fuckin' race of degenerates is completely worthless, and it's beyond our capacity to even attempt rehabilitating the boneheads," Zeus thundered. "I plan to eliminate those asshole Arcadians in order to ensure the continuation of tranquility upon this fragile globe that we call home. Those mortals down there are more fucked-up than both Medusa and the Cretan Minotaur are right now, combined!" the Lord of *Olympus* maintained. "I suspect that their brains are crammed inside their assholes, and some parts are stuffed inside their diminutive peckers. And I want to destroy the whole fuckin' moronic race before the rebels learn that their brains ought to be inside their damned heads, and not up their shit-filled asses!"

Prometheus contemplated Zeus's assessment of mortals for a moment. "But Lord Zeus," the Titan insisted. "Your proposed new race of men replacing the Arcadians will probably be just as quarrelsome, and just as obnoxious as the Arcadians' themselves are."

"Instead of kissing our asses," Zeus argued, "the Arcadians give each other blowjobs, and the newly-formed kinky females are becoming adept at lesbian cunnilingus, and also skilled at performing sadism and masochism. If my wife Hera ever learns *S & M,*" the chief god emphasized, "then *my* immortal ass is in mighty big trouble!"

"What's wrong with that?" Prometheus countered. "Maybe that's what you need; a good buttocks-spanking by Hera to whip your corpulent ass into shape!"

"Enough of your demented and deranged humor," Zeus lividly replied. "Men are going to have to learn how to serve *us*, the gods! If they don't, I'll blast them with so many lightning surges when they're having sex that their dicks and clits' will short-circuit with *ample* sparks flying all over the damned place. That's how I'll methodically kill them all off during one of their mass orgies! And if that electric experiment doesn't work," the chief *Olympian* yelled to his adviser, "I'll make them all choke to death by pissing out of their sinuses and shitting out of the throats!"

"Up here, safe and sound on *Olympus*," Prometheus interrupted, "you never consider the basic needs of these humans. You solely think about *your* need to be feared and to be worshipped. But Zeus," the chief councilor continued his prattle, "how could men learn and value wisdom when *you* stifle their knowledge with lightning bolts up the anus; with booming thunder; with intolerable hurricanes, and with horribly freezing winters!"

"Prometheus, you demonstrate too much compassion for those sorry excuses irreverently disrespecting and dishonoring the high ideals that the gods represent," Zeus bellowed. "And if you persist in extending any more sympathy toward those detestable mortals down there on the planet's surface," the omnipotent god loudly bellowed, "I'll definitely incarcerate you inside an electric cage, with revolving lightning bolts as its bars. Do you now understand my wrath?"

"But Lord Zeus, those sorry souls down on Earth have minds and hearts, and the race displays wonderful courage and enviable stubbornness from time to time, too," Prometheus verbally volleyed. "The perplexed mortals wish and dream to live and become immortal just like us, and the marvelous creatures are presently even pursuing the discovery of nectar and ambrosia?"

"If humans ever discover the secret food and drink of our immortality," Zeus hypothesized and articulated, "then you and I better contemplate certain suicide by not drinking nectar, and by not eating ambrosia. For as you know, Prometheus," the architect of all world disasters continued, "it is a much-revered law of *Olympus* that states once man obtains one of *our* treasured secrets, we should not take that knowledge away from his knowledge. What a fucked-up rule *that* dangerous bull-shit is! Who the *Hades* ever thought-up that ludicrous mandate, anyway?"

"You did, Lord. But dear Zeus; you must exhibit more patience and prudence!" the all-too-wise Titan adviser recommended. "You must show men that *you* are also benign and generous. Kindness will get you more substantial results than harsh devastations and earth-shattering calamities," the stouthearted, royal guidance counselor suggested. "Men will master morality only by imitating good example, and not by practicing revenge, or by being corrupted, or influenced, by your vindictive indiscretions."

"You're so full of shit you could dually be the happy cesspool for all of *Olympus,* and also for all of merry-faggot mankind!" the king-god vehemently criticized. "I've allowed you to live on *my* mountain after the revolution against the Titans," Zeus spoke in a threatening tone of voice, "only because you had collaborated with me in the coup d'etat against Cronus. But now, you're foolishly begging for a coup de grace after the coup d'etat had been completed," the monarch-deity preached. "And you're now going to need a resurrection instead of an insurrection, when I get the fuck through with you. Prometheus; that is, if you again dare to break my balls by defending those shit-faced, scumbag mortals down on Earth," Zeus boomed. "Then, I'll personally take great satisfaction in turning you into a cockroach, stepping-on and crushing your filthy body, and thus exterminating *you* from all existence! Is that highly-probable consequence perfectly clear?"

"Yes, King Zeus," Prometheus assented with his head crestfallen. "Your supreme will is my ultimate duty!"

Zeus then stepped into his black and white marble entertainment lounge to watch two dozen acrobatic dwarfs and a dozen kinky nymphs having a raunchy sex orgy, with two diminutive males for every well-endowed, horny, young female. Prometheus stood-up and stormed-out of the superb palace in a pissed-off mood, possessing a determined desire to spite "that fifty-foot-tall midget Zeus".

The all-too-considerate Titan swiftly paced out to the palace gardens, and then thought about the approaching winter season down on Earth, and how the pathetic humans would become even more miserable by freezing their balls, dicks, asses, tits and clits' off. 'I gotta' do something quick about the cold weather that Zeus had caused, or else those suffering mortals won't have any balls to produce seeds to shoot into their honeys' honey-wells, and those tit-less females won't have any milk to honey-suckle their hungry little weaners,' the sympathetic benefactor concluded and decided.

Prometheus the Titan possessed the wondrous gift of foresight, and the clairvoyant minor-god was the complete opposite of his brother Epimetheus, who could only recognize events (until it was too late) *after* they had happened. 'I know Zeus is going to chain me to the summit of *Mt. Etna* after the vengeful son-of-a-bitch finds-out I've betrayed his indomitable will,' the great prognosticator accurately imagined. 'But I really don't give a shit anymore! I want to do my own thing, and Zeus can go pound sand on the nearest beach, or *he* can kiss my fat Titanic ass if the petty tyrant doesn't like my radical ideas!'

After ascending the white marble steps to the palace's upper tier of splendid gardens, the emotionally-disturbed Titan leaned against an old elm tree and contemplated his ultimate fate; Zeus's ultimate fate, and mankind's ultimate fate. At the base of the mountain, Prometheus then noticed a handsome young prince about to enter Apollo's chariot, which was attached to four superb white stallions. "Hey you down there! Identify yourself or I shall report you to Zeus as a vagrant trespasser!"

"I am Phaethon, son of Apollo, god of music and medicine," the ambitious youth explained in an alarmed voice. "And I am about to drag the sun across the sky with my father's golden chariot. I must perform this task," the daring teenager elaborated, "to show everybody in the world that I am indeed Apollo's son, and that I can perform my daddy's work that only he and I can do!"

"Well then," Prometheus yelled-down through the cottony clouds to the base of the mountain. "What the *Hades* did you say your name was?"

"Phaethon, my Lord; proud son of Apollo, and my mother's fine name is Clymene; a beautiful mortal living across the big sea over in Ethiopia!"

"Well, Phaethon," the Titan hollered-down to Earth. "You happen to be trespassing in the wrong myth! Get your father's stupid chariot outa' here, or else I'll have to get Zeus to shoot your ass and balls right out of the fuckin' sky, sun or no sun; son or no son!"

"Yes Sir, I'm very sorry, Lord Sir!" the energetic and rambunctious lad *apolo*gized. "I don't want to get barbecued up my asshole, that's for damned sure! I'll be outa' your myth in just a second, right after I take a long piss!"

"That's much better," Prometheus amiably answered. "At least you have some respect for your elders and for your superiors. Usually, stupid-assed teenagers are insolent and rebellious little pecker-heads that think they're invincible, but you seem to have some good breeding. Good luck to you, young, frivolous Phaethon! May your' lunatic mission be blessed with success."

The Titan observed Apollo's chariot rise above the ground into the clear blue sky, and then ascending into the Heavens, the youth's route following the established path of the sun from east to west, and the proud and noble Prometheus aggressively waved to the helmsman' Phaethon, as the white stallions and the gleaming golden vehicle sped past *Mt. Olympus,* heading in the direction of Macedonia.

The gods' knowledgeable and wise councilor felt genuine empathy towards humans, knowing full-well that Zeus had banished *his* relatives to the black pit of Tartarus, which was really the pits' that was situated in Hades, somewhere near the Earth's central lava core. 'Cronus and every other Titan, except Atlas, my brother Epimetheus, and I are imprisoned in Tartarus,' Prometheus pondered. 'And Zeus only allows them to eat tartar sauce in Tartarus, and I can't think of anything worse to eat in such a detestable place, or swallowing-down something ever tarter than Zeus's tartar sauce in Tartarus!'

The Titan then meditated some more. 'Zeus is a greedy son-of-a-bitch for wanting dominion over both men and nature,' Prometheus rationally thought. 'So, I must help men learn culture and develop science, so that if Zeus becomes too avaricious, and more-proud and more-reprehensible than he already is right now, then mortals will be able to competently defend themselves against his totally excessive arrogance.'

As Prometheus floated-down toward Earth as if he was a chicken feather, the compassionate Titan considered other relevant factors in *his* mental equation of checks and balances. 'Men are pathetic, fearful, and shivering creatures, huddled together in their cold damp caves. Zeus is afraid of their potential,' Prometheus theorized, 'because if mortals ever acquire things like art, science and technology, which I vividly foresee happening in the distant future, the scrawny beings will be able to kick the *Olympians'* fat, lazy asses',' the Titan assumed. 'Men are *my* trump card, and if Zeus chains me to the top of *Mt. Etna, his* puny humans will reciprocate my favor given to them by eventually freeing me from that cruel reprisal.'

The kind-hearted Titan believed that men should not live like animals according to the laws of fangs, jaws and claws' survival. Prometheus generalized that if men possessed the gift of fire, the race could make tools, weapons, and machines. Mortals could sit in warmth around campfires, and have time to think, rather than dedicating all of their' strength and essence to merely surviving, reproducing and hunting. Fire could lead to knowledge that would checkmate Zeus's destructive tendencies. The gift of fire could allow men to eventually challenge and rival the assumed authority that the gods randomly exercised by the implementation of chance, consequence and fate, which the *Olympians* often abused by their own personal intercession; by their cruel sense of justice, and by their capricious condemnation of all human activity.

When the sunset finally descended on the western horizon, Prometheus stood tall upon a Greek beach, ready to initiate his plan to neutralize Zeus's absolute power over the Earth. The Arcadians lived in caves, situated along rugged cliffs that overlooked the sea, and Prometheus schemed to bring to those humble, intelligent creatures not only the comfort of fire, but also the understanding of how to ignite a blaze. "Zeus has got to learn how to chill-out!" The Titan contemplated as "the fire-bringer" carried a yellow metal reed to clearly demonstrate the art of fire making to the hungry-minded, very cold, mortal, cave dwellers.

The Titan glanced-down at the yellow metal length. 'Hephaestus the blacksmith god makes hundreds of these pieces daily, and I have stolen this one from his cluttered workshop. He'll never miss it,' Prometheus concluded. 'Hephaestus is too busy porking his lovely wife Aphrodite, and that's all the bastard ever thinks about: sticking his throbbing penis inside Venus!'

Then, Prometheus considered other behaviors of the eccentric *Olympians*. 'The gods never build fires around or near men, fearing that mortals would acquire the special talent. That is, the gods never *built* fires around men up until right now! I'll surely be banned from *Olympus* for doing this vital deed,' the merciful Titan thought. 'But who the hell gives a friggin' fart? Zeus and the other *Olympians* are even more fucked-up than Cronus and my family is, and was! In fact, all of the asshole gods in the whole universe belong imprisoned in Tartarus, eating tart tartar sauce that is tarter than any other tartar sauce in Tartarus, or in any other dumb-ass place!'

As the constellations began to appear in the cloudless, cold, night sky, the Titan gathered a pile of dry driftwood and some loose straw. Prometheus next carefully rubbed the metal stalk against a piece of flint, and as the friction caused heat to be released, sparks shot-out, and almost instantly ignited the dry straw, which then slowly began incinerating the dry driftwood. Soon, intense flames were leaping-up and licking the driftwood, giving-off comforting heat, light, and hope, for humanity, and for the promise of enjoying hot sex.

Amidst the shadows of the high mountain caves, crouched figures appeared at the entrances, and then the observers cautiously emerged out of their cliff dwellings while exhibiting curiosity, the parent trait of genuine learning. Families of intrigued mortals crept closer to the intensifying flames to better inspect the impressive, dazzling phenomenon. The night air was cold, and the warmth from the great fire was both inviting and alluring.

Soon, a large crowd of spectators assembled, with their circumference encircling the Titan, who had stooped-down and was fully aware of the throng that had gradually accumulated around him. Several of the astounded mortals had the courage to initiate introductory conversation with "Prometheus the Fire Giver".

"What the fuck's that?" an intrepid old dumb-fuck inquired. "It reminds me of my old flame back in Sparta!"

"Why my dear mortal, the gods call this spectacle 'fire', and you may call it that, too!" Prometheus suavely answered. "It is nothing to fear, although if not used judiciously, it has the capacity to destroy and to devastate. Once I teach you freaky clowns how to create and how to control flames, fire shall become your finest friend, and also your best ally!"

"We have seen this thing *you* call fire many times before," a young man in the group excitedly declared. "But the gods always carried it around in a concealed stone bowl, and never started one as you have just done. Is it caused by magic? If not, how the fuck do you get it' going? What in blazes makes it work?"

"Young, curious simpleton," Prometheus loquaciously replied. "Look and see what I do with this yellow rod. Just pretend it's *your* erect dick, and that there's no prostitute or whore's snatch, or gay guy's asshole around to stick it into. Then, you'll know exactly what to do with this here metallic rod. And if *your* rod is as long as this metallic rod is, then my illustrious friend," the helpful Titan stressed, "then the almighty gods have already blessed you!"

Prometheus finally took the eighteen-inch-long metal rod from the now-distracted-but-fascinated teenager, who incidentally had been momentarily preoccupied measuring his eighteen-inch-long erection with the thin metallic tube's length.

"Give me that metal tube, you' stupid jerk-off!" Prometheus yelled as all of the curious human bystanders burst-out in a roar of rare laughter. "How are *you* going to learn anything when there's more blood in your dick than there is in your goddamned brain!"

Next, Prometheus instructed all of the males to piss into the flames to effectively extinguish the fire, and the nitwits all obeyed his strong command; even the old fucks experiencing kidney failure. And all of the men and boys were then extremely disappointed and *pissed* that *they* had eliminated the source of the alluring flames, along with the mini-inferno's accompanying warmth, by pissing their foul-smelling urine. The driftwood was no longer burning, and the women in attendance were so infuriated that the angry whores all then wanted to tackle and *piss-on* the facetious Prometheus for "killing the fire".

"What the fuck did you make us do that for?" the tribe's oldest elder petulantly asked the amused Titan. "I'm so cold now that I could freeze to death, and I might have just taken my last piss ever, all because of *you!*"

"Relax old-timer, and pay strict attention," the Titan intelligently suggested. "Otherwise, I'll methodically crush *you* in my giant hands, and I guarantee you that *that* last leak will surely have been *your* last piss, you insane, hoary, fucked-up, jerk-off!"

The old geezer, suffering from chronic dementia, cleared his throat, gulped-down some thick phlegm, and then politely uttered, "Sorry Mr. Titan. I still want to piss some more later tonight, and even perhaps tomorrow morning, Zeus willing!"

The crowd watched in full amazement as Prometheus used a knife to shave chips of wood, and next sprinkle the pieces into a strange mixture of straw and tree bark. Then, the inspired teacher notched-out a piece of elm wood, and placed the blend of straw, bark and wood chips inside, and also around the notch, doing a top-notch job of it. After that instruction had been accomplished, the industrious Titan assiduously rubbed the metallic tube against a sturdy long piece of driftwood, just above the elm wood notch. As friction intensified, sparks began shooting-out, and soon the unique mixture of straw, bark, and wood chips ignited.

Red flames burst-out, and in due time, warm smoke billowed-up and wafted into the cold night air. The mesmerized crowd of choking mortals was astonished beyond belief, and then the audience acted like audiences everywhere from the beginnings of antiquity up to the present time by producing a round of applause for Prometheus's stellar performance of what previously had been stupidly evaluated and described as "magic".

"Geez!" shouted the feeble-but-appreciative tribal leader. "If my dick was bigger and longer, I could set my wife's shrinking bush on fire with that kind of intense friction against the dry walls of her putrid-smelling cunt, that stinks exactly like a dead fish cemetery! But I guess now I'll just have to repeat the method you so generously demonstrated!"

The Titan then scurried about the beach and found additional pieces of dried driftwood to rekindle the fire into a huge inferno. Prometheus threw the newly-acquired wood upon the growing blaze, and soon the amazed witnesses realized that more wood meant a bigger and longer fire, and that the flames could be raised or diminished with the amount of wood being applied. The humans mimicked the minor god's fine example, shouting gleefully about their new-found acquisition of knowledge that no longer was "a secret of the gods".

The excited mortals all sprinted-up the frozen dirt trails leading to their remote cliff dwellings to experiment with their novel discovery. Soon, massive fires were aglow in all-three-hundred mountainside caves, and the aroused natives were enthusiastically humping and pumping away in a sequence of wild sex orgies. And for the first time, babies would be born in the late summer and early fall, because sex was then being enjoyed in the wintertime without the victimized humans freezing their dicks, balls, asses', tits, slits and clits' off.

"What the fuck's goin' on down there on Earth?" Zeus asked his family of gods as the Mt. Olympus residents all leaned against a marble balcony ledge, their curious eyes looking-down from the lofty terrace upon Arcadia.

"The fire generators are not coals that the gods have taken from Hephaestus's hearth. I believe the humans have actually acquired the knowledge of creating fire!" Hermes the messenger god divulged to *his* very disenchanted head deity. "Holy shit! Creation is the business of the gods!"

"The end of *our* dominion over men is near," Zeus sadly lamented. "The mortals now grumble and complain, but I must admit that the species is admirably ambitious. Soon humans will develop science, and directly challenge *our* divine authority. This fire ability really pisses me off big time!" Zeus squawked and bitched. "Who the fuck taught those weirdo mother-jumpers how to make fire from everyday simple items?"

"I believe it was Prometheus," squealed Hermes, who never liked his distant cousin, and who was always trying to get *him* in trouble. Now was the messenger god's unique opportunity to get the Titan into gigantic difficulty with the mighty king-god Zeus.

"Have Hephaestus manufacture the heaviest chains with the strongest links immediately!" Zeus thundered so loudly that his voice reverberated way-down to the steep cliffs of the Arcadians. "Prometheus the Titan has authored his own doom; that deviant asshole maverick!" the king-god bellowed with *fire* in his eyes. "Chain him up to the summit of Mt. Etna over in Sicily right away! And I don't want to hear Apollo playing any damned unchained melodies on his out-of-tune lyre!"

"Colliding Myths"

Some ancient Greek myths are popular because the characters described in them are fucked-up. Even today, people love gossiping and reading about others of their species that are complete assholes, just to make the gossipers or the readers feel better about themselves. And even four thousand years ago, adults knew about what pains-in-the-ass teenagers are, and how the stubborn, adolescent dumb-shits think that they are invincible, which often leads to tragedy. When acne-faced, hormone-dominated kids believe that they know it all, then those know-it-alls either wind-up in the hospital, or in the cemetery. Consequently, it is absolutely amazing that any of us survive those ugly adolescence years, and luckily mature into wise adults. As it has so aptly been described, "It is too bad that youth is wasted on the young!"

Daedalus was a genius from antiquity that dared to learn the gods' treasured secrets. The creative Greek was a master architect and engineer, who designed many extraordinary temples, amphitheaters, agoras, buildings, whorehouses, public projects, and impressive co-ed' public restrooms. The inventor was commissioned by the wealthy *cretin,* Cretan King Minos to oversee the construction of the Labyrinth, a complex series of underground caves and tunnels situated beneath the king's opulent palace on the island of Crete.

"I'll commit to building the Labyrinth for your personal honor and glory," Daedalus told Minos. "But I'll need a lot of con*Crete* foreign material to finish the job. Also, I need to bring along my royal pain-in-the-ass, punk teenager to keep him out of trouble, and to teach the little thug how to value *constructive things,* so that hopefully, the blundering loser successfully makes it to adulthood."

"I know exactly what the fuck you mean!" King Minos, the *cretin'* Cretan, concurred. "I need this 'a-mazing' Labyrinth built beneath my palace to keep my monster the *Minotaur* contained in a safe enclosure. The grotesque creature has the body of a muscular man, and the head of a formidable bull. Every year, I plan to sacrifice seven young vestal virgins, and seven acne-faced, *bullheaded* punks to the *Minotaur* inside my subterranean, amazing maze, just to get rid of the know-it-all bitches and horny bastards, and also to appease the greedy gods," Minos related to the distinguished experimenter. "Daedalus, if you're lucky, your asshole kid might be one of the victimized, bullheaded, punk shit-heads to be sacrificed!"

"That's a deal!" Daedalus agreed, warmly shaking the king's already-broken hand. "My son Icarus thinks he can do no wrong; the callow fool defies my authority, and always impetuously attempts taking the 'bull by the horns' when the frivolous asshole should be exercising mature patience and 'discretion', which does not rhyme with 'excretion'."

"Your recalcitrant son Icarus sounds like the typical run-of-the-mill teenage jerk-off to me," King Minos surmised and agreed while examining his crushed right hand. "And Daedalus; I think that *'a minute' tour'* with the *Minotaur* ought to scare the shit out of your wise-assed punk kid! Ha, ha, ha, ha!"

After the intricate and complicated Labyrinth had been built for the king beneath his expansive-expensive palace, Minos loved its design and confusing maze-like passages so much that the monarch decided to keep Daedalus on Crete (against the genius's will), to creatively erect other architectural wonders.

"Daedalus, I want you to engineer a great reservoir for Knossus," the tyrannical king insisted. "Since I am one of Zeus's favorite sons, it will be built to honor my omnipotent father, the founder of *my* city! Do I fuckin' make myself' clear?"

"I'd like to stay residing on your ugly, barren, arid, desolate island," Daedalus politely refused, "but I have to return to Athens back on the mainland, and give my estranged wife money, or she has threatened me with divorce and with serious alimony payments that are certain to bankrupt my troubled ass!"

"Build me my damned reservoir for the taxpaying people of Knossus, or else, you'll most certainly be fed to the *Minotaur* along with your fucked-up, teenage, punk kid!" Minos boisterously threatened. "Get the message, you' derelict, egomaniac, lowlife shit-head!"

Daedalus intensively and extensively worked on the massive reservoir project for several years, but when King Minos (not King Your Nose) had learned that the renowned architect had tried bribing sailors to stash Icarus and himself' in a ship's cargo hull as stowaways to Athens, the ruler became mighty pissed-off. Minos had Daedalus and his insolent, know-it-all kid, locked inside a high stone tower situated upon a lofty cliff, overlooking the *Aegean Sea,* which gets older every single and married day.

From his open-air window overlooking the sea, Daedalus studied the graceful seagulls zipping-around the towering cliffs, looking for human heads to drop their raunchy wet crap bombs upon. The inventor marveled at the birds' elegant flight patterns, as the eagles and vultures circled the stone tower, and the inventor envied the creatures absolute freedom: soaring, drifting, and majestically gliding all over the goddamned cloudless sky.

"Icarus, I have some friends on this island who are willing to smuggle bird feathers and wood pieces to this tower," the father calmly explained. "We will make sturdy frames that will fit snugly over our arms and shoulders, and next, we'll cover them with feathers, and then fly-off of this Zeus-forsaken-island back to the mainland of Greece."

"Okay, I'll help you Pop," Icarus complied. "But only because I need to get back to Athens to shack-up with my old girlfriend, and to escape the danger of that horny *Minotaur* predator, who is said to be gay in addition to being fucked-up. I heard that the big mother wants to screw young boys up the ass with his pillar-sized dick! Let me tell you, Pop, I really don't need that kind of 'bull-shit' happening to my sensitive asshole!"

Within six months, all of the necessary materials the accomplished builder had specified had been successfully smuggled into the stone tower, and Daedalus and Icarus diligently manufactured the two sets of wings, using thread and wax to attach the essential bird feathers to the flexible wooden frames. Soon, the determined conspirators had almost-completed their ambitious project.

"Remember Icarus," Daedalus reminded his independent-minded, aberrant son. "Don't fly too high or too low. Take the straightest, most moderate course back to the coast of Greece. Follow my stellar lead, and don't deviate, you fucked-up, young punk deviate!"

"I'll do exactly what the hell I want," Icarus vehemently protested. "And that's all that I'll do, and nothing else. I know precisely how to use these stupid wings without ever having the need for further education from attending *Hermes' Aviation School and Flight Academy!*"

"I wish you wouldn't have such a defiant *mercurial* personality!" Daedalus maturely and vociferously criticized. "If you fly too high and propel yourself too close to the sun, the goddamned wax on your wings will melt, and you'll swiftly plummet into the sea."

"Pop, the sun's gotta' be more than seven miles away from the fuckin' Earth, contrary to what you happen to think it is," Icarus argued. "And besides, once I climbed a mountain, and noticed that the higher I ascended toward the summit, the colder the temperature got! I think you're trying to feed me a lot of nonsensical, superstitious, adult-mythological, non-scientific bull-shit about the sun melting my wings!"

"And son," Daedalus proceeded while ignoring his son's arrogant and obnoxious comments. "Don't snafu yourself and fly too close to the sea. Your wings might become damp and wet from the saltwater waves, and then you'll crash and splash into *Poseidon's* dangerous domain!"

"Pop, the word *don't* ain't in my friggin' vocabulary," the defensive, know-it-all retard challenged. "Saying the damned word *don't* to a teenager is just like saying, 'I dare you' to fuckin' do it'."

The following morning, a light breeze accompanied the appearance of dawn, and the two plotters diligently prepared for their clandestine escape mission. The father and the son donned their portable feathered wings, and Daedalus was the first to leap out of the stone tower's third-story open window. Icarus followed his father's steady example, and soon was also majestically gliding over the rugged mountain cliff, and heading out over the serene *Aegean Sea*.

"That's the gods' *Hermes* and *Cupid* flying up there!" King Minos's chief counselor erroneously indicated to the astonished monarch. "Even without filing a flight itinerary, those two chums really know how to wing it!"

"Minotaur shit!" Minos yelled and wildly cursed at his principal adviser. "Those nutcase idiots flying-around up there are that stupid shit-head Daedalus and his fucked-up kid Icarus, desperately attempting to escape my petty despotism!"

Soon, Icarus became infatuated and enthralled with the exhilaration of flying through the tranquil atmosphere. The excited youth had to test his physical limits: zipping, looping, and zooming all over the azure sky in violation of his determined, steadfast father, who maintained *his* straight and narrow course in the direction of the distant Greek mainland.

"I can fly like the gods!" Icarus screamed in absolute delight. "I feel immortal! I feel invincible! I feel like jerking-off!" Icarus was rising and swooping all over the sky, frenetically attempting to gain control of his erratic path from Crete to Greece, all the while randomly experimenting with the thrill of flight.

* * * * * * * * * * * *

Meanwhile, in the far-off land of Ethiopia, a punk teenager named Phaethon impatiently listened to his mother Clymene brag that *his* father was Phoebus Apollo, the Greek god of music, medicine, masturbation, and the sun. According to exaggerated ancient renditions, every morning Apollo would mount his magnificent golden chariot, and would commandeer four white stallions that would fly across the sky from east to west, dragging the sun on its daily celestial path from the eastern to the western horizon.

A schoolboy friend that pretended to be a son of Zeus scoffed at Phaethon's claim that *he* was a bona fide offspring of Lord Apollo. Naturally, Clymene's son became incensed at his pal's malicious ridiculing.

"Look, asshole," the other boy scornfully hollered. "I am a son of Zeus, and my daddy can kick your daddy's stupid ass any fuckin' day of the whole fuckin' year. How do ya' like them fuckin' apples?"

"But my mother," Phaethon said, paused, and then reiterated. "But my mother has told me this truth that I am indeed Apollo's son, and that someday, I might be able to perform comedy routines and revival music acts at one of my father's many theaters. As you know, Greek heroes, like Hercules, are born after a god of Olympus has sex with a mortal woman."

"Get a fuckin' life!" the other wise-ass punk suggested. "Your mother is nothin' more than a goddamned kinky whore-turned-prostitute, and you're *her* illegitimate son! This story she's giving you is a lot of stinkin' *Olympus* bull-shit! I know because my mother's a goddamned hooker, too! I ain't no goddamned son of Zeus! And you ain't no goddamned son of Phoebus Apollo! That's all a bunch of speculative, self-serving horse manure!"

Phaethon sadly walked home from school for lunch in a mighty depressed state of mind. "Mom, tell me the truth," the boy requested. "Are you a goddamned whore or prostitute? Or is this weirdo story that I am indeed the son of Apollo actually true?"

"Son, you are indeed of heavenly birth," Clymene swore. "And if I speak falsely, may the gods punish my arrogance and make my hyperactive vagina atrophy. I strongly suggest that *you* journey to the eastern horizon and visit the temple of my handsome husband Apollo. Ask *him* about *your* divine origin, if you don't believe me."

"Okay Mom; pack my lunch, and I'll go and check it out. How do I get to India? I was never too good in geography, and failed the damned subject last semester!" the all-too-curious, slow-learner teenager asked. "I hear that India is the exact place where Dad's new marvelous marble temple is located."

"Just keep walking east for about a century," Clymene informed her impulsive son. "And hurry-up and get the hell out of here, because I have a wealthy client arriving in about fifteen minutes, and I need to wash my stinky crotch and freshen-up a bit!"

Apollo's Indian sun palace had columns of pure gold and glittering jewels that magically glistened and sparkled in the morning sunlight. The walls were made of rich platinum ore, and the ceiling of gleaming ivory. Murals of Earth, sky, sea, and *Mt. Olympus* had been painted on the walls of every chamber in the splendid, colossal temple. Hephaestus had erected the fantastic edifice in tribute to Lord Apollo, who didn't know or care a shit about anything except music, medicine, masturbation, screwing beautiful mortal women, and tugging the hot sun across the sky the four separate seasons of each monotonous year.

Phaethon cautiously entered Apollo's charmed sanctuary, seeking confirmation of *his* true identity. The determined kid approached the radiant god, imperially sitting upon his glimmering, golden and jeweled throne, and the impetuous know-it-all punk soon had to cover his eyes for protection from the intense, dazzling glare. The sun god was wearing a fabulous diamond-studded purple robe to complement his overall supernatural appearance.

"Oh, Apollo, lord of the sun, and custodian of its daily trek across the sky; I request of your excellence," Phaethon bull-shitted. "Please provide me some proof that I am indeed your mortal son."

"Who is your whoring mother?" the sun god thundered in a booming voice that shook the entire throne room, pillars and all. "I have screwed so many gorgeous mortals that I really can't remember all of *their* unimportant names."

"My mother is Clymene, the finest prostitute in all of Ethiopia, with the firmest set of knockers this side of the *Euphrates River*," Phaethon boldly stated. "Do you remember her?"

"Wow, yes!" Apollo exclaimed. "How could I ever forget those fantastic tits she possesses? They were absolutely incredible! I'm getting a major hard-on just thinking about them!"

"Then, *you* really are my father!" Phaethon eagerly screamed-out while thinking: 'Why you dirty mother-fucker'! That asshole son of Zeus ought to have his balls busted and ground into dog meat! The lying bastard!' Phaethon's diminutive brain internalized.

Apollo beckoned for his bastard son to approach *his* stately- shimmering throne, so that the father could better admire the boy's strength and audacity. "You are indeed my son," Apollo informed Phaethon. "And *you* shall enjoy my genetics for the remainder of your years, and you'll have the stamina to screw at least sixty mature females a day, which comes to about three pussies an hour, if you don't sleep and decide to go non-stop. And to show you my appreciation of your surprise visit," the sun god continued in a booming voice, "I shall grant you any wish your little fart, er, I mean heart desires."

Phaethon contemplated Apollo's promise for a minute, and without giving the matter sufficient consideration, the dumb, overly-ambitious, proud kid blurted-out, "Please father; I beg of you; allow me to drive *your* exotic sun chariot across the sky for just one day to demonstrate to the world *my* true *Olympus* ancestry."

"But Phaethon, you don't even have a chariot driver's license yet!" Apollo objected. "You don't even have a goddamned learner's permit! I beg you' my son; do not attempt to surpass your bounds," the sun/archer god sincerely pleaded. "You're a mere aspiring mortal, and might suffer a mere mortal's fate unless you wise-up and make a more reasonable request! Not even Zeus could steer the flaming chariot without a week's worth of intensive lessons and flight training!"

But Phaethon was adamant in his persistence, so Apollo had no alternative except to honor *his* promise to his and Clymene's son, and permit the impulsive idiot to attempt the impossible. "Never lose your grip control of the four powerful horses," Apollo cautioned Phaethon. "And don't be distracted or lose your grasp on the reins when you get hit in the face by stenchy flying horseshit exploding out of the horses' smelly assholes. And whatever you do," Apollo continued, "never look-down to Earth, because that will make you as fuckin' dizzy as drunken *Dionysus.* And my son, the horses' lungs are also full of fire, and if the animals turn their heads toward you, be careful, for the flames from their nostrils can singe the hair right off of your balls, and might even set your hairy asshole on fire!"

Apollo looked into Phaethon's eyes, which were bloodshot from the long trek to India from Ethiopia via a detour through Russia, and also through ancient Palestine. Immediately, the divine father understood that all logic was futile, and that persuasion was a useless tool to implement against the cocky teenager's obstinate insistence. "I hope you've already gotten laid many times, because otherwise, you're going to die a fucked-up virgin!" the sun god declared to his haughty, adventurous, over-zealous offspring.

The scrupulous sun god accompanied his stubborn kid out the temple's platinum back door, where the fabulous golden chariot had already been hitched to the four immortal white stallions. "You still have time to change your mind," Apollo recommended, "because pretty soon, you won't have time to change your shit-streaked underwear! What do you have to say about it?"

"That's okay, Pop," Phaethon reflexively replied. "I don't wear underwear!"

The knowledgeable sun god then applied some protective oil (suntan lotion) to *his* son's rosy face, so that *his* nose and chin would not be seared from the fiery sun's heat, or from the horses' hot breaths. "Take the shortest route across the sky, and whatever you do," Apollo cautioned the oblivious punk-dunce Phaethon, "don't deviate from *my* daily course. If *you* allow the horses to take charge of your responsibility, then you might as well commit suicide right now, because otherwise, you're as good as fuckin' dead!"

Phaethon leaped-upon the rider's platform of the heavenly golden chariot, and anxiously grasped and held the reins. The nervous white stallions snorted fire, and then stomped their hoofs in anticipation of their daily flight across the majestic sky. The chariot zoomed-off toward the western horizon, and after a minute of careful flying, the four imposing horses realized that the highly-skilled and experienced sun god was not piloting their present excursion.

The chariot's intense speed was soon unbearable, and the task too overwhelming for any mere mortal to endure. Soon, the sun god's vehicle began to sway and vacillate as the chariot meandered between constellations, planets, the Earth and the moon, and then Phaethon became quite fearful, regretting that the lunkhead had ever pleaded with his divine father to drive the sun chariot alone from horizon to horizon.

The fire-breathing horses soon wildly ascended, and erratically descended, in abnormal flight patterns and zany oscillations across the morning sky; the magnificent steeds taking full control of the chariot from the alarmed and suddenly frightened asshole teenager, trying to do a god's job without proper training or practice.

'This excessive heat is intolerable!' Phaethon thought. 'And this hot horseshit smacking me in the face is far worse than any bullshit I have ever heard, ever seen, or ever smelled! Alas; I'm being justly punished for being so fuckin' over-confident and so fuckin' stupid!'

As the fiery chariot swiveled, rocked, vacillated, and then plunged toward the Earth, Phaethon frantically and desperately tugged and manipulated the reins. Finally, out of sheer fear of dying, the young rookie charioteer made a last-ditch effort to save himself from ultimate destruction.

Amazingly, the beleaguered youth regained control of the seemingly doomed chariot, as *he* miraculously managed to reverse his *crash course* in sun-pulling. The chariot astoundingly righted itself on a steady route, and the four white horses obediently responded to the courageous lad's loud commands. Apollo's impressive golden vehicle rose-up to a safer altitude, and eventually out of harm's way. Catastrophe had been temporarily averted.

Then, just as Phaethon finally regained his cocky confidence, and demonstrated admirable dexterity while vigorously piloting the heavenly, weaving, and bobbing chariot, an unexpected obstacle suddenly appeared before his eyes. "Who the fuck is that idiotic asshole?" the stunned son of Apollo exclaimed.

Icarus was rising and swooping all over the sky, frenetically attempting to gain control of his erratic path from Crete to the Greek mainland, after randomly experimenting with the thrill of flight. Meanwhile, Phaethon's chariot was on an unavoidable collision course with his teenage counterpart. The youth wildly tugged the reins to the left, but to no avail. A terrible impact resulted, and Icarus, Phaethon, the golden chariot, and the four great white stallions tumbled-down to Earth, causing mass destruction all over the damned hemispheres.

The forceful collision, and the resulting celestial chariot's crash, caused fires to scorch most of the Earth in northern Africa, thus, creating the *Sahara Desert*. The unperturbed-and-cautious Daedalus looked back, shrugged his winged shoulders, and then continued his steady flight path toward the Greek mainland. 'Father knows best!' Daedalus intelligently concluded.

"Baucis and Philemon"

In the ancient land of Phrygia (now Turkey, which is situated right next to Chicken), all songs strummed on the lyre had to be played in Asia Minor, and not in Asia Major. On the desolate high plateau section of Phrygia, the not-so-pleasant peasants all admired and frequently commented about a great gnarled tree. The extraordinary wonder was a weird combination of linden on the left, and oak on the right side, growing from the same roots, but the unique freak of nature was really considered the grandest of marvels, because it was the only damned tree in all of that section of Phrygia. This imaginative story confirms exactly how the tremendous tree had originated. The immortal gods often did fucked-up things for fucked-up reasons, just to prove to secular, atheistic, fucked-up mortals not to fuck with them.

On occasion, when Zeus and his confederate Hermes were tired of consuming ambrosia, eating immortal and mortal pussy, and drinking gallons of nectar and honey-sweet pussy juice to stay young, potent, and vigorous, the eccentric pair would descend from *Mt. Olympus,* because the duo also often became bored listening to Phoebus Apollo redundantly playing his repertoire of songs in B Minor, and sometimes in Asia Major.

"We must show the crazy humans that we're essentially 'down-to-earth' guys once in a while," all-powerful Zeus reminded Hermes, the mischievous messenger god, as the two were ambling through Phrygia. "I'm really fuckin' tired of watching those big-breasted Graces do couch-dancing in my face. Now Hermes, let's act meek, meager, and ordinary for a change, rather than hedonistic and fucked-up like we normally do! Sometimes, my dear messenger, *we* must attempt setting a good example for those irascible assholes residing down on Earth. The mentally deficient numbskulls will hypnotically imitate our behavior, as if the fools were ordinary mimicking monkeys."

"I fully concur My Lord," Hermes amiably agreed. "So, it's nice that once in a blue moon, we disguise ourselves as mendicant suppliants, and rub shoulders with mortal riffraff, just to see if the rabble lowlife still worships us. And don't forget, almighty Zeus; we ought to shrink-down from fifty-foot-tall to *their* diminutive height before we fuckin' indiscriminately encounter any mortals; clever disguises, or no damned clever disguises!"

"That's a great practical idea, Hermes," Zeus commended and endorsed. "That way our irritating, enlarged hemorrhoids will shrink-down, just like our fifty-foot-tall bodies!"

Hermes was indeed the most cunning and creative of the great ancient Greek gods. The winged-footed deity had suggested to his superior Zeus that the two should show-up in Phrygia to investigate how receptive and hospitable the natives would be to *their* anonymous, disguised Mt. Olympus guests.

"Ya' know Hermes," Zeus indicated as the chief deity magically traded his rich robes for pleasant peasant's garb. "I want to see exactly how the mortals in Asia Minor are honoring my controversial Law of the Suppliants. If you recollect, all god-fearing mortals should…"

"Should give food, shelter, and good cheer to traveling visitors, because luxurious lodges and hotels haven't been invented yet," Hermes interrupted his moody supreme boss. "According to *your* fine law, all itinerants must be treated with courtesy and dignity, even if they're traveling bandits, scoundrels, terrorists, or robbers; or else, the derelict homeowners not honoring your law will be visited by an earthquake, or perhaps a devastating tidal wave, or maybe wind-up having high-voltage lightning bolts flying-up their targeted, tender butt holes."

"We'll wander through this pathetic land where other strange local gods compete for the humans' loyalties," Zeus summarized to his more-jovial colleague. "Yes, dear Hermes. We'll knock on each door and request food and lodging, and if we don't get cooperation, then…,"

"Then Phrygia will be destroyed out of *your* arbitrary spite, and the worthless land will be left to the other fuckin' indigenous, obscure gods to fuckin' worry about," the immortal courier finished.

At every stop, the two nomadic guests were savagely cursed-out, treated with belligerent insolence, greeted and with hostile defiance, and that brutal rejection had occurred at least three-hundred-times, for the outlandish natives were pragmatic pagans, heathens and cynical, atheistic realists. The obnoxious Phrygians generally worshiped sex and perversion, much more than the natives honored impractical, arrogant, and egotistical foreign and local gods and goddesses, along with *their* stupid and inflexible laws, decrees, and bull-shit edicts.

Almost completely frustrated, totally mortified, and virtually out of patience, the dual *Olympus* travelers decided to try one more home before taking-out their mutual wraths upon the barbaric Phrygian cave and shanty dwellers. Finally, Zeus and Hermes arrived at a remote shack situated all by itself in the countryside, because the already-scorned occupants had been evicted and ostracized from the nearest city's numerous ghettoes and barrios.

After Zeus angrily knocked on the splintery door, the pair were greeted by a cheerful male voice, and courteously invited inside the raunchy, ramshackle abode. An elderly, thin gent with a long grizzly beard instructed the wayfarers to sit-down upon the only hard 'bench', which was normally reserved for unethical area judges and magistrates that occasionally showed-up at the old man's door, cold and lost, and asking for directions to King Midas's ornate palace, or how to find the nearest Phrygian cemetery.

"Where are ya' odd-lookin' strangers from?" the aged man's old-looking wrinkled wife asked. "We haven't had any visitors in these parts for over fifty years. As you already can tell, kind sirs, my husband Philemon and I live way out here in the god-forsaken boondocks, far beyond this accursed country's damned hinterlands and dangerous cities."

"What's your name old woman?" the omniscient Zeus inquired, just for the sake of polite conversation. "I'll have to enter it into my secret black date book!"

"It's Baucis," the old dame politely answered. "And my husband Philemon's two unfortunate brothers Philharmonic and Philanthropic were both philosophical philanderers that died from phlebitis over in Philadelphia, that ghetto town between here and Egypt. The two idiots treated the rare visitors to their homes with indignity and with violence. And consequently, both of my idiotic brothers-in-laws, namely Philemon's's fucked-up brothers, were punished by the gods with clogged arteries and with clogged sperm ducts. Shit, kind sirs," Baucis elaborated to the two weird-looking guests. "Philharmonic and Philanthropic were both glad that they died from blood clots, and not from excruciating, painful sperm clots inside their rotting-away crotches!"

"Baucis and I have always been cooperative with the gods' capricious laws, ever since the dreadful demise of Philharmonic and Philanthropic," Philemon added to his wife's testimony. "And neither of us want our assholes cauterized by some errant, high-voltage lightning bolts, or by some lacerating liquid lava shooting and squirting-up our sensitive, withered anuses. That's why we so eagerly answered our door this afternoon," the old codger explained to shrunken-down visitors Zeus and Hermes. "Ya' never know when a crazy pair of Greek *Olympus* wanderers will visit your humble dump for an unannounced, impromptu inspection, ha, ha, ha!"

51

"Do you enjoy living way out here in the middle of nowhere in abject poverty?" Hermes curiously inquired. "If I had to live in a shithouse like this one apparently is, I'd simultaneously contemplate blindness, insanity, starvation, and a most-welcome suicide."

"We are very poor as your keen eyes can determine," Philemon verified. "But Baucis and I have blithe spirits that rejoice whenever we recall and discuss the great sex life that we had shared six decadent decades ago. Our passion used to be hotter than the ashes and embers now-burning in our modest fireplace," the decrepit husband explained. "Let me fan the flames on the hearth, so that I may distribute more warmth for the four of us occupants to share. All I dream about now, kind strangers, is growing and maintaining a nice stiff erection, and planting the throbbing mother into a young Baucis's wet, pink love tunnel. But unfortunately," poor Philemon continued his sorrowful monologue, "her honey-well now is dryer than the barren Phrygian desert out there, and more regrettably, I haven't popped a decent load in almost a non-fuckin', fuckin' century!"

Baucis's water kettle that hung over the gentle fire began boiling and then steaming. Soon, the wife poured the container's contents into a pot of common cabbage, which had been selected from the couple's sparse garden. "*Let' us* be good friends and eat this boiled cabbage when it soon will be ready to consume and digest," Baucis suggested to her fully-amused visitors. "I'll stir the pot with a piece of pork that's hanging-down from that termite-infested, decaying beam up there. I stare at that pork every morning, wishing that it was a young Philemon's hard erection ready for some serius bed action. But alas, my aged husband now has a tiny rat's dick that looks like it belongs on a friggin' chipmunk!"

Then, Baucis methodically set the table with her gnarled arthritic hands that shook and exhibited an advanced case of Parkinson's disease, and next, the afflicted woman used a broken plate as a shim under one of the shorter bench legs, because the table had contracted a nasty case of polio in its youth. And finally, the domesticated old dame set some olives, carrots, and turnips upon the rickety old table, along with several eggs that she had been saving for area 'poachers'. Appalled Zeus and Hermes were then invited to sample the horrible food, and to flourish in the couple's genuine hospitality inside the dilapidated framed home, that itself, would have served a better purpose as winter kindling wood.

"Please accept this wine in wooden bowls. Its foul flavor tastes like vinegar," Philemon offered his incognito, neato distinguished guests. "I wish I had better vintage to give you two ugly vagabond travelers, and I hope my ears do not hear any sour grapes from the lips of either of you two strange-looking freeloaders."

"This is the best damned fuckin' wine I've ever tasted, either sober or drunk," Zeus commended his poverty-stricken hosts. "And may Dionysus bless your asses with a productive grape harvest in years to come. In fact, this rancid shit will kill every radical germ and bacteria in my whole friggin' body. And if it makes me piss vinegar," the king-god remarked, "then I'll definitely urinate into a decanter, and celebrate you Philemon, and your wrinkle-faced wife, as both being real pissers!"

Baucis and Philemon stared incredulously at each other when the pair noticed that no matter how much their' thirsty visitors and they drank, that the wine bottle incredibly remained full and undiminished in liquid volume. Then, the toothless host and the incontinent hostess stared at each other in utter astonishment, fully realizing that their gregarious guests were indeed immortals of the highest magnitude. Both mortals dropped to their knees in adoration of the two traveling *Olympus* itinerants, apparently masquerading as common wayfaring bums.

"Kind sirs," Philemon timidly stated as his eyes squinted and finally observed Hermes's shrunken winged sandals. "Baucis and I have a goose stashed-away that my wife would gladly prepare for you. I'll attempt to catch it, if you would like to observe my awkward frivolity. I mean, My Lords; my whole pathetic life has been one vast wild-goose-chase in pursuit of wealth, pleasure, pornography, and other idiotic, sinful. earthly nonsense, that you gods matter-of-factly enjoy all the fuckin' time."

"That's perfectly all right, old man," Hermes indulgently laughed. "We don't want to sit here all night and watch your quacky wife eat your skinny bird. Just the thought of such a gross sight makes me want to split my gut while laughing my ass off, before vomiting my guts out! Geriatric sex would be too much raucous entertainment for my weak heart to endure," the great messenger god confided. "I might then become the first fuckin' giddy immortal to die laughing, and wind-up going to *Hades*. Ha, ha, ha, ha!"

"You two mediocre and ridiculous senior citizens, who already look like walking zombies, have been generous hosts to me and to my dear companion Hermes," the chief god Zeus sincerely declared with a thankful smile. "I shall prodigiously reward you two hapless adult dolts for your wonderful acceptance of a pair of wayward travelers into your pathetic abode, that doesn't even have an outhouse to take a freakin' dump."

"What do you intend to do to the remainder of sinful Phrygia, Lord Zeus?" Baucis curiously asked. "Do I have to go through damned menopause again? What a lot of bloody bull-shit that messy business was!"

"The wicked inhabitants of your bizarre country shall be severely and *amply* punished for their blatant violation of my sacred laws, and also for their audacious mistreatment of Hermes and me," Zeus promised the elderly couple. "Those antagonistic, repulsive assholes will be deluged with the biggest catastrophe of their fucked-up lives."

"*Amp*ly punished usually means Zeus administering high-voltage electric lightning discharges up the old asshole," Hermes reminded his flabbergasted mortal listeners. "Your aberrant Phrygian countrymen back in the city' ghettoes and barrios will then think that they've become ancient Ass-Searians! Ha, ha, ha, ha!"

"Look over there at yonder fireplace!" Hermes directed the quivering old couple. "Your goose is cooked! Ha, ha, ha!"

Zeus opened the shack's squeaky door, brushed some active termites from his hands, and escorted the other three occupants outside. Amazingly, the king-god and Hermes instantly shot-up to their normal height of fifty-foot-tall. Baucis and Philemon trembled to their knees in sheer supplication of the show-off Olympus deities.

And when the elderly couple stared in all directions, the two penitent paupers frightfully observed that a gigantic flood had just devastated Phrygia in all four directions of the knoll upon which their' deteriorating house had been crudely constructed, eighty-years before. The visibly distraught pair wept for their' old age, and cried out loud, protesting to the majestic, radiant gods that the elderly couple had not also been drowned in the terrible calamity that Zeus had maliciously and vindictively caused upon baneful Phrygia.

And as the bleary-eyed duo perceived their hands, feet and each other's faces, all of their ugly wrinkles and crepey skin had miraculously disappeared, and Baucis's visage was once again young and beautiful, and her rejuvenated slit hole was now a bright pink and sporting well-lubricated walls; and her crotch again looking like a decent, healthy, brown bush.

Philemon looked-down and was delighted to see a large bulge sticking-out from his newly acquired, rich-looking, embroidered tunic. The two old farts immediately and passionately embraced, lowered their newly-acquired young bodies to the ground, and wildly screwed like horny lions in heat for three consecutive hours. And while the two were euphorically humping and pumping and changing positions like there was no tomorrow, their decrepit old shack magically transformed into a splendid marble mansion, featuring a magnificent golden roof, with a large quacking, non-edible, silver goose at its summit.

"Good fucked-up people. I have provided you with youth and a fine home, simply because you've shown noteworthy respect for us, the disguised, omnipotent gods," Zeus, the accomplished voyeur, related as he and Hermes gracefully ascended into the sky. "And I shall now form a shrine with large pillars, and send the two of you off to a distant future place called *Temple University* to study and learn to be my official priest and priestess in this fucked-up land of Phrygia, or what's left of Phrygia. And please remember," the supreme deity emphasized while partially hidden behind several cottony clouds. "All future incantations and chants to Hermes and me must be played and sung exclusively in the key of Asia Minor. Now, do you two raunchy, incompetent, lucky imbeciles have any further requests before my immortal, illustrious companion and I zoom back up to eternal *Mt. Olympus?"*

"Why indeed yes!" Philemon affirmatively answered and yelled- up with his hands forming a sort of megaphone in front of his now-vernal mouth. "I don't want to live forever and then have to be thoroughly bored to death like you two pedestrian assholes obviously are! With that remarkable remark being truthfully said, I would prefer that once Baucis and I enjoy each other's company and our new-found prosperity on our second splendid chance at married life," Philemon solemnly indicated to Zeus and to Hermes, "please grant that we may both die and be united as one soul, immediately after the next miserable millennium commences."

Zeus enthusiastically acceded and benignly granted the old gent's unusual request. Not one pilgrim (lost or otherwise), ever accidentally or purposefully visited the sensational white marble temple and accompanying pillared mansion during the next hundred years. After an eighty-year-tenure as appointed custodians of the recently-formed temple, which was conveniently situated next to the exquisite white marble mansion, the second-time-around, the old odd couple finally, mutually and sadly, died in a tender embrace.

But instead of turning into gruesome bony skeletons, Baucis and Philemon had an unusual bark miraculously form around their human remains, and Philemon's body became an oak tree, and Baucis's corpse coincidentally transformed into a linden tree, that remarkably also grew from the same entwined roots, because Zeus and Hermes were still *rooting* for the blessed couple up on *Mt. Olympus.*

And when archaic mythology finally evolved into the beginning of ancient history, flower-laden residents and pilgrims from all over Asia Minor and Asia Major trekked to the remote hill, not only to admire the gleaming temple and the magnificent mansion, but also to pay homage to a very extraordinary tree that is half-oak and half- linden. And all of the residents, and most of the *pilgrims,* knew nothing about a distant land called America.

"Bellerophon's Marathon Adventure"

Bellerophon, a conceited young numbskull, frequently observed spectacular high-flying eagles, hoping that a heavy errant bird turd wouldn't fall from such a great height and penetrate his thick dense cranium. The eagles would repeatedly squawk "Bellerophon! Bellerophon!" from lofty heights, because that was the only word or name the stupid creatures knew, or belched-out, before either disgustingly puking or crapping. In ancient Greek eagle language, "Bellerophon! Bellerophon!" meant "Fucked-up Stupid Asshole! Fucked-up Stupid Asshole!"

But Bellerophon assumed that the calling of his name and its reverberation off of the high mountain crags, and subsequent deflection into the valley below, was a profound prophecy that *he* would one day soar like an eagle, and possibly even fly over Philadelphia, a village of retards located in Asia Minor. Even though Bellerophon was indeed a "Fucked-up Stupid Asshole", the lad still possessed a bright shiny sword that the fool randomly brandished and wielded, using the dangerous weapon to intimidate young children, senior citizen' geriatrics, and the numerous filthy cockroaches crawling and scurrying-around inside his dark, dismal, damp cave.

'Shit!' Bellerophon thought. 'I'm the meanest mother-jumper in the entire neighborhood, and even Leroy Brownaculus and his fierce junkyard dog are afraid of me. But I must obey the stringent commands of a demanding King, who gives me entirely too many bullshit assignments,' the wannabe' hero grieved. 'If only I could change the tyrant into a cockroach, and frighten the shit out of him with my mean-assed sword!'

But King Proteus's promiscuous wife had the hots for Bellerophon, and each and every night dreamed about giving the youth oral sex, instead of being porked up the ass by her temperamental, bisexual husband. 'Bellerophon is so magnificent and beautiful compared to fat, ugly, bald Proteus, who drastically needs a high-protein diet and the Hair Club for Kings!' the Queen imagined. 'And I bet my true love's dick is longer and harder, while it is soft, than my husband's dingle is when it is erect. In other words, I'd rather suck Bellerophon than fuck Proteus!'

But every time the sex-starved Queen made amorous overtures to immature Bellerophon, the young cave dweller whipped-out his sword instead of his pecker, and brandished and wielded the sharp object around, pretending to be slaying invisible monsters and super-enlarged cockroaches.

The scorned Queen got pissed-off at being rejected, so she adamantly complained to the King that Bellerophon was contemplating raping her, while all along, the wily bitch was considering doing the exact same thing to Proteus. The jealous King had the young handsome pretender sent-away to a distant part of the land, a full half-mile from the capacious royal palace.

"You must go visit my nephew King Lykia (Lie-Key-Ya), who owns a small, bankrupt furniture store," King Proteus commanded Bellerophon. "Take these two concealed tablets and a glass of water, and present the credentials to my imbecile nephew. Lykia will read the instructions and drink the water; thus, gaining the knowledge of what the hell to do with you," Proteus eloquently elaborated. "And if you finally turn gay within the next few years, be sure to fuckin' come back to this god-forsaken section of the kingdom and visit my personal bedroom suite."

When Lykia opened the orders from his pathetically miserable Uncle Proteus, the penniless merchant yelled to Bellerophon, "You must slay the fierce Chimera, because my uncle and I are both cowardly shits, and are afraid to even look at the fierce son-of-a-bitch! The ferocious Chimera appears in the sky every day at noon, and scares the crap out of all my indigent taxpayers, who can no longer afford taxes and tribute to me, especially when the dumb fucks are devoured by the voracious monster's appetite. Now if you luckily kill the flying menace," Lykia specified to Bellerophon, "then I promise that you can live as a tax-free, green-carded, legal alien in my land, even if you never return as a citizen to my fucked-up uncle's, fucked-up domain, that has myriad shitting eagles, in addition to constantly-shitting citizens."

The legendary Chimera had the head of a lion; the torso of a goat; the tail of a dragon; the dick of a cockroach, and the asshole of a hippopotamus. It was indeed a most hideous, distorted, and horrible-looking creature that mercilessly bombarded Lykia's kingdom daily with square ten-pound droppings from its hippopotamus-like, gargantuan asshole.

"I shall slay the savage Chimera for you, Lykia, only if you give me a free kitchen dinette set with matching colorful chairs from your foundering, inferior furniture store," Bellerophon boldly stipulated. "I shall bring the monster's lion's head into your un-regal throne room, and exchange it for the requested kitchen set. And fuckin' throw in a decent hutch, too, for good measure, or else I'll then summon the eagles from my uncle's plagued kingdom to show-up here and shit thousands of heavy five-pound turds, rather than the mere hundred a day ten-pound-droppings that the Chimera is pooping out of its giant hippopotamus asshole. So, if you don't honor my specific terms," Bellerophon threatened neurotic Lykia, "then you'll have to put-up with the annoying eagles' crap all day long, and wish that you again had the troubling Chimera back terrorizing your fucked-up land!"

Lykia reluctantly assented to Bellerophon's most-reasonable request, and the hero set-out with his shiny sword to decapitate the raunchy, despicable creature that reputedly screwed giant cockroaches, and would indiscriminately shit heavy, life-threatening, hippopotamus-like droppings all over the damned kingdom.

As the tenacious young man ascended the land's tallest mountain, a goddess's voice beckoned to the foolish champion, "Bellerophon, you fucked-up moron! Why are you stupidly climbing this steep mountain? You must first mount the flying horse Pegasus that grazes in yonder pasture, and ride the white-winged-steed up to the heavens to slaughter the dreadful Chimera," the goddess's voice calmly suggested. "But first, my chosen hero; you must bridle the mighty Pegasus before you can ever attempt kicking the Chimera's ugly, fat, hippopotamus-like ass."

Bellerophon traded his clothes for a bridle outside a neighborhood bridal shop, and ventured-forth naked to harness the majestic beast known as Pegasus. The in-progress champion came upon the splendid wild, white creature as it fed upon lotus flowers near a local swamp. The winged horse's mane fluttered in the gentle breeze, and the now-nude Bellerophon approached the graceful winged equine with his bridle and sword. 'I hope I don't fart from all of those luscious lima beans I ate for breakfast!' the aspiring hero thought and feared. 'And I'm feeling mighty gaseous at this very difficult moment in my lousy, accursed life!'

Bellerophon could not get close to the great flying horse during the first day of carefully trailing it. Although Pegasus could not see Bellerophon, the steed smelled the lad's lima bean farts from a distance, and then simply trotted-off to greener pastures and murkier swamps to graze. But on the second day of the great pursuit, Bellerophon surprised Pegasus, who was busy drinking water from a toxic spring. The hero grabbed the legendary stallion by the mane, but the white-winged horse kicked the determined naked youth in the balls with its dainty-but-powerful hoofs. The panicky horse broke free from the young man's grasp, and soon flew-away to join and help the annoying voracious eagles shit upon King Proteus's kingdom, but every day, Pegasus loyally returned to the toxic earth fountain to drink more of the polluted water to which it was immune.

King Proteus's retarded subject (Bellerophon), assigned by Lykia to slay the formidable Chimera, suspected that putting a bridle on Pegasus would be no elementary task. 'I'll never be able to hold and control that horse long enough to harness and mount it,' the dumb-ass lad realized and lamented. 'Why couldn't that asshole furniture tycoon Lykia give me an easier labor to perform, like biting the tits off of a dozen caged female gorillas, or circumcising the world's largest bull elephant?' Bellerophon regretted. 'But on the other hand, I must slay the monster, or else have to obediently wipe both Lykia and Proteus's butt holes for the remainder of my un-prosperous, lackluster, doomed life, and I'll probably have to give each of those pathetic idiots three super blowjobs a day, too!'

One night, the goddess' Pallas Athene (who had nothing better to do) appeared to Bellerophon in a dream, along with *her* formerly anonymous voice. "I shall assist you in your important endeavor," Athene claimed, "because I admire your tenacity; your courage, and your fucked-up lunacy. I shall place a philter (a secret potent elixir) to tame Pegasus in a cup, and leave the formula next to your shield. So, when flying atop Pegasus, you may use your bronze shield to block the wind, therefore, inventing the world's first windshield! But I also must emphasize that the shield is not a good sun blocker!"

When the naïve dreamer awoke from his extraordinary slumber, Bellerophon discovered a cup filled with a wonderful red liquid, laid next to his heavy metal shield. Instinctively, Bellerophon held his shield up to his ass, when he felt a need to release a thirty-second fart. 'This windshield could serve as a terrific windbreaker, just like my spring jacket does!' the imbecile imaginatively thought. 'Now I must capture and control Pegasus long enough to make the winged steed my means of transportation to battle the Chimera. I must perform this arduous Promethean task, even though my fuckin' name is Bellerophon and not Prometheus.'

When Pegasus again arrived at the equine's favorite drinking place, Bellerophon was ready with his cup of magically divine philter. The determined youth anxiously leaped naked out of the nearby bushes, seized the white steed by its mane with his right palm, and then poured the potent aphrodisiac down the neighing beast's throat with his left hand. Momentarily, the winged horse became sufficiently tranquilized for the youth to bridle it, and then hop onto its back, inadvertently crushing *his* tender testicles in the process. "I command thee, Pegasus, to take me to the vile Chimera, so that I may behead the terror in the name of both benign, and malignant, human civilization!" the rider intrepidly shouted.

Soon, the immortal beast pranced forward, and then flapped its enormous stellar wings. The horse and its nude equestrian suddenly and gracefully launched-up into the atmosphere, and in a pregnant moment, were swiftly gliding towards the eastern horizon in the direction of the formidable Chimera, which was too preoccupied crapping large square ten-pound turds down to the ground to ever notice the unexpected intrusion of its air space.

Bellerophon gazed downward upon the Earth, and witnessed a plethora of rapes, murders, muggings, robberies, fights, beatings, molestations, gay rights' demonstrations, and other evidence of "civilized uncivilized" human enterprise. Soon, the nude champion recognized the fearsome Chimera in the distance, by virtue of identifying the vicious beast's unique physical characteristics.

The nasty monster breathed-out fire, pretending to be a flying dragon (but not a giant dragon fly), but Bellerophon was undaunted and unwavering in accomplishing his prospective quest. The hero held-up his bronze shield to protect his sensitive skin from the abominable, blazing-hot wind. Pegasus was unfazed by the extreme atmospheric inferno, since the flying creature (the Chimera) that *his* rider had chosen for an enemy, unlike himself, was merely mortal. But the flying horse knew how to take the heat, whether it originated from a volcano, from a furnace, from a conflagration, or from the Chimera's oven-sized nostrils and sinuses.

And also, Pegasus was amply stimulated by the philter' aphrodisiac it had drunk, and the famed flying horse now desired to screw the hideous Chimera. Ironically, the perverted aerial monster likewise desired to reciprocate and duplicate the flying horse's amorous, indecent, fucked-up behavior.

But the nude, impatient Bellerophon ruined everything by raising his sword in his right hand at precisely the correct moment, and then, successfully thrusting the sharp blade directly into the center of the venomous monster's heart. The Chimera winced, and then fell victim to gravity by plummeting two-miles down to the ground, and the loud impact of its tremendous weight with the Earth caused an enormous crater to be formed where its body had crashed.

Bellerophon valiantly rode Pegasus back to the natural spring, so that the marvelous creature could drink some more toxic water to thoroughly dilute and neutralize the powerful aphrodisiac that the winged-steed had swallowed. As legend has it, the Chimera had somewhat-disintegrated upon impact, and its lion's head; its goat's torso; its dragon's tail; its cockroach pecker, and its hippopotamus-like asshole all separated as if the young champion had actually dismembered the hideous beast, thus adding to *his* ever-growing reputation around Greece as "a highly-skilled butcher".

But some of the Chimera's poisonous blood had incidentally squirted onto Pegasus's erect dick during the fierce battle, so the agonizing horse whinnied quite loudly, and it leaped into the toxic stream to soothe the intense heat that had scalded its now not-so-erect sperm-juice shooter. However, Bellerophon never knew or even suspected that Pegasus had actually gotten the huge erection when the winged horse had first spotted the handsome, strong champion's impressive, muscular, naked body, and the flying horse desired sodomizing the brave lad.

'I guess that's what happens when Pegasus got the hots for the Chimera, which incidentally, was also a gay male creature just like the immortal flying horse is,' Bellerophon realized and acknowledged. 'And it's a good thing that those faggot kings' Proteus and Lykia don't have access to the potent philter elixir, or else I'd be sodomized by both of those asinine homos' day and night for the rest of my goddamned, pathetic life! Oh well,' the hero concluded. 'I ought to retrieve the Chimera's body parts before the kingdom's scavengers get around to devouring them. I'll then obediently take the lion's head and the slain beast's other sections and present them to King Lykia, so that I could be publicly 'lionized', and officially receive my deserved rewards.'

"Here, my faggot King Lykia, are the various remaining body parts of the Chimera," Bellerophon sincerely announced to the astonished Ruler. "Now, please keep your promise and give me my solid oak dinette kitchen set, along with an accompanying matching hutch."

"Bellerophon, you may now have and own my entire bankrupt furniture store," King Lykia surprisingly answered. Then, the Ruler covetously admired the Chimera's various body parts, including the cockroach-sized dick, and the hippopotamus-sized butt-hole. "And I now intend to go into the taxidermist business. I can make a fantastic fortune selling these initial Chimera body parts. And young man," the lunatic king continued while addressing the audacious but thick-headed Bellerophon, "there' are only a thousand more nasty monsters in my realm for you to slay before you finally gain your independence. After I sell those ten-thousand, high-priced monster body parts to eager collectors for astronomical profits," Lykia very deliberately stated, "I'll then be the richest fuckin' king this side of the harvest moon, and you, Bellerophon, will have finally earned your freedom!"

"Daphne's Daft Daffiness"

In prehistoric times, before mankind knew how to write alphabets, or even wipe their smelly asses, or have raucous group sex in full cesspools, the sun god Phoebus Apollo exited his white marble palace, and roamed the Earth searching for compounds necessary to invent toilet paper, and also ribbed prophylactics. During one of his enterprising expeditions, Apollo encountered Stupid Cupid, another renowned archer, who was then in the pride of his youth.

"What do you have in your *quiver?*" Apollo asked the neurotic boy wonder. "My dick always quivers and becomes straight as an arrow whenever I see a beautiful mortal woman."

"Arrows that I shoot at young males and girls, right after they go through the ordeal known as puberty," Stupid Cupid aptly answered. "I have to always check their armpits for hair, just to make sure the lovebirds are no longer children or birds. In the future, though, I intend to use my bow and arrow, and become the big shot around these parts."

"Stupid Cupid," Apollo critically replied. "You don't sound like a real mean guy. But don't you know that I'm the best archer to be found anywhere in ancient Greece? I once *slew* the fierce viper known as the Mighty Monty Python, along with a whole *slew* of other venomous serpents. The beast's hot breath will no longer scorch peoples' asses or ass hair anywhere on the Earth," the sun god haughtily bragged.

"Yes, I have heard of that famous killing!" Stupid Cupid replied. "The Mighty Monty Python kept on screaming at you, 'A-pollo is a chicken! A-pollo is a chicken'! Then, you reactively eliminated its ass, anus and all!"

"Aren't you aware, Stupid Cupid, that war weapons like bows and arrows are for mighty warriors like me, and not for young, precocious, ambitious dumb-fucks such as yourself? I mean," Apollo expounded and clarified, "you can keep your fuckin' dinky darts, but leave the use of the sacred bow to a highly-skilled expert such as myself. Do you now fully comprehend *that* obvious, rudimentary detail, you young, moronic hooligan?"

Apollo's arrogance really pissed-off Stupid Cupid. "I need not *apolo*gize to you for anything on Earth, or in Heaven," the brash youth answered in a typical Stupid Cupid inane pun. "My trusty bow will impress you with its accuracy, and you'll really regret insulting my ass way out here in the middle of nowhere. When I get done with you, you' classic freak show," the punk upstart threatened, "you'll wish you were fuckin' *bow*-legged! You'll indeed have trouble on how to dodge my dart!"

Without wasting another second, and before Apollo could get over *his* excessive laughter, Stupid Cupid flew-up into the air, and withdrew two small magic arrows from his leather quiver, situated between his fluffy white wings. The first projectile was a glistening golden dart that had a barbed point with the word "Love" etched onto it. The second little projectile had a shiny, silver, barbed point that had the word "Hate" inscribed. As Apollo cackled-away, holding his gut, Stupid Cupid (who indeed was a real mean guy) took aim with the more dangerous silver arrow, which was a good solution to conflicts and arguments, centuries before mankind had invented and utilized such things as silver bullets.

Apollo ducked-down just in time as the silver "Hate Arrow" whizzed-by his head and accidentally implanted itself into the left breast of Daphne, a beautiful maiden, who had been washing her pink panties at a stream on the other side of the forest.

Daphne was the daughter of the River King Peneus, who immorally pimped his daughter out for prostitution, so that the greedy asshole could save sufficient money to open an unlicensed riverboat casino. But Stupid Cupid's silver arrow inspired the emotion of 'Hate' to dwell and thrive in Daphne's heart, for as everyone from Athens to Sparta knows, Hate is really Love upside down, and it is often difficult to distinguish between the two abstract qualities, especially when jealousy and pride enter into the emotional equation, and really begin further complicating matters.

Stupid Cupid then took his bow, and more-carefully aimed his second projectile. When Apollo's eyes perceived the painful golden Love Arrow (which actually had been aimed at his super-productive testicles) approaching *his* heart, the arrogant sun god quickly pivoted-around, and Cupid's second sharp arrowhead penetrated the right cheek of *his* noble, delicate ass. The proud-but-embarrassed god raced through the woods, and finally yanked the golden dart from his buttocks while still on the run.

Finally, the fleet *Olympian* (who appeared to be individually competing in the *Ancient Greece Summer Olympics*) encountered the disreputable forest nymphomaniac, Daphne, whom the sun god immediately fell in love with, although she instantly despised and loathed his egocentric personality.

The elusive girl sprinted in the opposite direction, but Daphne was aggressively and amorously chased by sexually-aroused Apollo. The focused god of music and medicine had the biggest erection of his entire life, several millennia before the popular drug *Viagra* made its wonderful appearance inside Earth pharmacies, and on world black markets, which are presently controlled by both homosexual and heterosexual African priests, and other treacherous and unscrupulous *white-collar* criminals.

"Slow-down, oh gorgeous Nymph, daughter of that insidious river gambler Peneus," Apollo futilely yelled-out. "My dick-stick is so long right now that it scrapes a deep furrow into the ground every time I attempt dashing after your unrivaled beauty. I entreat you, lovely forest doll," the sun god beseeched. "My two-hundred-pound body now contains a nine-pound-dick, being fueled by a nasty hundred-and-ninety-pounds of explosive sperm juice!"

"I shall flee from you like the lamb runs from the wolf; like the deer from the lion; like the dove from the eagle, and like diarrhea from an overactive asshole!" Daphne exuberantly exclaimed as the alarmed nymph rushed-forward along the cluttered forest trail. "Thank goodness this path is too narrow for you to speed your chariot and your four, white, fire-breathing stallions upon. Their terrible exhaling would set the whole fuckin' forest on fire, and into a roaring inferno during their hot pursuit!" Daphne panted as the beautiful girl bolted forward in sheer determination. "Shit! My gorgeous golden bush might have also caught on fire, too!"

"You forget, gorgeous Daphne, that I am no common man, either with or without a damned enviable hard-on!" Apollo shouted as the horny pursuer carefully lifted his huge, long erection out of the trench he had just burrowed. "I am no mere shepherd; blacksmith, or farmer. Almighty Zeus was my regal sire. And although I am a renowned and accomplished archer," the sun god hypothesized and yelled-ahead, "that little runt Stupid Cupid's aim is much more accurate than mine is. My heart is seriously wounded, and has pumped all of my rich blood from my cranium down to my magnificent throbbing god-hood!"

"You *are* the illustrious god of healing," Daphne laughed as the beautiful chick sprinted towards her father's illegal river and casino barge, which was still under construction. "But there is no cure for a heart filled with desire such as the one you possess. That frivolous Stupid Cupid runt has you wildly chasing the nearest available cunt, and nothing more!" the foxy vixen cutely rhymed.

The vivacious girl's sexy, transparent, sheer garments fluttered in the wind, as the nymph dashed ever faster through the enchanting, maze-like forest. While Daphne's golden locks waved in the breeze, Apollo realized that not even a greyhound (or any other similar kind of bus, oxcart or chariot) could catch her, especially a horny greyhound, featuring a nine-pound erection. In an act of total desperation, Apollo stopped his advance, and then the horny god inserted an arrow from his quiver into his reliable second-best bow in the country.

Daphne turned her head to again verbally antagonize her obstinate pursuer. "Oh Apollo, you cretin fool; you lust for my curvaceous, hourglass body!" the knockout young broad shouted. "You are taking measured aim at me, you ridiculous Nim*rod!"* Daphne yelled as her eyes gaped at his immense, red, throbbing *god*-hood, a mere two-hundred-feet behind her.

The sex-driven sun god could not resist Daphne's charms any longer. While still running, Apollo accidentally released a lethal arrow from his bow, and it pierced his female idol in the center of her left breast. Soon, Daphne's tits were covered with brown bark, her golden hair and bush magically grew into green leaves, and her slender arms and solid legs had transformed into sturdy branches. When Apollo arrived and witnessed the remarkable transformation, the moron finally realized that he had in his haste accidentally used his detrimental "Laurel Tree Conversion Arrow", instead of the more resourceful and required, "Female Hormone Inducing Arrow."

"Shit!" Apollo exclaimed in despair and regret. "Just look what the fuck I've done now! What the fuck am' I goin' to do with this massive erection I've achieved?"

Apollo embraced the recently converted laurel tree, sorrowfully pulled his arrow out of its trunk, and then stroked its soft green leaves, and kissed its brown coarse bark. 'If I chop this tree down and cut it in two,' the disconsolate sun god speculated, 'then I could finally rest on my laurels.'

Suddenly, the glorious Mt. Olympus deity became inspired. Stimulated by the tree's wonderful textures, the still-aroused sun god thrust his enormous three-foot-long erection into a squirrel hole on the right side of the laurel, which Phoebus Apollo imagined to be Daphne's wet, pink honey-well. Remarkably, the tree was well lubricated on the inside, and grateful Apollo relieved his anxiety by popping a tremendous explosion of sperm juice into the laurel tree's spacious interior, instantly killing a resident squirrel family.

'Now, I know exactly where to come when I need to come!' Apollo aptly concluded. 'That pleasing pleasure sure beats the hell out of jerking-off. This laurel tree shall be held in high esteem, and in great honor, in the Pantheon of my divine, endless, demented, totally sick mind.'

And ever since Apollo saw fit to screw the laurel tree (which he actually thought and believed was Daphne's luscious vagina), laurel has been used as the crowning symbol for all athletes winning Olympic sporting events.

And famous kings and emperors from Alexander the Great to Julius Caesar also honored the fine laurel leaf tradition that Apollo had established on that legendary afternoon in the anonymous enchanting forest. Every time in future history when Greco-Roman rulers had erections, the monarchs would seek-out the nearest laurel tree, and pump the hell out of it, in remembrance and in reverence honoring the inimitable Apollo, along with his two awesome arrows.

"Psyche and Stupid Cupid"

"Psyche and Stupid Cupid" is an illogical mythological story about the relationship of the soul to love, but the myth has little to do with people that love soul food, so don't be miffed by this myth. An ancient Greek king had three beautiful daughters, and was always teased by friends, "It takes a man to make a man, you weak-spermed asshole!" But the youngest daughter, Psyche's pulchritude, rivaled that of Aphrodite herself, in spite of the goddess's very prosperous Sahara-based diaper service, then fondly known as "the Afro-dite Company". And Psyche's two lovely sisters were so jealous of her reputed charms that the girls were all-psyched-up to harm or injure the beauty by scarring-up her perfect face in a much-anticipated, female hair-pulling, nail-scratching catfight.

Psyche's fame spread all over the Earth, which back then in antiquity meant a ten-mile 'radius', minus an ulna. Local yokels with nothing better to do with their spare time, or with their lackluster lives, journeyed from as far as nine miles away to admire and adore Psyche, who ignored their special homage, because the beauty basically had lesbian inclinations, ever since she had vacationed on a wild spring academy break on the notorious Isle of Lesbos.

"Aphrodite herself is not as gorgeous as Psyche," men would say, just to break the goddess's non-existent balls. "Let's abandon the deity's temples and leave her altars neglected. We'll forget all about Aphrodite's prodigious charms, until she finally wises-up and becomes 'Venus in Blue Jeans'."

"I've had just about enough of this mortal bull-shit about Psyche!" Aphrodite shouted at her very innocent and inanimate reflection pool image. "I'll have my devoted son, the winged Stupid Cupid, use his illustrious love darts to help solve my nasty problem. This fuckin' Psyche is makin' me fuckin' psychotic!"

Stupid Cupid arrived on *Mt. Olympus* after being summoned by Hermes, the messenger god, whose erratic temperament was indeed very 'flighty'. "Use your potent arrows, Stupid Cupid, and have one hit Psyche right in the center of her crotchola," Aphrodite commanded her immature son. "I want the vixen to fall madly in love with the most hideous-looking creature residing down there on Earth. Men will become too afraid to worship the glamorous bitch, and will soon again show their staunch allegiance to *my* celebrated beauty. We Mt. Olympus gods and goddesses are sick and tired of putting-up with so much prolific bull-shit being generated by vile. ambitious mortals."

Now Cupid himself happened to be very much in love with Psyche, and did not fully heed his mother's definite instruction. 'To hell with mother's perpetual horse crap!' Cupid thought. 'If it were fuckin' centuries later in history, I could send the fair Psyche a goddamned Valentine! Why must I have such a temperamental bitch like Aphrodite for an arrogant, deadbeat mom?'

Years passed, and Psyche's two older sisters married important kings of unimportant cities. Men still craved her charm, but then feeling inferior to the maiden's awesome beauty, the sagacious suitors married more ugly and fatter women that were good cooks and terrific housekeepers.

The *Oracle of Apollo at Delphi* augured to Aphrodite that Psyche must be placed on a distant mountain's summit to have a summit meeting with a gruesome bisexual monster that would make her his lawful wedded wife, for the beast was a sexually-confused, dick-less creature that liked aloof lesbian women, whether they originated from Lesbos or not.

Psyche dressed herself in her most radiant purple gown, and that day appeared on top of the sacrificial mountain. The sorrowful girl maintained her courage, but desperately wished to lose her virginity. "Aphrodite, I mean you no harm!" Psyche prayed to the apathetic, unsympathetic heavens. "Why are you so envious of me? Your pussy must be just as hairy as mine, and maybe even more juicy!"

"Go tell it on the mountain, you' narcissistic little bitch!" an angry female voice yelled-down from the thick clouds to Earth. "You' young, witchy, wannabe' will soon have a historic rendezvous with destiny! Ha, ha, ha!" Aphrodite's loud voice cackled and crackled from the sky. "And I hope you meet your doom sometime before fuckin' doomsday! Ha, ha, ha!"

Psyche wept and shivered at her horrible fate on top of the nameless, insignificant, sacrificial mountain. Soon, the cool breath of Zephyr came wafting-up through the crags to the peak, and the strong gust unexpectedly whisked-away Psyche. The beauty floated, drifted, and then glided like a bird from the rocky apex to a lush green meadow laden with flowers, which stimulated the girl's allergies so badly that she sneezed her lungs out for three solid hours, until the victim finally passed-out. Back then in mythology, a person could easily pass 'Out' since there were no dumb parlor board games where Psyche could pass 'Go' and collect two hundred Drachmas, or a thousand Staters. In fact, there weren't even any damned parlors (ice cream, funeral or otherwise) around during those miserable, ancient, backward times.

Psyche awoke from her unconscious state without any Staters (to coin an expression) in her possession. The vivacious doll surveyed her immediate environment, and observed a flawless, immaculate-looking mansion situated next to a scenic river. The stately residence had pillars of gold, and inside (looking from outside) could be seen splendid jeweled floors, and spectacular silver walls. The landscape was abundant with fragrant flowers that again seriously activated the damsel's sensitive sinuses.

'This fantastic house must be reserved exclusively for me!' Psyche thought. 'But what the hell is the good of being a damned horny lesbian when a person is all alone?' she conjectured. 'And if I'm the only one around these parts, this magnificent mansion can't even be a house of prostitution for straight assholes, let alone a hopping bordello for amorous queers and kinky faggots!'

The mortal beauty cautiously entered the impressive mansion, took a refreshing bath, masturbated for a whole hour with a squash and a cucumber, and then dined at a feast table that had been mysteriously prepared just for her appreciation. Sweet music swirled around her head, and blessed her ears, and Psyche wondered what her husband would look like when he would eventually arrive home for a well-deserved piece of ass.

'I hope he sodomizes me up the old exit hole!' the girl wished. 'Oh well, if he eats me out, I'll just pretend that he's one of my sisters or girlfriends! I can't wait to get lewd and nude! I don't want to disappoint him, whoever the fuck he is! I just can't wait to tingle his dingle!'

That night in bed, Psyche' felt a warm form lying beside her inside the dark chamber. His soft voice whispered in her ear, and kept inanely repeating: "Sweet nothings! Sweet nothings!" Then, the anxious and curious girl pondered, 'He does not sound like an evil, hideous monster at all! He just sounds like a goddamned stupid parrot who, just like history, ignorantly repeats himself!'

'I'd rather have sour somethings in my mouth than fuckin' sweet nothings in my ears!' Psyche concluded. 'And I don't even know what the hell my husband looks like, even though he sounds somewhat gentle and tranquil when he isn't farting. How do I know that my fucked-up, anonymous spouse isn't just a trick, artificial, goddamned ventriloquist's voice?' the knockout girl wondered. 'On the other hand, what kind of naïve, beautiful dolt like me wants to sleep with Medusa's fraternal twin brother?'

One night, Psyche's psychic husband warned her in the dark that her two jealous sisters would arrive at the mansion and plot against her, and also, conspire against her stable marriage. "And if you allow the two troublemakers to see and converse with you," the suspicious husband cautioned Psyche, "it will erode my passion for you, and your immense stubbornness will ruin your life. You might even die a fuckin' virgin, you lustful, licentious, lesbian bitch."

Psyche pledged in the dark to her monster husband that she would not meet and consult with her envious sisters, both of whom were AC/DC bisexual broads. The young bride thought about having oral sex with her older sisters Leslie and Lezzie, and when Psyche finally fell asleep, all her subconscious mind could think about was eating out, but definitely not at any ancient Greek, fast-food, Spartan restaurant.

The following night, the mysterious, secretive husband rolled into bed and sensed that his sex-starved wife had been dreaming of having lesbian sex with her deceitful siblings. "Do what you want to do," the psychic husband related to Psyche' in her latest fantasy dream. "But you're undoubtedly courting disaster. And Psyche, you must not allow your lustful sisters to see me, or else you'll suffer retribution that you will surely regret. Now continue sleeping, while I jerk-off and relive my ever-mounting tension that I feel when desiring to be mounting you; and then mounting my horse, to be followed by mounting the mountain."

As Psyche was about to orgasm in her sleep from having her crack being double munched in her dream by her horny, kinky sisters, the sleeping beauty screamed-out in her Morpheus state, "Yes! Yes! Yesssss!" while her preoccupied husband exploded his colossal load clear across the bedroom and out the open window, killing and decapitating an innocent ostrich taking a night shit outside the opulent mansion.

The next morning, the two envious sisters were conducted down from the sacrificial mountain to the meadow below by the breath of Zephyr, who had nothing more urgent to do with his time except to blow everyone he saw, either male or female. After Psyche greeted her reprehensible siblings, the three engaged in wild, perverted, lesbian activity for three consecutive hours, until their honey-wells were dry and chaffed from excessive licking, lapping, gnawing and fingering. Finally, the threesome re-entered their clothes, and Psyche gave Leslie and Lezzie a personal tour of the resplendent palatial mansion.

"Where is that beautiful music coming from?" Leslie asked. "It sounds just divine, as if Apollo has his sturdy penis and hairy balls caught in his lyre's strings."

"The enchanting melody is my secret husband's doing, and is probably generated by some form of immortal witchcraft," Psyche answered. "Isn't his bird-like trilling thrilling?"

"What does this mysterious and elusive husband of yours actually look like?" Lezzie inquired. "We could arrange for him a wonderful sex transformation operation, and then shave our pussies and glue the soft-textured hair around his newly formed bare slit hole. Then, we could all share your husband, when your spouse decides he can no longer be a fucked-up, straight, male heterosexual."

"My handsome husband is presently away on a hunting expedition with several immortal friends," Psyche liberally lied. "But I shall tell him of your marked curiosity. Here now, my jealous sisters. Take these marvelous lustrous jewels back to the sacrificial mountain. I shall summon Zephyr to transport you there, even though neither of you have dicks to be administered adequate blowjobs." But the extravagant gifts only made the two elder sisters more cunning, more despicable, more envious, and more avaricious than ever.

In her deep sleep that night, Psyche's strange husband again warned his wife in the dark of her abhorrent, aberrant, disobedient deportment. "Don't you dare allow those raunchy, greedy bitches to visit you again!" the powerful voice implored in the middle of a nightmare. "I'm fully aware of your gay, deviant activities, and find them both mentally and emotionally repugnant. Still, dear Psych; I intend to love you despite these terrible fuckin' conflictive feelings we're both now experiencing."

'Am I forbidden to see all other humans?' Psyche contemplated in her sleep. 'Must I be deprived of seeing my own flesh and blood, all because of your tyrannical, nonsensical, incomprehensible commands? Give me an answer, you friggin' omniscient asshole!'

"Okay; I'll surrender that point and concur that you may see your pernicious sisters," the monster's voice compromised. "But no perverted lesbian sex, you understand! Your delightful pussy and maidenhead are to be saved exclusively for me, and I don't want one of your sister's inferior tongues breaking your sacred hymen! Got that, you damned, unfaithful, unreliable bitch!"

Again, the diabolical older sisters arrived from the sacrificial mountain to the incomparable mansion, but the siblings had to honor Psyche's new rules of engagement. "I will lick, suck, and masturbate the two of you one at a time," the youngest sister stipulated. "But since I'm having my period, my own love tunnel is presently off limits to both of you horny dykes. Got that, you faggot bitches!"

After three hours of intense lesbian activity, the visiting sisters and Psyche dressed themselves, and sat impatiently at the mansion's elegant white marble banquet table. Soon, the conversation turned from pleasurable female homosexuality to Psyche's luscious right titty, and finally, the three discussed the nymph's husband's anonymous identity.

"Dear Psyche; I have heard from random gossip in the village marketplace that your spouse is not a man, but a wretched monster," Leslie confidentially disclosed. "And the hideous thing you sleep with possesses a devastating thick, six-foot-long dick, that could stretch from one person's yard clear into a neighbor's yard. It is no fuckin' wonder that the grotesque creature's pecker is a staggering fuckin' two *yards* long!"

"And Apollo's *Oracle at Delphi* has recently revealed that after your husband, the awesome monster, finally gets around to pumping the holy shit out of you, my dear Psyche," Lezzie profoundly interrupted, "then the vile menace will eagerly commence eating your love tunnel in imitation of Leslie and me, but then while you're delighting in your rapturous pleasure, the odious creature will devour you right-up, starting with your heavenly pubic snatch and your delicious, squiggly, honey-sweet, cantaloupe-sized clit."

"What should I do?" the bewildered Psyche asked her 'siblings' without any indication of rivalry. "I've never had my snatch eaten by a male mouth and tongue before, be the male either human, or animal, or a combination of both!"

"Listen to us, Psyche. You must hide a sharp knife and a small lamp under your bed," Leslie seriously advised. "When your phantom husband is sleeping, leave the bed and carefully light the lamp."

"Then what?" the perplexed girl worriedly asked. "Should I stab the lamp with the knife, and then light my husband's fire?"

"No Asshole!" Lezzie critically and cynically countered. "You must figure-out where his heart is; stab the son-of-a-bitch creature to death, and then inspect his appearance using the lit lamp. I suggest you fuckin' first study, and then master chronological order, which is also known to serious kindergarten students as 'sequence of events', you moronic bitch."

Psyche's heart was suddenly filled with aggression and terror, which caused the immediate evacuation of all love and affection from her 'auricles'; the violence that had been prescribed by several oracles. The comely maiden angrily dismissed and chased-away her conniving, covetous sisters from the luxurious mansion, threatening with her brandished knife to have their tits displayed as trophies on the fabulous edifice's walls, right next to elephant, rhinoceros and giraffe butts, dicks and balls. Then, the confused maiden entered her lonely mansion.

'Why is my husband such an evasive prowler?' Psyche asked her inanimate bedroom mirror. 'Why is he so brutal in keeping me sheltered from my own family, and for that matter, from the entire Zeus-damned human race? Why does my anonymous spouse have to be so fucked-up? Why does my weird husband shun daylight, and act in a clandestine manner at night?' the girl wondered and pouted. 'Does he think he's the fuckin' dark side of the moon? That's it! That's why my husband is a goddamned *luna*tic! He believes he's the fuckin' dark side of the moon! Maybe I'll embarrass and shock the shit out of him tonight by holding the lit lamp up to my bare ass, and then mooning the unpredictable idiotic bastard!'

For the remainder of that same afternoon, Psyche' rationally assessed all of the circumstances involved with, and surrounding, her introverted husband. 'I don't have the courage or the strength to brutally kill him as my wicked sisters suggest,' the girl thought and sobbed. 'But I am very curious and determined to discover what the Hades my phantom spouse looks like. I mean, for Zeus Olympus's sake,' the girl mentally cursed. 'He *is,* after all, my fuckin' lucky, un-betrothed husband!'

That night, Psyche woke up at 3 a.m. and remembered to initiate her meticulous plan. As her anonymous husband lay sleeping next to her horny body, the new bride intrepidly-but-foolishly lit the lamp, when her sisters' specific instructions were to first stab and kill her suspected monster spouse, and then light the damned lamp. The young woman held the dull light up to his facial features, and was relieved to see a handsome young man, and not a grotesque creature, lying beside her as had been expected.

'Holy Hermes!' Psyche thought as she gazed upon her mystery spouse. 'He's a real doll, with a nice firm, muscular body, and not Medusa's horrible-looking brother after all! Now I despise my sisters more than ever for lying to me. And to add to my fuckin' quandary,' the girl speculated, 'my sweet husband will know that I have betrayed his faith should he suddenly awake, and rightfully beat the shit out of me.'

And just as Psyche was imagining some warm sperm went shooting out of her husband's outstanding sexual apparatus, when several drops of hot oil simultaneously spilled out of the lamp, searing *his* left shoulder. Stupid

Cupid (Psyche's bed partner) instantly awoke, realized that Psyche had the hots for him, and next leaped out of bed and sprinted out of the bedroom, as if his wife had brutally scalded his sensitive dick, instead of scorching his very masculine shoulder.

The aroused wife dashed-out of the mansion in hot pursuit, but could not locate the agile winged Cupid's whereabouts. But her ears perceived his distraught voice originating from a far distance.

"Psyche; I am Stupid Cupid, your husband substitute for a most heinous and grotesque monster intended for you by *Olympus*. My nefarious mother Aphrodite had ordered me to condemn you to the sacrificial mountain, but I considered you to be so beautiful that I disobediently deviated from her austere command, and decided to marry you," the notorious Symbol of Love divulged. "Although I inspire love in others with my tiny arrows, I am very shy, and have never gotten laid. But now I must tell you that goddamned love can't possibly exist where there is no trust; so therefore, dear Psyche, I must spend the rest of my life jerking-off because *you* have un- necessarily treated me like a mortal jerk-off!"

The enchanting male voice ceased speaking, and Psyche was now fully aware that her insulted husband had indeed abandoned her. 'The God of Love was my husband, and I was too concerned about being a damned lesbian that I relinquished being the most-happy wife in the world; that is, once Cupid would finally get the balls to pump the poop out of me,' the dream girl regretted. 'I could've started him out with a little sodomy up the tight exit hole, and gradually taught Cupid how to pork my love tunnel like there's no tomorrow. Damn it!' Psyche admitted with obvious remorse. 'Why am I such a stupid, selfish cunt? That's even worse than being a stupid, selfish asshole!'

Then, some other interesting thoughts paraded around inside Psyche's unsettled mind. 'I could spend the remainder of my mortal existence searching for him as a token of my love, and as evidence of my guilt,' the upset young woman sadly lamented. 'But I have no idea where to begin to search, or where to go. Now, just wait a goddamned minute!' the knockout doll considered. 'Where does a man usually go when he leaves his wife? Exactly! He always goes to see his goddamned mother, that's fuckin' where he goes!'

Stupid Cupid did journey up to celestial *Mt. Olympus* to consult with Aphrodite, who immediately put a wet, dirty, used diaper on his gross-looking shoulder wound. The Goddess of Love listened to her melancholy son's solemn and lugubrious recollection of recent events, and after learning that he had chosen to marry *her* mortal nemesis Psyche, the resolute Goddess of Beauty became excessively pissed-off and rebuked Stupid Cupid for his disrespectful, disloyal disobedience.

"Why the fuck didn't you follow my specific directions?" Aphrodite chastised. "I hope right now that your fuckin' shoulder snaps and falls off! You could then use the joints as several of your damned inaccurate arrows!"

"But Mother, I was smitten with love!" Cupid readily admitted. "Now I know what the fuck it feels like whenever one of my' tiny arrows pierces someone's emotions. It makes the arrow between my legs rise and want to shoot millions and millions of wriggling sperms all over the fuckin' place!"

"Either jerk-off or fuck-off, that's my sage advice to you, my unappreciative son!" Aphrodite sternly admonished. "Any female who prefers another woman's pussy to a nice long firm erection like yours is truly fucked-up! That's the short and the long of it, my son!" And with that harsh rebuking, Aphrodite vanished into thin air to travel down to Earth to have some decent down-to-Earth heterosexual intercourse with a most-fortunate, randomly selected, mortal male.

But after getting laid by thirty different ordinary men at half-hour intervals, Aphrodite plotted to have her sweet revenge on Psyche for stimulating her virgin son's vulnerable libido.

In the meantime, Psyche creatively offered used tampon sacrifices to Zeus, to Apollo, and to Hermes, to win those *Mt. Olympus* gods' sympathies over to her maniacal cause; but unfortunately, none of the male gods desired having a treacherous female deity such as Aphrodite as *their* eternal immortal enemy, or as their eternal immortal friend, either.

'I have only one fuckin' option left!' Psyche brilliantly deducted. 'I'll go directly to Aphrodite and request to be her dutiful servant. Perhaps she'll relent and ease her resentment of my beauty, and allow my marriage with her foxy son to continue, and eventually be divinely sanctioned.'

When Psyche finally did encounter the goddess outside a prominent Athenian whorehouse, Aphrodite was not-too-enthused about the impromptu meeting. "So, Psyche," the Goddess of Love and Beauty declared in a nasty, condescending tone of voice. "You almost-scalded your husband to death with flaming hot oil, and now you seek my blessing, you scurrilous, lesbian, harlot, little bitch! Do you think I look like a fuckin' queer dyke from futuristic Holland, or what?"

"Oh, dear Goddess; please have mercy on my unfortunate plight," Psyche pleaded. "Give me a daunting task to perform, so that I may prove my sincerity to you, and also demonstrate my genuine intention to serve you, and faithfully service your quite-remarkable, sex-starved son."

"Very well then," the scheming goddess reluctantly agreed. "Here, inside this bag I am holding, is a mixture of seven pounds of grain seeds: a pound each of oats, rye, wheat, poppy, millet, rice and corn. Your asshole assignment is to assiduously sort and separate the seven seeds into seven smaller one-pound bags. If you successfully complete that particular duty, I'll then consider your extraordinary situation, and perhaps decide to break your goddamned ovaries some more!"

And after uttering that formidable challenge, Aphrodite rose-up into the air, and miraculously and divinely disappeared into the lower atmosphere.

Psyche immediately stepped behind the aforementioned Athenian brothel, and poured the seven pounds of various seeds onto the ground. Then she manufactured seven small bags from the one large one, using a thread and needle she had acquired from a seamstress gay whore friend, employed inside the popular bisexual house of prostitution. 'This pile of seven different seeds is a real heap of trouble!' Psyche contemplated as she scrutinized the high mound of seven various tiny grain seeds. 'This pile is worse than any pile I've ever had anywhere, either inside or hanging outside my goddamned almost-flawless butt! I suppose that's why I'm a perfect asshole!'

The girl's mind was in an amazing maze, as she examined the pile of maize seeds, along with the six other grain-types mixed-in. But although no humans or immortals rendered any assistance to her present dire need, a colony of industrious ants marching-up in neat columns from the soil, and made themselves useful to Psyche's immediate concerns. The helpful insects meticulously divided into seven armies, and each group specialized in sorting the seven different seeds into seven distinct piles, each of which Psyche gladly gathered and deposited into the seven tightly-sewn bags. And when Aphrodite returned to the famous whorehouse to again masquerade as a horny slut, the itinerant goddess was very displeased at Psyche's very apparent, and quite extraordinary, achievement.

"Your labors are certainly not over by a long shot," Aphrodite angrily remarked. "This punishment matter is indeed a very seedy business, as you've already discovered," the goddess indicated to the now-apprehensive girl. "But since you've surprised me with your exceptional problem-solving ability, I must put you to sleep until I can fabricate another fuckin' difficult chore for you to perform! Now young bitch, you must soundly sleep, while I deviously develop another challenging labor for you!"

The following morning, Psyche was sleeping in Cupid's impeccable mansion, dreaming of becoming a bona fide bisexual, when Aphrodite rudely-awakened her with a plethora of obnoxious ranting, and dictatorial imperatives.

"Wake-up, you drowsy Bitch!" the goddess screamed while shaking the beauty out of the rest of her beauty rest. "Assuming that you have the get-up and go, get-up and go down to the meadow having the *thick dark bushes* that are fluffy, just like your lovely snatcheroo, and also, just like my splendid pubic garden, and pluck some of the shiny golden wool from the sacred sheep fleeces," the jealous goddess emphatically instructed.

When Psyche arrived at the smooth flowing river, the beauty had to resist a very strong temptation to fling herself into the stream and drown by suicide, because her soul had been so sadly laden with despair and grief. "Oh, don't sacrifice your life!" a zany frog hollered from a remote lily pad. "We distraught frogs are the only ones allowed to croak in this goddamned pristine river!"

"How am I to collect the golden wool from the bleating sheep?" Psyche asked the humorous, distant *bull*frog, who had long hard horns on his head, like-a-bull has. "I feel so disconsolate that I don't even want to visit the Greek consulate," the melancholy girl honestly indicated to the sympathetic amphibian.

"Just hang-out near the bushes, and the many branches will soon catch enough golden wool from the sheeps' backs to entirely fill your two sacks," the droll frog revealed. "And if I were a horny toad, instead of a lethargic, impotent bull-shitting bullfrog, I'd hop right into the friggin' sack with you! And if you think a goddamned frog in your throat feels funny, just imagine experiencing one inside your smelly crotch!"

Psyche politely thanked the comedic creature for his wise counsel, and was able to successfully transport back to Aphrodite two full sacks of wonderful golden wool. But the attractive girl's success predictably again drew Aphrodite's vehement wrath.

"Someone had to fuckin' help you with accomplishing your mission," the enraged goddess protested. "If I find out who it was, I'll immediately turn the brazen son-of-a-bitch into a goddamned bullfrog, just like I usually do. Now, I'm so aggravated that I'm going to assign you to a new task that is virtually impossible to perform. Even that asshole simpleton Hercules would balk enacting this new accursed labor I shall contrive and institute!"

"Does my new project entail that black water flowing from yonder hill?" Psyche reflexively and perceptively asked. "Do I have to fuckin' paint the black water blue?"

"No, naughty vixen, but that was not such a bad fuckin' idea," Aphrodite complimented Psyche with a false smile exhibited upon her countenance. "That black water is coming from the underground *River Styx* that divides the Land of the Living from Hades' macabre, morbid Kingdom of the Dead. Here is a large gallon flask," the perturbed goddess pointed-out. "Your fuckin' assignment is to completely fill the huge tube with the deadly, poisonous, highly toxic cascading *Styx* water."

"Styx and stones may break my bones," Psyche eloquently chanted, "but your fucked-up words will never hurt me, you distrustful vulture bitch. I wish that you contract Alzheimer's disease along with amnesia, before I ever complete the dangerous black water mission, so that you won't remember to relentlessly curse my ass again and again in the future, you mangy Mother!"

When Psyche finally approached the roaring waterfall, she realized that only a large winged creature could effectively reach the cascading river, and fill the enormous vile vial with deadly water. 'These algae-laden rocks are slippery, steep and slimy,' the beautiful maiden decided. 'And only a graduate student from *Slippery Rock,* or a large winged animal could possibly reach and contend with the wild turbulent flow.'

An *Eagle* from Philadelphia was cognizant of Psyche's dilemma, and instantly came to her assistance. The big bird grabbed the mammoth flask with its powerful beak, mistaking the tube for a *beak*er. Soon, it brought the tube, filled with venomous black water, back to Psyche's location next to the ominous giant waterfall, spewing water from the subterranean *River Styx.*

"Thank you, dear *Eagle,"* the indebted girl declared. "And I only wish that my husband's bird will be half as big as you are."

But Aphrodite persisted in giving Psyche another abominable quest to attempt. The divine bitch handed her already-discouraged mortal enemy a box, and the restive recipient was directed to journey to the underworld, which at that crazy era in mythology, was not governed by the dastardly ancient Greco-Roman Mafia. The girl instantly fathomed that her next exploit would be borderline insanity to perform.

"Well, mortal Girl, possessing only temporary beauty that will fade within the century," Aphrodite sarcastically began. "You must carry this common box to the dreadful afterworld, and have Queen Persephone fill it with all of her beauty she can fuckin' stuff inside. Tell the pallid-faced Death Queen that I need it, after having the harrowing experience of tending to my son's terrible burn injury," Aphrodite instructed. "And Psyche; while down in Hades, just make sure that you don't have your own hairy box stuffed by some stiff corpse's stiff erection, or the whole deal of you being my servant and having a shot at winning Stupid Cupid from me is off," the devious goddess explicitly specified. "Now get the Hades out of here, and don't accept any damned help from that wild and reckless chariot gang, Hades Angels!"

Several dysfunctional area priestesses on drugs gave the girl inaccurate directions to Hades, but upon inaccurately following all of the inaccurate instructions, Psyche finally came to a great hole in the Earth, and a steep vertical tunnel led her down irregular slate steps to the legendary *River Styx,* where Psyche' gave Charon the Grim-Reaper-type ferryman a Drachma for a one-way toll passage. Soon, the nervous girl found the dark path that eventually led her to Queen Persephone's bleak, morgue-like palace.

Cerberus, the freakish immortal, three-headed, rabid dog guarded the solid oak doors, but Psyche flashed her hairy beaver, and showed the ferocious animal some savory wet, pink inners, and the bellicose-but-distracted monster forgot all about being vicious, and began euphorically licking its erect dick with all three of its bobbing heads.

Since Psyche was the first visitor that Persephone had had in the last fifty thousand years, the Death Queen gladly accommodated her benign and courteous guest, and related that an ample sample of her eternal pale beauty had just been conveniently squeezed into the designated box.

Upon reaching the surface after her ten-mile climb, Psyche had a tantalizing need that paralleled the one experienced by Pandora, who according to mythology, was the first woman: she felt a strong compulsion to open her box, even though the girl was not in the mood to masturbate, or vigorously toy with and manipulate any huge squash or cucumber. 'Shit; if I open the box just a tiny crack, my crack might coincidentally turn to cement,' she greatly feared. 'And I might never get my substitute bed partner Stupid Cupid back, and I might also risk Aphrodite turning my dainty pubic hairs into tiny poisonous vipers. Oh well,' Psyche concluded. 'My curiosity is overwhelming, so I might as well open the fuckin' lid, anyway.'

A heavy mallet, belonging to the lame blacksmith god Hephaestus, came falling down from *Mt. Olympus,* and the plummeting hammer impacted Psyche on the noggin, totally knocking her into la-la land. The tool had fallen out of Stupid Cupid's grasp when he was attempting to smash his way out of the marble room's window atop *Mt. Olympus,* where Aphrodite had kept her clumsy son prisoner. Stupid Cupid anxiously flew-down to Earth, because naturally, he was basically a down-to-Earth guy, who instinctively despised pompous *Olympus* arrogance and haughtiness.

After gracefully landing near the dreaded sacrificial mountain, Cupid gingerly wiped the sleep from his wife's eyes, placed the sticky material into the box, and then closed the squeaky lid. And after performing that important service, Stupid Cupid awoke his lovely spouse from her unconsciousness by slapping her face silly a hundred and seventy-six times.

"Here Psyche'," Stupid Cupid declared. "Climb *Mt. Olympus* and take this significant box to my conniving Mother Aphrodite, while I fly-up and confer with Zeus about all this dumb bull-shit we've both been valiantly putting-up with."

"But why can't you just latch onto me, so that I can zoom up there too, and conserve my energy in the process?" Psyche vehemently challenged. "I've got a fuckin' headache that won't quit from going down to Hades to retrieve this container, and it feels like I've been fuckin' zonked on my delicate cranium with an enormous hammer, or perhaps, even an axe!"

"Because that's the fuckin' rules of the game that have been prescribed by Zeus!" Stupid Cupid replied to his incensed potential wife. "Life for immortals like myself, dear Psyche, must be easy, and life for accursed mortals like you, must be hard. Do ya' now get the fuckin' message, my dear devoted wife, and immortal wannabe'?"

Zeus feigned being pissed-off while negotiating Earth diplomacy with obstinate Stupid Cupid. "Your powerful, errant love darts have made me experience the indignity of being changed into animals like bulls and lions," the king-god complained. "But I really wasn't extensively disappointed, because I had found animal sex with mortal women to be just about as rewarding and gratifying as normal sex with goddesses was. And so, young Cupid," Zeus pontificated. "I really enjoyed sex from an animal's point of view, and when I was a happy bull, once I really popped a tremendous load that blasted a beautiful mortal woman right up into the fuckin' stratosphere, after I exploded my imperial essence into her wet, pink vagina while we were standing!"

Zeus granted Stupid Cupid's unique request, and the chief god's justice overrode nefarious Aphrodite's subordinate curse on Psyche. Stupid Cupid and the salvaged beautiful maiden were formally married up inside the largest marble temple on stately *Mt. Olympus,* and Zeus begrudgingly bestowed immortality upon Psyche when the beauty was officially proclaimed (much to Aphrodite's chagrin) a "secondary goddess".

And every night, before Psyche administered a fabulous blowjob to the grinning Stupid Cupid, the wife first smeared nectar and ambrosia onto his two-inch erection, before applying her soft tender lips, thus ensuring that the new goddess's joyful immortality would continue with each successive suck.

"Atalanta's Last Race"

In Greek mythology, references to two different Atalantas exist, and neither of the dolls lived anywhere near Athens or Atlanta, Georgia. One particular Atalanta was the renowned Huntress that carried around the land a *bow,* and the other was a rapid-running speedster (the daughter of King Schoeneus of Boeotia), who was desperately searching for a *beau.* Although the more notorious second Atalanta was very fast afoot, her dim-witted father King Schoeneus was not too swift.

Atalanta had pledged to the Mt. Olympus gods that she would only marry a man that was a faster sprinter than she was. In fact, the girl was speedier than any naval *fleet* known to the ancient world. Young, horny ambitious youths from all over Greece often arrived in Boeotia to race against the speedy lady, and each left the city-state kingdom disappointed and defeated.

King Schoeneus eventually became so pissed-off at all of the foolish, parasitic gigolos showing-up in his isolated land, seeking fame and fortune, that the ruler made an explicit proclamation: "Any dumb-fuck jerk-off with a death wish that comes to Boeotia to challenge my daughter Atalanta to a foot race will be condemned to death at the hands of the official executioner, immediately after losing the contest."

And then the volatile King Schoeneus turned to his beautiful daughter and said, "Atalanta; we need fewer male *racists* in Boeotia, so I made this special law to discriminate against the dirty, intruding, foreign bastards," the elderly, cantankerous ill-tempered, totally soulless monarch preached to his lovely offspring.

One fine morning, an impractical youth name Hippomenes arrived in Boeotia from an unknown *fishing village* (that really only knew how to catch sea bass), the remote, unidentified hamlet being situated on the other side of the vast mountain range. The happy-go-lucky young fellow was really a worthless, idealistic vagabond that lethargically appeared in the inhospitable country, only because his aimless aspiration in life was to wander all over the general topography without ever accomplishing a single damned thing.

"Why is everyone in attendance shouting over there near the pissed-off King?" Hippomenes asked a local resident. "Has a ferocious rogue lion maliciously scratched *their* tender balls, tits and fat asses'?"

"No curious stranger; four young men have recently challenged the King's daughter Atalanta to a foot race, and when the dumb fucked-up aliens lose, the fools will be promptly slaughtered by the royal executioner," the jubilant spectator disclosed to Hippomenes. "We Boeotians are basically cannibalistic and sadistic. We then, according to the King's new edict, will barbecue the four doomed losers' butchered flesh, and have a great picnic feast with lots and lots of delicious grilled meat! That's why everyone in the gallery is cheering and prematurely celebrating their next nutritious meal!"

"Unlucky idiots!" Hippomenes answered, referring to the bold male challengers, and not to the carnivorous citizens of Boeotia. "How foolish the cocky assholes are to risk their lives simply for a permanent piece of ass, and the acquisition of great wealth," the critical wanderer commented to the excited bystander, while the pair both watched the four young men limbering-up their leg muscles for the start of the all-important "life-or-death race".

'This girl Atalanta must be a witch; a powerful enchantress, or a rich bitch with an ideal snatcheroo,' Hippomenes speculated. 'She might even be an evil sorceress, who possesses the ability to attract so many unfortunate, distant, young men to their deaths. This remote desert place Boeotia seems like a foolish paradise. I'm not so sure that I want my life abruptly abbreviated, simply over stupid things like money, prestige, power, good sex, and beauty.'

Soon, the talkative and callow visitor observed Atalanta approaching, and his dingle began throbbing and bobbing under his orange tunic. 'That deadly witch is really a tough-looking bitch!' Hippomenes noted and mentally rhymed. 'My blood-drained brain is so empty and light-headed that I feel like racing her myself, right this very moment.'

The trumpeters' shrill signal to commence the race gradually broke the naïve young man's highly-focused infatuation. On the count of three, the five contestants zoomed-off their starting blocks, but Atalanta soon moved out into the lead with her gorgeous, light-brown tresses blowing and waving over her shoulders in the morning wind.

Hippomenes further evaluated all possible circumstances. 'I hope those four male participants lose the damned race! That way, Atalanta will still be available for me to vanquish in a future sprint,' Hippomenes selfishly thought. 'I'll simply eat a pound of baked beans tomorrow morning and take-off like a falcon out of Hades, making a run to the first outhouse just beyond the finish line. But right now, I must admit, I've never attended a real-life human barbecue before,' the itinerant youth acknowledged. 'And

I'm enthusiastically looking forward to voraciously eating and licking other men's meat!'

Atalanta easily and deftly crossed the finish marker, and won the race by a wide margin. King Schoeneus placed a victory laurel wreath on his athletic daughter's head, and announced to the boisterous crowd that a barbecued meat smorgasbord would be set-up in one hour after the royal executioner, royal butchers, and royal chefs completed their particular tasks.

The moody, fickle King looked-down on the throng and spotted the ever-plotting, lazy Hippomenes, while the almost-hypnotized traveler kept his eyes fastened upon the very charming Atalanta's heavily breathing chest. 'These friggin' races are killing my military draft,' the highly mercurial King grieved and mentally weighed. 'That's four more soldiers I could've easily enlisted into my personal bodyguard.'

But soon, the irritated King's daughter's attention turned toward the young newcomer, and the big-breasted girl immediately discerned that the lad would not be satisfied until he became un-mystery meat for a future "Bountiful Boeotian Beef and Ale Barbecue".

"Speak, oh visiting youth!" Schoeneus boomed at the thoroughly-entranced Hippomenes, who was busily admiring the King's daughter's firm tits and voluptuous curves. "Tell us what brings you to Boeotia, as if we all don't fuckin' already know! Can't you get laid in your own fuckin' town, or what?"

"Your vivacious, curvaceous daughter only races wimpy faggots to achieve athletic fame," Hippomenes arrogantly criticized. "She has not gone-up against any man that has superior physical prowess like I possess. I am a son of Poseidon, the immortal sea god," Hippomenes boasted. "And if I lose and am executed and barbecued by you friggin' assholes, then my Big Daddy will seek vengeance by deluging Boeotia with a major tidal wave coming over yonder mountains, and efficiently drowning all of you raunchy bastards and bitches as if your second-classed city was inhabited by a colony of filthy rabid rats!"

"You might want to re-think the possibility of actually losing a race," Schoeneus gulped and whispered to his extremely talented daughter. "This young sucker seems to mean business, and I'm intimidated by his threat that we'll all suddenly drown out here in this desert community, right in the middle of fuckin' nowhere. I wonder if the fool has the wherewithal to actually do what his brazen mouth claims?"

"Don't worry father!" Atalanta supportively answered. "I'll easily defeat his ass, and we'll just call his bluff about Poseidon being his father, and turbulently causing a major aquatic catastrophe! And if I am to drown to death, I can think of no person on this planet whom I'd rather do it with than you, Big Royal Daddy-o!"

But the swift Princess, in her vulnerable heart, also didn't desire to see the young handsome visitor become the next day' menu's barbecue entrée. "Brave, stupid, foolish asshole," Atalanta personally addressed Hippomenes. "Either Apollo, Hermes or maybe even Zeus must be envious of your muscular physique, and each wants to see you aptly eliminated from the rolls of the living by voluntarily becoming 'dead meat'. I strongly suggest that you not meet your imminent doom, and wisely retract your announced intention of racing me," the gorgeous girl begged. "When a simpleton such as yourself races against death and fate, the invincible, almighty gods' opponent, namely me, always wins! I implore you, handsome stranger," the fair maiden continued. "Abandon your unreachable dream and leave Boeotia as soon as possible. The afternoon four-door-chariot to Corinth leaves in two short hours."

"No go, my fair lady," Hippomenes courageously replied. "For I shall enter tomorrow's race and wager my mortal life, just for the privilege to be your dedicated husband. I cannot live with sadness and cowardice, once I have gazed upon your slender beauty, and lustfully admire your firm, hard tits that stick-out from your magnificent chest like perfect dual female erections!"

Atalanta fearfully stepped-away from her fascinating, fascinated challenger, bent-down to adjust her right sandal, and waited for her stern, psychotic, dominant father to answer the eager stranger's brazen remarks. Seconds later, the egomaniac King cleared his parched throat and gave the predictable response.

"Face your destiny at noon tomorrow, young fool!" the King definitively stated. "Prepare to meet your ultimate downfall, you outrageously covetous, wet-behind-the-ears neophyte! Tomorrow you fuckin' die!"

Hippomenes left the belligerent King, *his* stunning daughter, and the fanatical barbecued beef banquet and ale crowd, and hurried into the woods to first vomit, and then take an extended dump in that exact sequence. After the youth mechanically wiped his sore butt with dried leaves and prickly, painful tree bark fragments, the intrepid stud studied the sandy course upon which he and the swift girl would compete. 'Perhaps I spoke too prematurely without analyzing the whole situation properly,' the young fellow regretted. 'Maybe I'm an even bigger asshole than everyone actually thinks that I am? A premature decision is almost as bad as a goddamned premature ejaculation!'

As Hippomenes raised his eyes toward the cloudless blue sky, the ambitious adolescent saw a remarkable heavenly figure drifting afar on the horizon, and then quickly moving towards him at break-neck supersonic speed. "Sacred *Mt. Olympus!*" the amazed and presumptuous youth gasped and exclaimed. "It's Aphrodite, goddess of beauty and love, coming to give me guidance, confidence, and a certain erection!"

"Greetings, dear Hippomenes," the almost-impeccable goddess saluted with her right hand raised over her head, showing an abundance of ugly underarm hair. "You have the stout heart of a *hippo* (Greek for "horse"), and a case of the *meanies,* like no other human presently alive on this whole damned Earth!"

"Then, you've come to succor me and give me strength and courage?" the lad inquired. Hippomenes avariciously peered at the goddess's wonderful solid breasts. "I'm a little deficient in abstract qualities like love and beauty, so I often think with my blood-engorged penis, rather than with my brain-drained noggin that's devoid Type-O Negative red fluid."

"You must win the impending race and wed the King's comely daughter," Aphrodite insisted to her new-found champion. "Here, inside this scruffy bag, which my left hand is holding, are some valuable tools that will aid you in your current dilemma. I hope you find them practical, and figure-out how the Hades to effectively use each of them!"

Hippomenes carefully opened the dirty, blood-stained, goatskin sack, and examined the weird array of objects stashed inside, while majestic Aphrodite continued her rather odd discourse. The young champion conscientiously listened to the gorgeous goddess's authoritative and imperative rhetoric.

"I was just recently visiting distant Africa, and have taken three golden apples from the immortal tree that grows near the northern mountains, along with the sturdy, thick, foot-long branch that the golden fruit had matured upon," the goddess loquaciously explained to her chosen hero. "Since I am an immortal *Olympus* goddess, I have a license to do what the Hades I like with complete impunity, whenever I feel motivated to act. And incidentally, my dear mortal," Aphrodite proceeded. "Here is a little utilitarian gift from your sea-god sponsor Poseidon; it's a small six-inch-long trident attached to a circular belt, fastened midway around."

"What am I to do with these wonderful-but-peculiar items?" Hippomenes urgently asked. "Sell the golden apples on the immortal bough, and use the trident as a fork during a future Boeotian barbecue?"

"That's where your noteworthy imagination is supposed to kick-in," the goddess impatiently-and-vaguely revealed. "Use your limited brain capacity, and implement the unique things in the bag, along with the souvenir trident in a creative manner. But I'll mercifully give you a good hint," Aphrodite declared out of pity for her new, favored champion. "Put all five gifts inside your tunic, and your essential clue is: 'Four to rod, and one to prod!' Get it, my favorite, thick-skulled Earth asshole! 'Four to rod, and one to prod'. Remember it, you dense-headed, Earth asshole!" And without providing any more helpful directions, the beautiful deity then *vanished into* thick oxygen, which hadn't adequately learned to diet properly, and therefore, naturally would have been ordinary *thin air*.

"Four to rod and one to prod!" the inquisitive youth kept introspectively thinking and then repeating. "There's only one thing those fuckin' words, constituting a really dumb-ass riddle, could possibly mean."

The next morning, just before noon, Hippomenes first placed and next fastened the trident belt around his lower abdomen, so that the three-pronged fork would repeatedly slam against his buttocks when the 'dashing young man' would run, and painfully "prod" the youth forward in his quest for the finish line. Then, the visitor to Boeotia ungracefully shoved and stuffed the long-branch along with the three attached, large golden apples down his girdle inside his tunic, making it appear that his genitals were ten times bigger than their normal, non-aroused size. Hippomenes then awkwardly walked towards the King's official starting line, as everyone in the gallery gawked, scoffed, jeered, and pointed at *his* very exaggerated sexual apparatus.

'Look at his grand, protruding dick and massive balls!' Atalanta thought in sheer astonishment, as the thoroughly-amused spectators all roared and heckled with laughter. 'With equipment like that, this city doesn't need any damned fire department to extinguish raging infernos!'

And then, the angry, tiny-peckered Schoeneus, who didn't have the balls to do what Hippomenes had audaciously enacted at the starting-line, raised his imperial right hand for silence. "Hear me one, and hear me all. This gullible, idiotic, poverty-stricken youth Hippomenes seeks to gain my daughter Atalanta's hand in marriage by winning the upcoming foot-sprint against her. If the empty-headed dunce somehow is victorious, and escapes the axe of the official royal executioner, then we'll all have to turn vegetarian this afternoon at the King's fruit and produce buffet, along with the accompanying ceremonial country salad bar!" the King reminded his peevish and suddenly-irate subjects and predicates. "Let the dolt Hippomenes's death be a clear message to all other silly, frivolous youths that have the crazy notion to think that they can run faster than my winged-footed little girl!"

Then, the determined Atalanta crouched-down in the regular starting position, but being encumbered by all of the paraphernalia stuffed inside *his* burgeoning girdle, poor beleaguered Hippomenes could only stand there, and wish that the King would immediately articulate the numerical countdown to begin the race. 'Four to rod and one to prod!' the trustful, callow imbecile kept thinking over and over again inside his puzzled and befuddled mind. 'Four to rod and one to prod!' Soon, the familiar shrill-sounding trumpets were blown, and the King sanctimoniously gave the traditional three-number countdown.

The young male challenger managed to maintain his initial dash side by side with his highly-skilled opponent, despite the handicap of having five uncomfortable objects jiggling around inside his extremely uncomfortable girdle. But about one third into the five-hundred-yard sprint, Atalanta began distancing herself from her tenacious rival. The girl then felt sorry for her inferior pursuer, so she slowed-down sufficiently for Hippomenes to run alongside of her. The princess's right hand accidentally touched *his* exaggerated crotch, and that unexpected wild sensation momentarily stunned and aroused the ordinarily very competent, female athlete.

Hippomenes instinctively used his innate intelligence, removed one of the three golden apples from under his tunic, and tossed it several-hundred-feet ahead, so that its falling would attract the attention of his spirited competitor. As the distracted young lady bent over to pick-up the priceless golden apple, the determined challenger approached the king's daughter's behind from behind, and rammed the sturdy, protruding tree branch into his rival's crotch, directly up her butt hole, making Atalanta shriek with both pain and pleasure.

The revitalized wannabe' champion yanked his artificial dork from his formidable female opponent's tail-end, and then conscientiously continued sprinting towards the finish line with the six-inch-long trident repetitiously goosing and penetrating his severely-lacerated buttocks all the way. Atalanta got over her momentary, aberrant sexual deviation, and again hustled-back into the thick of the race. The fleet-footed girl was quickly catching-up to her inventive contestant, as Hippomenes neared the booing, jeering, incensed, carnivorous crowd, assembled at the finish line.

Much to everyone's disappointment, Hippomenes had won the race *by a rod* (a massive hard-on), and also had simultaneously won the right to ask for King Schoeneus's permission to marry *his* royal attractive daughter. When the chagrined King announced to the already-dissatisfied throng that a vegetarian buffet was to be served in an hour, all of the disgusted spectators belligerently pelted the regal asshole with pebbles, stones and rocks, and then the agitated crowd angrily left the area in both miserable and disenchanted frames of mind to demonstrably boycott the lousy vegetarian smorgasbord.

Then, ecstatic Hippomenes secretly reached-down into his girdle and removed the long sturdy branch with the two remaining golden apples still attached. He happily handed one of them to Atalanta, and romantically said to his prospective bride, "A golden apple a day keeps rabid cannibalism away!"

Atalanta pulled-up Hippomenes's orange tunic, looked-down inside his pink girdle, and innocently-but-humorously exclaimed, "Where's the beef, you dumb-ass meathead?"

"Orpheus"

Before there was Elvis Presley, the Beach Boys, Madonna, and the Rolling Stones, there was Ludwig van Beethoven, Johann Sebastian Bach, and Wolfgang Amadeus Mozart, who *broke* away from the 'baroque' style of composing because he had no money. When those celebrated men died, the artists had left composing, and quickly got into decomposing. Before musical history had 'Wolfgangs, there were roving howling *wolf packs*, and before there were roving howling wolf packs, the ancient Greeks had Orpheus.

The Greeks loved music as much as they loved adventure, lesbians, vacationing on the Isle of Lesbos, and wild unlimited sex orgies. When famed Achaean Orpheus sang, trees would extend their boughs downward and shade him from the sun, because the wandering minstrel was a damned albino with milk-white skin. The poison ivy vines reached-out their tendrils in response to Orpheus's majestic music, and everybody in the vicinity that already had venereal diseases didn't like the notion of doing additional skin scratching, so the worried area residents very discreetly stayed out of the forests, ponds, streams, marshes, marketplaces, and swamps.

When Orpheus sang and played his sensational tunes on the lyre, rocks would rumble and tumble-down mountainsides, causing widespread devastation to nearby villages and outhouses. Wild beasts skulked around low to the ground, because the dumb-ass creatures felt like continuously pissing and shitting, and woodland gods would stop masturbating and screwing each other up the yazoo, just to benignly listen to the boy wonder's glorious, enchanting music melodies.

Orpheus *madly* loved a girl named Eurydice, who inspired the minstrel to go beyond "madly" straight, right on to "insane", and then on to totally "crazy" lyrics. The musician's creative powers to organize imaginative love songs had originated from *his* passionate longing to lose his disgusting virginity, and pump the excessive poop out of Eurydice's eager beaver. All nature celebrated with the 'mythology period bard' on his wedding day, but unfortunately, Eurydice didn't want to get laid, or have her box munched, because the moody bitch was starting her own bloody *period* cycle during the aforementioned 'mythology period'.

On the morning of the wedding ceremony, no priest arrived to officiate, because religion had not yet been invented in ancient Greece. Disappointed by no priest showing-up, and pissed-off because she was having her monthly period, Eurydice ambled-down to the riverside to have lesbian sex with her equally pissed-off bridal attendants. The despondent girls gathered bunches of flowers to shove down the throat of the first Greek priest to show-up, and then the aggravated bridesmaids were fully prepared to choke the sanctimonious son-of-a-bitch if and when the suspected pedophile priest should ever come-around to their village after the eventual establishment of religion.

Unfortunately, Eurydice was suddenly bitten in the foot by a huge, poisonous snake, and her totally shocked maidens instantly became frightfully snake-bitten themselves, and then quickly serpentined their' exit the hell away from the river before the foul, venomous viper reloaded its fangs for a second lethal attack.

Orpheus became quite despondent when the minstrel heard the bad news about Eurydice, and the horny adolescent was so pissed-off that he couldn't get a hard-on to jerk, no matter how hard he tried. The singer's somber songs were now very sad, and reflected *his* totally disconsolate disposition, and all of the wild male forest beasts got pissed-off too, because suddenly, the creatures could no longer lick each other's long dicks, and also couldn't get laid either, after vainly attempting to achieve even weak erections. "Go to Hades, you dumb, stupid bastard!" the pissed-off animals all repeatedly yelled at Orpheus, no matter where he roamed.

The rather depressed Greek minstrel picked-up his lyre and made his way to the wide cave that led down to eerie Hades; yes, the Greek underworld, where as you already might know, ancient gangsters and mobsters hung-out after the ill-tempered scoundrels had died. Orpheus believed that Eurydice's soul had already journeyed down to bleak Hades, and the young lover theorized that *that* was where her *spirit* could ultimately be found. 'Who the hell wants to have sex with a damned thin, two-dimensional ghost?' Orpheus objectively conjectured. 'Eurydice no longer has a body, and her massive tits are now probably just hollow air bubbles; her ass is probably two noxious farts glued together, and her former hot-wet pussy is probably like a primitive air pump. Who needs this kind of fuckin' shit in their already-troubled life?'

The melancholy minstrel descended a vast vertical tunnel inside the nearby ominous cave, and successfully clambered-down a twelve-mile-long rocky, subterranean cliff to reach the dreadful *River Styx*, which historically separated the Land of the Living from the morbid Kingdom of the Dead. Charon, the macabre, hooded, skeleton-ferryman monotonously rowed his barge to shore to pick-up his next passenger for transportation across the stranger-than-fiction underground river to mysterious, dark and dismal, Hades.

"Hey jerk, ya' gotta' be dead in order to get to the *other side*," Charon chastised his still-living mournful guest. "Ya' just can't look dead, asshole! Ya' gotta' *be* fuckin' dead! Go back to Earth and get assassinated or murdered. Have you ever fuckin' considered chugging-down hemlock or arsenic, or be eaten by a famished shark, or maybe a hungry lion?"

"But my spirit is dead already!" bitterly grieved and argued Orpheus. "So, what's an empty, pitiful mind and body to do?"

"Just hand me a coin to pay the toll of passage, and then simply commit suicide," the ghastly, ghostly specter firmly recommended. "Then, you'll officially leave the *sticks,* and I'll take ya' across the *Styx* to some other part of the even more incomprehensible post mortem' *sticks,* ha, ha, ha!"

"Permanent death?" Orpheus exclaimed. "I'm not ready for that type of esoteric bull-shit yet! I just gotta' find-out if I can get my rocks off with my girlfriend's ghost, and that's all I wish to accomplish on this particular expedition."

The *dispirited* musician had to devise a fast solution to remedy his present dilemma. So, the disenchanted minstrel went into his mystic, creative mode and sang a haunting love song that completely mesmerized the heartless Charon. The ferryman felt wonderful ecstasy for the first time in his eternally dismal life, so the skeletal figure voluntarily led Orpheus onto his barge, which would allow the saddened passenger to *barge-in* on the pathetic, silent underworld. If the minstrel could enchant the god Hades with his powerful stirring lyrics, then the singer might be able to retrieve Eurydice's ghost and transport it back up to Earth, where the departed spirit could be reunited with its no-longer-active 38-24-36 hourglass figure.

Cerberus, the three-headed dog that growled ferociously and snapped its jaws and bared its fangs, was steadfastly guarding the narrow portal leading into Hades' interior. The fierce monster was so hypnotized by Orpheus's song that the awesome beast cowered-down like a tame puppy, and then the mutt was so thrilled by his newly-discovered blithe nature that Cerberus began wildly using all three heads to lick its erect dick, and then did the same to Charon's *boner*, giving the ferryman a pleasurable "triple *head*er".

As Orpheus entered the dismal, gloomy world of Hades, pale spooky ghosts crowded and flitted-around the apprehensive hero, with all the attracted shades being wholly captivated by his beautiful song. The visitor's extraordinary voice resounded throughout the myriad caverns and stagnant dark marshes, artificially giving the appearance of life to the formerly silent and ominous fucked-up place.

The determined musician cautiously stepped into the well-manicured, flowered fields of Elysium. And all of the daffodils, the petunias, the dainty dahlias, and the 'creeping' myrtle that ordinarily gave everyone the creeps, leaned towards the sound of the lad's marvelous voice. The suddenly-happy dead danced and frolicked through the colorful floral meadows and shadowy dells, finally experiencing delight and pleasure as part of their' eternal boredom. The jubilant ghosts held hands, and jumped and pranced around, inadvertently crushing a plethora of beautiful flowers, and giggling incessantly, while acting like a billion faggots and gay-spirited lesbians.

Then, Orpheus advanced through a shadowy cave and entered the spooky area of atonement where the pathetic, grieving ghosts of dead individuals were posthumously punished for violating the capricious gods' supreme laws. Even Sisyphus, who labored for all eternity pushing an enormous rock up a steep, curved hill, only to have it roll down the incline so that the process would have to be repeated over and over again, stopped his labor to enjoy and appreciate Orpheus's unique song. Sisyphus was so inspired by the marvelous melody that the ghost immediately organized his own underground band called "The Rolling Stones and Pebbles", and instantly began mimicking Orpheus's fine example. Even the crackling flames that blazed and flourished in leaping fences of fire in that section of Hades, danced-around, and soon heated-up the whole damned area.

Next, Orpheus and his music encroached upon thirsty and hungry Tantalus, who had been eternally punished by having to stand chained inside a pool that was filled chest-high with delicious water. An abundance of fruits on tree limbs dangled above the hungry and thirsty man's head. When Tantalus was 'tantalized' to drink, the manacled figure would bend-over, and the cool water would rapidly drain out of the tank. When the penalized apparition would reach for a ripe peach, or for a savory apple, the fruit would either disappear or be blown away by a sudden wind gust. The penalized ghost was so enraptured and entranced by Orpheus's singing that the brain-dead specter ceased performing his eternal sentence, and Tantalus's rejuvenated spirit fondly recalled what it was once like to be alive.

Finally, Orpheus arrived at the stone-cold, black-granite pillared *Halls of Hades*. The ashen faces of great Greek heroes were sadly sitting at the god Hades' ebony table. Even King Hades and his pallid-faced Queen Persephone showed animation, and began smiling in the direction of the young troubadour, dually acknowledging his wonderful music. The gods' cold hearts knew all misery, and cared not one iota about any of it, but amazingly, Hades and his pale, morbid wife were touched and moved by the magical rhapsody that their dull ears were wondrously hearing.

At length, Orpheus became fatigued from his difficult descent down into the underworld, and also, the musician had become exhausted from his extensive singing and meandering. The shades of the assembled, swirling ghosts mingled-in with the gentle winds, and at least temporarily, all nature in Hades was one and the same. Then, King Hades addressed his latest visitor, and the awesome god's deep bass voice reverberated throughout *his* usually silent, cavernous, dark world.

"Go back Orpheus to the sunshine, while my monsters are still under the spell of your songs," Hades imperatively advised the hero. "Climb-up the steep, vertical tunnel to the warmth of broad daylight, and I promise you, the spirit of Eurydice will follow. But there is one caveat to this special arrangement," Hades austerely warned. "Whatever you do, don't turn-around for verification of my words, and therefore, by doing so, doubt my promise. If you dare turn-around, Eurydice will return down to the underworld, and your fond hopes will immediately vaporize into utter despair. If you learn to trust and believe my imperial decree, you can have living and breathing Eurydice back as your three-dimensional fiancee!"

"Yes, go back Orpheus," Queen Persephone implored from her dark ebony throne. "My crotch is getting wet for the first time in three centuries, and I actually feel like getting laid. Get the hell outa' here, and give us some damned privacy! I'm as horny as King Hades is right now, and I need to be vigorously pumped and humped!"

"Yes, go back quickly," Hades anxiously concurred. "I'm getting a massive erection, and I think I know exactly what the fuck to do with it! Show me some pink, Persephone! I'm headin' right toward the center of your hot, juicy, love tunnel!"

Orpheus turned and retreated from the great *Hall of Hades,* and the teeming ghosts separated into two divisions, and made sufficient room for the wanderer to exit. The young musician desperately searched on both sides, and in front, for any sign of his lost Eurydice's spirit, but dared not look behind him in honor of Hades's stern edict. No sounds were discernible anywhere around him, as the talented minstrel advanced through the major dark, rock-mineral corridors, moving past Tantalus and Sisyphus, and then through the now-wilting flowers in the tranquil Elysian Fields. Soon, the inconsolable lover passed Cerberus's narrow portal, and then assertively stepped onto Charon's barge, which quickly sank-down two-feet in reaction to *his* weight being onboard.

"Is Eurydice behind me?" Orpheus anxiously asked Charon. "I dare not look and violate Hades' weird prophecy."

"Behind every man there is a woman!" Charon diplomatically and arcanely answered. "If you are *that* curious, you asinine asshole, why not turn your damned neck around, and fuckin' see for yourself if Lord Hades had been bull-shitting you?"

"No thanks!" Orpheus answered in response to a very compelling temptation that he felt. "You must have virgin ears Charon, because what woman in her right mind would want to suck on a piece of cartilage dick for the remainder of eternity, or have sex with someone that looks like the fuckin' Grim Reaper's twin brother?"

"Did you feel any additional weight shift the boat's equilibrium after you had entered?" Charon replied with a question, enjoying his self-appointed role as an accomplished and sophisticated eternal ball-breaker.

"No, but I must value Hades' promise in spite of your biased sarcasm, your pessimism, and your fucked-up cynicism," Orpheus proudly volleyed.

Finally, the surreal ferry left Hades' bank, and slowly made it across the dreary *River Styx* to the opposite, shadowy shore. The ascension to the upper-world of mortals was an arduous climb that was filled with strange shapes and alien forms floating around inside the tight, chimney-like cavity's tomb-like silence.

Orpheus ceased his scaling to listen for any remote sign or sound of his beloved Eurydice, but there was not a trace of a noise, or a hint of an echo of her soft voice. 'Maybe Charon was right, and Hades was just bustin' my balls about Eurydice following my ass back up to Earth?' Orpheus suspiciously thought. 'I wonder if that miserable bastard is still getting it on with Queen Persephone? Both of those imperial, pallid-faced assholes looked like they needed ten blood transfusions each.'

Orpheus feared that the God of the Dead had deceived him, and that *he* was alone and isolated between two worlds, but his soul had been belonging to neither one. 'What if I climb up to the bright sunlight, turn around, and Eurydice is not there?' the adventurous romantic skeptically considered. 'I had fascinated Charon, Cerberus, Sisyphus, Tantalus, Persephone and Hades once with my spellbinding music, but could I repeat those remarkable results with a second daring expedition into the underworld? Maybe I have lost Eurydice with my naïve eagerness to believe any and all bull-shit from men and from gods?' the mirthless singer lamented. 'Gee; I wonder if Hades has enough blood to sustain an erection for a full century? I wonder if the immortal prick has any blood at all?'

With every step upward that the befuddled hero took while carefully ascending the precarious precipices, Orpheus became more and more dubious of Hades' promise. The frustrated climber diligently labored-up the last treacherous stretch with his sad heart laden with doubt and despair. The darkness soon converted into a grayish mist, indicating that the fatigued minstrel had finally advanced close to the Earth's surface. The air was cleaner and more breathe-able, and as Orpheus inhaled the fresh oxygen, his brain realized that the entrance to the dreary, huge cavern was just ahead. Still, the musician's beleaguered mind questioned Hades' veracity.

Orpheus could not bear his heavy emotional burden any longer. Acting on impulse, in the ominous grayish light that belonged to neither the Land of the Living nor the Land of the Dead, the confused trekker veered-around, and his eyes beheld a thin, misty shade at his rear, and quickly, the indistinct, vague female specter with the beautiful face loudly cried, "You really fucked yourself over this time, you stupid, dumb-dicked, virgin asshole!"

Orpheus cried-out "Eurydice!" But the faint female specter soon crystallized, and then evaporated into nothingness. A slight echo of "Farewell Orpheus" resonated throughout the deep, dark, vertical tunnel directly below his shaky feet.

The disconsolate lover gathered his sensibilities and hurried back-down the now-familiar, steep, dangerous path which the explorer had just laboriously ascended. The depressed lover's efforts were greatly thwarted by his extreme apathy, and also by his overwhelming sorrow. Charon was deaf to the singer's prayerful voice, which lacked the innocence, and the romantic quality of its first authentic presentation to the inhabitants of Hades.

"Stop trespassing where you aren't supposed to go," Charon imperatively warned in a bellicose tone of voice. "You must have a death wish, Orpheus, but if you want to achieve your fatal dream, you must honor tradition and go back to Earth and commit suicide like I had originally advised you to do."

"Shove your rotten oar up your' stinkin' bony ass!" Orpheus angrily replied. "How in Hades do you manage to get into your house? With a goddamned skeleton key?"

"Fuck-off, you insignificant, puny, jerk-off mortal!" Charon vehemently yelled. "You should have more respect for the custodians of the dead!"

"Go home and work your skinny-dicked boner!" Orpheus screamed like a demented maniac. "Instead of white semen, you must surely shoot-out pink marrow from your bony dingle, if you aren't already impotent!"

Orpheus tried duplicating the original beauty of his song, but eventually, acknowledged that his meaningless endeavor was a total failure. For a whole week, the glum singer sat upon the eerie banks of the bleak river, watching Charon transport doomed souls to their final resting places in Hades' black kingdom. The pathetic wailing of the morose *River Styx* canceled-out any cheerful love song that the depressed musician could muster. The swirling ghosts also ignored Orpheus's entreaties, and the melancholy lover finally realized that his sad intonations no longer had any tangible effect upon his completely apathetic, inhospitable, now-alien, horribly-wretched environment.

"I guess I really pissed-away my one and only chance of reuniting with Eurydice," Orpheus sobbed and regretted. "I'm so depressed I feel like slicing my balls off!"

Disgusted and defeated, Orpheus rose from his sitting position, and then trudged and stumbled-up along the dark, steep path, which he knew so well. When the dejected youth eventually arrived back to Earth, all bedraggled and begrimed, his lyrics and voice sounded both pitiful and hopeless. Orpheus could tolerate human company no longer, and the irate minstrel chased people away when the area natives came-around to hear his exceptionally haunting melodies, along with sad love themes, which he kept *harping* upon the lyre.

In the end, the disillusioned lover met his ultimate demise. Women of Thrace were angered at Orpheus's refusal to play upbeat, romantic melodies for them, so out of sheer contempt, the scornful bitches attacked, molested and attempted to rape the young man. And when the victim couldn't achieve an adequate erection, the crazy females choked and killed the unfortunate minstrel by shoving unsanitary sanitary napkins down his throat.

Legends maintain that as the body of Orpheus smashed against jagged rocks in the *River Hebrus's* many rapids, and the deceased musician's waxen dead lips faintly uttered "Eurydice" all the way down to the subterranean *River Styx*.

In the daffodil meadows of Elysium, Orpheus's specter met-up with the ghost of Eurydice, and since Orpheus no longer had a pecker, his shade used a daffodil stem as a vagina-insertion-device, which soon became known all throughout Hades as a "daffy-dildo"! And where the main path in the complicated underworld network becomes particularly narrow, Orpheus's apparition goes first into the unexplored tunnel, and thereafter, his flat form admiringly looks back, and then beckons the spirit of its one true love, Eurydice, to obediently follow.

"The Three Golden Apples"

A hero in Greek mythology was a lesser god whose father was a Mt. Olympus deity, and whose mother was a mere, gorgeously stacked, horny mortal. One such legendary hero was Hercules, whose pappy was king-god Zeus, and whose mom was a vivacious princess named Alcmene. That particular genealogy resulted because the divine king of the gods nonsensically (don't ask me why) preferred human, juicy pussy to heavenly, juicy pussy.

Hercules was doomed (or fated) to live a life of struggle, unhappiness, and strife. Hera, the jealous queen of the gods, and Zeus's spiteful wife, despised Hercules, since *he* was the offspring of her husband's infidelity after having an intense affair with a mere mortal woman with a nice hairy, juicy, pink pussy. Hera used her supernatural powers, and compelled Hercules to temporarily become insane by burning-down his own house; then killing his wife and children, and after the blaze had subsided, the muscular fellow discovered that *their* charred bodies hadn't been barbecued.

Since there were no psychiatrists, psychologists, advisers, guidance counselors, and social workers around in mythological times to fuck-up people's minds, Hercules trekked to Delphi to consult the *Oracle,* which in this particular case, was not a chamber of the heart, even though *she* often gave advice about love. The lady prophet instructed Hercules that in order to atone for his egregious crimes against his family, the perpetrator had to perform twelve arduous labors for *his* cousin Eurystheus, King of Argos.

For his eleventh labor Hercules had to journey to northern Africa and select three golden apples from an enchanted tree that grew in the Garden of Hesperides, which was monitored by four voluptuous dancing sisters, all having alluring, hairy, golden-blonde beavers.

Before the Garden of Hesperides had been overrun with wild weeds and crabgrass having really sharp claws, people all around the known world were skeptical about the story of a glorious tree that bore gigantic golden apples. Many young imbeciles, eager to visit and see other countries, desired to journey to the legendary garden and bring back a golden apple to give to their girlfriends in exchange for a de luxe piece of ass at an acclaimed Argos hotel featuring Spartan accommodations.

Many of the bold adventurers never returned from their expeditions, preferring to munch on the pussies of the four Daughters of the Evening

Star for the rest of their short-lived, choking, mortal lives. And the worst part about the whole ordeal was that a nasty dragon with a hundred heads (fifty slept while the other fifty kept watch guarding the Golden Apple Tree) would unexpectedly devour the would-be hero right when *he* began licking the pink inners of the first delightful sister's golden blonde snatcheroo.

Hercules had just finished wandering through the land of Italy, looking to buy a Sicilian pizza with anchovies, but the fabled hero couldn't find any such commodity, because the strongest of Greek champions was on the prowl in mainland Italy, and not meandering-around in circles on the island of Sicily. The renowned fellow wore a lion's skin, which had been given to him along with his heavy club, by the generous King Eurystheus at an *Argos Lions Club* Meeting attended by all two members.

At every cave, whorehouse, or village that Hercules had visited, the wanderer inquired about how he could locate the famous Garden of Hesperides. Many of the Italian residents said that they had heard of the notorious garden, and of the famous Golden Apple Tree, but none knew exactly where to find those two obscure references. "I think it's not far from where you can buy Sicilian pizza with anchovies!" one senile village elder explained to the rambling hero.

"Where the fuck is that?" Hercules demanded, raising his club with his right hand while intensively scratching his balls with his left appendage.

"If I knew that," the old demented, hoary-bearded ignoramus answered, "I'd be eating Sicilian pizza with anchovies right now, rather than talkin' to a traveling asshole like you about it!"

At last, Hercules arrived at the brink of a pristine river, where the trekker first took a lengthy piss, and then spotted four beautiful young blonde damsels twining flower wreaths, and incessantly gossiping while intermittently checking-out each other's hairy golden beavers through the sheer transparent white gowns that the four darlings were wearing. The muscle-bound demi-god thought that he was at foreign Bush Gardens rather than at the fabled Garden of the Hesperides.

"Please confirm to me, you dazzling, young, sexy maidens," the powerful-looking stranger began in an uncharacteristic cordial voice, "is this the right way to the Golden Apple Tree? I'm temporarily blinded by your outstanding beauty, and can only see and appreciate what looks like Bush Gardens at the moment."

"The Garden of the Hesperides, indeed!" one of the four vivacious Daughters of the Evening Star amazingly shrieked. "That is what you are seeking?"

"We thought that mortals stopped searching for it after others had experienced so many failures and aborted missions to steal golden apples from the ancient, gnarled tree," the second fair damsel with the hairiest blonde bush chimed-in. "What a pity that all of those young, well-endowed studs have died in vain!"

"And pray tell, wandering hero," the third fantastic virgin articulated. "What business brings you in quest of the great tree from antiquity? Tell us all about your current exploit, if you will."

"A certain insane king with a long fucked-up name too difficult to pronounce has ordered me to pilfer three of the finest golden apples growing upon the tree," Hercules confided, as the visitor started to achieve an enviable erection, which was *hard* for him to conceal.

The four damsels saw the hero's tool rising and pulsating beneath his loosely fitting lion's skin, and began giggling as if they had feathers rubbing against their armpits. "And I must tell you, well- endowed traveler," the fourth maiden piped-in, "that most young men with average-sized peckers go in quest of the apples to retrieve one for their girlfriends, or for their mistresses, in the name of love. But I can plainly see from your throbbing glory that you are not an ordinary, tiny-dicked asshole. Do you love this retarded king so much that you would risk your life for him? Are you fuckin' gay, or are you some sort of demented, side-tracked pedophile?"

Hercules felt very uncomfortable being interrogated in such an unfamiliar manner by the fourth *damsel in this dress*. "Where do you nice pussies, er, I mean golden-haired maidens live? Where is your home?" the brute of a man inquired as Hercules deftly changed the controversial subject from himself to the four horny bitches.

"Oh, we don't live in a house, a cave, or a ghetto!" the first maiden replied.

"And we don't live in a mountain tunnel," the second maiden with the fluffiest blonde beaver added.

"We just hang-out in this garden and dance around the Golden Apple Tree over yonder, when we aren't doing cunnilingus or sixty-nine on each other," the first maiden informed the impressed wanderer. "As our father always told us when we were mere youngsters, 'eat out more often'!"

"I see, indeed," Hercules answered in an admiring fashion. "I'm so glad to hear that you fair young ladies do not live in a house, because I do have a certain propensity for pyromania when it comes to family dwellings. But I have approached you in friendship," the champion of great deeds continued. "And after I successfully obtain the three golden apples, I'll allow all four of you to suck on my humongous tool, all at the same time. It sounds like you four pretty bitches need a little diversion to your sex life, besides all of that dull lesbian bull-shit you sisters have alluded to!"

"That sounds like an appropriate diversion, all right," the first damsel readily admitted. "If we suck you off, we can retain our virginity and still dance our cute asses off, monotonously prancing around the Golden Apple Tree, just like Almighty Zeus wants us to do!"

"Your mission sounds like a *Herculean* task!" the broad with the hairiest blonde bush contributed. "Who are you stranger?"

"I believe that you've already heard of me," the hero with the *two* massive 'clubs' chuckled. "My name *is* Hercules."

"That's just great!" the third attractive blonde acknowledged. "And after you pop your massive load and shrink your apparatus down to normal size, you can then use that wooden club as a dildo, and shove it repeatedly up each of our assholes!"

"Oh Hercules, your magnificent accomplishments are famous all over the known world," the first maiden melodramatically complimented. "We do not think it extraordinary any longer that you are in quest of the Golden Apple Tree and its divine fruit."

"My dear 'comely' maidens," Hercules answered as he almost prematurely ejaculated all over the damned place. "Now that you know my name and have examined my exposed, long, thick, male equipment, can you tell me which way it is to the singular Garden of Hesperides? I am near-sighted and can only see 'bushes' that are close by. Since eyeglasses haven't been invented yet, I can't see shit far away. I can only smell it!"

"We shall provide you with the best directions we can," assured the four damsels all together. "But as you know," the third maiden continued, "in Greek mythology, nothing for mere mortals is easily achieved. You must first go to the seashore's beach and locate the Old One. Then, your big challenge is that you must convince or force the stubborn curmudgeon to inform you precisely where the prized Golden Apples are to be found."

"Look ladies," Hercules objected. "I'm fuckin' nearsighted and can't see this damned tree you're alluding to that I know is fairly close by. Just tell me where it is, and that will save me a lot of valuable time and wasted effort with finding and interrogating the Old One, whoever the hell he is!"

"How's this for incentive for doing things *our* way?" the second maiden answered. And with her verbal preface completed, all four damsels lifted-up their transparent white gowns, got-down on the ground lying on their backs, and then simultaneously opened their luscious blonde beavers and pink slits for Hercules' visual approval.

"Okay, okay, you win!" Hercules exclaimed before he popped a huge load that knocked the loose lion's skin' garment right off his body. "Sorry about that!" the famous champion apologized as he embarrassingly picked-up his lion's wrapping and reentered it as his four female admirers giggled and laughed in astonishment at the white sticky wetness hanging from all over their bodies. "I'll surely return for the blowjob I had been promised. And it's to be administered after I finish the special three golden apples' assignment," Hercules vowed. "By then, my limp tool should be reloaded and ready to explode another jet of sticky semen into your lucky faces!"

"Remember Hercules," the third damsel reminded their temporary guest. "The Old One is really the Old Man of the Sea. He possesses remarkable abilities that you will soon discover."

"Yes," the fourth maiden confirmed. "And whatever he attempts, be sure to latch onto his form and hold tight until he gives you the vital information that you seek. Until then," the blonde babe proceeded, "we'll just hang-out here next to the Golden Apple Tree you have sought, and dance around, and then twine flower wreaths while gossiping about your fantastic manhood. Too bad you're so damned near-sighted and have to go through all this additional bull-shit just to get the golden apples, but unfortunately, that's the way fucked-up mythology works!"

Trekking to the north, the hiking champion heard the sea roaring in the distance, so Hercules increased his pace, and soon arrived at a hard-sanded beach having loud surf and great waves. Some green shrubbery was rather abundant growing upon a hill next to a cave, so Hercules decided he'd investigate the area to see if any edible fruit grew there. The new-arrival clambered-up the steep, treacherous ridge, and then ambled across a lush green carpet of wild grass, blended-in with thick clover.

An old man (or what appeared to be an old man) was sleeping at the cave's entrance. As Hercules more-closely inspected the snoring figure, the observer determined that it was a combination of a human being and sea creature, having fish scales on its extremities, and the thing also was web-footed, much like a mallard or a goose worthy of taking a *gander* at. The Old One's beard was more like a seaweed tuft than an actual accumulation of gray or black whiskers.

The courageous hero grabbed the slumbering Old One's arm with one hand, and the old coot's miniscule dick with the other, and the disturbed creature awoke from its deep sleep in a very startled-but-belligerent frame of mind. The Old One instantly transformed into a stag with long antlers, but Hercules maintained a strong grip on its front leg and aching pecker. Then, the Old One converted into a tremendous female eagle without *a bird,* so Hercules had to move his left arm and latch onto one of the ferocious animal's razor-sharp talons, and hold as tightly as the famed wrestler could.

Immediately afterward, the Old Man of the Sea changed into a fierce, barking three-headed dog, baring six-inch-long fangs in each of its mouths that were desperately attempting to bite the hero's fadorkenbender off. But Hercules was so determined in capturing the talented shape-shifter that the inspired grappler held-on with all his great might. Next, the incredible Old Man of the Sea magically switched into Geryon, a savage six-legged man-monster that instantaneously pissed into Hercules' face with all six of its dingles.

The Old One was now becoming both exhausted and frustrated from fruitlessly expending so much energy, and as a last resort, became a huge viper, which vainly tried to coil around the champion's chest, and constrict the air out of his lungs. But the brave hero squeezed the enormous serpent's head so tightly that it hissed in absolute agony. The Old Man's power to change into anything else had been effectively neutralized by the visitor's steadfast resolve. Its magic was no longer a surprise, or a deterrent, to Hercules's superhuman mettle.

Finally, the Old Man realized that it was absolutely futile to battle and resist the formidable strength of his new-found adversary, so *he* voluntarily relinquished *his* stubborn opposition, and reappeared in *his* natural, geriatric-looking form.

"Pray powerful mortal, what the fuck do you want with me?" the very fatigued Old Man of the Sea panted. "Your indomitable grip almost squeezed the breath out of my gills, and the shit out of my ass! If you do not let me' go, I shall evaluate you as a very uncouth and uncivil member of your moronic species!"

The hero retained his disabling clutch. "My name is Hercules, a stranger to this African seashore," the boulder-lifter proudly and loudly announced. "And I shall never release you from my death grasp until you reveal the nearest and quickest route to the Garden of the Hesperides. If you fail to surrender those specific directions, I guarantee that I will turn you inside-out, and then squeeze the breath *into* your gills and the shit back *into* your intestines! So, just cooperate, and stop givin' me a lot of your stupid, evasive, ever-changing bull-shit! And don't dare try turning into a damned Cretan Bull, either!"

"Okay, I concede defeat," the Old One begrudgingly answered. "You should venture south, and at the division of the road, turn left, and follow that path to where you shall encounter a very colossal giant that holds the sky upon his big brawny shoulders. And if the Titan should be in good spirits, the brute shall tell you where the Golden Apple Tree is situated. And," the Old One shrewdly added. "I don't think you'll be able to subdue the Titan like you had so easily done with me. Now, get your diabolical hands off my arm and also off my dick, and use some seaweed over there to wipe the three gallons of disgusting yellow piss off of your sorry-looking face."

"You stupid shit!" Hercules vehemently chided. "You should've turned into the giant you've just alluded to!"

Hercules then thanked the Old Man of the Sea for *his* accurate instructions, and resumed his seemingly nomadic itinerary, proceeding in the aforementioned direction, and then shortly thereafter, taking the appropriate branch in the road. After several hours of exhaustive walking, the burly, strong fellow approached an island with a tremendous mountain in its center, but upon closer examination, what the hero thought was a volcano was really the figure of a huge behemoth holding the sky upon his mammoth shoulders. It was indeed a very marvelous and spectacular sight for mortal eyes to behold.

Stationary, cottony clouds around the Titan's waist looked-like an immense white girdle, and those resting under his chin made the gargantuan hulk appear to have an old man's light-gray goatee. A gentle breeze slowly moved the cumuli from around the Titan's face, and Hercules finally beheld the enormous ogre's full countenance. The monster had eyes as big as ponds, and a mouth as wide as a lake. A very lugubrious expression was evident upon the giant's visage, suggesting that the Titan was completely bored and depressed about his monotonous burden of holding-up the azure sky, while standing on the Earth.

A forest was actively growing and spreading between the Titan's sizable toes, which each had *a corn* just like each of the tall oak trees had when it had originated from 'a corny' *acorn*. The towering-yet-despondent Titan finally looked-down from his high elevation, and spotted Hercules standing below, waiting to be recognized.

"Who are you loitering and dawdling down there near my toenails?" the frightful figure thundered.

"I am Hercules!" the hero bellowed back in a vibrant voice that almost rivaled the volume of the giant's awesome bass. "I am seeking the Garden of Hesperides."

"Well; I am Atlas, the mightiest Titan the world has ever known," the formerly lackadaisical brute replied. "I've been punished, er, assigned by Zeus to act like a mythological bandit and *hold-up* the sky!"

"I understand now why you appear to be in such a miserable quandary," Hercules sympathized. "But dear Atlas; can you tell or show me in which direction is the Garden of Hesperides? I have already visited Bush Gardens and enjoyed it very much!"

"What dumb-fuck business do you want there?" Atlas challenged. "You must desire getting killed! Ha, ha, ha!" the tremendous phenomenon boomed as the Titan's mood oscillated from gloomy to buoyant in five short seconds.

"I need to pilfer three of the golden apples," Hercules explained, "to give to my fucked-up cousin, the lunatic king of Argos. If I don't bring them back to the insane monarch, he'll tell me to 'Ar-go fuck myself'! I'm sick and tired of hearing that fucked-up joke over and over from him!"

"Good one, ha, ha, ha!" the amused Titan cackled and then coughed as the Earth beneath his feet quaked. "Good one indeed, Hercules! But let me tell you that there is no one except me that can trek to the garden and snatch those golden apples for you. If it weren't for this stupid bullshit of me having to hold-up the sky for Almighty Zeus," the beleaguered giant emphasized, "I would make six long steps across part of the Mediterranean Sea and secure the three bitchin' objects for you."

"But I thought the Golden Apple Tree was in northern Africa, not far from where the fabulous Daughters of the Evening Star always dance; twine floral wreaths; masturbate, and eat each other out!" the muscular mortal revealed.

"Their imitation apple tree is just a fuckin' decoy for the real one," Atlas readily clarified. "I can easily execute your errand in a jiffy."

"But can't you just place the sky on one of the nearby mountains?" Hercules inquired. "That seems like a relatively easy solution."

"None of them are quite high enough to be effectively utilized," the melancholy giant bitterly lamented. "But noble Hercules; if you stand on yonder mountain over there, your head would be on a level equal with mine. You could temporarily relieve me of my eternal penalty, while I could ramble-over and fetch your gleaming golden apples, and personally deliver the marvelous fruit to King Ar-go fuck yourself! Ho, ho, holy shit, I made a funny! Ha, ha, ha! I made a fuckin' hilarious funny!"

The itinerant hero was puzzled for a moment, and then Hercules advanced a rather relevant question to the ponderous figure before him. "Atlas," he stated. "Is the sky exceptionally heavy? I am but a mere mortal, and perhaps not equal to such a *titanic* undertaking!"

"Not at first Hercules," the Titan boomed as thunder echoed throughout the neighboring mountain valleys. "But after a millennium or so, it gets to be a pain in the neck, not to mention being a royal pain in the ass. I need to take a lengthy break, so that I could relieve my kidneys and flood and fertilize the entire *Sahara Desert* with abundant piss!"

Hercules was still dubious of the giant's motives. "And how long, Atlas, will it take you to acquire the three golden apples, and then return here to repossess the sky from my humble mortal shoulders?"

"That can be accomplished in only a few minutes," the Titan promised. "I shall take giant steps of fifteen or twenty miles at a stride, and be at the garden and back before your balls even develop a double hernia. How do ya' like those friggin' apples, Hercules?" the colossus laughed, causing massive destructive earthquakes that comprehensively obliterated seven afflicted villages and eighty-seven brothels in the immediate vicinity.

"I have limited options, Atlas," Hercules reluctantly admitted. "So, I shall climb the mountain behind your back, and then you can transfer the sky to my unworthy shoulders. I always wanted to stand head and shoulders above other men, so I suppose here's my unique opportunity to distinguish myself' from the cowardly masses. I mean to say Atlas," the garrulous journeyman proceeded, "I want to do something great in my lifetime, and not just kill a hundred-headed dragon, or wrestle and destroy a family of irate gorgons. When I get to the mountain peak, then hand me the fuckin' clear blue sky! That deed will be my most-vital contribution to posterity!"

Soon, the sky was shifted from Atlas to over-confident Hercules, who immediately discerned that the prohibitive weight was more than unpleasant to bear. 'What if Atlas skips town and never returns?' Hercules pondered. 'Oh well; it's too late to do anything about it as long as the Titan has his freedom to ramble all over goddamned creation, looking for virgin cherries to bust!'

The giant's first instinct was to stretch in order to expand his many contracted muscles. The Titan certainly was an impressive and prodigious sight, and the huge fellow then happily abounded-about, capering and prancing all over the area, while causing three major cities on the northern coast of Africa to crumble, and then catastrophically tumble into the vast Mediterranean Sea.

Then, Atlas's voice bellowed-out, "Ho! Ho! Ho!" so loudly that Zeus heard *his* exclamations reverberating on top of *Mt. Olympus*, hundreds of miles away from the sound's source. The giant finally remembered his recent pledge to Hercules, and stepped into the wine-dark Mediterranean. Ten miles out into the sea's basin, the waves came-up to the giant's knees, and twenty miles out (the greatest depth), the water rose to Atlas's chest.

'I just hope the knucklehead remembers retrieving the friggin' three golden apples,' Hercules prayed. 'If the Titan decides to start swimming and churning his arms, Atlas will surely drown the entire population of the whole fucked-up Earth!' the hero on a mission realized. 'Maybe that's not such a bad idea after all! But I really pity poor Atlas. If this weight seems irksome to me after only five-minutes, how horribly irritating it must've been for him after three millennia of this stupid, monotonous bull-shit. The lofty giant's only satisfaction is that he could be a successful voyeur, watching from this height thousands of people getting their freakin' rocks off on three separate continents!'

Fifteen minutes later, Hercules's heart began palpitating wildly when the strong mortal observed Atlas returning from *his* incredible trek across the sea. In his right hand were three fabulous golden apples that were four times the size of cantaloupes. When the giant emerged from the sea and stepped onto the shore, Hercules commended the Titan for his promptness and for his diligence.

"I'm quite happy to see you have safely returned," the Greek champion sincerely related. "And I'm quite thrilled that you've wonderfully absconded with the three golden apples I had requested!"

"Without a doubt! Without a doubt!" the smiling Titan aptly summarized. "I helped myself to the most beautiful apples growing on the enchanted tree. And the fucked-up hundred-headed dragon was quite a spectacle to behold. He was rather defensive and hostile at first, but then the stupid shit finally realized that the viper didn't want to fuck with me! It's too bad *you* had to miss all of the wonderful bull-shit I got to witness first hand!"

"You had a most splendid ramble indeed," Hercules concluded and declared. "And I must confess that you have completed the project just as easily as I could have done myself'. And now, since I have to finish the labor that you've so graciously assisted me in doing," Hercules elucidated,

"I must transport those fantastic apples to my cousin, the asshole king of Argos. It's now time for me to give you back your unlucky burden. Here Atlas; let me exchange the rare-aired atmosphere for the coveted three golden apples. To tell you the truth, I'm getting a bit dizzy and giddy from a lack of oxygen, way up here on this jagged mountain peak!"

"Why as to your recollection of recent events," the imposing Titan roared as the colossal-sized fellow deftly juggled the three huge golden apples with his right hand, sending them each twenty miles or so into the stratosphere, and then nonchalantly repeating the process. "I consider you, Hercules, to be a little too illogical. I can deliver your precious apples to your mentally-challenged cousin, the king with the fucked-up name, much quicker than you can," Atlas pragmatically suggested. "I'll take my longest strides, even if I occasionally devastate a fragile city or two along the way. Now that I have many liberties to merrily enjoy and pursue," the Titan firmly indicated, "I have no interest in obeying Zeus's unjust edict any longer."

Hercules shifted his body around on top of the adjacent mountain summit, becoming uncomfortable with both the weight of the sky and with Atlas's new-found independence. Two stars in the night firmament tumbled from horizon to horizon, and everyone in a hundred-mile vicinity, witnessing the phenomenon, thought that the end of the world was imminent.

"Oh Hercules, you need more practice at performing your new art!" the Titan criticized with abundant laughter. "Believe me when I say; I have not lost as many stars tumbling from the sky in the last ten centuries. Patience and fortitude will be the virtues that will enable you to perfect your new craft! Ha, Ha, ho, ho, ho! You don't know a toilet bowl from your asshole!"

"What the fuck!" Hercules exclaimed in astonishment. "Do you plan to make me perform your shit-eatin' responsibility forever? Zeus will definitely punish your ass even worse next time, after *he* finds-out about your blatant insubordination to *his* divine authority!"

"Fuck Zeus!" Atlas yelled, causing a devastating sonic boom that leveled stone houses and wrecked gay marriages on three continents. "Zeus only does shit *to* you, and never *for* you. Now Hercules; I might return to this place in a hundred-years, or maybe in half a millennium, in order to relieve you of your inhumane encumbrance," the giant considered. "Well then, if in a thousand years, I happen to become bored with the world's wondrous variety, I might return out of sympathy, and switch places with you. If you can prove you can do the work of a Titan," Atlas amply chuckled, "then history will honor and revere your name, dear Hercules. You'll receive many well-deserved accolades from acolytes!"

"Stop bustin' my balls with your haughty bull crap, and cease breakin' my back with this great agonizing sacrifice I'm enduring!" the mortal hero adamantly complained. "I'll gladly hold-up the sky until you return, if you will promise to do me just one small favor!"

"And what exactly is that?" Atlas curiously asked as the antagonist continued to adroitly juggle the three incomparable golden apples skyward, while looking at and negotiating with perplexed Hercules.

"This great sky weight is chafing my sensitive shoulders," Hercules complained and admitted. "And I would like to use my lion's skin as a cushion to protect my delicate mortal skin. I cannot endure standing here for countless centuries without any skin upon my shoulder bones. I need fuckin' protection!"

"Bend over, and the friction will certainly chafe your ass in addition to lacerating your shoulders," the giant mockingly laughed while totally amusing himself. "But your request is certainly a legitimate one. I shall take back the sky for just five minutes to give you' a breather, so that you' can adjust your lion's skin and make it into a soft blanket," the Titan fairly agreed. "Next, I shall be off to Argos to deliver your apples, and then roam the Earth, and even descend down into the dark Pit of Tartarus in hope of reuniting with and emancipating my fellow Titans that have been unjustly sentenced and punished by that conceited anarchist, Zeus."

The jolly giant tossed-down the three golden apples; cheerfully took back the sky from Hercules's supposedly chafed shoulders, and then transferred the heavens onto his own upper anatomy. Hercules wasted little time in sprinting-down the high mountain, picking-up the three treasured apples that were four times the size of cantaloupes, and then heading for the nearest road leading back to the virgin Daughters of the Hesperides.

"Hey, where the fuck do ya' think you're goin'!" the victimized Titan bellowed at the clever mortal trickster. "I've been fuckin' hoodwinked!"

"I'm gonna' get the blow-job of my life from the four *comely* sisters with the terrific blonde bushes!" Hercules smartly answered. "And as for my cousin, the fucked-up king, he can wait and twiddle his thumbs for his three golden apples. I might hang around the beautiful Daughters of the Evening Star for a few terrific decades, and really get my reproductive pipes cleaned-out!"

"But you're breaking your goddamned promise!" the infuriated giant screamed, causing a hundred-foot-high tidal wave to instantly disintegrate the city of Argos, and consequently drowning its deranged king along with most of his innocent subjects.

"You shouldn't vehemently protest and be so extremely jealous, just because I'm going to get the ideal blow-job of the millennium!" Hercules ridiculed his very immense victim. "After all, Atlas; look at it this way! You've been really royally *fucked* by this most recent development! You oughta' feel greatly satisfied!"

"I hope you become impotent, and that your worm never again becomes firm!" Atlas futilely bawled and rhymed.

"Not a tiny bug's chance caught in a thick spider's web," Hercules insisted with an air of *cock*iness. "You can enviously watch the whole damned blow-job thing from a distance, you arrogant, unscrupulous, perverted voyeur!"

Eventually, Atlas became fatigued of his grueling chore, and over centuries of toil, converted into a solid mountain, and to this day, those high summits in northern Africa are still benignly referred to as the *Atlas Mountains*. And when thunder is heard in the local valleys, some superstitious, asshole natives still believe that the loud booms are the sounds of pathetic Atlas yelling and pleading for Hercules to return to complete *his* long-neglected promise.

"Theseus and the Minotaur"

Theseus was an ancient Greek hero from Athens that led a very Spartan existence while living his childhood in southern Greece and later visiting Crete, which was an island situated next to Excrete. In fact, many college literature students have written their theses on the legendary Theseus. The popular champion was featured in three of Euripides' plays, and after another playwright named Sophocles tore-up the three Theseus' scripts, a third drama writer named Aeschylus shouted at Sophocles, "*You rippa' these*? Why are you' such a dumb destructive fuck! *You menna' these* now, you stupid shit!"

Theseus was the son of Aegeus, King of Athens, but his strange estranged father thought that his kid would be an embarrassing nuisance, so the ruler had his progeny live with *his* bitchy mother in southern Greece. Aegeus was very superstitious, and religiously honored a silly prophecy that a blind, deaf and dumb soothsayer had once predicted to the easily-influenced, paranoid Athenian king.

'I'll bury this sword and soldier's sandals in this hollow,' the king worriedly thought after dropping-off his pregnant wife in southern Greece. 'And then, I'll place this miniature boulder over the items in this hole. I hope this rolling stone gathers no moss while I'm pushing it toward the buried articles in the hollow,' Aegeus reflected without even using any mirror. 'When my son becomes strong enough to roll the giant rock off the hollow all by himself,' the king imagined, 'then the punk will be mature enough to live with me in Athens, where I can corrupt his morals, and make his mind totally fucked-up and decadent, just like mine is.'

When Theseus became older and strong enough to move the rock, the youth consulted two stone-rolling engineer friends, named Mik and Jagged, to render advice, so after Theseus's mother showed him the small boulder for the thousandth time, the prodigious lad easily moved the object, and discovered the buried bronze sword and soldier's sandals stashed underneath.

"Now I can go to Athens and sleep with father instead of shacking up with you," Theseus told his proud, promiscuous mother.

"The time has come for you to get the *Hades* out of here," the disgusted mother related to her discourteous, ambitious son. "Your grandfather wants to see you leave the city, too, because he believes you're an absolute arrogant, thug-hooligan. Now Theseus," his distraught mother stressed. "Go' directly to the dock and climb aboard the next friggin' boat sailin' to Athens."

"I refuse to make the trip by water," Theseus protested. "The voyage would be too safe and too simple to complete. I mean, Mom; if I am to ever become a great hero, I need major challenges and problems. How the fuck am I ever goin' to become a legend by just sailin' around in a dip-shit wooden boat with asshole senior-citizen sightseeing tourists, all the way to fucked-up Athens?"

"Your older cousin' Hercules rides in boats and ships all the time," the teenager's mother reminded him. "And *he's* already regarded as an accomplished hero. I believe that the younger generation always has to make things more difficult than they really have to be!" the mother chided. "Why do you always have to impetuously prove something without thinking it through?"

"May you grow a second asshole, and may the exit cavity appear between your tiny tits!" Theseus exclaimed, while indirectly favoring his father and denouncing his mother, along with her wimpy, aristocratic, cowardly family. "You'll never grow or have balls for as long as you live!" the boy disrespectfully chastised his already-insulted mother.

"I hope you live a dangerous and adventurous life, my son," Theseus's mother prattled. "For I can plainly see that you're just as conceited and just as egotistical as your pretentious father is. So, it's gotta' be *my way* or the freakin' highway, if ya' don't want to shape- up and ship-out!"

"Mother; I only wish that we ancient Greeks had last names, for if we did, I'm certain that *your* last name would be Fucker!" Theseus wildly cursed, as the stubborn youth set-out on foot north in the direction of scandalous Athens.

"You will lead a hard, harsh life, and your ship will never come in!" the mother shouted. "Become a starving playwright, and get your freakin' act together!"

"Eat my royal salami!" Theseus turned and hollered back. "Then you'll have a major reverse *edible co*mplex!"

The overland journey to Athens was long and arduous. Many avaricious, heinous thieves and bandits stayed hiding along the trail, waiting to pounce on any itinerant traveler, but magnificent Theseus was not stifled by any sinister lowlife threats jeopardizing his safety.

"Give us your money," the leader of three robbers demanded in one particular ambush.

"I have no money, and I don't give a shit what you say!" Theseus boldly answered. "Now fuck-off, assholes!"

"Then, kneel-down so that after *we* pilfer your gold and silver coins, we may lift and toss you over the side of the cliff into the sea!" the second belligerent robber insisted.

"I've already told you to 'fuck-off', assholes!" Theseus demanded. "What you have threatened me, I shall certainly do to you! Fuck-off, and find someone weaker and richer than I am to abuse and rob!"

The infuriated Greek hero then grabbed the first surprised trail thief, hoisted the scumbag over *his* head, and flung the screaming bandit off the precipice into what would become known as the Aegean Sea, which would be named after the lad's aging father Aegeus, ages later. Then, Theseus violently knocked the other two bellicose aggressors fully unconscious, adroitly utilizing his bare, clenched fists. When the pair of hostile highwaymen finally revived, the now-delirious shit-heads found themselves tethered to two pine trees that had been bent to the ground.

"What the fuck's goin' on?" the first thoroughly paranoid villain yelled. "Damned *Oracle of Delphi!* Your terrible prediction has come to fruition! This pugnacious asshole is gonna' tear me limb from limb!"

"I hope you two villains are prepared to go your separate ways!" Theseus laughed. "And splittin' headaches are nothin' compared to the splittin' bodies I'm about to administer!"

"Untie us and we'll promise to do anything you ask!" the third robber pleaded. "I'll wash your grimy feet; wipe your dirty, smelly ass clean; lick your raunchy dick every hour; well, we'll do just about anything you command!"

"Fuck you!" Theseus yelled as the angry prince released the trees from their tethers with one swift swipe of his trusty bronze sword. The two men were simultaneously catapulted into the air, and in a second, separated into severed appendages that soared-off the precipice, and into the yet-unnamed Aegean Sea, a hundred-yards below. "That oughta' teach you dunce-headed hoodlums from ignorantly fuckin' with me!"

Theseus had killed over a hundred diabolical bandits in his arduous trek from Sparta to Athens, and finally it was now safe for politicians, priests, pedophiles and other less dangerous crooks to travel about ancient Greece unmolested. When Theseus finally reached his destination, the Athenians had heard of his successful campaign against BASTARDS (Bandits Association for the Systematic Thievery of Athenians, Retards, Dumb-asses, and Spartans). King Aegeus had also been briefed of a bold young hero that had triumphantly entered his city. The ruler invited the yahoo by messenger (but not by *Yahoo Messenger*) to attend a banquet that was coincidentally being given on that very day to honor no one, or nothing in particular.

'I'll poison the young punk at my exquisite banquet,' the king thought while not realizing or caring that the callow vigilante might indeed be *his* exiled son. A witch named Medea had planted that evil thought in Aegeus's underdeveloped brain. Medea wanted to have full influence over the Athenian king; knew by virtue of prophecy that Theseus was the ruler's son, and wanted the kid out of the picture so that the greedy witch could continue running the city and its profitable businesses, while using the dummy king as her obedient puppet.

At the raucous, regal banquet, Medea was about to hand Theseus a chalice filled with wine laced with poison, but the young hero inadvertently dropped his bronze sword onto the palace's stone floor. The king instantly recognized the bronze sword as the one that *he* had surreptitiously buried under the boulder in southern Greece, which was even worse than being buried for seventeen years in ancient greasy grease. The king instinctively knocked the poisoned cup out of Medea's hand onto the stone floor, and the witch used her magical powers to disappear to Asia Minor, where minors under the age of eighteen were officially allowed by law to drink wine, beer, liquor, sperm juice, and poison.

"People of Athens," King Aegeus announced. "May I introduce to you my son and heir, Prince Theseus!"

"Fuck both you and him!" everyone in attendance sarcastically jeered. "Get some new, worthwhile genetics in your cursed family tree!"

"When's the royal orgy going to begin?" another impatient guest yelled. "I feel like a *bisexual* tonight!"

"I'd rather be *introduced* to venereal disease than to a slime-ball like Theseus!" another celebrator boomed.

"Just what this already fucked-up city needs is another perverted, pompous, royal asshole!" the thousand guests all amazingly shouted *in unison,* even though they all were *in Athens*.

All the while, the scheming King Aegeus was contemplating a contemptible plot to eliminate the threat of Theseus prematurely stealing the monarch's power, wealth, concubines, sluts, dildos, and glory. The king escorted the pure-hearted Theseus out of the royal banquet chamber and into *his* private, ornate lounge, to make the chaste lad a special offer.

"My son by incest, Theseus," Aegeus began his remarks. "I have a special 'proposal' for you to consider."

"I don't want to marry any damn man," the hero replied, "especially a psychologically-dysfunctional idiot that happens to be my fucked-up father!"

"No-no, my son," the king indulgently laughed. "I want you to go on a special quest to rid my soul of a certain guilt that persistently haunts me."

"Special quest!" Theseus's eyes lit-up as the ambitious punk evaluated the prospect of finally experiencing a real adventurous exploit that could make him famous. "Do you want me to break-up lesbian love triangles in Corinth? What about me eliminating all homosexual romantic trapezoids trapped in Attica?" the young handsome prince inquired.

"I assure you, Theseus, that you will be living under aging King Aegeus's aegis until I die!" the father persuasively alliterated.

'I would rather be standing at the base of *Mt. Olympus* when it finally crumbles and tumbles to the ground,' Theseus cynically thought, but did not share.

King Aegeus proceeded to tell his ambitious son about the legendary King Minos, ruler of the island of Crete, situated right next to shitty Excrete. Minos had lost his only son Androgeus. The cretin Cretan king had sent Androgeus to Athens to discuss with King Aegeus the exciting plan of trading wives for whores.

"Theseus," Aegeus said to his pristine, idealistic son. "I foolishly told Androgeus about a very dangerous, horny bull that was terrorizing the outskirts of Athens, and the outskirts and undergarments of all women living around or near Athens. The lustful, horny beast wanted to screw beautiful women, instead of simply obeying nature and being content porking cows."

"What did you do to Androgeus that was so foolish?" Theseus innocently asked without suspecting how big of a conniving, devious prick his father actually was.

"When Androgeus heard me talking about this special perverted bull," duplicitous Aegeus continued, "he volunteered to go and kill the sex-crazed creature, and I stupidly allowed him to pursue his fancy. Then, the horny bull mercilessly gored and killed Androgeus, and King Minos became excessively pissed-off about *his* son's unnecessary death."

Aegeus then explained that Minos sent his best elite soldiers to invade Athens, and threatened to burn *his* splendid metropolis to cinders if the beleaguered king didn't send seven fair maidens and seven virgin males to Crete every nine years to be given in sacrifice to the Minotaur to devour.

"The minute tour?" Theseus asked. "How could a *minute tour* of any government building devour fourteen innocent teenagers?"

"My dear fucked-up son," interrupted Aegeus. "The Minotaur is a horrible, huge monster that has the head of a bull and the body of a man, and I tell you that that's no goddamned bull-shit. The grotesque creature was the offspring of Minos's wife, Queen Pasiphae, and a studly bull kept in the palace's basement. Pasiphae preferred having sex with bulls, horses, donkeys, and elephants, or just about any animal that had a dick longer and thicker than a man's leg."

"Wow!" Theseus marveled and exclaimed. "Then, Minos's wife never had sex with a rooster, so that this perverted tale you're now relating could never be misconstrued as your typical cock-and-bull story."

"Exactly," King Aegeus petulantly concurred. "Queen Pasiphae hated roosters with a passion, and would often repeatedly scream-out during nightmare orgasms, 'Any animal's cock'll do, besides a cock-a-doodle-do'!"

"How did King Minos get possession of such an extraordinary creature as this Minotaur you've been graphically describing?" Theseus asked his demented, degenerate father.

"A magnificent bull was given to Minos by the sea-god Poseidon," Aegeus explained to his fascinated son. "Poseidon strictly instructed Minos to sacrifice the bull to the gods, but Minos refused to do so. The asshole king was an impotent voyeur, who only got half an erection watching the horny bull fuck the shit out of Queen Pasiphae twenty-four times a day," Aegeus disgustedly elaborated. "Then, a son was born to Pasiphae, and the offspring was the gruesome-looking, big-dicked, very horny Minotaur."

Theseus learned from his father that Minos had commissioned the services of a great architect named Daedalus, who had designed and supervised the construction of a vast network of underground caves and tunnels that formed a virtually inescapable dark maze beneath the Cretan palace at Knossus. Every nine years, the fourteen young Athenian virgins were cruelly placed inside the incredible labyrinth, and were eventually individually, brutally slaughtered, and then voraciously consumed by the heinous Minotaur.

"So, what the fuck does all of this damned stupid Minotaur bull-shit have to do with the reason for my quest?" the now-perturbed Theseus inquisitively asked his amnesia-stricken, daft father.

"Within a week, the next fourteen Athenian youths are scheduled to leave Athens and voyage to Crete, only to be thrown to the wretched beast," Aegeus divulged. "And you, my son, must venture to Crete and slay the vile Minotaur before the innocent virgins are sodomized, screwed, and then ultimately devoured."

"I volunteer to be one of the young males to be sacrificed!" Theseus cavalierly announced to his father. "I gotta' get my first big exploit under my belt. And besides; I might actually enjoy being sodomized by the monster."

"Are you a virgin?" Aegeus curiously asked.

"Fuckin'A!" Theseus proudly declared and lied. "Before the ship returns to Athens, I shall lower the bad news black sail, and raise the good news white one, so that *you* will know in advance of my conquest of the Minotaur," the eager prince confidently stated. "Now father; please leave me the fuck alone while I formulate a clever ruse to employ!"

"That is good, my brave son," Aegeus meditated and answered. "But how the hell could you ever raise the black flag if you have been killed by the ferocious monster? After you are slayed by the beast, my debt to Minos will have been erased, and my imperial dominance as the kingpin here in Athens will be unchallenged by Crete! Good luck on your quest, my quixotic son!"

The fourteen young, designated victims arrived in Crete, and were forced to march in a procession that paraded throughout the city of Knossus, which had only two one-way streets. The fourteen prospective victims were showered with bull sperm; cow ovarian eggs, and the teens felt and heard lots of heckling bull-shit yelled at them. Ariadne, the daughter of Minos, was in the crowd throwing hard and soft bull manure at the fourteen unfortunate Athenians when she noticed Theseus's muscular body, and immediately fell in love with his impressive body.

"Daedalus," Ariadne said to the drunken reveler standing next to her. "Tell me'; how does one escape the labyrinth that you and your son Icarus had designed and had constructed beneath my father's mammoth palace. How does a person like myself', who doesn't have the gift of tunnel vision, get out of that freakin' underground maze?"

"Okay, Ariadne. I'll tell you everything in detail, if you promise to give me a good blow-job, and then sit on my face with your bare ass and maneuver your wet pussy over my nostrils for at least an hour," Daedalus sternly stipulated.

"It's a deal!" Ariadne enthusiastically replied. "But I don't want your long nose bustin' my cherry before my chosen lover has the opportunity to pump the poop out of me!"

Later that afternoon, Ariadne had several soldiers escort the chaste-hearted, courageous Theseus to her royal bedroom. The young hero eagerly listened to the princess's proposal as his eyes remained fastened on Ariadne's rock-solid tits with beautiful round protruding nipples showing through the young lady's sheer, thin, white tunic.

"I shall help you escape the labyrinth if you promise to take me to Athens and then marry me," Ariadne directly suggested. "I need to escape outa' this fuckin' desert-island dump, and get the *Hades* away from my fucked-up voyeur father, and my mentally-sick, sex-crazed, bull-screwin' mother."

"I promise to take you home to Athens as long as you don't fuck-around, having abnormal sex with bulls, horses, donkeys and elephants!" Theseus honestly returned. "To tell you the truth, Ariadne, their long, thick dicks make me feel rather inferior."

"I promise!" the obliging princess agreed. "Now, take this ball of thread, and I'll tell ya' exactly how to use it."

That night, Theseus entered the pitch-black labyrinth through a well-concealed palace secret door. The hero tied a loop of string around the wooden door's latch, kissed Ariadne for good luck, and then proceeded into the dark, perilous labyrinth. All the while, the wannabe' hero unwound the ball of string that was now his sole connection with Cretan civilization.

Theseus ventured forward in the cold, dank blackness, searching and listening for any sound of the dreadful cellar-dweller. The young champion soon heard a loud snoring in the far distance. The clumsy intruder fell-over the suddenly startled Minotaur, and then took the bull by the horns, smashing the beast's skull repeatedly against the dense rock walls. And then, Theseus beat the living bull-shit out of the snarling creature by pounding it relentlessly with his clenched fists, alternately in the balls, and then in the face. Soon, the defeated creature had been brutally battered to death, and breathed no more.

Theseus lifted himself up from atop his terrible adversary; luckily found the ball of string upon the ground, and followed its path back to the concealed palace door from which he had audaciously entered the amazing maze.

"Oh, my wonderful hero; you have returned alive!" Ariadne yelled as she threw her arms around her new-found idol.

"I don't play *second string* to nobody, not even a fuckin' Minotaur!" Theseus boasted as the Athenian Prince dropped what remained of the ball of string to the palace's white marble floor.

The thirteen virgins (excluding Theseus and Ariadne, both of whom were definitely not certifiable virgins) fled with their two bodyguard rescuers back to the Athenian ship. In no time, the couple was heading north by northwest, and the following morning, the vessel smoothly docked at the island of Naxos.

"Oh, Theseus," Ariadne uttered. "I'm extremely seasick, and have already vomited-up half my lungs and a third of my stomach. Please leave me on this island, until I fully recover from my nausea," the ailing princess wept. "Then, by all means, return to Naxos, and take me to Athens with you!"

"Okay, Ariadne!" Theseus consented. "I approve of your weirdo recommendation. But I insist that if you would simply give me a deep-throated blowjob, then all of that nasty sour stomach fluid would quickly exit your mouth, after I pop my biggest load ever down your gorgeous throat!"

When the Athenian ship left Naxos and finally neared its ultimate destination, Theseus was thinking about Ariadne giving him the best fellatio ever, and the slayer of the Minotaur forgot to take-down the bad news black sail, and hoist-up the good news white one.

King Aegeus was watching the black-sailed ship from the summit of the *Acropolis*. 'This is great!' the evil ruler thought. 'My son Theseus is dead, and the black sail has been raised, indicating that wonderful bad news. I now can rule Athens unimpeded and unchallenged by any young, idealistic, punk-whippersnapper!'

Theseus's mind broke-off from its idle reverie long enough for the passenger to realize that he had been morally obligated to his royal father to lower the black sail, and then raise the white one, signifying *his* glorious victory in Crete over the ghastly Minotaur.

Seeing the white sail being hoisted-up the ship's mast, Aegeus became depressed, paranoid, crazy, despondent, melancholy, neurotic, and lugubrious, all at the same time. The reprehensible monarch leaped from a hill of the *Acropolis* and plummeted-down, crashing into a small temple of Pallas Athene, where the king instantly ruptured both of his *temples,* and immediately died upon impact. Aegeus's body then continued rolling all the way to the nearby sea, and finally fell-off another cliff, into the dark blue water. Hence. the geographic area is now known as the Aegean Sea.

125

And that's precisely how the intrepid Theseus had killed the contemptible Minotaur, and then easily became by default (through no fault of his own) the rightful king of Athens.

"Olympus Lives"

Mt. Olympus has been a source of awe and wonder ever since ancient times to the present age. Situated between Thessaly and Macedonia, the massive mountain rises to a celestial peak that towers nearly ten-thousand-feet above the Earth. From prehistoric to modern times, shepherds have loyally tended their bleating flocks near the mammoth wonder's base. *Olympus's* grassy slopes gradually surrender to snow-clad crags, and human eyes can observe, and fully appreciate, the mountain's total grandeur from a distance. *Mt. Olympus's* glorious crest is often shrouded by a veil of fog, or by a mystic halo of cottony clouds.

The majestic peak was thought by both educated and uneducated ancient Greeks to be the very center of the then known world. Many dumb-asses foolishly believed its summit to be the official residence of the twelve Olympian gods. Poets and bards, on and off drugs and alcohol, imagined that splendid palaces were supremely situated atop the mountain's stately crown.

The decline of Greece as a dominant civilization occurred when the power base of the *Western World* eventually shifted from Athens to Rome. Knowledge of the ancient civilizations had been almost completely forgotten during the *Dark Ages,* before electricity had been harnessed to create artificial light. The *Renaissance*, the *Age of Enlightenment,* and the *Industrial Revolution* had drastically altered man's methods of thinking, working and screwing. By the time of Shakespeare, mythology had diminished in prestige when compared to *Globe Theater c*omedy and tragedy play presentations. And later in human history, science and technology became the most powerful cultural forces of the twentieth century besides the dysfunctional "gay sexual revolution".

Humans are no longer primitive, fearful, and superstitious creatures. Mortals have evolved into haughty, proud, and ambitious beings, who can invent computers that are smarter than Apollo; who can build skyscrapers that would give Hephaestus an inferiority complex; who can film the most erotic pornography better than Aphrodite could ever imagine, and who can generate atomic energy that would make Almighty Zeus's electric thunderbolts seem like mere child's-play.

Ancient beliefs handed-down from classical bards have been reduced in importance by modern education and evolving hedonism. Anything not originating from science and technology is subject to cynicism, mistrust and doubt. Materialism and humanism are presently contributing to the decline and fall of now-suspect, classical wisdom. Homo sapiens and homosexuals don't have time for Zeus, Hera and Apollo anymore. Instead, the species reveres televisions, automobiles, computers, the *Internet,* music disks, dildos, ribbed condoms, sex vibrators, and thousands of other prized technology "things". Religion is no longer the dominant world influence, but has been replaced by modern science and technology.

Humans have become egocentric pleasure machines, worshipping wealth, mobility, peep shows, and convenience, all offspring creations of the *Industrial Revolution* and the *Sexual Revolution*, which incidentally doesn't fight *AIDS*. Compare those ideas to what Zeus and the Olympus gods had to offer mortals: poverty, travail, sacrifice, punishment, venereal disease, and burgeoning misery. Modern men have little time for paying homage to ancient gods. Their new religion is science, and science has made mankind selfish, defiant, and agnostic.

Greek mythology has suffered a terrible demise over the past two millennia. Children prefer to believe in pixies, dragons, magic, witches, Santa Claus, the Easter Bunny, the Tooth Fairy, and Satanic sorcerers, rather than in Zeus, Poseidon, Hades, Ares, Hephaestus, Apollo, Hera, Hermes, Aphrodite, and Athena. But a little-known, esoteric fact is fully comprehended by a small nucleus of erudite "New Age" mystics. The family of the Greek gods of antiquity are indeed still alive.

Mt. Olympus's present facade suggests a lazy, august serenity. Neither mortal nor immortal activity seems to be existent anywhere upon its dignified surface appearance. The mountain's noble tranquility suggests that the once almighty Olympus deities have evacuated the entire vicinity. Presented in this disclosure is secret documentation that supports the contrary.

Over the centuries, a vast network of silver labyrinths has been surreptitiously built inside the noble mountain. The subterranean kingdom is coordinated and connected by a maze of resplendent marble tunnels. The internal city of *Olympus* is so self-contained, and so self-sufficient, that its immortal inhabitants need never venture outside its perimeter. The well-concealed fortress grants the gods refuge from humans, and it safeguards Zeus and his haughty, divine family. The Olympus deities are served by legions of appreciative and well-fed slaves, who have been generated and bred from Mediterranean ancestral stock. The descendants of the original servants have been in the gods' service several centuries before Julius Caesar's Rome.

Zeus's colossal, resplendent palace dominates the subterranean Olympian Empire, which is lit by millions of candles burning in golden sconces, and by thousands of brilliant torches attached to sturdy ivory holders, which are anchored into the marble walls. The king-god's magnificent edifice towers over the other deities' smaller-but-most-impressive, gleaming structures. The impeccable temple is the property of the still-conceited Zeus. His singular mansion has marble and bronze floors, golden ceilings, and glittering platinum roofs.

One side of Zeus's majestic temple looks like the original Athenian *Parthenon*, only it's ten times as large in dimension. Another side is similar to King Minos's former great palace at Knossus on the isle of Crete; a third side is modeled after King Priam's much-heralded castle at Troy, and the fourth is comparable in design to the famous oracle's shrine at Dephi. Ornate Corinthian columns, and incredible statues of major and minor gods and goddesses, have been erected everywhere at key intersections inside the fantastic mountain metropolis. A gallery on the right side of Zeus's palatial residence leads to a special chamber, the official meeting place of the "Supreme Olympus Council".

The vindictive and isolated gods have reluctantly relinquished the Earth to ambitious mortals over the last two millennia. When men had built thousands of factories in the nineteenth century, their knowledge of chemicals, compounds, and combustion soon greatly surpassed even the most-spectacular achievements of the immortals. The divine ones, under the aegis of Zeus, now borrow ideas and steal patents, just to play catch-up with mankind's illustrious and formidable ingenuity.

Electricity is generated inside *Mt. Olympus* by an underground river's waterfall. The transferred kinetic energy produces sufficient light for streets, parks, gardens, and buildings. The principles of the gasoline engine, stolen from old Henry Ford blueprints, enabled Hephaestus to power underground "mass transportation", designed to conveniently shuttle slaves from one mountain palace to another. "It's a good fuckin' thing we gods are immortal," Zeus had told Ares at the last Council meeting. "Or else, we would suffocate to death from all this noxious subterranean pollution."

Zeus owns a fleet of seventies-styled *Cadillacs* and *Lincolns*, but the other gods, depending on their rank in the divine pecking order, must drive less-extravagant renditions of *Fords*, *Chevrolets,* and *Pontiacs*. Cable television has recently been installed, but the gods must watch black and white '50s reruns, siphoned from nearby Greece satellite transmitters. "Man has gone from slave, to nuisance, to rival, to conqueror," Zeus lamented to Hera the night before his next scheduled Council forum.

"We need more spies and special agents out there stealing their innovative technology," the queen goddess suggested. "Maybe your brother Hades could cooperate and lend us Benedict Arnold, Nathan Hale, and Mata Hari's essential services."

"We can't even keep-up with what these remarkable, fucked-up creatures had achieved in the early twentieth century," the philanderer Zeus confessed to his attentive spouse. "And now, with atomic power, Star Wars technology, the *Internet*, gay sex, and space travel, let me tell you Hera, those damned perverted humans scare the living Hades out of me!"

"The children of Arcadia have gone from your humble servants dressed in tawdry rags to being the insane terrors of the universe," Hera alertly added. "They're quite imaginative, in addition to being insubordinate to *our* whims and intentions."

"Prometheus and I had molded those creatures from mud, do you hear me Hera, m-u-d," Zeus emphasized as the frustrated god stared into his wine chalice. "Those first men were mere, puny jerk-offs. I should've snuffed them out right then and there, before the rogues had a chance to make fire and use it to manufacture weapons. Now, I must rely on *them* for such crazy things as shampoo, dog food, jock-itch-spray, and tacos. By Cronus, how I love Mexican tacos! And burritos, jalapeno peppers, and enchiladas, too!"

"Zeus, when can I have my first *Lexus* automobile?" Hera inquired. "I need to drive all the time, just like your mighty penis needs to drive all the time."

"Whenever Hephaestus or Hermes can steal the fuckin' plans," Lord Zeus answered in a disgusted tone of voice. "Then you'll get your new set of wheels."

Olympus still has many time-honored laws. The words in one ancient edict state that once mankind has acquired a particular knowledge, skill, or secret, then the gods would never take that "gift" away. But the discovery of electricity; the evolution of telecommunications; the creation of the microchip; the practice of biochemical warfare, and the decadent influence of *MTV* and *VH-1* have all given the Greek gods gross inferiority complexes.

The gods refuse to confront men directly, because the divine ones now feel inadequate to *their* creation. Zeus and company evade contact with their former suppliants at all costs. Even Zeus has a phobia of 'evolving humanity'. The Olympus gods' energies are now exclusively devoted to subversive tactics, sabotage, and counter-intelligence. Their prime goal is to have men and women quarrel and battle amongst themselves, or as Athena aptly calls it, "A clever divide and conquer strategy."

"Father, if we could get men quarreling and fighting each other," Athena commented at family discussion time at the great marble-slate dining room table, the night before the next upcoming Council Meeting, "then mass discord could trigger the fall of modern civilization."

"Yes," Hera promptly agreed. "The gods could enter the vacuum caused by world chaos, and assume power again on Earth."

"Then, I could regain dominion of the Earth *and* the sky!" Zeus exclaimed. "Our glory would grace this despicable planet once more. Our meritorious greed would again reign supreme, all over the fuckin' planet!"

"I hope we can steal *MTV* and *VH-1* before the asinine humans eradicate themselves," Athena complained. "I want to see what this disco stuff is all about, and what this Fleetwood Mac group looks and sounds like. I don't even know what the Beatles, or even the Rolling Stones look like. But I like their music cassettes I hear on my new tape player that Hermes managed to pilfer for me from something called a *Walmart* store!"

"Athena, that is exactly what's wrong with immortal children nowadays," Zeus admonished. "I mean, you've been a child, my child, for over three thousand years now. Don't you get it! You idolize retarded human entertainers and movie stars just like ordinary asshole earthling kids do, but *they're* supposed to worship *you!* Athena; I'm hereby warning you. I want you to stop acting like a mentally deficient and emotionally horny Greek geek!"

"Daddy, I also like soap operas, poodle skirts, '50s music, mosh pits, and *Disneyland!"* Athena revealed before she raised her body up into the air and effortlessly drifted into another part of the palace.

The dejected gods knew a few secrets that still gave them some distinct advantages over mortals. One was nectar and ambrosia; the drink and the food of the gods. Even that wonderful knowledge was in danger of being discovered by, as Zeus called them, "Those fucked-up, monstrous mortals living down on Earth."

"Hera, genetic research done down in those rooms the mortals call laboratories is analyzing the structure of the *DNA* molecule," Zeus informed. "I had casually created life, and I have no idea what in Sparta a fuckin' *DNA* molecule is! I mean, all I said was 'Let there be formed a

131

smaller version of an Olympus god that is mortal, and designed to serve us, the gods.' I mean, I never said anything about a silly, stupid, son-of-a-bitchin' *DNA* molecule!"

"Zeus, when can I get a credit card?" Hera asked while deftly changing the subject. "I'm especially tired of these obsolete tunics and cumbersome sandals I've been wearing for over three thousand Earth years now. Then, I could shrink-down to five-foot-six-inches in height, go to shopping malls, disguised as a svelte lady, and purchase some new modern clothes like bras, strippers' outfits, G-strings, and pantyhose."

"Hera!" Zeus hollered in a thunderous voice. "You aren't fuckin' listening to me, as usual. This repulsive race I had created is on the threshold of mastering a synthetic formula for immortality. The obnoxious shit-heads don't even waste their time trying to find nectar and ambrosia, anymore. The rebels want to do *it their* way, just like that crazy Frank Sinatra fellow!"

Zeus sadly missed his involvement in, and intervention into human history. Thec chief god used to enjoy manipulating men's destinies, and tinkering with their fates. When he didn't perform those interferences himself, the son of Cronus used surrogates like his wife Hera; like Ares, the god of war, or like the Fates and the Muses to execute *his* divine will.

"Remember the good old days, Hera," Zeus fondly recalled as the egomaniac sat erect without an erection on his golden throne. "Men were our puppets, and we fancifully pulled and manipulated the strings. Remember all the great fun we had producing and directing the sensational *Trojan War*."

"Do I!" Hera fondly recalled and exclaimed. "We staged the whole *Odyssey* as if the adventures of Odysseus were strategic moves in a challenging chess game."

"You've done it again, dear wife," Zeus adamantly grieved. "Mortals invented chess, not us. That's what really disturbs and aggravates the hell out of me the most. Mankind invents ten times more than we can create. Those insolent assholes down on Earth seem to have much more inherent imagination and creativity than we supreme gods do, and I had created the insolent scoundrels."

Zeus and his Council felt threatened by humanity's recent, arrogant insurgence, ever since the introduction of the microchip and the computer. At first, the gods ignored man's aspiring quest for intellectual independence. But over the past two millennia, the race's indifference to the gods has evolved into unbearable contempt, balanced by apathy. The overall general defiance had now reached intolerable proportions. The gods, especially Zeus, no longer felt rivaled. The Mt. Olympus residents now feel imperiled and overwhelmed. Their former narcissistic, self-concepts have been atrophying into a malaise of "poor self-esteem". Zeus despised the Earth dwellers' disinterest in his avaricious family members, and he specifically resented their "disgraceful and shameful irreverence" towards him, their illustrious creator.

Every hundred "Earth-years", ever since the time of Julius Caesar, Zeus had convened his Olympian Council to discuss current events, and to analyze the gods' general progress and strategies. Plenty had happened in the last century to cause the gods to be alarmed. Nuclear weapons, spy satellites, space exploration, cable television, new medical technology, computers, the *Internet*, jet airplanes, X-rated films, and the invention of the automobile were just some of the major accomplishments developed down on Earth that had eclipsed anything that the gods could collectively conceive.

The Mt. Olympus game plan was rather simple. The divine family believed that they should live in isolation until mankind terminated its existence through war, decadence, rap music lyrics, weapons of mass destruction, and death resulting from excessive body piercing and mutilation. In fact, the conniving gods are presently plotting sinister schemes to accelerate the mortals' declination from power.

Zeus's Council assembled, and was about to convene on December 31, 2000. Aphrodite and Athena respectively wore glamorous yellow and teal silk tunics of different designs, and also flaunted stunning diamond diadems upon their heads. Hera was dressed in purple, and wore a brilliant sapphire and ruby tiara. Ares, Poseidon, Hermes, and Apollo sat at the other end of Zeus's long emerald and marble table, which was trimmed with pure gold. Dionysus and Hades were exchanging anecdotes as the pair stood next to their topaz thrones that had soft, velvet cushions. Hephaestus, the lame blacksmith god, was the last arriving council member, limping into the chamber and locatimg his ruby throne.

The meeting room was quite dazzling and regal. The chamber had more sparkling jewels embedded into its walls and ceiling than the total number of rare gems in all the world's jewelry stores put together. Zeus imperatively called the meeting to order by hurling a wicked thunderbolt at an enlarged black and white photograph of Manhattan. The lightning bolt immediately obliterated the city's skyline. The other gods in the assembly ceased their casual prattling, and rather quickly came to attention.

Artemis was the only major deity absent from the Council. Zeus had given the female archer permission to go on a hunting mission to Ethiopia to capture an elusive sub-human specimen known as *Big Foot*. Zeus believed Artemis's story, even though the goddess knew all along that the creature would more likely be found in Saskatchewan, Canada than on the African continent. Such a feat would definitely boost Zeus's ego, but only Artemis knew and thought: "It ain't gonna' happen."

"My fellow immortals," Zeus prefaced his somber introduction. "We need discipline among our own ranks in order to defeat the wicked scourge that plagues us on all major fronts. My biggest mistake was modeling the human mind after my own."

"My dear husband," Hera boldly interrupted. "You should be edified. After all, every achievement man enjoys is indirectly *your* achievement, because their minds are really reproductions of your most noble genius."

Zeus raised his massive white eyebrows, shifted about on his gigantic golden throne, smiled briefly at Hera, and then proceeded with his prepared text. "Fellow deities; I regret ever giving mortals intelligence, cunning, courage and stubbornness. These bold, brazen creatures have, believe it or not, ascended to a level worthy of our admiration, and also our vengeful condemnation."

The other Olympians nodded their heads in tacit agreement. Zeus proceeded with his angry rhetoric, which his speechwriter Apollo had actually prepared on the backside of a scroll that was positioned upon an easel, directly situated to the now-standing lord-god's right.

"Initially, we derived amusement from watching their awkward folly," Zeus pointed-out. "Man's futile effort to merely survive was indeed a novelty to behold. The fools feared us; worshipped us; respected us, and sought our protection. We even gave the mendicants a benign code of ethics, based on moderation, just to safeguard the assholes from self-destruction."

Everyone in the magnificent chamber concurred with Zeus's cogent assessment. The Council gods were all anxious to present their own assigned oral reports, and get the meeting over with, so that the divine audience wouldn't have to see Zeus, or hear his dictatorial narrative for another peaceful hundred-years.

Hera wanted to read the latest *Hollywood* tabloids; Athena wanted to listen to her cherished '50s music tapes; Hermes desired studying how *Federal Express* and *UPS* operated, and horny Aphrodite wished to look at the centerfold in the latest available heisted copy of *Playgirl Magazine*.

"Yes, my fellow Olympians," Zeus cautiously resumed his lengthy preface. "I recall brave men like Odysseus, Agamemnon, Jason, Achilles, Orpheus, Perseus, Hercules and Daedalus. Those mortals respectfully paid homage to *us*. They showed fortitude and mettle. The men of Homer's time were what I had in mind when I had molded the first puny Arcadians out of clay," the chief god pontificated. "Now, I must share with you that I regret that I had inadvertently molded and fabricated a curse, a plague that has haunted me for over three thousand years."

"Yes," a drunken Dionysus interrupted. "Now-a-days, *Arcadians* are those young humans who addictively play pinball, poker machines, and raunchy video games."

"Enough of your vile drivel, Dionysus," Zeus commanded. "Stop acting like a human jerk-off!"

Ares could not control his nasty temper any longer. The god of war cleared his throat, and proudly stood-up to be recognized.

"Your Eminence; if I may say something significant," Ares requested. "I believe our problems all began with that treacherous traitor, Prometheus."

Zeus became enraged at the mention of *that* wholly despised name. "Don't ever even think about that obscene, traitorous Titan again. Prometheus had deliberately violated Olympus's most sacred rule!" Zeus's voice blasted-out so loudly that it shattered the delicate crystals in an overhead chandelier.

"That demented law which stated that only male gods could be promiscuous?" Hera humorously asked.

"No!" Zeus boisterously bellowed. "The undeniable rule that gods should never give men tools, or bestow on them knowledge. As you all know, once man acquires a gift, it should not be taken away. Oh, how I regret establishing that monkey-shit mandate around the time of Medusa's unfortunate demise, caused by that intrepid fiend, Perseus."

"So what?" Pallas Athene defiantly challenged. "Men got fire; men stayed warm; and men got laid more often. Big deal! Prometheus felt sorry for the afflicted race, and decided to enhance their sex lives."

"Athena," Zeus corrected. "Men did not learn how to make fire on their own. Prometheus gave them fuckin' fire, and taught them how to fuckin' make it. With fire, man changed his mind from figuring-out how to survive, and almost-immediately transformed into a cultural mechanism having free time to think. Humans then used fire to make bronze," Zeus elaborated, "and after men knew all about bronze, the ambitious assholes made dangerous weapons from bronze. Soon, the industrious fools had manufactured swords, helmets, and shields. *Thinking* was indeed the beginning of man's insubordination to the gods' authority."

"Where is Prometheus now?" Ares, the god of war, curiously asked. "He's no longer chained to *Mt. Etna* as punishment for defying you, oh great Zeus!"

Zeus explained that Prometheus had to be moved to a less conspicuous location after humans had invented the device known as "the camera". Pictures would have been taken, and eventually, Prometheus would've been interviewed by the media and by meddling television talk show hosts. The easily influenced humans would feel sorry for Prometheus, and then would try to liberate "the victim" from his shackles. "My eternal command would've been reversed by the implementation of stupid human compassion," Zeus loudly protested. "I could've never lived with that bullshit mortal opposition. Prometheus is now imprisoned in a dark dungeon a mile beneath this very chamber."

"King Zeus," King Hades asked his brother to be recognized. "You are too kind in so eloquently describing the human vermin."

"Hades; you take care of the underworld and the afterlife, and let me and Poseidon take care of the rest of the fucked-up world," Zeus defensively answered. "But confidentially, I must say I am angered by human conceit and disdain. I did not create men for the gods to envy *them*. Their token remembrance of us is limited to occasionally naming rockets and planets in honor of our sacred Greek and Roman appellations," Zeus hesitantly acknowledged. "The planet Pluto honors you, dear Hades; Mars honors Ares; Mercury honors Hermes; Venus honors Aphrodite; Neptune honors Poseidon; and of course, Jupiter, the largest damned planet in the solar system, pays special homage to me, Zeus."

"And please don't forget the summer and winter *Olympic Games,* too!" Apollo reminded his Commander-in-Chief.

Poseidon was just as perplexed as his brother Zeus has been, ever since the time of Homer, so the sea god decided to speak. "Unfortunately," Poseidon declared, "these earthlings have forgotten the original purpose of the *Olympic Games*, which was to praise and worship *us*, the Olympians. Now, the retards egotistically carry on *our* proud games simply to edify themselves! How spiteful and inconsiderate could those degenerate imbeciles possibly be?"

"Enough of this hollow sentimentality!" Zeus loudly thundered. "Our *Golden Age* is long gone, but the purpose of this scheduled meeting is to restore our legacy to past glory. I'm going to call upon each of you to report your subversive activities of the past hundred-years. Hermes, we'll start with your explicit testimony."

"Thank you, your Excellency," Hermes commenced. "I am saddened to report that the earthlings have learned how to build great machines that enable them to fly three times faster than sound. These jets, as they call them, could fly ten times faster than any god now sitting in this room. I beg your pardon. Of course, gods can't fly while they're sitting, but just yesterday, I was almost-rammed out of a cloud by the careless pilots of a *Boeing 747*. The wings almost fell off my helmet, and also from my sandals, resulting from the terrible turbulent air currents that instantly enveloped me."

Zeus stopped Hermes' monologue, and told the messenger god to refrain from his personal experiences, and to stick to telling exactly how the divine courier had thwarted "the demented descendants of Pandora and Epimetheus". Zeus then politely cracked a small smile for the first time in seventy decades, and Lord Hermes proceeded with his most-demonstrative and animated oral presentation.

"As the appointed messenger god," Hermes continued his dissertation, "I've tried contaminating all sorts of communications on Earth. I really got aggravated when the *United States Mint* discontinued the Mercury dime. The government removed my image, and put someone by the name of Franklin D. Roosevelt on the back instead, and that blatant disrespect really pissed me off."

"You're deviating off course once again, but tell us Hermes; what did you do to get even with the humans' coin mints? Do you intend to make *mints-meat* out of them?" Zeus asked.

The dedicated messenger god ignored Zeus's weak attempt at corny humor. "Thousands of people overreact to one another, simply by imitating the violence that I encourage the imbeciles to watch on cable television," the messenger god informed. "Negative behavior in movies, newspapers, rock n' roll, and rap music on the radio and TV, and also, what people see defined as daily activity on *Action News,* have all contributed to man's overall decadence. It's only a matter of time before Earth cultures will crumble and disintegrate from a lack of civilization and organization."

"I object!" Athena vociferously disagreed as if she were a defense attorney. "What's wrong with soap opera television, *MTV* and *VH-1*? And please tell me; what the heck is rap music? I'd like to listen to it, and see if it is enjoyable to my ears. That sounds as if it is good enough to make my hips hop!"

"Nothing is particularly wrong with *MTV* and *VH-1,* my erudite, dear daughter," Zeus replied. "It's perfectly all right for the gods to be decadent. What Hermes is saying is that he is trying to use decadence to have mankind self-destruct, caused by their cultural behavior fuckin' imitating us. Continue please, won't you Hermes?"

"I'm glad to say, if I might use a human expression, that we're 'all on the same wavelength'," Hermes indulgently laughed. "Thanks to decadence in the mass media, there are more crimes being committed down on Earth than ever before. Misdemeanors and felonies are rampant everywhere on the accursed planet. Weaker-minded men and women are mimicking the violence that their eyes see enacted on television, and that the dumb-shit fools also hypnotically watch in the movie theaters. Arson, theft, homicides, muggings, and greed are all definitely on the rise across the globe."

Hermes also reported that he believed the avaricious species dwelling down on Earth would be positively extinct in another hundred-years. The messenger god finished his formal presentation by promising that the Olympians would soon live in the sunshine once more, because destructive events were happening fast instead of as slowly as wars had developed during the stagnant *Dark Ages,* before men had electricity, and when peasants were too cheap, or too poor, or too dumb, to use candles.

"And if *we* don't come to power again?" Zeus promptly challenged. "What then?"

"Well, my King. I could always get a job with *FTD Florists* delivering roses if things really get rough," Hermes cleverly responded. "I might even become a pediatrician, and *deliver* babies outside abortion clinics."

Poseidon was the second speaker on the agenda, who was slated to address the Council. The sea-god had a very haggard expression on his hoary, wrinkled face. The ocean deity raised his silver trident into the air to get everyone's undivided attention. King Neptune's role in the Olympian conspiracy was restricted to the ocean floors. The sea god was Zeus's favorite brother, who had introduced *him* to the pleasures of Maryland crab soup and *Bumblebee Tuna* fish, even though neither he nor Zeus knew how to *tune a* guitar or a lyre. The king-god held the marine sage's excellent advice in high regard.

Poseidon possessed a strong, resonant voice, because the nutcase would always gargle salt water whenever he slept and snored on coral reef' beds at the bottom of the sea. The ocean denizen had become quite laconic over the centuries, mainly because it is hard talking to anyone seven-miles below the *Pacific Ocean,* since there aren't too many people or gods living or traveling seven-miles below the *Pacific Ocean,* even when it is tranquil. The sea god sounded rather pessimistic and skeptical as he initiated his oration.

"My *fellow* deities," Poseidon chauvinistically began. "I have relentlessly encouraged, through mental suggestion, that humans should excessively pollute the oceans. This will have a devastating effect on the balance of nature. Sea contamination will change weather patterns, and there will soon be a myriad of hurricanes, typhoons, and monsoons all year round, all over the damned planet."

"Excuse me Poseidon," Hera spoke-up before clearing her throat. "But if *you* contaminate the oceans, isn't the sea *your* home? Aren't you destroying your own precious environment?"

"Hopefully," Poseidon replied, "there will be enough left to work with, so that I, Thetis and the sea nymphs, and also Charybdis, and Triton, and all the rest of my gang, can start ocean evolution all over again."

"Continue with your discourse, my good brother," misogynistic Zeus commanded. "My wife is a little wet behind the ears, and dry within her crotch, when it comes to either the sea or sex," the king of gods laughed. All the male gods roared with delight, while the lady deities frowned and grimaced, sharing Hera's deep contempt and humiliation.

"When the oceans are adequately polluted," Poseidon proceeded, "fish and aquatic vegetation will die by the billions. Whales are already in short supply in three oceans, right this minute. Other sea creatures are *currently* classified as endangered species. Quite soon, mankind will eventually become an endangered species, too," the sea god declared.

"Very perceptive and surreptitious," Zeus commended, "because I am aware that even land animals are in jeopardy of extinction. Humans are happily trashing-up their fresh water rivers and lakes, as if those pristine places are their own fuckin' private back-yards. My dear brother, is there anything else informative you'd like to contribute to our forum?"

"As a matter of fact, there is," Poseidon recollected and articulated. "I absolutely loved the movie *The Poseidon Adventure.* The humans still remembered my glory by naming the disaster flick after me. And I'll bet you didn't know that I was instrumental in the sinking of the *Titanic,* and also the *Lusitania,* even though those stupid humans down on Earth credit a large iceberg and an errant torpedo as being responsible for those particular catastrophes. And I also hated and detested that celebrated Jacques Cousteau jerk-off. He had the audacity to name his ship *Calypso,* plagiarizing right out of Homer's *Odyssey.* As you recall, Lord Zeus,

Calypso is the stunning goddess who had offered Odysseus immortality," Poseidon vehemently complained. "And then, that Cousteau character was brazen enough to invent the aqua-lung. With advanced *SCUBA* equipment and submarines, men and women can now stay underwater almost as long as I can. Even I must surface occasionally to check-out some pretty sirens, and hot-looking sea nymphs' big firm knockers."

Zeus told Poseidon that the sea-god was deviating from *his* report's theme, and that *he* should forget his particular likes and dislikes, and his personal opinions, in order to be more objective during the 'sophisticated symposium'. "Stick to the facts!" Zeus objected and reprimanded his brother. "This meeting ought to be over in less than one human month, if we all agree to practice terseness and patience!"

"Thank you for pointing-out my apparent mental distractions," Poseidon answered with a trace of guilt. "Those vain creations known as humans have built dreadful battleships and submarines. I now feel very leery and uncomfortable swimming-about in my native environment. Presently, many smaller channels of water are completely unsafe to enter. I have a big scar on my left arm from a wayward harpoon, and another one on my right shoulder caused from a large ship's propeller that also almost savagely castrated me when I bent-over to examine my painful shoulder injury. And those new-fangled noisy jet skis flitting-around on the surface are fuckin' driving me nuts, too!"

The annoyed sea god then related that in 1995, he had to scramble behind a coral reef when a Russian submarine picked him up on their radar screens, and fired two torpedoes in his direction. "It required all my nautical skill just to avoid being fuckin' blown all the way to Neptune," Poseidon wryly reported. "And I assure you, Lord Zeus, that I can think of much better ways of being blown!"

The other Council gods gave Poseidon their approval by loudly clapping their divine hands. Zeus thanked his brother for his vigilance and allegiance while experiencing "drastic dire straits".

"I too fear the dangerous pestilence that Prometheus and I have inadvertently created," Zeus indicated to his peers. "What's to stop the human dolts from discovering *our* present location, and then evilly demolishing *Olympus* with a fifty-megaton nuclear bomb? And it might not even be a legitimate government that does us away, either! It might be some maverick international terrorist group out to make a shit-eating name for themselves!"

Throughout his royal three millennia reign, Zeus had always been chauvinistic, even three-thousand-years before Napoleon's cavalier General Nicholas Chauvin appeared marching-around on the Earth. The king-god preferred masculine domination of the universe, as long as *he* was the chief male overlord. Goddesses were always subordinated to male gods' whims. That was why Hermes and Poseidon's reports had been scheduled before any female deities could address the Council. Feeling satisfied that male dominance had been effectively asserted, Zeus asked his wife to articulate her conniving activities during the past century.

The beautiful queen goddess stood-up from her regal throne and smiled toward her all-too-familiar audience. Hera's pearly white teeth added a distinct power to her wonderful charm. Zeus's spouse's grace was matched only by her sagacity. The queen's beguiling eyes communicated her notorious shrewdness, and her haunting voice exuded charisma. Everyone, including Zeus, sat captivated on his or her throne, virtually hypnotized by the influential goddess's compelling radiance.

"Thank goodness the humans' calendar still recognizes the month of June, which was named after my Roman name, Juno," Hera graciously commenced her presentation. "And the the dunces still honor Ares with March; Mars being our esteemed war god's Roman designation," the chief goddess indicated.

"Humans absolutely love war!" Ares yelled from the other end of the grand marble table. "The assholes are lost without it. That's why mankind will remember me until the bitter end! The red planet is symbolic of bloodshed during war. And truthfully, I almost have to admire mortals for naming the red planet, Mars, after me!"

Everyone cheered Ares' rather perceptive remark. Even the gods enjoyed fighting among themselves more than they relished cooperating with each other. The fickle, self-infatuated fools regarded *sharing* as being "a petty human enterprise".

"My beloved husband and other deities," Hera saluted as she continued her comprehensive report. "I've been extremely busy this past Earth Century. I've adopted a sociological approach in my relentless campaign against humanity. To use the enemy's appropriate terminology, 'I am currently involved in the spread of mortal misery'. I once read *that* interesting passage on the last page of the insurrectionist *New York Times.*"

"Could you be more specific?" Zeus requested. "Please provide us with more poignant pithy details."

"Certainly," Hera amenably obliged. "By convincing women that ladies must have equal rights, I have sown the seeds of distrust between the sexes. Most men now fear their ruthless mates, even more than the idiots fear the scheming plans of other men."

"My dear wife," Zeus interrupted. "Make sure you restrict this women's rights' liberation business to Earth. It could cause real serious governing problems up here inside *Olympus.*"

Hera waited until the other gods stopped their cackling along with their' ridiculous chattering. "I am thrilled to announce the deterioration of the family structure all over the globe. Conflict abounds everywhere. Separations and divorce are rampant on every continent. Infidelity teems everywhere. It's actually growing at epidemic proportions," Zeus's wife proudly affirmed. "The basic moral fabric of Earthly societies is being slowly-but-surely eroding away. In another hundred-years, I predict that lesbians, especially dykes, will rule all families, clans, tribes and nations! The destruction of the traditional nuclear family will become more devastating than nuclear energy itself!"

Hera paused to evaluate the extent of her speech's impact upon her audience of peers. Seeing that her power had its usual bewitching and captivating effect, she proceeded with her forceful dissertation.

"Men are already disenchanted with their spouses, who aspire to surpass them in every facet of achievement. Since women now work, females are no longer exclusively dependent on their husbands' incomes. The wives are becoming more and more independent of male authority," Hera insisted. "Millions of female spouses now cheat on their already-cheating husbands. Jealousy and spite are flourishing in most every country, corresponding with the collapse of male jurisdiction. This new mass conflict will make Lenin and Marx's class conflict of the nineteenth century look like a school picnic," Hera predicted. "Soon, there will be global pandemonium, not between countries or alliances, but between men and women, both inside and outside of the standard family structure."

"Forget Lenin and Marx," Athena rudely interrupted. "What about Lennon and McCartney?"

"Silence daughter!" Zeus nastily yelled while almost ejecting his tonsils from his enormous throat. "Either respect your parents or go to your temple sanctuary and pray!"

Zeus also felt threatened by his wife's insistence on women's liberation, in addition to Athena's defiance of his almighty autocracy inside his family's structure, especially when evident at important Council meetings.

142

The paranoid god also believed that Hera was giving women mental powers, that when coupled with female physical attributes, would overwhelm all males, gods included.

"Hera, I think you're giving women too much guile to complement their sexual allurement," Almighty Zeus diplomatically challenged. "Please be more prudent and discreet."

"Indeed, my dear husband," Hera suavely answered. "Earthly women, just like men, are seeking variety with the opposite sex. They're responding to my mental transmissions like hungry bees lusting for sweet honey. Quarrels, fights, suspicions, accusations, insinuations, and domestic violence abound. Eventually, family unity is certain to rot away," Hera elucidated.

"Is that good?" Apollo interrupted. "Would it help *our* family?"

"Yes, Apollo; it is consistent with *our* needs, because the ingredients of lust, disloyalty, insincerity, and infidelity have been added to my subversive recipe. In the end," Hera convincingly maintained, "physical sex will be the deciding factor, and since women have and control what men want and need, women will be able to stack the deck, and those same powerful women will deal the cards, while the females hold all the aces, and all of the trump. And as for *our* family, we've never had absolute unity anyway, so it really doesn't matter what happens to the human condition."

Athena and Aphrodite gave Hera a standing ovation, while the male gods, including Zeus, passively clapped their hands in mock applause.

"My dear wife, thank you for your dramatic, most informative presentation," Zeus falsely praised and commended. "Your graphic exposition was laden with truths mingled-in with half-truths. At this time, I would like to deviate from normal procedure and make a public confession to this Council."

The assembled gods seated in the ornate chamber suddenly became absolutely silent. The colossal, opulent meeting room was as quiet as the deepest, unexplored tunnels of Hades. The Council had never before heard ostentatious Zeus apologize for anything. His will had always been paramount, and his guilt had always been concealed from *their* scrutiny. The other gods leaned-forward to intensively hear every syllable to be uttered.

"I suppose it's more of an admission, than a confession," Zeus clarified. "Nevertheless, you are all obviously aware of its reality. In the past, I've been unfaithful to Hera on numerous occasions. Those minor affairs were but casual, token, spur-of-the-moment romances I had had with only a handful of mortal women, or should I call them incidental encounters with two handfuls of mortal women," Zeus indicated by raising all ten massive fingers before his now crimson face. "At any rate, those incidental rendezvous' trysts have haunted my conscience for many centuries. Hera, I beg forgiveness for my three-thousand-years of foolish indiscretions and marital infidelity."

"Let there be soap operas!" Athena called-out. "My unfaithful father is attempting to show good faith. What a divine travesty!"

Hera blew a derisive kiss at her philandering husband, and the Council of deities incessantly laughed in unison for the first time since the emergency session that the gods had held in late 1492 about some dis*oriented* fellow named Christopher Columbus discovering America.

Hephaestus, the lame forger of metals, who still made bronze helmets, swords, and shields for the Olympians, was the next speaker listed on the agenda. The ugly deity rose slowly, and soon, the self-conscious, crippled blacksmith god spoke in a very deliberate manner. His words reflected his skepticism with the ineffective way the Olympian campaign against humanity had been progressing. Hephaestus' speech's content did not share the contrived optimism of the other more theatrical, flattering immortals.

Zeus hoped that lame Hephaestus's address would be brief. He did not want the hammer and anvil god's lethargic mood to become contagious among the other represented deities. The Council members were already feeling jittery and uncomfortable.

"I regret to report that humans are doing fantastic things with metals," Hephaestus began his antithesis. "Their discoveries have made my greatest attainments seem like mere child's play. I've borrowed many of their methods, and implemented them in my motley furnace room two-thousand-feet below this hallowed palace."

The hobbled metals' forger went on to explain that he had difficulty keeping-up with the latest scientific technology. Hephaestus asked Zeus to requisition an updated computer system in the next fiscal budget, so that *he* could keep pace with the latest advances in metallurgy. The bronze fabricator had recently entered the iron and steel ages, and Hephaestus needed better technical machine assistance to produce more advanced mechanical inventions. The blacksmith god disclosed that computers on Earth had "memory banks" full of valuable information that could reduce the great "technology time gap" between mankind and *Olympus* to only a few hundred years.

"Maybe I could soon arrange to have Bill Gates and Stephen Jobs help you?" Hades, the Lord of the macabre Underworld, suggested to Hephaestus. "Once they journey down to Hades, I'll immediately transfer their ghosts to *you* for them to labor in your boiler-room, and obediently serve as your private slaves. In a matter of nine short decades, Hephaestus, I promise you'll be fully automated and able to effectively compete with the humans!" Hades declared.

"These confounded Earthlings," Hephaestus continued, ignoring Hades' optimistic suggestion, "have developed many uses for new metals like steel and aluminum. I've finally gotten the making of steel down to a science, but aluminum needs much more research. I'm trying to get two uncooperative spirits named Edison and Carnegie to help me out solving the essential problem. Thank you, Lord Hades, for lending me *their* services!"

"Are you into heavy metal?" Athena asked and laughed.

"Heavy metal? What do you mean?" inquired the very provincial blacksmith god.

"Heavy metal rock and roll groups," Zeus's amused daughter clarified. "Haven't you ever heard of Metallica and Led Zeppelin?"

"Athena, you said you haven't heard that trashy acid rock music ever being played!" Zeus chastised. "Why must you always fuckin' persist in fibbing?"

Athena did not want to make an embarrassing public confession to her assembled relatives. "No father. I haven't exactly heard the trashy music, but I've *heard about* the rock groups that sing the trashy music," the delinquent daughter defensively stammered.

"Please forgive my obnoxious daughter's prevaricating prattling, Lord Hephaestus," Zeus apologized. "Now kindly continue with your gloomy description. But make it short and sweet. I feel a damned triple migraine coming on."

"These clever-but-resourceful humans, King Zeus," the charcoal skinned god proceeded, "somehow use metal wires to send messages around the world at the speed of light. Their scientists have developed alloys that would take my overworked, underpaid staff, consisting of three imbeciles and two morons, a million years to duplicate. The mortals' progressive initiative is dauntless. No obstacle seems to thwart or handicap them," the crippled god reported. "And besides that very amazing, bizarre bull-shit occurring," Hephaestus divulged, "the mortals are now going wireless."

"Is there no hope?" Hera seriously asked. "Are we fighting a losing battle?"

"Our only hope," the austere blacksmith god insisted, "is that the pollution from the industrial smokestacks and automobiles disrupt the precious atmosphere the humans have to breathe. Already, they've created a 'greenhouse effect' that is warming the seasons, and melting the polar ice caps. Cities in the future will be deluged from rising oceans and seas, possibly by the time the next Council meeting convenes. That prospect is the only cheerful news I can presently relate."

"For being a crippled nincompoop, you've done an admirable job against staggering odds," Zeus commended Hephaestus. "Keep things under surveillance. At our next banquet, we can celebrate our ultimate victory over those overachievers known as humans. My will shall be vindicated!" Zeus prophetically bellowed.

"When are we gonna' eat?" Athena asked out of turn. "I'm getting tired of gobbling-down nectar and ambrosia all the time. I wanna' have some custard, hot dogs, French fries, pizza, hamburgers, and enchiladas for a change."

"My ornery daughter," Zeus abruptly admonished. "You're beginning to be corrupted by those despicable land beings. Your enunciations are grotesque, in addition to being entirely fucked-up."

"Sorry Big Daddy, but I only wanted to *chow down* before I *chill out!* Get with the program, will ya'!"

The rest of the Council members cringed-down in their seats at Athena's defiance to her almighty father's assumed authority. The others waited for the king-god's response to her unorthodox lingo.

"My dear insolent daughter," Zeus chided with a forced smile. "Please do not embarrass me in front of our extended family. And for *your* information, we shall, according to tradition, feast right after our vital meeting. And most certainly, it's gonna' be nectar and ambrosia instead of pizza and burgers, and the music is gonna' be flutes and harps instead of alien barbarians like Guns n' Roses and the Beach Boys, ya' dig my jive, baby doll!" Zeus yelled in mock imitation of his offspring's slang-type vernacular.

Zeus's mental equilibrium had also been intimidated by a particular "political invention" of modern-day man, "Constitutional Democracy". The practice of freedom had made men and women exceedingly enterprising, individualistic and independent. Liberty fomented total disrespect for monarchy; for autocracy; for aristocracy; for dictatorship, and for ancient gods.

"Fellow distinguished gods," Zeus implored. "Who would have ever thought that such fantastic achievements could have blossomed from man's feeble and miserable origin? These malignant creatures have demonstrated tenacity and stubbornness that we all should fear. The despicable race seems to thrive on catastrophe. The dip-shits welcome tragedy. They love fuckin' adversity. I have created mortal monsters down on Earth, worse than all the reprehensible Minotaurs, Gorgons, Centaurs, Cyclops, and Titans put together!"

As weary Hephaestus and playboy Apollo began dozing-off out of complete boredom, Zeus expounded on his cynical observations. The king-god explained that his spirit had become fatigued from lack of human worship. "I crave and need sacrifices; lots and lots of sacrifices, to bolster my deflated ego," the chief god lamented. "Apollo, are you ready to speak to the Council?"

Poseidon gave Apollo a sharp nudge to the ribs with his rusty trident. The god of music, hunting and medicine blinked his eyes, and his physical reaction to Poseidon's elbow was *his* reflexive banging into Hephaestus to his left, waking-up the sea god, also. Apollo awkwardly stood with bleary, bloodshot eyes to narrate to the Council his disclosure.

"The past fifty-years, Ares and I have collaborated in furtively assisting the humans in their deployment of nuclear weapons," the sun god began his memorized dissertation. "Several atomic bombs have already been dropped on Japanese cities. A global debacle is waiting on the horizon."

"How do you know this probability?" Hera skeptically asked.

"I went to see a bisexual tarot card reader at a carnival in New York," Apollo admitted. "Her rather queer name was Henrietta David Tarot."

"Were you on official Olympus business in New York?" Zeus suspiciously stormed. "I remember paying you overtime for that particular reconnaissance expedition."

"Why certainly, King Zeus," Apollo apologized. "You all know how I love music, and how music is in *my* jurisdiction. I was coincidentally attending an important concert at the *Apollo Theater* in Harlem."

"Well, all right," Zeus approved. "Your excuse is a valid one. Proceed with your revelations, and keep the horse-shit and the chicken-shit down to a minimum."

"Ares and I had collaborated and caused a terrible explosion to happen in Russia at Chernobyl, and we had a near miss at the *Three Mile Island's* atomic energy plant in Pennsylvania in 1969," Apollo informed. "But then, clever American scientists and engineers figured-out *our* subterfuge at the last minute, and somehow averted a nuclear meltdown."

"Wow!" exclaimed Athena. "That explosion would have really been *dynamite!*"

"Child, stop you're perpetual stupid harping right this instant!" Zeus thundered. "Find a more peaceful musical instrument like the lyre to play, instead!"

"I don't play the harp or the lyre, but I want Keith Richards to someday teach me the electric guitar," Athena answered. "I get sexually aroused the way he uses his fingers."

"Forgive my reckless daughter's lack of respect, Apollo," the Chairman of the Council counseled. "She's going through the classic rebellion phase of maturation, and I'm afraid that in the next hundred years, she's going to grow into an even bigger bitch than Hera is."

"Anyway," Apollo apathetically proceeded. "Nuclear arsenals are being accumulated in many *Third World* countries. Being the sun god, I have learned all about fission and fusion. Worldwide detonations of hydrogen and atomic bombs will bring about an unimaginable nuclear holocaust. When the radiation clears, the Earth, or what's left of it, will be *ours* once again."

"Bravo," Zeus complimented as the other Olympians politely applauded. "Now Ares, please give us *your* fucked-up thoughts about thwarting human enterprise."

"I wholeheartedly support Apollo's convictions about the future demise of those puny-but-amazing Homo sapiens," Ares stated. "Our star will rise, like the legendary *Phoenix,* from the ashes of destroyed human civilization. With our negative influence, man has begun authoring his own self-destruction. I guarantee that his societies will be obliterated by military science's advanced weaponry. Those that survive will be relegated to the slave echelon, to again serve us, and our selfish whims."

The Council warmly applauded Ares' "positive speech". The Olympians were finally organized in a sophisticated crusade against their chief nemeses, man and his new-found genius.

Ares next told of his specialty, which was arranging invasions and revolutions through the power of mental suggestion. When men saw other men involved in carnage, the witnesses would become influenced by their accurate observation, and then mimic and duplicate the heinous deeds. According to Ares, humans were "stupid antagonistic chimpanzees" who

148

often feel compelled to imitate one another, so once one major nation attacks another world power, the whole planet would be doomed to disaster by "the deployment of man's imbecilic propensity for retaliation".

"Your persuasive arguments make much sense," Zeus praised and acknowledged. "These humans behave like monkeys all because of some extraordinary jerk-off named Darwin, who falsely taught the fools that they actually came from monkeys. It now makes a lot of sense, doesn't it; monkey-see, monkey-do."

"Yes, my distinguished Lord," Ares concurred. "And Apollo and I have used suggestion and persuasion to cause a number of brutal conflicts and battles in the last hundred-years. *World War I, World War II*, the *Vietnam War*, the *Korean War,* the *Gulf War:* need I say more? We've both been very, very busy."

Aphrodite, goddess of beauty was the next speaker on Zeus's docket. Her external enchantment disguised the cunning that dwelled deep inside her scheming heart. The skilled mistress of deceit claimed that she had been concentrating her efforts on decaying and corrupting the morals of men, women and children. The Goddess of Love and Beauty desired to cripple human emotions, just like her embittered, lame husband, Hephaestus, ironically had been physically crippled.

"I shall shrewdly debilitate humanity with my stealth," Aphrodite predicted. "Their ultimate doom is rapidly approaching!"

"You're always coming-up with lame-brained ideas," Athena criticized Aphrodite. "Your lame ideas are even lamer than your crippled husband is!"

"Forgive my discipline-problem daughter's nasty rhetoric," Zeus apologized to Aphrodite. "Proceed with your sage report."

"Malice and slander will dominate the vile creatures," Aphrodite uttered while, ignoring Athena's annoying juvenile prattle. "With the help of my loyal associate, Eros, prostitution, homosexuality, and pornography are proliferating all over the globe."

"Now you're talkin' my damned language!" Apollo said without realizing his subconscious fascinations, or his impact on the other assembled gods' libidos.

Aphrodite insisted that she relied heavily on the primitive instincts that often guided the "unwary mortals' behaviors". She claimed that first she affects their "lower subconscious minds" with erotic fantasies. Then the cunning goddess "mesmerizes their vulnerable senses with passion". "Perverting the species is very simple, once you utilize those easy proven methods of attack," the Goddess of Love and Beauty professed.

"Bravo, bravo!" Zeus raved like an immortal maniac. "Please Aphrodite; kindly tell us' some more. I'm actually getting quite aroused while *boning* up on the subject."

"The sight of a lady's ankle, let alone an open vagina would be enough to arouse my horny husband," Hera laughed and revealed. "Men are such visual idiots; quite stimulated and aroused by even the smallest of breasts and nipples."

"Eros and I first focus on stimulating the libido," Aphrodite continued her profound report. "We've done a lot to lower the world's population by promoting gay rights and gay conventions. Homosexuality, when you think about is, is actually a form of sterility. Eros and I look at it as a basic method of birth control," Aphrodite related. "Gays don't reproduce by natural means. And so, homosexuality is without a doubt good for *Olympus,* because fewer humans on the planet translates into less headaches for the gods!"

"Thank you, Aphrodite; thank you very much. And it all started on our wonderful Greek Isle of Lesbos!" Zeus perceptively observed and reviewed. "Now, let's waste no time in hearing some rather intoxicating remarks from our di*vine* colleague, dear Dionysus; our inimitable, effervescent god of wine and merriment."

"Thank you so much, my Lord Zeus," Dionysus slurred in a drunken tone. The wine god held a goblet of red vintage, which he drank from between sentence' stutters, lisps, and mumbles. He wobbled back and forth, from right leg, to left, to right again, staggering, slurring and blabbering his way through his rather peculiar oration.

"Fellow Olympians," my *back is* killing me," Dionysus awkwardly shouted and punned. Everyone hooted and hollered in response to the idiotic, silly joke. "I'm happy to report that over twenty percent of the Earth's fucked-up population can now be classified as chronic alcoholics," Dionysus hiccupped and disclosed. "Half the soldiers in the Russian Army are hooked on vodka. Recently, I diversified into the propagation of drug addiction and narcotics trafficking. Marijuana, cocaine, heroin, opium, and morphine are in plenteous supply all over the blasted planet," sputtered blundering Dionysus. "The whole fuckin' world is becomin' mentally sicker by the minute, thanks to little ole' me and a little heroin."

"What's wrong with a little heroin?" the petulant Zeus instinctively challenged.

"Nothin' major at all," the wine god answered. "Now Joan of Arc; that was a little heroine who didn't use heroin. Ha, ha, ha!"

Everyone laughed incessantly, even the normally glum Zeus. Dionysus belched twice, and then loudly farted, and next, the daft ignoramus adroitly imbibed another serious mouthful of "Vino".

"Drug addicts need money to feed their raunchy habit," Dionysus informed the drowsy Council Members. "They gotta' commit crimes like robberies, thefts, looting, and burglaries to keep their' vile habit goin'. My powerful drugs and alcohol have guaranteed the future of anarchy, and the future of mass chaos, I'm fuckin' very happy to report. Hic."

"Dionysus, quit your infantile *whining*," Athena laughed. "Your brimming cup spilleth over!"

Dionysus burped and loudly passed gas, and then again farted even louder. "How would you like it Athena if I came to your side of the table, and my vomiting throat suddenly made your nice new tunic turn stained with burgundy," the drunken god threatened. "Next to relentless drinking and farting, I really love to fuckin' belch and regurgitate."

"Now, now!" Zeus imperatively exhorted, standing and waving his hands in the air to subdue the boisterous laughter emanating throughout the sacred chamber. When order was finally restored, Dionysus proceeded with his triumphant, extemporaneous discourse.

"All I gotta' say now is that almost as many people are addicted to, and killed by harmful legal pharmacy prescription drugs than by illegal drugs," the lord of festive occasions divulged. "I have nothin' more in the line of bull-shit to report, except what sailors do when they enter their various submarines. 'Down the hatch'!" Dionysus enthusiastically exclaimed as the ignoble moron swallowed-down the remainder of his delicious wine.

Hades, the miserable god of death, was the next speaker slated to lecture the demented congregation. The pallid-faced king of the afterlife possessed sunken gray eyes, and colorless lips that certainly magnified his gloomy personality. The death god addressed the Council in his familiar macabre, morose, wretched voice. Several of the more uncomfortable gods and goddesses began squirming on their purple velvet cushions in response to *his* haunting-but-beguiling monotone.

"The bright reflections in this Council chamber hurt my sensitive eyes," Hades grieved and protested. "Maybe I'll journey to Italy and have special bifocal glasses made with Venetian blinds on them."

"You're finally seeing the light!" Athena obnoxiously blurted-out and childishly punned without heed or discretion.

"Silence my impulsive, embarrassing, petulant daughter!" Zeus shouted. "Any more outbursts from you, and I'll see to it that my brother Hades gives you a hundred-year tour of his dismal subterranean kingdom."

"It is good to get away from my underworld home once in a while," Hades observed and shared. "Immortality can be a very boring, tedious thing when one happens to be the eternal custodian of the dead. Like you, King Zeus, I too am concerned about the deplorable mortals studying the very complicated *DNA* molecule, whatever the Hades that fucker is! If man ever learns immortality, it would put me completely out of business. On the other side of the coin, business is currently prospering. Hades itself is more overcrowded than either Brooklyn or Baghdad is right now."

"How do you now transport the ever-increasing multitude of deceased souls to Hades?" Ares academically asked. "Do you have a modern mass transit system?"

"Loyal Charon now operates a fleet of twenty-four motorized barges to ferry souls across *River Styx* from the world of the living to the morbid catacombs of Elysium," Hades explained. "And poor old Charon only works with a skeleton crew."

"Wow! If I visit you in Hades, dear uncle, can I get to meet the Grateful Dead?" Athena ecstatically asked. "I've heard all about Jerry Garcia."

"Athena!" Zeus yelled with the walls shaking. "I'm warning you. Enough of your juvenile, impudent clown-show! If you interrupt my brother Hades one more time, you're outa' here. I'll swiftly send you down to the underworld, where you'll be forced to bone-up on the true meaning of death! Physical decomposition!"

"I was wondering," Hera interrupted. "Are Al Capone and Frank Nitty in Hades? They were *underworld* figures when they were alive, weren't they? How about Jimmy Hoffa?"

"Hera, sometimes you're worse than Athena when it comes to making ludicrous nonsense in the form of comments," Zeus loudly chastised. "Stop making a travesty out of *my* most significant conclave! Now, please continue, my dear brother, before lightning strikes twice; once at Hera, and the second time at Athena."

"Thank you, sagacious brother, for skillfully re-establishing order," Hades assented and complimented. "We recently had to make an extensive addition to the Elysium sector. Ten thousand new acres of daffodils had to be planted to accommodate the ghosts of the happily deceased," the death god declared in his dismal, listless tone of voice.

"Athena would ask you if there are any '70s Flower Children resting there in Elysium, but since she is not allowed to talk again, I'll ask for her," Hera said with a wry smile exhibited upon her countenance.

"Why yes," Hades admitted. "Most of those dim-witty assholes that attended the first Woodstock concert are already-dead. Now those bizarre hippies can frolic, or eternally sleep, with Elvis, John Lennon, Otis Redding, and Frank Sinatra. I'm still trying to figure-out that weird Otis Redding fellow. He doesn't do anything except keep sitting at the dock of the *Styx.*"

"Well then," Zeus wondered out loud. "What about the restricted Area of Atonement?"

Hades reported that the Area of Atonement was where the most rapid growth was taking place. The punishment zone had to be quadrupled in size in order to accommodate the billions of souls that required special purification by fire. The god of death informed the Supreme Council that a dozen new tunnels had to be burrowed deep into the Earth's mantle during the last century. "This perplexing problem is expanding exponentially," Hades regretfully revealed. "It's all quite ironic. The more immorality that occurs on Earth, the greater the Area of Atonement must become. It's all simple, basic cause and effect stuff, ya' know," Hades emphasized. "The more decadent mankind becomes, the more exhaustive my labor and responsibility must be," Hades acknowledged. "That fucked-up guy Hitler set me back a full century. If the Earthlings have any new incidents of mass genocide and world destruction, I'll be backlogged for another hundred million years."

"That's perfectly all right," Zeus strangely replied. "You can handle it. What about those laboring idiots Tantalus and Sisyphus? Are they still down there atoning?"

"Indeed, they are," Hades confirmed. "But the impenitent fools have filed official grievances, along with another militant dissident soul named Lazarus of Israel. They're all complaining about the lowlife spirits from the Woodstock generation partying all the time, and having to listen to loud irritating rock and roll music," Hades related. "Tantalus still stands chained inside his pool, being tantalized by overhead fruit and water. When he bends-down, the water filters out of the tub. When Tantalus reaches for a peach or an apple, or even a piece of ass, it immediately disappears from sight. Hephaestus did a noteworthy job designing that particular novel tub punishment for me."

"How about my favorite soul, poor Sisyphus?" Hera wanted to know. "Is he still stubborn and rebellious?"

"Sisyphus still must roll his huge boulder up the steep inclined plane, over and over again, for all eternity. When it tumbles-down from the force of gravity," Hades explained, "old Sisyphus must repeat his task until the end of infinity, whenever the fuck that is. Anyway, the dumb-ass, obstinate bastard had surrendered his free will when he died."

"Wow!" Athena hollered. "I wonder if Mick Jagger knows that Sisyphus was *the first* Rolling Stone? I also wonder if Keith Richards knows about that?"

"Athena, I can't tolerate any more of your inane asshole quips!" Zeus stormed. "Now you're officially grounded, so go to your palace immediately. And don't fuckin' listen to any of your repugnant Elvis music tapes, or call Ethiopia long distance and talk to Artemis's faggot friends on the telephone. Your long-distance calls are putting a wicked strain on my royal treasury! Now get along daughter dearest, or else I'll place you into Hades' cruel custody!" Zeus's voice boomed.

Athena stood-up, curtsied mockingly to her all-powerful parents, and as she left the splendid Council Chamber, the bitchy girl yelled-out to her father, "You Ain't Nothin' but a freakin' Hound Dog!"

Zeus shook his head in complete dismay. "It's a good thing my daughter is only allowed to listen to dead artists' music," the bored board chairman indicated with a frown. "When the punk rockers, the hip hoppers, and the rappers start to die in large numbers, I'm going to need a new set of eardrums. This abominable rock and roll music is fully corrupting Athena's morals, and it's making me want to abdicate my throne," Zeus remarked, momentarily losing his train of thought. "Now, where the hell were we? Oh yes, finish-up with your report, my dear brother."

"You're absolutely right, omniscient and wise King Zeus," Hades agreed. "These fucked-up humans have the appetites of miniature gods. Could you imagine what would happen if they all were fifty- foot-tall, just like us? There would be no goddamned Earth ground left to burrow tunnels into, with the plethora of cemeteries being ten times their usual size!"

"What about your expense budget?" Zeus inquired. "Are you showing financial prudence and keeping costs down?"

"Well, let me tell you," Hades responded with his cold, metallic-gray eyes focused on his almighty brother. "The bookkeeping alone has become a horrendous problem. I'm just getting computerized, and I have two intelligent spirits named Newton and Einstein helping me to become more

154

organized. Unfortunately, the task at hand is quite formidable and overwhelming."

"Enough of your myriad, shitty, petty difficulties," Zeus insisted. "What about your successes?"

"On the other side of the ledger," Hades replied, "I have discovered many neat new ways to cause death." The underworld god then differentiated between new methods of accidental death and new techniques of suicide, along with other forms of deliberate deaths. "Many of these mortals have a low tolerance for emotional anguish. They lack coping skills; become frustrated, and then go-out and kill others before the dolts decide to terminate themselves," Hades told the generally disinterested Council Members. "The idiots now call these types of spontaneous executions 'going postal'. The death business is indeed booming, even better than the cannon business ever was," Hades cleverly finished.

Zeus finally stood to give his evaluation of the past hundred-years. His fifty-foot-tall form towered over the others still seated at the marvelous marble and emerald table, trimmed in gold.

"I must admit," Zeus concluded and muttered. "My soul still craves tribute from the humble creatures I had molded out of mud and dust for *our* benefit. Man's science and technology have been terrible threats to the gods. Let them now be curses to the mortals!"

The Council cheered and shouted accolades and kudos at their leader and mentor. The king-god held his hands high above his regal head to re-establish quiet.

"When I had Pandora's box constructed," Zeus prefaced, "I filled it with hate, famine, war, disease, pestilence, despair, and death to drastically encumber the mortals. I beg your forgiveness for me also placing the gift of *hope* into that historic chest."

"Your daughter Athena calls Pandora's box a *hope chest!*" Hera cackled. "And our erratic daughter still hopes that her chest will become larger."

"Wife, let me finish my solemn speech and then we will have time to feast, gossip and have hot sex," Zeus admonished. "I found all of *your* meticulous presentations most illuminating. I promise you that we Olympians shall again have established dominion over what is rightfully ours, and triumph over the reprehensible race, that unfortunately, I have unselfishly created."

Zeus summarized by explaining that the sophisticated materialistic world which the Earthlings had built was too complex for even the immortal gods to comprehend. "Things were much easier to understand in the good old days when Jason; Perseus; that heel Achilles, and scheming Odysseus roamed the Earth. All we had to govern-over then was land, wind, fire, water, sky, monsters, and intimidated mortals," the king-god fondly recalled.

Zeus culminated his concluding remarks by saying that mortals had besieged the Olympians with too many inventions, innovations, and discoveries. The lord-god Zeus had created all the electrons, protons, neutrons, and atoms, without even bothering to name them. But the "scurrilous upstart mortals" had analyzed and changed those same atoms and molecules into amazing compounds that thoroughly confound even the most-advanced reasoning of the smartest of gods.

"My *fellow* deities," Zeus chauvinistically continued. "Robots, androids, radioactivity, dynamite, nuclear bombs, laser beams, and telecommunications; it's all basically just mind-boggling! And add to those extraordinary creations, ideas like capitalism, socialism, communism, democracy, science, technology, and rock and roll music, and you'll fathom that our former simple pastoral lives have become an all-too-complicated equation. Science has become the mortal's new god, and I don't relish that ugly violation one iota!"

The other Olympians applauded Zeus's latest perceptive comments. The king-god thought it most appropriate to dismiss the parley on a more positive note.

"My loyal family, in the much-needed absence of recalcitrant Athena, I must commend all of you for your dedication to, and your support of, my supreme authority. I truly cherish your most-recent superlative labors, and your steadfast faithfulness. The next great upheaval is within our grasp," Zeus emphasized as the Olympus Chairman raised his two clenched fists to chest level.

"Let our greatest opportunity not slip away into the clutches of infinity. We must initiate an unprecedented, awesome counter-revolution. I officially adjourn this Council until January 1, 2100," the chief god's voice thundered with new-found hope and energy. "Now let's all eat, drink, party, and get laid."

"Perseus and Medusa"

Acrisius was king of Argo, and the nutcase was so full of shit that the monarch daily sat on a golden toilet, instead of on a golden throne. Besides always taking lengthy craps, slapping his monkey, and scratching his royal ass most of each day, the king (just like all other past rulers of Argo) was notorious for telling anyone and everyone who asked about his city-kingdom, "Ar-go fuck yourself'!" The worst part about the entire fiasco was that chronically constipated King Acrisius thought that *his* single, redundant, hundred-year-old, bad joke was actually funny.

The King of Argo had a beautiful daughter named Danae, who had a bad habit of walking in the woods, and then dreaming about getting laid by some horny forest god having multiple dicks. One day, Danae was picking daffodils near a grotto when Zeus, king of the gods, happened to be sauntering by on his way to Ethiopia to visit his fellow Olympian Phoebus Apollo, who had recently had a new magnificent temple erected in *his* honor in that distant African land situated below ancient Egypt.

Upon seeing Danae's many charms, Zeus immediately got a gargantuan hard-on, and felt that he had to plant it inside the nearest mortal vagina. Danae was mesmerized by the king-god's magic wand, which of course was erect, huge, long, thick, and throbbing. The pretty nymphomaniac then made a major mistake in judgment. Instead of giving Zeus a super-duper good blow-job, she got on her back, opened her hairy eager beaver, and had the royal poop pumped out of her until her face nearly turned as purple as Zeus's pulsating bazooka.

A month later, Danae missed her period, and discovered that she was indeed pregnant. Her child would be half-*divine* and half-human; whereas, grapes are totally "the vine" fruit, and her child might also be *divine fruit of the womb* if he or she (the potential fruit) turned-out to be gay, either male homo' or lesbian.

Danae rushed to her constipated father Acrisius, who was seated upon his golden hopper, and told the idiot the bad news. The thoroughly upset, full-of-shit king got instant severe diarrhea, and almost died from a bad case of dehydration.

"Danae; first Zeus screwed the crap out of you in *the mating woods,* but now he's going to screw me really good, too!" the king lamented while awkwardly wiping his smelly ass with rough cabbage leafs.

"I don't understand exactly what you mean father?" Danae replied. "I didn't know you had a vagina!"

"Danae; I don't have a goddamned vagina, and if I did, I'd pour cement in it, and seal the fucker up! Anyway, my dear daughter," Acrisius continued. "A few years back, I journeyed to *Delphi* to visit Apollo's *Oracle* there, and find-out my future!"

"That was more stupid than being screwed by Zeus!" the daughter answered. "The Oracle always predicts gloom and doom, and never augurs happy tidings. You would have been better off father, seeing Medusa's treacherous face and being turned into stone. Then, you wouldn't have to shit brick turds into your golden hopper, and suffer extreme dehydration all of the damned time!"

"Anyway, dear daughter," the king went on as the dolt wiped his fat ass with red onion peels, since he had used-up all the coarse cabbage leafs. "I asked the Oracle if I would ever have a son, but she predicted that I would only have a rebellious daughter, who would eventually bear a son that would grow-up to kill me! And now it's fuckin' happening!" the king insanely screamed. "That blooming seed in your womb is half-divine, and when the boy grows-up, he's gonna' eliminate your old man's shittin' ass right off the fuckin' planet!"

"How do you know the sex of the baby that has not yet been born?" Danae challenged. "How do you know I will definitely have a boy?"

"Because I trust the fucked-up Oracle a lot more than I trust you and your abominable, promiscuous snatcheroo!" the king countered. "And besides Danae; the fucked-up Oracle has cement up *her* crotch, and wouldn't bull-shit me for sex, or anything else cheap and vulgar, just to get her freakin' rocks off like you always desire doing!"

Nine months quickly passed. Acrisius became very distraught and disconsolate, and not wanting to have Danae executed by the royal hangman, the neurotic monarch placed his daughter and her child in a large chest, and had them cast out to sea. The indiscriminate waves carried the floating box to the island of Seriphos, where a handsome fisherman named Dictys retrieved Danae and her crying baby from the pounding surf, that was smashing into dangerous rocks.

Dictys shared his home and possessions with the lovely, disowned princess and her strong-lunged, crybaby son. The fisherman never had sex with the attractive woman, because once that he had learned that the boy's father was the chief *Olympian,* the discreet fellow didn't want to be shafted up the ass by one of Zeus's dazzling, electrified, billion-volt lightning bolts.

Fifteen-years had elapsed, and the boy had matured into a young, strong sailor, who journeyed to many islands in the vicinity to engage in trading whores for harlots, and prostitutes for hookers. Danae had named her son Perseus, but all of the natives of Seriphos believed the lad to be a "son of Zeus", because of his terrific biceps, his firm abs', and his cute compact butt.

Perseus was adept at boxing, wrestling, bull-shitting, and javelin throwing. And the youthful mariner possessed admirable social qualities that engendered courtesy, virtue, humility, and justice. But trauma was certain to accompany drama in Perseus's life on the small island of idle gossipers, pedophile priests, and mentally sick, perpetual masturbators.

Dictys' brother was Polydickdees, ruthless King of Seriphos, who incidentally had three uncircumcised penises. The ruler was also evil, cruel, villainous, conniving, greedy, and arrogant. And when Polydickdees saw Danae, his *privates* began *publicly* throbbing and pulsating like a divining rod, or just like Zeus's divine rod. While Perseus was at sea and unable to defend his mother's welfare at home on Seriphos, Polydickdees took Danae away from Dictys' jurisdiction and said to her, "If you will not be my wife, then you will certainly be my servant. What is your response, woman?"

"I wouldn't marry you if you had the only dick and the only set of balls in the whole wide world!" Danae snottily retorted, not knowing that the freak-of-nature king had three uncircumcised peckers and seven uncircumcised testicles. "I'd rather fool around with bananas, squash, and cucumbers than have any kind of sex with you, oral or otherwise, you big selfish, avaricious, dumb, braggart asshole!" Danae lambasted Polydickdees.

Meanwhile, on the island of Samos, where Perseus's ship was taking on a cargo of harlots, hookers and slaves, the handsome sailor stepped into a nearby woods to take a long leak. A twelve-foot-tall woman approached with a bronze helmet on her head, and she was carrying winged sandals, a bronze shield over her shoulder, and a bronze spear in her right hand.

'When the hell are we Greeks ever going to get out of the damned *Bronze Age?*' Perseus thought. 'There must be more to this stupid age than ridiculous copper and tin alloy!'

The tall, luscious babe then spoke to the awed sailor, who blushed as the modest young man tucked his pecker, still dripping urine, back under his tunic. "Perseus, you must perform a special errand for me," the tall deity requested.

"Who are you lady, and how do you know my name is Perseus? Are you a glamorous spy, or are you a gorgeous woodland prostitute? If you want my opinion about woman that put out," the young sailor declared, "I'd prefer if you were a gorgeous woodland harlot, for I am virtually destitute, and have no money to pay for a gorgeous woodland prostitute!"

"I am neither," the voluptuous woman disclosed. "I am Pallas Athene, daughter of Zeus, and goddess of *Olympus,* and I can read goodness in a man's heart, and I have readily detected that quality in yours. Tell me, dear Perseus," the goddess continued. "Would you rather have a soul of fire, or would you prefer a soul of clay?"

Perseus considered the enchanting goddess's proposition, even though she was not trying to proposition him. "Definitely, a soul of fire," the sailor wisely answered, "for it's a lot better to know adventure and die in the flower of youth than to be like a cow, chewing its cud in the field for an entire boring lifetime. For fame and honor go to those possessing souls of fire," the youth eloquently elaborated, "even though those possessing souls of clay often become rich kings; live in colossal palaces; get laid every night, and can afford all of the best hookers and prostitutes available in the whole damned ancient world!"

"You have chosen wisely," Pallas Athene commended, while holding up her bronze shield, so that Perseus could view an image that was being reflected from it. "See here, Perseus; do you have the courage to slay this terrible monster, Medusa the Gorgon? She has vipers for hair; talons and claws for hands and feet, and the creature bites men's dicks off when giving very bad, unprofessional blow- jobs. What do you think of the ugly bitch?"

"She's the most hideous creature my eyes have ever beheld, and I will certainly cross my legs and eat a pound of saltpeter before I confront her," Perseus promised the heavenly goddess. "Where can I find the ugly beast?"

"You are too young and not yet ready to assassinate her," Athene chastised, "so kindly return to Seriphos, and when the time is right, you shall answer the challenge and be equal to the task," the goddess promised.

"Okay; I'll be glad to kill Medusa, as long as I don't have to lose my virginity and my sensitive dick screwing the venom out of her," Perseus agreed. "For all I know, the Gorgon might have metal jaws planted up her snatch, and that fate might even be worse than receiving a damned fatal blow-job from her ravenous lips, and from her dagger-like fangs!"

The benign goddess then instantaneously vanished *into thin air,* because goddesses, like magicians, wizards, and sorcerers, hadn't yet mastered the technique of vanishing into thick air, since factories with smokestacks didn't exist back then to heavily pollute the atmosphere. So, Perseus obediently returned to Seriphos, where he heard that his mother had become a lowly slave in the very ostentatious King Polydickdees's opulent palace.

The livid young mariner dashed the full mile to the pretentious king's residence, and darted from room to room, desperately searching for his captive mother. Perseus came across Danae, turning a hand millstone, and crying her tits off. Evil Polydickdees then entered the confinement chamber, followed by his brother, the pleasant-minded Dictys.

"Craven tyrant!" Perseus recklessly and imprudently shouted at the always-scheming king. The enraged *Adonis* quickly lifted-up the simple hand-operated machine that Danae had been rotating. "Mom," the incensed sailor said. "Has *this* mother-fucker been screwing you against your will?" Perseus yelled as *he* raised-up the run-of-the-mill, basic, everyday grindstone to use to split the suddenly fearful king's cranium open.

"Please, my son; show tolerance and restraint!" Danae begged. "We are but lowly strangers in this oddball land, and must act humbly, and not haughtily, although I wish you could break Polydickdees' head, ass, and balls open before I have to again diligently *put my nose to the grindstone!"*

"Your mother is right!" counseled the passive and wise Dictys. "If you do to my wicked brother what we'd all like to do to my wicked brother," the honorable fisherman opined, "then all of the people of Seriphos will fall upon us and then viciously kill our asses. That' is because all of the fucked-up people of Seriphos love being governed by my fucked-up, evil, reprehensible brother. How could I ever explain it to you more logically?"

Polydickdees had been trembling as if he had been experiencing a one-man earthquake. Perseus lowered the hand-mill that had been elevated above his head, set it onto the stone floor, and then quickly ceased being so *mill*itant. The son of Zeus grabbed his mother's hand and conducted her to the island's temple of Pallas Athene, where Danae was accepted by the resident priestess as a floor and altar sweeper, and also as a temple 'marquee' dust and ass wiper, because vacuum cleaners, feather-dusters, and toilet paper hadn't been invented yet.

Now Polydickdees was a cunning old bastard, so the heinous scumbag plotted to somehow get Danae back into *his* custody, and permanently removed from the temple's safe sanctuary. Of course, the king could have sent his soldiers to kidnap Danae at the temple, or dispatched his guards to kill impudent Perseus and benevolent Dictys at home, but the sinister monarch had never endorsed simple solutions to complex problems, and preferred living and anguishing with difficult decisions.

So, the nefarious king schemed-up a rather complicated trap to send his chief nemesis on "an impossible mission of no return". Polydickdees organized a massive feast, and invited all of the island's nobility and dignitaries, including Perseus, to the grand banquet, in order to pay homage to the ruthless king, and to *his* very prosperous land.

Every guest brought an expensive gift, and presented it to the ignoble monarch. Then, the villainous dictator summoned Perseus to *his* throne for everyone to witness a confrontation, and the shrewd ruler cunningly asked the embarrassed lad, "Perseus; I have invited you to my splendid celebration, but where is your gift to present to your honorable king?"

Perseus was unaware of such a custom, and stood humiliated before the curious assemblage of pompous aristocrats. The embarrassed sailor blushed, and then was extremely nervous when the future hero stuttered, "I have not brought anything, because I am an impoverished dunce, who can barely provide for my own basic needs, that incidentally, don't include expensive hookers, couch dancers, and costly prostitutes."

"This insolent young man," the king preached to the pride and flower of *his* corrupt realm, "had been washed ashore onto our peaceful island. We have dutifully given him asylum and residency, and now the ungrateful nincompoop demonstrates his gratitude by not bringing his king a worthy gift. You even claim to be the son of Zeus! I say to you, dumb-ass Perseus, that you are an illegitimate vagabond pretending to be of divine descent! How do you account for yourself, you ludicrous, preposterous, foolish, fabricating, fucked-up simpleton?"

The insulted young sailor grew angry with shame and pride, and cried-out for all of the shocked audience of prominent guests to hear, "I shall bring your majesty a present nobler than any you have thus received at your feast!" Perseus pledged without having any specific idea of what such a gift might be, or what the hell he was even talking about.

"Well then," Polydickdees pressed-on. "Exactly what might this superior gift be? Pray tell Perseus; let the people of Seriphos know its description and its true value!"

Everyone in the crowded throne chamber laughed at the king's derision of the almost-indigent young mariner, who boasted that he was indeed the son of the chief-god of the universe. The young man then remembered the beautiful tall woman whom he had encountered on Samos, and reckoned that now was the time to exhibit the courage she had instilled in him.

"King Polydickdees," Perseus uttered in a stronger voice than the future champion had ever exhibited before. "I shall bring you the head of Medusa the Gorgon. That awesome prize will be my belated special gift to you!"

All the guests in attendance gasped at hearing the young man's bravado. The naïve sailor had played right into the king's plan to get the boy off the island, so that Polydickdees could then capture Danae from the temple; take her to his palace, and then screw the shit out of her ten times each night with his incredible three dicks and seven testicles. "You have foolishly promised to bring me Medusa's head?" the king indulgently chuckled. "Well then, junior jerk-off. Leave Seriphos immediately to engage in your frivolous quest. And don't come back to this island until Medusa has given you some head! Ha, ha, ha, ha! Even your penis and rocks will turn to stone! Ha, ha, ha, ha!"

The son of Zeus and Danae finally realized that the sly king had cleverly tricked his ass, and the crestfallen youth left the great feast being jeered and mocked by the five-hundred jovial attendees, who all loved being governed by the cruelest and most deplorable king east of the *Pillars of Hercules.*

Perseus was wholly disgusted with his own gullibility. The disconsolate 'victim' slowly ambled-out to the island's high cliffs overlooking the sea, and prayed that Pallas Athene would come to assist him in undertaking *his* extremely dangerous exploit. Three times the youth wept and begged that the goddess should appear, and when despair had virtually saturated his vulnerable soul, a wonderful mist appeared upon the eastern horizon, and drifted over to the cliff where the hoodwinked adolescent was standing. A sparkling, celestial figure gradually emerged from the illuminated haze.

"Perseus," Pallas Athene greeted. "Raise your head up high, and be proud of the noble virtues that inhabit your heart. Take this bronze sword, shield, helmet, and these winged sandals, and wear them proudly on your daring quest. Now, it is time for you to achieve glorious honor, and convincingly slay that horrendous menace, Medusa the Gorgon," the goddess sternly announced. "Then, you will take her head back to Polydickdees, just as you have so valiantly promised. Your will shall be vindicated by beating the shit out of Medusa!"

"Gee, Pallas Athene. I really made a complete asshole out of myself at my opening act at the palace!" Perseus admitted with an innocent smile. "Please show me how I can redeem my lost credibility and establish a favorable reputation."

Athena explained that her hero had to venture-out on a perilous, seven-year-journey to the end of the known world, and that if he was ever overcome by cowardice, then the youth would surely perish with a *soul of clay* in the ominous "Unshapen Land".

"But how can I slay Medusa if her despicable face will turn me into stone?" Perseus insisted on knowing. "It's bad enough that I now have rocks in my head, let alone a petrified matching stone face to boot!"

"All of that you will learn in due time," the goddess sincerely pledged. "This expedition of yours must be accomplished in many small steps. First, you must go north and visit the three Gray Sisters. The blind bitches will give you directions to the famous Daughters of the Evening Star, who dance around the *Golden Apple Tree* like horny lesbians. The daughters will provide you with the precise directions on how to find Medusa's diabolical lair!"

"But how the fuck can I ever kill Medusa if one brief glance at her despicable face will simultaneously freeze my ass, dick, balls, and sperm into stone!" Perseus demanded knowing.

"You shall see her reflection in your invincible bronze shield, and then smite the detestable monster with this magic bronze sword," Pallas Athene divulged to her fascinated listener. "Then, you'll stuff her shit-ugly head inside this shit-ugly goatskin sack, and transport it to King Polydickdees for *his* personal inspection."

"But how can I fuckin' cross the seas without a ship?" Perseus inquired. "I can't even swim a stroke, even though I'm a goddamned experienced sailor!"

"Put these divine, winged sandals upon your feet. They will guide you across the winds to your particular destinations," the goddess patiently explained. "Wear them proudly, along with the bronze shield, bronze sword, and the bronze helmet. Now Perseus; venture-out into mythology and start kicking some serious ass!"

"Can't I at least say goodbye to my mother and to kind Dictys?" the soon-to-be hero asked. "They've done much to develop my personality and character!"

"No, you may not!" Pallas Athene imperatively stated. "It is now time for *you* to trust the will of the gods, and to discard all emotions and human associations aside. Cast your fate to the winds, Perseus. Aspire to attain a higher power, and then glory and fame will be yours forever!"

The glittering cloud descended from the stratosphere, and again enveloped the celestial goddess, who soon glided-out over the sea, and quickly disappeared over the eastern horizon from where it had come. Perseus adorned his feet with the splendid winged sandals; placed the bronze helmet upon his head; lifted-up his new sword and shield, and then gently floated up into the air. Soon, the aspiring hero became adept at regulating both his speed and his altitude, and after an hour of assiduous practice, the prospective champion set-out on his great quest, possessing a joyful, stout heart.

The enthralled lad was thoroughly enjoying the thrill of flight, and after beating several falcons in impromptu sky races, the motivated flyer buzzed the cities of Athens and Thebes, scaring the shit and the piss out of the daily pedestrians shopping in the busy marketplaces. And after several months of showing-off his aerial skills all over Greece, brave Perseus came to an ominous moor, which after a hundred-miles, eventually converted into a vast sheet of ice. The courageous fellow then followed an obscure mountain trail through an intense blizzard, until he finally reached the isolated cave of the notorious Three Gray Sisters, who were too ugly and wicked to be ancient nuns, or to even be over-the-hill hookers.

The three old, blind hags were grotesque-looking, warty-faced witches that were preoccupied passing their single eye amongst themselves, while arguing incessantly about *its* possession. The illustrious young hero immediately pitied the Three Gray Sisters, who actually didn't give a shit or a damn about pity for each other, or for that matter, pity for anyone else residing on the entire goddamned planet.

"Oh, eminent Three Gray Sisters; I am Perseus," the young stud formally introduced himself to the hideous hags. "And I need to learn some vital information. Please tell me the directions to find Medusa the Gorgon, for I don't have a map, or even a damned primitive compass!"

"You have the voice of a child of man," the first perceptive sister answered. "Who are you really, oh intrepid mortal?" the curious bitch asked, for in her heart, the old whore really wanted to get laid because she hadn't had any good sex from a stiff cock in over five-thousand-years. "Holy Hera! I haven't been pumped since I had 'menopause' over five millennia ago," the former harlot admitted. "And the *men* have *paused* porking me, ever since my once juicy love canal dried- up, just like the fuckin' Sahara!"

"The rulers of *Olympus* have dispatched me to find the formidable Gorgon, and to gain knowledge of her whereabouts from you Three Gray Sisters," Perseus announced and claimed. "Don't you three 'sisters' have a *Mother Superior* I can speak with?"

"Look jerk-weed!" the second cantankerous sister remarked. "You might have to eat all three of our ancient, dried-up, smelly, lice-infected, cunts if you don't cooperate with our demands. We are kin to the Titans, and also to the Gorgons, and to the brutal Monsters of Antiquity, too," the old bag laboriously explained. "And we want *you* to know that we despise the new rulers of *Olympus,* along with their fucked-up human worshipers!"

"Listen carefully, twisted Sister," the bold young adventurer answered the most horrible-looking hag of the three. "I would rather jerk-off naked in that wicked blizzard out there, than eat or screw any of your raunchy, smelly, dried-up, arid pussies. Now then," Perseus adamantly continued. "Tell me the way to find Medusa!"

"Who is this insolent mortal pecker-head who dares invade our privacy?" the third withered, pallid-faced, crepey-skinned Gray Sister insisted on knowing. "Give me the eye so that I may evaluate *his* appearance, admire his muscular physique, and imagine and fanta*size* the 'size' and length of his hairy cock!"

As the three ugly, warty-faced, pallid sisters grappled and groped for the eye, which the zany trio had been passing amongst themselves, Perseus reached-out his free hand and grabbed *their* only window to the world. "Now then, you' ugly ingrate bitches," the hero shouted. "I now have your sacred only eye in my possession. I insist that you please tell me where the Gorgon resides, or I shall confiscate your eye, fly to the moon, and deposit it in an active volcanic crater," the impatient cave visitor threatened. "And try pissing me off some more, and I'll cut-off your distorted heads, and also your flaccid tits with my magic bronze sword, and gladly donate the hideous relics to the *Athenian Mythological Museum of Unnatural History.*"

"You wouldn't dare!" the first wretched-looking old hag exclaimed. "You haven't the testicles or the sperm to attempt that!"

"If you don't cooperate and give me accurate directions to Medusa's lair," Perseus emphatically predicted, "then I'll make all three of you pathetic, stubborn, miserable, blind bitches' lick and suck on my stenchy hemorrhoids until they magically disappear right out of my hairy, infected asshole!"

"Okay, you win this time, you conniving young bastard!" the first ornery witch acknowledged and compromised. "Go south toward the sun, and you will arrive at the *Golden Apple Tree* with three young maidens dancing around it. The maidens are the *Hesperides,* daughters of the Titan Atlas's brother, and the chicks will give you the essential directions to Medusa's secluded island," the old bag disclosed. "Now give us back our essential eye, so that at least one of us can view your form, and fantasize about having hot sex with a young stud-meister such as yourself!"

The motivated hero returned the portable eye to its rightful owners to quarrel over, rapidly left the dismal, isolated ice cave, and continued southward, flying over desolate mountains and weedy meadows until Perseus observed a tremendous form in the distance holding up the sky, and separating it from the Earth. 'That is the Titan, Atlas,' Perseus reckoned. 'And someday, he'll be relieved of this important duty, and then finally go into the lucrative business of manufacturing reference books for libraries and for classrooms.'

Then, the young champion heard sweet, angelic female voices singing, so the flying fellow descended down from the clouds, and viewed the aforementioned *Daughters of the Evening Star,* prancing and dancing around a magnificent apple tree, featuring large golden fruit suspended upon its wonderful limbs.

The beautiful, cheerful *Daughters of the Hesperides* held hands and danced around the fabulous *Golden Apple Tree,* which had an apparently listless, lazy dragon coiled around its base. The blithe nymphs ceased their merriment upon detecting the unexpected arrival of the crusader against evil injustices.

"Who the hell are you?" a blonde-haired beauty asked with half of her golden bush, and all of her firm tits, hanging out of her loose-fitting tunic. "Are you *Hercules* come to again steal golden apples from our incomparable tree?"

"No, fair maidens," the young champion candidly replied. "My name is Perseus, but you're absolutely right about one thing. The goddess Pallas Athene has sent me on a *Herculean* labor. You must show me the way to Medusa the Gorgon's secret lair!"

"Not just yet!" the second blonde-haired and blonde-bushed maiden answered. "Come dance with us. Then, we'll let you play with us, too!"

"Well, I must admit, that's a mighty big temptation you've offered me!" Perseus exclaimed as the guest asshole licked his lips while thinking about *those* other lips between the comely girls' perfectly structured legs. "You just aren't paying *lip service* to what we'll be doing, are you?" Perseus begged for verification.

"No, but you can masturbate any and all of us," the third horny nymph informed. "But you cannot penetrate our maidenheads, because, according to Almighty Zeus, we must remain virgins. But we do give good blow-jobs that are guaranteed to make you come again!" the *comely* nymph confidently stated.

"Well, that's all very nice and proper," the hero promptly agreed. "But I'll have to take a rain-check on your offer. I'm obligated by sacred promise to perform a vital errand for the Immortals, but after I am finished that *Promethean* chore," Perseus informed, "even though I am not Prometheus, I can then also lose my virginity, and even my maidenhead too, if I have one!"

Then, the fair damsels cried and slobbered all over the place, and all over each other, whimpering, "Medusa will surely turn you into stone. Then you'll never have the pleasure of massaging our hot, wet, pink, blonde beavers, or sucking on our firm, erect, succulent nipples," the first nymph regretted. "Won't you please reconsider? That scumbag Medusa lives in an alien *cunt*ry."

"I assure you fair maidens. I will not be converted into stone by some ugly hussy!" Perseus warranted. "Now, if you'll presently tell me the precise directions to her secluded lair, I can then be on my way. The sooner I can leave, the sooner I can return here and learn some fine, hands-on hedonism."

"Very well, then!" the second blonde damsel agreed, as the gorgeous maiden scrutinized the impressive bulge protruding below the center of Perseus's sexy orange tunic. "The knowledge you seek is not within our scope of experience, but if you request that same information from Atlas, who can see far into the distant Unshapen Land from his position of holding-up the sky, the Titan will probably help you."

The favorite mortal of Pallas Athene accompanied the luscious blonde knockouts up the side of a steep mountain where their inimitable uncle was busy keeping the sky separated from the Earth.

"Uncle, please assist this young explorer," the first maiden yelled-up and requested. "He requires knowing the location of Medusa the Gorgon's den. Is it somewhere in Denmark?"

"I can see the Gorgon resting in the shade of a distant island, but kind stranger," Atlas cautioned, "you cannot approach the territory unless your identity is cloaked by the *Hat of Darkness*. Then Medusa might be able to smell your presence, but won't be able to see you, even with *her* keen eyesight."

"Well then, kind Atlas," Perseus boldly stated. "Where is this unique *Hat of Darkness?* Where could I locate it?"

"*The Hat* is hidden in the depths of *Hades,* but my immortal nieces could easily retrieve it for you. But in payment for rendering that favor," Atlas continued, "I must receive one in return."

"What would you like me to do for you?" the bronze-helmeted champion curiously asked. "Would you like me to scratch your balls, or massage your ass?"

"No, Perseus. This fuckin' task of holding-up the sky is too tedious and monotonous for even a Titan to perform," Atlas aptly complained. "So, if you are successful in butchering Medusa's head off, show it to my face, so that I may be turned to stone. Then, my horrible, gruesome assignment will be that much less arduous for the remainder of eternity!"

"That's a deal!" Perseus euphorically acceded. "You can be the envy of every drunk's most passionate desire. Atlas, my friend; I want you to just think about your future status for a second. You will be *stoned* for all eternity!"

The *Daughters of the Evening Star* took a secret passage leading into the side of the mountain, which led to a macabre tunnel, that descended down fifteen miles to the Earth's core. A full week transpired until the trio finally completed their perilous mission, and ascended to the Earth's surface, carrying the incomparable *Hat of Darkness* as their prized trophy.

"Thank you, kind sisters of mercy, for obtaining this terrific gift," the young adventurer from Seriphos declared. "And I'll be thinking all about your hot, wet, pink, blonde pussies, and your firm erect succulent nipples, all the way to Medusa's private lair, I assure you." And then the young stud placed the extraordinary *Hat of Darkness* on top of his bronze helmet. In seconds, the sailor-turned-hero vanished from sight, laughing like a maniac as the jolly crusader cavorted around in his invisible state, tickling the fair maidens under their arms, and then feeling and squeezing their firm tits, featuring very erect succulent nipples.

Perseus, wanting to retain his virginity, a quality necessary to successfully complete his quest, flew onward toward the Unshapen Land that had been alluded to, and had been indicated by Atlas. Ahead, he could see the Gorgons' talons glistening in the morning sunlight, and the airborne encroacher instantly forgot about contemplating playing with the fair damsels' blonde pussies and firm tits, while concentrating all of his mental dynamics on the immediate task at hand. 'Pallas Athene suggested that I should first fly aloft and glance at Medusa's image in my bronze shield,' the daring fellow thought. 'If my back is to the sun, then I could more easily accomplish *her* expectation.'

The determined hero's invisible form flew above the three lethargic, inattentive Gorgons, all sleeping and basking in the sunlight, as if the monsters were lazy dinosaurs grazing in prairie lands, unaware of a fatal meteor hurtling through the atmosphere, ready to destroy their existence.

Perseus's hand trembled as the on-a-mission trespasser held his bronze sword aloft, for the Gorgons looked rather formidable, even while resting in their non-aggressive state. Medusa was rolling and tossing back and forth in her sleep, perhaps having a premonition of impending disaster.

Pallas Athene's champion gazed into *his* bronze shield, which served as a reliable mirror, and the aerial hero viewed the beast's horrible locks that were now identifiable as moving, living, lethal serpents. Her sharp fangs protruded out of the sides of her evil mouth, and even as the monster slept, the reprehensible beast hissed intermittently. Medusa was so foul, and so wicked-looking that Perseus felt inspired to immediately initiate his "supernatural errand". Looking into the bronze shield, the boy wonder savagely swung his sword, and his aim and effort had been true to the mark. In one mighty twist of the arm and wrist, the repulsive creature had been marvelously decapitated.

The thrilled victor reached-down, and without directly looking, grabbed the bloody head, and adroitly inserted it into the goatskin sack. 'Now I gotta' get the fuck outa' here in a hurry!' Perseus anxiously thought.

Medusa's body flipped, flapped, and flopped all over the rugged terrain, abruptly waking-up her savage sisters from *their* deep slumbers. In a second, Perseus was airborne, and as the perplexed sisters searched in vain for the invisible assassin, the murderer was entirely hidden from their scrutiny by the very effective *Hat of Darkness*. The enraged Gorgon sisters flew-off, and four times circled the rocky ledge where the surprise assault had occurred, but no evidence of any assassin was anywhere to be seen or found. Only a flying goatskin bag could be detected in the distance, speeding-away toward the western horizon.

"Serve me well, my swift-winged sandals," Perseus implored. "Give me the lightning speed of Hermes to escape the vindictive beasts hot on my trail, lusting for bitter revenge."

The euphoric victor flew south across the Mediterranean Sea, and soon Perseus came to northern Africa, the land of the *Golden Apple Tree,* and also the renowned *Daughters of the Evening Star.* The two determined Gorgons finally abandoned their futile pursuit, with the approach of evening, along with the nearby Mediterranean Sea, marking time and geographic boundaries for *their* exhausted bodies to honor.

After landing on the peninsula bordering the spectacular *Golden Apple Tree,* Perseus gallantly trekked over to Atlas to fulfill his grateful promise to the grieving Titan.

"Satisfy your pledge to me!" Atlas urged the ambitious youth. "Show me the bitch's fuckin' ugly puss so that I can escape my *Olympus* punishment, and be transformed into stone for all eternity. I demand that you turn me into an inanimate mountain crag, right this fuckin' minute."

And Perseus honored his stated responsibility to the melancholy, woeful giant by removing the bloody Gorgon's head from the goatskin bag, and then showing its' cursed, horrible face to the colossal figure. Instantly, the Titan changed into a mountain peak, and the surrounding northern African ridges still bear the giant's name to this very day, the *Atlas Mountains.*

Then, Perseus enclosed the Gorgon's head inside the thick goatskin sack, so that no further damage or transformation could accidentally result from its exposure. The three blonde maidens came sprinting-up the mountain trail to inspect their uncle's new, radical, rock-hard appearance.

"He's now as solid as *Gibraltar,*" the first nymph attested.

"Uncle Atlas can now be one of the *Pillars of Hercules,*" the second golden-hair vixen marveled and stated.

"Uncle Atlas is finally out of his perpetual misery!" the third *Hesperides'* daughter gleefully shouted. "Now Perseus; just point Medusa's head at your pecker, so that your fadorkenbender might turn hard, too! My sisters and I want to get laid really badly!"

"Sorry ladies," the chaste-hearted noble idealist suavely answered. "I promise to come back someday with a huge erection to satisfy all three of you young, horny bitches. But right now, I must consummate my important journey."

"Perseus, take with you *this* wonderful fruit," the second nymph insisted as the fair maiden held-out one of the lustrous golden apples. "It has sufficient energy to sustain you for a full week!"

"And don't forget to come back to northern Africa, so that you can fondle our tits, and do anything you'd like to our golden blonde pussies!" the third young maiden reminded the intrepid son of Zeus and Danae.

"Now fly eastward over the drab Libyan shore, and from there, zoom north to the land of Greece," the first lovely damsel instructed. "And please Perseus; retain your sacred virginity and save it for *us* to gleefully claim!"

The three blonde maidens then all kissed Perseus upon his lips and face, and the ecstatic favorite of Pallas Athene ascended into the air, and followed the three daughters' directions, heading straight to the Libyan coast. From there, the son of Danae would continue his odyssey to the island of Seriphos, where the condemned returnee would discard the goatskin sack outside the palace, and then nonchalantly have the vile Polydickdees admire Medusa's hideous face and head.

"King Midas"

Midas was King of Phrygia in Asia Minor, and most people living inside and outside Phrygia didn't give a fast fart about the egotistical ruler, or about any of his irrelevant, imperial bullshit. Despite the public's apathy about their royal guardian, Midas was extremely wealthy, and very powerful, because the tyrant taxed his subjects and predicates to death, and used their labor and their money to break almost everyone's balls, or puncture their inflated tits. The emperor never took any crap from anyone, preferring to pursue his own foolish inclinations, while making hasty and irrational judgments without the consent of his distinguished transvestite advisers, whom *he* thought were simply charlatans and mediocre assholes, instead of harmless, deviate transvestites.

One day, Dionysus, the always drunk Greek god of wine and frivolity, was traveling through Phrygia with his entourage of naked nymphs and retarded satyrs (creatures half man, half goat, and fully fucked-up). One member of the troupe was Salenus, an old, fat, bald-headed prick who was barely sober while nodding his noggin upon his donkey, which all of a sudden smelled some asses' asses a mile away in King Midas's royal stables.

The donkey surreptitiously lagged behind, and then strayed from the caravan of merrymakers, who continued to party without even realizing that the old fart and his mount were missing from their elite company. The independent ass took Salenus's ass west, and an hour later, arrived at the king's totally incomparable rose garden, where Salenus's ass fell off *his* ass, and tumbled into an *asinine* clump of asshole thorny rose bushes.

The King's alert gardeners discovered Salenus bleeding and laughing upon the ground, and helped the comical idiot stagger to his feet, and think of salient words to say. Meanwhile, the gardeners searched in vain for Salenus's eight other asses.

"Where the fuck am I?" the fat, bald-headed, old codger inquired. "Who wants to fuckin' tickle my armpits and scratch my balls with both ends of an ostrich feather?"

The notorious traveling revels of Dionysus had become common knowledge throughout Phrygia, and the alert gardeners perceptively recognized that Salenus was one of the wine-god's intimate colleagues. The laborers wrapped a wreath around *his* neck, consisting of assorted flowers and discarded marijuana butts; dragged his corpulent carcass up the palace steps, and gracefully dumped the intoxicated Salenus upon the marble floor. Greedy King Midas was then summoned to entertain his new eminent guest.

The affable monarch introduced himself to Salenus, who was still so inebriated that the retard believed *he* was speaking with a male prostitute in a city ghetto. Midas was thrilled that one of Dionysus's close acquaintances had visited *his* remote palace, and the ruler insisted that Salenus stay for a feast that would rival any that Dionysus had ever attended or provided.

"You must stay and enjoy my warm hospitality! I say hospitality because after you get done thirty days of partying, drinking, eating, and screwing, you'll fuckin' wind-up in my royal hospital," Midas told the still-dysfunctional Salenus. "In this isolated country, there is always feast, and never famine! And when we run out of food, we suck on each other's genitals."

"That's perfectly wonderful!" Salenus exclaimed while groggily staggering around and hiccupping. "My throat, my stomach, and my loins are all famished! Bring on the strippers, the switch-hitting lesbians, and the goddamned male couch-dancers, you stingy, parsimonious bastard!"

Much preparation and attention to detail at the palace was done, with servants flitting-around setting tables, carrying wine jugs and baskets of food, and placing sweet-smelling, ancient aphrodisiac elixir at strategic places.

A fantastic orgy followed, that lasted for ten whole days and nights, until all the men ran out of sperm fluid, and all the women's hairy, pink honey-wells went dry. Lyres and pipes were played by female minstrels having their menstruals, and the musicians were exempted from participation in the orgy, and when not tooting-away, the orchestra members had to sit all by themselves at a designated "periodic table", where they had some "good chemistry and lousy biology" to share, while periodically taking their daily physics.

Midas next conducted Salenus through the festooned halls to the king's favorite palace bath, where the two frolicked and toyed with each other like a pair of horny, homosexual chimpanzees. Those flirtatious activities went-on for another two whole days, until Midas collapsed on the bathroom's mosaic tile floor from sheer exhaustion, and Salenus had drunk all of the dirty, scummy water from the hot tub, thinking and believing that it was sweet-tasting wine, mingled with aphrodisiac elixir.

Dionysus heard about Midas's wild celebration, and soon arrived at the king's palace to retrieve his wayward friend Salenus. When the god of wine learned of the wonderful hospitality Midas had extended to *his* "salubrious comrade", Dionysus promised to grant the emperor any gift *he* so desired, either reasonable or extravagant.

The king's heart possessed many non-virtuous, negative qualities, such as lust, greed, pride, hedonism, and vanity. So, naturally, *his* exploration of pleasure was predicated on satisfying one or more of those particular vices. Midas's mind was still-fatigued from all of the ten-day biological indulgence, followed by the two-day private orgy with Salenus, so his selfish brain was now in total disarray; a facsimile of his fat, bald-headed guest's erratic thought patterns.

Midas's cerebrum envisioned the golden cups his wild revelers had dented and hurled upon the palace marble floors, and the ignoramus thought about *his* golden honeycomb that the famous Greek architect Daedalus had engineered especially for the king's honor. 'Those drunken, shit-faced imbeciles have ransacked my entire palace; have vandalized my cherished golden honeycomb, and have smashed or ruptured all of my treasured golden possessions,' the emperor imagined and concluded.

"Dionysus," Midas answered the quasi-deity, who preferred reveling with scumbag mortals down on Earth, rather than associating with *his* condescending, almighty, pompous peers on *Mt. Olympus.* "I wish to have golden statues of you and Salenus to commemorate your fine visit to Phrygia, and also, to pay tribute to your amusing friend's memorable stay at my luxurious palace." The king then realized a once in a lifetime, very *golden opportunity.* "Therefore," Midas continued, as the greedy bastard finally announced the true reason for his veiled plan. "Give *me* the power to transform everything I touch into solid gold. This gift will protect me from gold diggers; from goldbrickers, and from the disreputable *Golden Fleecers.* It will be like my own personal golden parachute, sheltering me from potential poverty, even though I don't know what the fuck a parachute is, let alone a goddamned golden one!"

"I suggest you give the matter some serious thought," Dionysus advised, while wisely cautioning his new acquaintance to engage in sober deliberation and somber discretion. "Don't do anything 'rash', for I have no ointment or lotion that can cure major skin irritations!"

Kings of Asia Minor tended to be obstinate and stubborn after committing to, and announcing, their intentions, so Midas was adamant about his innermost desire. "Dionysus, that is my wish," the already-wealthy moron selfishly maintained. "I would like to be conferred with the

Golden Touch. Now, I insist that you keep your promise, and afford me that special ability!"

"Okay Your Motley Majesty, you win!" Dionysus replied, shaking his head left and right to demonstrate his obvious skepticism and objection. "When Salenus and I exit your magnificent gardens, the *Golden Touch* will then go into effect. But always remember, dear Midas," the god of wine and frivolity lectured. "The only things' that should be golden' are silence, sunrises, sensational sunsets, and your later years."

Ten minutes later, Midas was so exhilarated from the official implementation of *his* new magical power that the enthused emperor couldn't decide what object he should touch first to convert into solid gold. The excited asshole chose a branch of a tall oak tree in the garden, not far from the palace wall, and after the stupid-shit touched the tree's lowest limb, its leaves slowly made a spectrum transformation from green, to yellow, and then to pure solid gold.

"These stellar leaves are better than the ones that Daedalus and his son Icarus had manufactured in the royal workshop!" Midas marveled and uttered. "They're worth a small fortune, and I have only begun to proliferate my wealth," the King greedily laughed. "I can't wait to fuckin' touch the royal falcon, and make it into a golden eagle! Ha, ha, ha!"

Midas was now the greatest and most demented king in the ancient world. The imbecile stooped-down and touched his garden's lawn, and the blades of grass instantly converted into strands of gold. He grabbed a stone, and it astonishingly transformed into a lump of pure solid gold. The experimenter next touched a familiar root crop vegetable growing in his private garden, and the object immediately turned into *twenty-four 'carrot' gold.*

The joyful king was delirious upon contemplating his new-found ability. Midas playfully held his hand out, and sprinted past a row of six white marble pillars, and after he touched each one, they all magically changed into solid gold. The euphoric ruler hypothesized that he would make his entire palace into a beautiful gold edifice, but then he considered that the six golden pillars were a nice contrast to the majestic white marble structure that rivaled any god's temple in either Greece, Egypt, Philadelphia, or anywhere else in Asia Minor.

Then, Midas had an inspiration. The avaricious prick grabbed a golden delicious apple from a fruit bowl, and held it up to his lips. 'This apple is already *golden*,' the drunk-with-power, asylum case mused. 'I wonder what will happen if I attempt biting into it!'

The anxious monarch bit into the apple, and much to his dismay, chipped two of his formerly perfect-shaped front teeth. 'How stupid I was!' Midas acknowledged. 'I should've asked Dionysus to grant me the *Golden Touch* in just my left hand, so that I could use my right hand to eat; to write edicts, and to fuckin' jerk-off. I must experiment more to evaluate the extent of this remarkable gift. Then, I should be able to ascertain whether it is, or is not an evil, wretched curse in disguise!'

The regal idiot ordered his royal servants to set their master's table, and Midas amusingly entertained himself by converting the dishes, saucers, cups, and tablecloth into pure gold. The covetous asshole accidentally touched the table, but then realized that it had been pure gold *before* he had acquired the phenomenal *Golden Touch.*

When Midas's chatty, gossipy servants had finally exited his personal dining room, the king tampered some more with his newly-acquired special talent. He gingerly grabbed a slice of bread and inserted one end into his mouth. The emperor nearly lost several incisors from *their* crunching-down upon the flat, solid, metal surface. The apprehensive king suddenly became extremely terrified by his "new damned power".

'I'll attempt biting, chewing, and swallowing a morsel without using my hands!' the worried fool theorized. 'If I just use my lips, I ought to be able to eat that second ordinary slice of bread on the table. Thank *Olympus* my lips don't fuckin' have fingers!"

The nervous king bent-over and used his nose to move the slab of bread closer to his mouth. Then, the dipshit bit into the slice, but it too had become solid gold. Midas's emotions quickly shifted from disappointment, to frustration, to shock, and then to exasperation. "What the fuck's goin' on here!" the royal dumb-fuck finally yelled-out to his intimidated servants, who perceived their master's anger, and hid behind the six golden pillars inside the botanical garden. "If only I had waited and thought the situation through," the afflicted king regretted. "Then, I would have wisely wished for the *Golden Touch* to only exist on the index finger of my left hand! Shit! Now I can't even finger Mrs. Midas's wide love canal! On second thought, that's not such a bad fuckin' idea!"

Midas reached for a 'goblet' of wine, but soon became aware that he could not drink from nor *gobble it.* The substance solidified inside his mouth and throat, nearly choking the incensed imbiber to death. The distraught King violently spit-out the golden chunk, finally fully fathoming the futility of his extraordinary gift of touch.

"This is fuckin' insane!" Midas angrily exclaimed. "If I hold my dick while I'm taking a piss," the upset ruler orally considered to a wall mirror, "then my bird will turn into a goldfinch, and my balls will transform into golden nuggets. Holy shit!" the emperor cried-out as he experienced sudden *social insecurity.* "And I'm still two decades away from my goddamned Golden Years! And if I feel or scratch my ass with the *Golden Touch,* my ass will become a *golden tush,* and I'll be shitting out gold bricks that'll scrape the feces right out of my colon, and also clear out of my semi-colon!"

Out of sheer desperation and extreme anxiety, the now-penitent monarch lifted his cursed hands into the air and earnestly prayed, "Oh great and wise Dionysus. Forgive my greed and my lustful need for excessive ostentation. Please show me mercy by removing the *Golden Touch* that *you* have so generously conferred upon your humble suppliant!"

A familiar voice descended from the sky and instructed, "Midas; you would've been better-off if you had discreetly requested a dozen additional assholes to complement the big one you already carry around with you. Go to the mountain of Tmolus, who as you know, was a minor god that had been punished by being transformed into a solid precipice. Bathe in the nearby stream," Dionysus's voice loudly directed, "and then the *Golden Touch* will be washed-away. And the next time a powerful asshole like me offers you a favor, make sure you have assessed all of the *goddamned* consequences. In the future, show more prudence and less impudence, you' stupid, ingrate, fucked-up, jerk-off!"

Midas was very grateful to Dionysus for providing him with the solution to *his* very terrible dilemma, but in his haste, the king heeded the wine god's instruction, but unfortunately, ignored *his* sage advice. The cursed dunderhead journeyed to the mountain of Tmolus, cleansed his entire naked body in the gentle, shallow stream, and noticed that the sand at the bottom of the narrow river reflected a bright gold color, that incidentally, has been that same particular hue ever since.

The Phrygian King was absolutely delighted to have been returned to normal. However, Midas still retained much of his arrogance, vanity, and greediness. The obdurate fellow soon resented, and then despised gold, as well as all of the other trappings associated with massive, limitless, decadent wealth.

Midas soon became a quasi-environmentalist, appreciating the sounds of babbling brooks, singing meadows, and whispering pines. The ruler distanced himself from his splendid palace; from his gossipy staff; from his marvelous festivals; from his fancy embroidered clothing and tunics, and from his fantastic harem of fifty horny harlots, all sporting eager beavers. While partaking in *his* "communion with nature", Midas coincidentally neglected the important political and economic affairs presently going haywire inside his chaotic, burgeoning empire.

Now the satyr mini-god Pan had made himself a pipe to play, and it just so happened that the minor deity of amusement was cavorting around in the woods near Mt. Tmolus. Pan delighted in playing his new flute when the forest wanderer wasn't exercising, thrusting, or having his own impressive skin-flute sucked on by some blind local nymph that always craved oral gratification, while providing sexual satisfaction in return. Hence, the well-endowed satyr had the appropriate nickname "Peter Pan".

As a result of Pan giving his new flute a major blow-job, because the sex-enthusiast had just received one from the aforementioned blind forest nymph, the beasts and the creatures of the woods became very active and happy, making exotic sounds and enchanting dissonance, and loudly farting all over the "Fuckin' Forest".

Midas encountered Pan inside the deep woods, and formally requested that the goat-god continue playing *his* alluring melodies for hours and hours, until the chirping birds, and the buzzing bees, and the squealing squirrels all developed chronic laryngitis and genital atrophy.

"Apollo, god of music and the lyre, will be proud of my new musical instrument," Pan told Midas. "I'll be glad to serenade you and the forest animals, until my lips grow weary, or until the end of the world arrives, or until my dick falls off; whatever happens first!"

But if Midas possessed one major fault, in addition to greed, vanity, and arrogance, it was the fact that the dumb-fuck never learned when to keep his big mouth shut.

"Great!" the idiotic emperor turned idiotic naturalist answered the forest satyr. "I'll ask *Olympus* in a solemn prayer that Apollo and *you* compete in a musical contest, and that the honorable Tmolus will judge who is the more skilled musician. The mere pleasure of listening to the music will be much more satisfying to me than possessing the *Golden Touch,* or having a dozen additional assholes to crap out of!"

Now naturally, Tmolus himself was a woodland deity, and would be biased toward selecting Pan while simultaneously discriminating against Lord Apollo. The god of music's harmonies had a classical rhythm that edified the diabolical *Olympians,* that extolled Greek heroes, and that praised dignified, rational virtues, such as justice, truth, honesty, and generosity.

But on the contrary, Pan's revolutionary music suggested emotional expression and freedom of thought; loose social and immoral behavior, and the pursuit of physical pleasure. It was a competition between "mind and conscience" versus "heart and body," and Pan had the definite advantage as far as Tmolus was concerned, because Tmolus used to enjoy getting laid, getting blown, working his stick, and wiping his ugly asshole, a thousand times a day. Hedonism appealed much more to Tmolus than art, science, and intellectual activity ever had, so Pan was destined to emerge victorious in his not-so-amicable rivalry with vindictive Apollo.

But Tmolus soon discarded his favoritism for Pan, and abandoned his prejudice against Apollo. The pragmatic personage awarded the coveted laurel wreath prize to the god of music, being fully aware that Apollo was an *Olympian,* and had far greater clout among the immortal "Powers That Be" than the less-influential Pan had. "I don't want to be a friggin' immobile mountain for all eternity," Tmolus said to a neighboring ridge named Cliff. "I don't even have hands, or a throbbing dick to jerk-off with!"

Midas, however, was not quite as prudent and as diplomatic as Tmolus had been. He too was biased in favor of Pan, and had completely shut and covered *his* ears when Apollo had been singing and playing his splendid lyre. The king was spoiled, because in the past, when *he* would yell "Leap", his courtiers and servants would always request knowing "How high"? And then, the subordinates would always-jump to the exact height that the deranged emperor had arbitrarily stipulated.

"No one has dominion over the way I think!" Midas muttered to his reflection showing inside a crystal-clear blue forest stream. "It's now time for me to speak-up for what is legitimately the forest god's triumph over that pompous *Olympus* loser, Apollo!"

The King of Phrygia eventually came-out of his self-induced stupor, and vehemently protested to the heavens that Pan had decisively won the musical competition, and not Phoebus Apollo. Tmolus peered-down at Midas indignantly, wishing that 'the implausible asshole should incinerate himself in a nearby active volcano's crater. Perceiving Tmolus's rejection of *his* boisterous verbal appeal, Midas beckoned to Apollo, furiously criticizing the "unfair judgment rendered by Judge Tmolus".

"Go suck a wet one, you incompetent dumb-fuck!" Apollo nastily retorted. "Oh, fucked-up King. You must most certainly have defective ears," the chariot sun-god continued his rant. "I now feel compelled to give *them* their true shape."

The falsely victorious god of music, medicine, literature, and the lyre, swiftly whirled-around, and then proceeded northwest toward *Mt. Olympus,* thoroughly convinced that *his* final judgment pertaining to "that asshole Midas" was far too lenient.

Midas raised his hands up to his long furry ears, and screamed-out to the sky, "Great Zeus in heaven! I've been given an ass's ears. At least Apollo could have granted me a long donkey's dick to go along with these exaggerated donkey ears!"

Upon returning to his palace after his bizarre Mt. Tmolus and woods' escapades, Midas felt ashamed of his animalistic appearance, and wore a large purple turban to camouflage his abnormally large ass's ears. The Ruler attempted to explain to his advisers and counselors that wearing the purple turban was a privilege that only the majestic king could exercise, and the chief consultants were happy to hear *that* singular proclamation, because no one desired to look so horribly unstylish and unfashionable as the "fucked-up, eccentric Monarch" did.

After the king's hair grew so long that his tresses and braidy bunches had to be sheared and trimmed, Midas summoned the services of the royal barber, who was also a royal gossiper, and a royal pain in the ass's ears.

"Cut and groom my straggly, shaggy locks," King Midas austerely commanded. "And if *you* dare tell anyone of my secret, you'll have to sleep with the royal zoo's 'twelve dozen' female gorillas when they are all in heat. Can you think of any punishment more fuckin' *gross* than that?"

The royal barber was quite tempted to relay the King's personal problem to almost everyone he saw or met, but *he* intensely feared he would be mauled and mangled by a hundred forty-four aggressive, sexually-aroused, affectionate, hideous, very dangerous female gorillas. Consequently, the intimidated fellow quietly bit his tongue so often that it was now two inches shorter than it normally would be.

'I don't know what's worse,' the worried barber painfully thought and anguished. 'Being emulsified by twelve-dozen, horny female gorillas, or sleeping with my corpulent five-hundred-pound wife; that choice is really a very tough decision. I'll have to seriously think about this lousy option. The ugly gorillas are looking better and better in my mind every damned minute!' the neurotic palace barber concluded. 'And besides *that* rather complicated consideration, crazy King Midas also might get pissed-off at me, and send my ass all the way to future America to fuckin' become a Yankee clipper!'

In bed, the troubled barber tossed and turned, and his obese wife rolled over on top of him, thinking that the poor fellow desired sex, when actually, all that *he* wanted was more oxygen. The paranoid barber even made mysterious noises and nebulous utterances in his sleep, and when *his* subconscious was about to reveal the king's awful secret, in desperation, the diminutive barber would beg for more sex, and his steamrolling wife would accommodate his irregular request at least five times every single night, until the hair-trimmer was steamrolled as flat as a pancake.

Feeling as flat as a table, one afternoon the bedraggled barber strolled-down to a distant meadow to take a leak in a waterlogged pond. When the pisser noticed that no one was in the vicinity to observe his *private* behavior, the barber then stuck his head inside a groundhog hole to relieve his extreme tension by then loudly shouting into the cavity. A belligerent woodchuck surfaced, bit a chunk of flesh out of the bad-luck barber's scalp, and then burrowed back down into its dark den.

"I'll have to dig my own hole to get the necessary relief that I seek," the aggrieved hair trimmer said to himself. "I will not despair, despite my great apprehension! I fuckin' never want to become a goddamned Yankee clipper!"

It required six minutes of assiduous excavation, but then the resolute barber finally accomplished his prime objective. Without hesitating, the mental case pressed his head inside the newly-created hole and twice bellowed, "King Midas has ass's ears!"

The hole eventually filled-up with scummy, stagnant pond water, and several weeks later, a colony of wild reeds began growing all around the cavity's circumference. When the thin reeds sprouted even higher, the growths rustled, as the wind briskly blew between them. A court messenger will kidney problems happened to stop at the distant "pissing pond" to take a healthy leak, and then *his* ears sensed a rather peculiar refrain. The young courier dashed to King Midas's majestic palace, and alerted everyone he knew of the strange articulations originating from "an enchanted hole" down near the isolated palace swamp.

A hundred or so curious, imperial employees darted-down to the secluded pond area, to observe and listen to "the most fascinating phenomenon ever". As the crowd gathered nearer to the hole that had been dug by the neurotic barber, the naughty reeds were melodically whispering and repeating, "King Midas has ass's ears; and King Midas's ass has ass" ears, too! King Midas has ass's ears, and King Midas's ass has ass's ears, too!"

182

"Odysseus and Cyclops"

In 1184 BC, King Odysseus was returning home from the *Trojan War* to Ithaca, his native island, off the coast of Greece. The Greek hero had an armada of twelve ships upon leaving the siege of Troy, and his famous confrontation with the contemptible Cyclops was one episode in a ten-year mis-adventurous journey after departing Troy. The *Trojan War* had taken ten-long-years to fight, and the lengthy conflict was finally won when Odysseus, a brilliant schemer and ball-breaker, had two famed Trojan horses built, and then had the army situate the structures outside the main gates of Troy. The city was strategically located at the Hellespont between Greece and Asia Minor (now Turkey).

The first wooden horse contained fifty horny Greek harlots that exited-down a hidden ladder, and then proceeded to service the Trojan guards (after distributing to them ribbed prophylactics, which the dunderhead Trojan soldiers naturally wore over their sandals, instead of over their sexual apparatus). While the Trojan guards were humping and pumping the nymphomaniac Greek whores, a dozen Achaean soldiers descended the hidden ladder to the second smaller *Trojan Horse,* and quickly killed the fifty Trojan guards while the idiots were busy screwing and happily climaxing inside the fifty insatiable Greek harlots. The hero Odysseus had thought-up the ideas of the dual *Trojan Horses,* because the mastermind wanted to return to Ithaca and pump his old lady Queen Penelope, whom the itinerant king had heard was being wooed by a dozen or so worthless suitors, walking around the island with massive hard-ons.

The *Odyssey,* like the *Iliad* (the story of the *Trojan War* and the Fifty Trojan Whores) took ten years to complete, so Odysseus was destined to go twenty lousy years without porking and sodomizing his faithful wife. He and his crew sailed twelve warships from Troy across the wine-dark sea, which tasted more like salty vinegar, and because of that irrelevant fact, Odysseus called the body of water "the *oddest-sea".*

"Damned, I wonder if Penelope's beaver is still black, its lips pink, and its interior wonderfully wet, pink, and juicy," Odysseus commented to his first mate.

"Who fuckin' cares?" Eurshiddenme, the first mate answered. "The sex between you and me has been good," the first mate continued. "So,

Odysseus; why the fuck should I really give a silly shit about your wife's eager beaver? I really hate straight sex, anyway!"

After a week of listless drifting at sea, Odysseus and his don't-give-a-shit sailors arrived at the island of the Cyclopes, who were giant, lawless hermits that lived in virtually inaccessible mountain caves. The Cyclopes were illiterate, and never read about themselves in en*cyclope*dias. The mammoth one-eyed idiots never planted crops, or plowed their fields, because the dumb-fucks were basically lazy, worthless, and indolent shit-heads. And worst of all, the cannibals ate men (but were not homosexual, but celibate), and never munched-on pussy.

The one-eyed freaks also ate wild grapes, wheat, and barley that grew without any cultivation. That was their basic problem. The Cyclopes lived without cultivation, neither agricultural nor cultural cultivation. But Lord Poseidon always provided the heinous ogres with ample nectar and ambrosia, conveniently stolen from Mt. Olympus. The Cyclopes voraciously ate the donated nectar and ambrosia, not knowing that the food was what actually was making them stay immortal.

However, in all due respect, the Cyclopes did learn how to make grape juice, mixing it with semen to have a nice white froth resembling the *head* on a cold mug of beer. This outlandish concoction the Cyclopes drank morning, noon, and night, so each of the one-eyed monsters always had what looked like a milk mustache showing above his upper lip, that really was a 'semen cocktail' mustache instead.

As had been alluded, the Cyclopes had no laws, no councils; no judges or courts; no government; no schools; no raucous Bingo halls; and no legislatures, so in many respects, the ignorant creeps were much better-off than fucked-up civilized men were. Each Cyclopes was a government unto himself', and the dangerous assholes never helped each other, and were often arrogant, antagonistic neighbors. As a result, each Cyclopes had to live a good distance from any others of *his* species; otherwise, the society would self-destruct within a year's time. The Greek bard Homer makes no reference to any female Cyclopes in his epic poem the *Odyssey,* but we have to believe that women existed among that peculiar colony of one-eyed creatures, simply to reproduce the idiotic race.

Now, Odysseus observed that a fertile islet, that remarkably wasn't pregnant, was situated about a half-mile from the land of the island of the lawless Cyclopes. The wayward Greek king commanded that *his* twelve ships be anchored off that smaller wooded territory, and the guileful commander planned on raiding a cave or two on the larger island to do what the ancient Greeks knew best: pilfer, plunder, pillage, and possibly pedophile little nude, unwary boys and girls.

Now, there was a multitude of goats pastured on the smaller wooded island. The Cyclopes were too stupid to invent or build boats to sail the half-mile distance to bag the wild goats, and the imbeciles were too mentally-challenged to ever attempt learning how to swim, or even how to wade across the shallow harbor. Fresh water streams abounded on the "goat island", but the dumb-shit Cyclopes were content living in misery on their less abundant, larger island, and killing and eating their fellow uncivilized cavemen whenever the opportunity presented itself', or whenever the food supply ran short.

"This looks like a fine island to beach our ships and to search for food and water," Odysseus told his second mate. "We are safe, as long as there are no fucked-up, hostile human residents dwelling around here."

"Don't bother me when I'm trying to flirt with and feel-up and tease the first mate!" Eurballsourout, the second mate answered. "Eurshiddenme is really pretty well-endowed!"

"Are you shittin' me?" Odysseus challenged Eurballsourout.

"No, my friggin' name is Eurballsourout," the second mate replied. "Eurshiddenme is your goddamned first mate! You oughta' know that common bull-shit by now!"

That first morning, in the uncharted area of the Mediterranean, Odysseus and *his crew* left the other eleven ships in order to explore the smaller island for food and water. The troop carried their spears and bows and arrows, and divided into three *bands* that sang and danced to mediocre Greek folk songs. It was hard labor, shooting the wild goats while singing and doing ancient Greek versions of *vaudeville*-type dance routines, so finally, the men quieted-down, so that the zany revelers were able to stealthily sneak-up on their intended prey.

Altogether, the hunting expeditions had killed a hundred and eight goats, and then the merry men from all twelve ships feasted, drinking sacks of wine the plunderers had stolen from the Cicones, a city of imbeciles *they* had recently marauded. The Greeks had obtained the 'sacks' of sweet mellow wine when they had *sacked* the city. Then they 'ran' away. That's how the soldiers had effectively *ransacked* the victimized Cicones' one and only mini-metropolis. But the macho men managed to kill most of the village people!

From the smaller island, Odysseus and his crew could see the campfires glowing inside the Cyclopes' caves, a half-mile distant. Odysseus called a military council meeting the next morning to organize a raid upon the unsuspecting, dumb-ass Cyclopes, who all didn't care a tiny shit about the outside world, or give a damn if they themselves, or anybody else lived, starved, disintegrated, or died.

"Stay safe here on this magical island," Odysseus had told his other eleven crews earlier that morning, "while I and *my* vanguard of men from *my* ship pay a visit to that larger inhabited land over yonder. I want to determine if the natives are uncivilized savages, or hospitable, cunning, and detestable civilized barbarians like we are."

Odysseus and his special bodyguards boarded their sleek commando landing vessel, and after loosening the hawser ropes that had been used for mooring the boat, the team clandestinely rowed to the land of the Cyclopes, with visions of committing theft by looting, if random experimental conniving, and ordinary trickery failed. After anchoring their boat in a remote harbor obscured by rocky cliffs, the daring hit squad furtively climbed-up the steep mountain ridge to an area where the spies could clearly view an unoccupied cave.

"Look at the size of that chair inside that cavern up there!" Odysseus marveled and remarked to his first mate. "Whatever creature lives there must be as big and as tall as Zeus himself'."

"Yes, Captain," agreed Eurshiddenme, the needed to be castrated first mate. "The monster's dick is probably longer and larger than any of us are tall and wide. It must be a real monstrosity!"

"The cave dweller might not be a human being at all!" Eurballsourout, the second mate, speculated and opined. "He might be half-beast and only part human! The asshole might be even more genetically fucked-up than the Trojans were!"

"Listen carefully, men!" Odysseus demanded. "If you enter with me into that mysterious cave, some of you might never see your wives or your children again!"

The brawny crewmembers all looked at each other and shrugged their muscular shoulders. None of them desired to ever want to see their fat, ugly wives, or their bratty, parasitic kids ever again, and would gladly die first in a dark cave on an unknown island at the hands of a cruel indiscriminate brute/monster.

Odysseus had selected his twelve "best men" (none of whom were ever in any wedding party) to accompany him the last hundred-feet up to the ominous hollow. The "guests" had brought along a goatskin filled with sweet-tasting wine, which had been given to Odysseus by Maron, a priest of

Apollo, after the Greek King had threatened to castrate Maron if *he* did not present a favorable gift of tribute. So, Odysseus often practiced receiving fabulous gifts by intimidation and by extortion.

Upon reaching the Cyclops (one Cyclopes) cave, the single-eyed monster was not inside, but instead, was out shepherding his hungry flock. Odysseus and his neurotic scouting patrol bravely advanced inside, leaving mounds of wet crap all the way from the entrance to a hundred-feet inside the dreary, dismal cavern.

"Look at those racks loaded with cheese," Odysseus related to his almost-mesmerized subordinates. "And the resident of this horrid place has more lambs, hoglets, and kids than his pens could contain. He must certainly be a very prosperous fellow, living on this apparently forbidden island!"

"And look," noted Eurballsourout, the second mate. "His pails and bowls are as big as we are, and they're filled to the brim with milk and whey."

"Get out of my *whey*!" Odysseus exclaimed, as the scouting party leader stuck his cupped hands into a shoulder-high bowl, and then voraciously drank some of the rich dairy product. "*Whey* to go Odysseus!" the brave hero praised himself.

The men then begged their boss if they could steal some cheeses and a kid each, but Odysseus commanded the other trespassers to just take the cheeses, and not get involved in any felonious, legally-complicated "kidnappings".

"Men, we are humble guests in the owner's house," Odysseus declared. "So, according to *our* customs and tradition, our host should present us with gifts under the Law of the Suppliants. If you recall," Odysseus lectured, "any strangers visiting a person's home while traveling through a distant town or village is to be extended hospitality and generosity," the leader boringly reviewed. "I say we *not* steal the cheeses! Let's instead wait until the *big cheese* gives us his cheesy cheeses, under the protection of almighty Zeus's Law of the Suppliants."

"I say your logic is really fucked-up!" the first mate criticized. "Why should we risk injury, or maybe even death, just because *we* honor *our* dumb-ass laws and our fucked-up traditions?" Eurshiddenme adamantly indicated. "This creature that lives here might not favor us, or our asshole laws, gods, or traditions!"

"If he's more fucked-up than we are," the second mate emphasized, "then we're undoubtedly in for a very long day, that's for damned sure!"

Eurballsourout observed and shared. "Has anyone brought along any knitting needles and a rocking chair to pass the friggin' time away?"

Inside the dark, dank cave, Odysseus and his men lit a fire, and then sacrificed some cheeses to the gods before the intrepid encroachers ate any of the remaining ones themselves. Some of the soldiers became restless and picked their noses; twiddled their thumbs; squeezed various pimples, and scratched their itchy balls.

"Why do we sacrifice these good cheeses to the gods, when we could've stolen the food and eaten the pieces ourselves!" the first mate questioned. "Sometimes we really do some stupid, shitty things!" Eurshiddenme perceptively concluded and stated.

"Because Dip-shit!" Odysseus yelled back. "There might really be gods up on *Mt. Olympus* that might be offended if *we* didn't think of *them* first, before considering *our* own selfish, biological needs. And if we start getting our asses kicked by the creature that lives here in this putrid-smelling cave," the Greek king supposed, "we might require the emergency services of some supernatural divine intervention in a fuckin' hurry!"

"But still," the second mate challenged. "If there really aren't any gods on *Mt. Olympus* to be pleased by our offering, then we will have wasted all of that lousy burnt cheese for nothing!" Eurballsourout stubbornly argued. "And besides; what insane god, in his or her right or left mind, would ever desire burned-cheese that is no longer cheese, anyway? You tell me that answer, Captain Asshole! Who the hell wants or needs evaporated or burnt cheesy cheese? A skinny mouse about to die, perhaps?"

"I never thought of that stupid bull-shit," Odysseus reluctantly admitted. "But who's willing to take the risk if your supposition is wrong? I mean," the somewhat-puzzled king philosophically explained, "when's the last friggin' time you had one of Zeus's shocking lightning bolts penetrate-up the center of your smelly, hairy asshole?"

"Great Zeus! I really never thought about such a dreadful consequence!" the second mate exclaimed in a terrified tone of voice. "I don't need to be divinely shocked into reality by that kind of electrifying experience!"

An hour later, the horrible Cyclops finally entered his dark cave, accompanied by an obedient herd of bleating sheep. The monster carried with him a big load of firewood to light near his wooden supper table, still loaded with whey and rancid goat meat. The hideous-looking giant flung the heavy timbers onto the ground, and the impact sounded like a wicked clap of thunder, almost scaring the entrails out of the Greek trespassers' unlucky thirteen rectums.

The gargantuan Cyclops then used a wooden rod to drive the remainder of his fattened ewes and she-goats inside the cavern, leaving the horny male goats, and the rambunctious rams, outside to gaily screw one another, rather than penetrate the females of their own species, now trapped inside the colossal cave. Then, the ugly, fierce behemoth, demonstrating the strength of two-dozen strong, healthy men, rolled a huge stone in front of the cave's entrance, preventing any of the domesticated creatures from randomly escaping to the outside.

"We're trapped inside this freakin' hellhole!" Odysseus whispered to his frightened crewmembers. "Who says a 'rolling stone' gathers no moss!"

"I think it was Mik Jagged that once said that fucked-up cliche, and he's the lead singer in a major 'rock' group back in Mycenae!" the first mate aptly recalled and replied. "Jagged's notorious for inventing silly, meaningless, hackneyed, bull-crap aphorisms like that one you just mentioned!"

"Quiet, Asshole!" Odysseus uttered, a little too loudly. "Quit farting out of your mouth! That big jerk-off might overhear your zany, nauseous comments!"

The men's ridiculous conversation echoed throughout the cavern, and the dialogue had distracted the Cyclops, who was about to piss a hundred-gallons of urine onto a sidewall of the already-stenchy, foul-smelling cave. "Strangers; who is foolishly speaking so loud over there that a deaf person could hear your inane drivel?" the Cyclops asked in a booming voice. "Are you A) traders, B) rovers, C) soldiers, D) thieves and trespassing pirates, or E) A combination of all of the above?"

The intruders were scared out of their wits until Odysseus mustered sufficient courage to address the towering, malicious ogre. "Kind Sir; we are Achaeans returning from the vanquished city of Troy," the Greek champion proudly began. "And Zeus's supreme will has detoured us to your beautiful land. We have come in peace!"

"Oh ycah!" bellowed the grotesque one-eyed giant. "You' dumb- fucks have come in peace, but you'll most certainly leave in pieces! Ha, ha, ha, ha!"

"I beg you, Lord," Odysseus continued a little 'bolder' from standing behind a boulder. "Please show some fear of Zeus's wrath, and demonstrate some respect for the almighty *Olympians*. We've come to you as suppliants, under the protection of Zeus, the travelers' god, and the avenger of all foreigners, and the faithful ally of legal and illegal aliens in distress, while aimlessly wandering on the world's highways, or sailing upon the high seas!"

The unimpressed-and-nasty Cyclops laughed lustily, and then disrespectfully answered, "Stranger; *you* are certainly an ignorant dolt coming to this land so naively. I fear not your asshole gods, and I mock their puny vengeance," the monster insisted. "I'm much more potent that any of your timid, weakling gods, and I shall now show my great animosity towards you and your absurd laws and customs," the one-eyed brute boasted. "And if your' midget-god Zeus were to appear inside this cave right now, I would pull down my animal furs from my torso, and then directly shit on *his* pointed noggin, while the fuck-head is standing erect next to me. Ha, ha, ha, ha!"

"You speak quite haughtily for a fellow who merely lives in a primitive cave!" Odysseus ridiculed his new-found adversary. "For the amount of advanced culture that *you* have developed on this wretched island, you must sleep, shit, and jerk-off all day long for how much progress you've achieved since the ancient dawn of mythology!"

The Cyclops didn't like being harassed and chastised by a mere six-foot-tall man, so the deformed giant figured he would stall for time, so that the cave-dweller could capture and kill his egocentric, antagonistic tormentor. "Tell me, brave Intruder," the big bruiser replied. "Where is your ship anchored? Is it around the inlet, or is it moored straight off the land?" the monster asked as *he* began systematically searching and sniffing around, attempting to trace the exact location of the little wise-ass mortal that had been mercilessly berating him.

Odysseus knew *he* had to think quickly, but the Greek warrior was too foolish to realize that the Cyclops didn't give two flying turds about anything the Achaean king would say. The reprehensible stalker only wanted to discover the location of the voice's origin, and then exterminate the mocker's vocal cords, along with any companions that might have stupidly strayed into *his* domain.

"Poseidon, awesome god of the sea, forced my ship to crash upon the rocks at the south end of this miserable, forsaken place," Odysseus lied. "And it is so severely shipwrecked that neither my friends nor I will ever be able to repair the extensive damage to the hull! Thanks to Zeus's mercy, my crew and I have evaded the jaws of death!"

The Cyclops stretched his grimy, vile hand into the dismal shadows, his grasp reaching behind a prominent boulder, and the ruthless brute clutched two of the paranoid, crouching crewmen. The creature easily picked-up the pair of warriors into the air, and then smashed the petrified bodyguards' skulls against the rock-solid floor, splitting open their craniums, with their worm-like brains oozing-out. Then, showing no compassion for human dead, the pagan Cyclops ripped each of the two soldiers' limbs from their torsos, just like pulling the legs off a dead crab. And without even heating the fresh meat in the crackling fire, the fearsome fiend disgustingly gobbled-up the chewed flesh, and spit out the bones from the victims' mangled appendages.

The eleven appalled human witnesses to the cave carnage knew not what to do, except gasp in horror at the totally despicable, cannibalistic act, and solemnly pray for the souls of the dearly-departed, who were now the dearly-separated, and also, the very dearly-consumed.

When the carnivorous Cyclops had filled his tank-like stomach, and after he had washed-down his meal with ten-gallons of whey, the mammoth creature further exhibited his great disdain for trespassing Greeks. The Titan-sized barbarian lied-down on the ground in ankle-deep sheep shit, resting among squealing goats, and then dozed-off like a bear that had gorged itself' with a winter's supply of fat and protein.

Odysseus was profoundly motivated to grab his sword and drive it deeply into the Cyclops' inhuman heart, but then the discreet leader considered something rather salient. If the hero were successful at killing the evil monster by thrusting *his* sword into the vile creature's heart, then surely, *he* and his remaining men would never be capable of moving the enormous stone away from the cave's entrance in order to exit. So, the Greek hero and his men simply sat there all night long thinking, 'Fuck! Fuck! Fuck!' a hundred-thousand-times each, until shafts of light filtered through the circumference of the cavern's blocked entrance, signaling that welcomed morning had finally arrived.

The Cyclops arose from his deep slumber, and then brushed some of the excessive sheep and goat crap off of his fur clothing; his arms; legs; and face. The vile villain again ignited his woodpile, milked his ewes and goats, and then remembered that he had trespassers hiding somewhere within the cave's confined perimeter. The disgusting, heartless dickhead gathered-up two more of Odysseus's personal bodyguards, and thrust their heads onto the cavern's solid-rock floor, dashing-out their brains with pints of blood squirting into the air in all directions. Then, *he* breakfasted as the fierce cannibal had supped, licking his fingers that were coated with layers of human blood and smelly sheep shit.

"He just ate two more of my men!" Odysseus panted to his knee-knocking companions. "He's a lawless fanatic!"

"The giant is too uncivilized to even be a homosexual," Eurshiddenme, the gay first mate regretted, "because the Cyclops just doesn't suck dick. He swallows the man's pecker, along with the rest of the victimized victim, in one tremendous gulp! What a fuckin' pitiful waste of humanity!"

The primitive brute then rolled the huge circular stone back against the cave's sidewall, allowing his ewes and his goats to venture-out into the sunshine to graze and be screwed by the lustful rams, and by any other animals waiting outside. Then, the monstrous hulk adroitly rolled the huge rock back from outside the cave, as if the twenty-ton object weighed only twenty-pounds. Finally, the shrewd Achaean king had time to plot a definite plan to defeat his extremely treacherous, unethical foe.

"Let's slice his balls and dick off and barbecue them over the fire!" mate number one intelligently recommended. "I haven't sampled Greek meatballs in over twenty years."

"No, Asshole," Odysseus emphatically disagreed. "This Cyclops doesn't have any wife or kids, nor does the ugly bachelor bastard want any of those fucked-up headaches. His penis and testicles bring him no natural pleasure, except maybe by means of masturbation and urination! Boy, I'd hate to be splattered against this solid rock wall by one of *his* prodigious ejaculations!" the itinerant king ejaculated. "I hope that's not a *coming* event!"

"Well then, we could pierce his jugular vein with our spears and have him fuckin' bleed to death!" Eurballsourout, the second mate, smartly suggested.

"No, Jerk-off; that would be too damned messy!" Odysseus objectively countered. "The wacky brute might have some unknown contagious venereal blood disease that might kill us a month from now. And besides," the Ithacan king deliberately proceeded and lectured, "if *he* moves, and we miss the jugular while attacking his neck from both sides, we might accidentally pierce his ears, and the fucked-up giant might get the idea of wearing two of us as decorative earrings. I can't take that remote chance. And furthermore," Odysseus elaborated, "we could never roll that immense stone back, and be able to escape from this shit-laden cave. We must decisively punish the gargantuan asshole, without killing him!"

The brazen Achaean king then disclosed a nifty plan to his perceptive subordinates, who wholeheartedly endorsed the proposal, after Odysseus promised the remaining commando idiots than each one could screw Queen

192

Penelope, and munch on her delicious pink pussy-hole upon their safe return to Ithaca, which *he* believed was highly unlikely to ever really happen.

The Cyclops kept a great club, the size of a ship's mast, lying next to one of his sheep pens. The fearless king instructed the remaining crewmen to use their swords and cut off a ten-foot-length of the massive staff, and then carefully shave-down the head until it was shaped into a hard, sharp, wooden point. The beam's tip was soon charred in the fire as phase one of the "stake-out" had been satisfactorily completed.

The mighty Cyclops eventually returned from outside, and after re-entering the dismal cave, again rolled the tremendous stone to effectively block the entrance. The monster next snatched-up two more of Odysseus's men, and heinously snacked on them, just like he had done with the other unfortunate victims.

"Well," the king said to his remaining, apprehensive companions. "We started-out with unlucky thirteen, and now we've been dwindled-down to a mere lucky seven. Just think men," Odysseus eloquently revealed. "This is really to your advantage, because now, with six men dead, you'll all have more-time shafting Queen Penelope, day and night, and chomping on her sumptuous, wet, pink vagina upon returning to Ithaca."

"Boss," said Eurshiddenme, the gay first mate. "We would stand more of a chance of living after drinking a five-gallon jug of hemlock than ever having the pleasure of either screwing your beautiful wife, or lapping and buttering-up her moist muffin! And anyway, I would only sodomize Penelope if she's a goddamned practicing lesbian!"

Showing his magnificent, steadfast courage, Odysseus stepped forward with a large bowl filled with the delicious black wine that the priest of Apollo, Maron, had maron-ated and given to him. "Here kind sir," the clever interloper offered the Cyclops. "Sip some of this splendid wine I had originally brought to your home as a gift, as is the custom of travelers seeking Lord Zeus's protection. My illustrious host, please drink man's rich wine to wash-down the taste of man's rich flesh!"

The Cyclops hesitated, but then accepted the bowl, and drank-down its fabulous contents; the imbiber had never before tasted wine, because the brute had never learned how to ferment liquid from grapes, and produce the wonderful substance.

"Er, da, that tasted very good!" the ugly one-eyed monstrosity conceded. "It tastes better than grape juice, or even better than pussy juice, for that matter. This drink indeed must be the nectar and the ambrosia that strangers to this land have told me about. It is definitely the drink of the gods that'll indeed make me immortal!" Cyclops generalized. "Give me some more, so that I may live beyond all eternity! Ha, ha, ha, ha!" the crazed behemoth chortled like the demented lunatic that *he* was.

Odysseus filled the bowl three more times, and the dumb-fuck Cyclops greedily consumed the fine, smooth-tasting wine, stating that he never tasted such a wonderful "elixir-type laxative". And then, the inebriated giant asked the stouthearted Achaean king, "What is your name, oh generous stranger?"

"My damned name is No Man," Odysseus wisely answered. "And my mother, father, friends and enemies all address me by that terrific title. I hate my friggin' name with a passion!" the king exaggerated. "So, watch exactly how you use your smart-assed *No Man*-clature!"

"You're more fucked-up than your fucked-up gods are! Do you know that logical fact, No Man!" the Cyclops bellowed until he nearly started a serious landslide, or a turbulent earthquake outside the cavern. "You're so funny you ought to do stand-up comedy in an amphitheater without any seats! Ha, ha, ha, ha! Suck a red rooster's red cock, you little cock-sucking dick-licker! Ha! Ha! Ha! Ha!"

"Odysseus, watch what you say to this horrible, ungodly thing!" Eurshiddenme, the first mate cautioned. "This fellow does not honor any laws, and respects nothing that *we* value! Not even luscious pussy or homosexuality!"

"That's right!" Eurballsourout, the second mate, concurred with Eurshiddenme. "This big lummox respects *no man,* gay or fuckin' straight!"

"That's precisely my goal," Odysseus honestly replied. "This big jerk-off is gonna' learn to respect No Man!"

Then, the cruel fifty-foot-tall oaf' temporarily cleared his groggy head and declared, "I'll greedily eat all of No Man's comrades first, and then save *his* tender skin and dick for last. This is the gift I shall give to No Man in exchange for this savory wine from your fucked-up priest's vine! This juice is for Zeus!" the crazy, pea-brain oaf laughed as *he* held-up his half-full bowl toward the cave's curved ceiling.

After the repugnant giant bragged, and again sarcastically mocked Odysseus's chief deity, the intoxicated Cyclops tumbled onto, and then sprawled upon the cave's rock-floor, stoned out of his mind, which indeed was a very mini-mind in proportion to the enormity of *his* total anatomy. The drunken monster became quite animated, and then while lying there, soon belched-up a gallon of wine, along with the semi-digested flesh of his last two consumed humans. He next spit the essence of his guts to the posterior area of the cave, and the horrible debris splattered onto the faces of the seven remaining Greek survivors.

"I hope he barfs-out his intestines, and then goes to sleep," Odysseus told his comrades as the giant cretin, not a giant Cretan, wiped the repulsive vomit from his arms and from his cheeks. "This uncouth Cyclops is gonna' pay for his insolence to our honored values, and for his sacrilegious defiance of our gods!"

"How's he gonna' pay?" Eurshiddenme asked. "They ain't got no money system on this freakin' freak-show island of totally demented freaks!"

"I meant that the Cyclops is gonna' be punished for committin' cannibalism, and for doing sacrilegious things in excess. Hubris will ultimately sentence this impudent, fat, barbaric asshole to a deserving fate," the Greek king bluntly asserted.

"This over-inflated shit-head thinks he's a god, so let's smash him with the stake right in his *temple!*" Eurballsourout candidly suggested.

"No Eurballsourout!" Odysseus objected. "I have a much better idea to implement!"

After the Cyclops finally stopped vomiting all over the damned place in his sleep, the Greek king and the remaining crewmen lifted the wooden beam the 'guests' had hidden under three-foot-deep sheep and goat dung. The six warriors and their itinerant captain again heated the charred tip inside the blazing fire, and after rotating the pole for a full ten minutes until the searing beam sizzled inside the roaring flames, the enraged entourage madly ran forward, and violently thrust the red-hot spike into the center of the Cyclops' single eye.

"Take that, Shit-head; since you think you're such hot stuff!" Eurshiddenme yelled at his avowed enemy.

"Now your eye will be a real eyesore!" Eurballsourout frankly hollered at his avowed enemy, adding insult to injury.

"The center of your eye has now become one of my *pupils!*" Odysseus gleefully shouted like a proud schoolmaster. "Now you can't keep an eye out for us any more, you dumb bastard!"

"Yowllllllll! Owwwwww!" the pained Cyclops thundered as the brute was rudely awakened from his drunken slumber. "Hey, I can't see a goddamned fuckin' thing! What's this damned hissing sound coming from inside my eye!" the huge retard hideously screamed as the giant twisted, and then yanked the sizzling, flaming timber from the center of his now-scorched and blinded eye.

Other Cyclopes in the vicinity heard the noisy racket, and were curious as to what the source of the clamor might be. Three of them gathered outside the cave and yelled inside to their awesome, bellicose neighbor.

"What is the matter, Polyphemus? What is bothering you? Did you accidentally ejaculate a ten-pound load backwards into your balls, or what?" a somewhat-concerned Cyclopes yelled inside the still-closed cave entrance.

"Polyphemus, what has happened? Did you accidentally crush your dick on a rock while slamming-down a sledgehammer?" a second inquisitive giant hypothesized and shouted inside.

The still-delirious and drunken Polyphemus boisterously shouted from the cave's interior, "No Man is killing me! No Man is fuckin' killing me!"

"Surely, Polyphemus; no man is capable of killing a fearsome giant like you," a surprised and amused neighbor replied from outside. "You must be hallucinating. *No man* has the strength, or the physical force to do you any significant harm!"

"Listen fuck-heads. I need your goddamned help!" the wounded and distraught blinded giant vehemently answered. "I tell you, neighbors; No Man has attacked and blinded me! No Man has fuckin' attacked and blinded me!"

"Well then, Polyphemus; if no man has attacked and blinded you," the first mountain cave resident concluded, "then what the fuck are ya' complainin' about? Stop annoying us with such bad, illogical, nonsensical riddles! Everyone knows that one puny man can't assault and blind a fifty-foot-tall jerk-off like you! It's just not fuckin' plausible!" the Cyclopes neighbor chided. "Just fondle and flog your log; pop a big load, and go the hell back to sleep! See ya' tomorrow, ya' big pouting crybaby!"

"No! Stop! Listen to me!" Polyphemus screamed and shrieked like a raving maniac. "No Man has blinded me! Do you hear me? No Man has fuckin' blinded me!"

"Why don't you do something constructive, like committing suicide!" the third voice remarked from the cave's exterior. "Goodbye Polyphemus, you dumb, melodramatic, thespian fuck!"

Odysseus and his crewmen laughed incessantly at the blinded Cyclops' very apparent frustration. The clumsy, injured ogre sat with his back leaning against the rock wall, regretting that he had been born with only one eye in the center of his head, and now was blinded for the rest of his accursed tenure on his ass-backwards island. But the creative Odysseus, who was renowned for inventing clever solutions to difficult dilemmas, still had to devise a viable method of escaping the cave and its blocked entrance.

It was now daybreak, and time for Polyphemus to rotate the incredibly huge stone, and allow his ewes and goats to leave the cave to graze, to screw, and to shit in the sunshine. The big, hulking, blinded bully sat at the cavern's entrance and felt in front, on top, and in between the evacuating animals to ascertain that "No Man" escaped *his* intensive search. Odysseus keenly scrutinized the giant's careful practice, and planned a strategy to counteract the wounded creep's predictable habit of "feel and seizure".

Odysseus pondered and meditated, knowing full-well that a poor decision would cost him his life, along with the lives of his remaining bodyguards.

Quite ingeniously, the following morning, the Greek king found some leather straps, and tethered together large sheep in groups of three. Each of the anxious surviving warriors crawled under the belly of the center sheep, and fastened his legs inside the straps, holding-on to the middle animal's fleece with *his* raised bare hands.

The hungry, healthy sheep rapidly rushed-out into the sunshine to feed. The vengeful Cyclops meticulously felt the fronts, sides, and tops of each set of three sheep passing by his tactile inspection, but not once suspecting that the conniving Greeks had escaped under the belly of the center sheep in the groups of three that passed-by.

As Odysseus's set of three sheep finally made it to the cave's entrance, the Cyclops reached-down, felt the top of the center animal and declared, "My favorite, most-treasured sheep. Why are you last to leave today? You are usually the leader; the proudest of my flourishing flock!"

Odysseus's heart was pounding so loudly inside his chest that the wandering Ithacan King feared that the blind Cyclops might detect the abnormally-distinct beating. Right when the petrified Greek Captain started pissing himself, the Cyclops delivered some additional, sentimental monologue.

"I know kind and faithful animal," the horrible monster proceeded with his sad commentary, "that you must feel badly because you sense that your master can no longer see. No Man has blinded me, and I must make retribution and kill the dirty, son-of-a-bitchin' scum. I know that if you could talk, you' pathetic beast," the Cyclops affectionately stated, "you would tell me exactly where my principal adversary is hiding. I would crush his bones with my bare hands; collide his head with the walls, and then impact his skull with the solid rock floor; spilling and smearing his brains all over the fuckin' cave, until there is not an ounce of blood left in his petty, rotten, human heart!"

When Odysseus finally escaped the cave, the hero freed himself from his straps, and then assisted his men in being un-tethered from the center sheep in each set of three animals tied together. And with the attitude of genuine plunderers, the ecstatic Greeks led the sheep and goats in a bizarre parade down to the anchored ship, where the remaining crewmen accepted the procession of pilfered animals aboard.

Then, Odysseus told his well-disciplined men not to weep for their deceased comrades, for their cries of mourning might be discerned by Cyclops's sensitive auditory perception. The Greek king still feared that the horrendous freak might still be capable of doing significant damage to the main warship, despite Polyphemus's recent blindness handicap.

When the vessel lifted anchor and quietly sailed a hundred-yards out into the clear-blue harbor, Odysseus garnered enough courage to spitefully and scornfully address his blinded enemy. "Cyclops!" the haughty mariner yelled-up at the top of his lungs. "You have sinned against omnipotent Zeus, and against the sacred laws of *Mt. Olympus.* You have rightfully been punished for the evils that you have egregiously committed, and you justly suffer for the outrageous disrespect you've shown toward guests visiting in your land, and toward *their* gods and customs!"

The furious giant lividly grabbed hold of a nearby mountain crag, and flung the ultra-heavy object in the direction from which he believed Odysseus's taunting had originated. The Cyclops's heave landed and splashed in the shallow harbor, and came within a breadth's length of destroying the ship's rudder. An enormous wave surged, and its force then propelled the vessel back near the island's desolate beach.

Odysseus tacitly signaled to his crew to row and not to speak, for the chief raider dreaded that the desperate avenger would become even more provoked; would manage to get lucky with another mountain peak toss, and would successfully sink the warship with a broadside hit.

"That idiot almost-demolished my Bireme and murdered my crew!" the commando leader finally admitted. "I'm glad we had blinded the savage bastard, and I'm also happy that it is now time to relish the taste of sweet revenge!"

"The asshole has thrown one boulder already, and driven us all the way back to the friggin' shoreline," Eurshiddenme protested. "So please, Boss; don't antagonize him any more until we're outside his firing range!" the scared-shitless first mate implored his sometimes all-too-arrogant captain.

"I hope I will be still-born in my next life, because I never want to experience any more fucked-up misadventures like this one!" Eurballsourout confided to his very excellent king.

"Cyclops!" Odysseus loudly challenged when the vessel was officially three-hundred-yards or so out into the harbor. "If anyone ever asks you who had taken your eye out and blinded you, tell that inquiring asshole that the brave warrior was Odysseus, King of Ithaca, and son of Laertes!"

The incensed Cyclops then recalled the essence of an old prophecy told to him by the soothsayer Telemus, son of Eurymus, who had predicted that a man named 'Odysseus' would handily blind the fanatical bastard during a major dispute. But Polyphemus was expecting to confront a hundred-foot-tall *Adonis* kicking *his* big ass on *his* own turf, and not a little runt like the Ithacan King, getting the arduous job done under the alias of 'No Man'.

"Come back Odysseus," the Cyclops hollered-out to the apathetic, deaf sea. "So that I, the son of the sea-god Poseidon, can give you gifts to take back to Ithaca. Come back, and I shall treat you like the royalty you really are!"

"Go fuck yourself', you big, cock-sucking asshole!" Odysseus screamed as loud as he could. "Do you think me half as stupid as yourself? You're just as blind to truth as you are to sight, you oversized, dumb-ass, no-eyed, blind fuck!"

Then, vengeful Polyphemus cupped his hands to his mouth and grievously shouted skyward, beckoning, "Oh great Poseidon; hear my plea! If I am indeed your son, as everyone on this fucked-up island claims that I am, see to it that Odysseus's shipmates never make it back to Ithaca alive! Let all of his scumbag sailors perish, and let Odysseus return home as a passenger in a foreign ship, and discover his palace in full disarray, and later finds his wife pregnant with another man's triplets!"

Poseidon heard his distraught son's urgent plea, and so the sea god yelled-back to his begotten son, "You stupid shit! I am the god of the sea, and I rule all the oceans from underwater with my trident as my royal scepter! Why are you praying up to heaven, when that is my brother Zeus's fuckin' domain!" Poseidon loudly reprimanded his orphaned offspring. "Now I know why I never visit you and your shit-eating Cyclopes' friends anymore! What a fuckin' waste you; they, and your whole asshole island subculture happen to be! Your land ought to sink into the friggin' sea, and be quickly swallowed-up in its eddying maelstrom!"

"Well, men," Odysseus announced to his crew of hardy rowers. "Poseidon has now disowned his own blinded son, but the fickle god has promised to kick our asses good in future episodes of our most-difficult, ongoing *Odyssey*."

"We're all going to die because of your insolent aggressiveness, and because of your inflexible impudence," Eurballsourout complained to his noble-but-imprudent king. "And if we never had sailed to that forbidden island behind us, we would not now be cursed and abused by the ruthless sea-god, nor would we have lost our colleagues to that terrible, blind, sore-loser monster, pouting and whimpering up there!"

"You're absolutely right," Eurshiddenme aptly agreed with Eurballsourout. "And Odysseus, thanks for earning *our* execution from Poseidon as retribution for blinding *his* damned ugly, freak of a son. And as for you," Eurshiddenme continued his tirade, "my King; your punishment will be the greatest of all! You'll have to live for at least twenty more years in Ithaca, after both Eurballsourout and I are fuckin' dead and gone. Our spirits will be resting in the Elysian daffodil fields planted in the good sector of *Hades,* while you're still alive, trying to fuckin' govern your screwed-up kingdom."

"You're absolutely right in your prediction, Eurshiddenme," Odysseus glumly acknowledged. "For I am the one who is really cursed at sea, and later fated to be doomed in Ithaca, by having to live through the bulk of Poseidon's wicked wrath!"

"Oedipus"

Oedipus did not have eight strange-looking arms like his deformed, ugly, twin brother Octopus had. Octopus had been hurled into the sea, where he and his descendants have been denizens, molesters, and predators ever since. Oedipus was the great-great grandson of a cad named Cadmus, who was a great-great pain-in-the-ass, who was so fucked-up that the gods decided all of *his* degenerate future generations (including Oedipus) should be doomed to suffer great hardship and adversity, in order to make them even more fucked-up than the dumb-shits already were.

King Laius of Thebes (who liked to get laid, but had a bisexual wife that inexplicably had cement formed inside her narrow vagina), was the third ruler of that dysfunctional ancient Greek city, a half-century after Cadmus had reigned in Thebes. According to his regal family's fucked-up tradition, the royal pain-in-the-ass Laius married a first cousin, whose name was Jocastra.

Soon, Oedipus came under the influence of Apollo's *Oracle at Delphi,* which was far worse than being under the influence of drugs, tobacco, *MTV* and alcohol. The Oracle actually fucked-up Oedipus even more than his fucked-up genetics had biologically fucked-up both his twin brother Octopus and himself.

Apollo was the Greek chariot god of music, medicine, legal and illegal drugs, and of truth or consequences. The Mt. Olympus deity communicated with humans through his famous *Oracle at Delphi,* a lesbian priestess with a clitoris bigger than all five of her tits put together. Laius had gone to the despised *Oracle of Delphi* to get laid, but when the nut-job discovered that the priestess was a lesbian nymphomaniac with a clit bigger than his erection, the wimpy dunce reluctantly asked her to tell him his future, instead.

"Laius, you will die *at the hands* of one of your sons; that is, after you throw Octopus into the sea for good riddance," the totally gay, demented priestess predicted.

"How could that be?" Laius incredulously challenged the Oracle's omniscient prophecy. "Octopus is more likely to kill me with eight arms, and my other son Oedipus has only two hands. How then am I to die at the hands of Oedipus? I could just cut his damned hands off by creating a new "Hands-off edict" in my totally-bizarre kingdom of Thebes!"

"Apollo says in these chicken entrails that it's *your* fuckin' problem, Asshole!" the faggot Oracle told Laius, who was now doubly disappointed, because the numbskull couldn't get laid with his gay wife, who had mysteriously formed cement in her crotch, and now because he had learned that his son Oedipus was going to brutally murder his ass.

When Laius had tossed Octopus into the sea one rainy October morning, Oedipus was still an infant, but not old enough to join the Theban infantry. Laius realized that close genetics indeed did have certain physical and psychological repercussions, and that the famous Greek maxim "Incest is best!" might actually be a blatant fallacy, if indeed, Oedipus was destined to slaughter the king.

'Octopus was genetically defective, and looked-like an absolute disgusting monster,' Laius lamented. 'And now, Oedipus looks all right physically, but the kid might be a fuckin' crazy lunatic, mentally-speaking. I gotta' dispose of the insane bastard before he eliminates my ass from this insane Earth! My mother always warned me to stay away from gloom and doom fortunetellers! Sometimes, I wish I weren't such a stupid, stubborn, retarded jerk-off!'

Laius gave a faithful servant the *complex* baby *Oedipus* to carry to a secluded mountain, which was so distant that area mountain goats had not yet even discovered it. The obedient servant tied the infant's feet together, but did not have the heart to leave Laius's remaining son on top of a lonely precipice to die.

'I can socially engineer my future much better than that homosexual dyke Oracle's predictions can,' Laius obstinately thought. 'By Zeus, her goddamned clitoris was twice as large as my biggest erection! That freakin' Oracle was more of a freakin' freak than my ugly son by incest Octopus was!'

Twenty-years later, King Laius came to a very important crossroads in his life. He and his traveling entourage of bisexual bodyguards got into an intense argument with a young punk' hooligan over the right-of-way at an intersection that was devoid of a "Stop Sign". The pugnacious hooligan leaped-out of his souped-up chariot; accosted Laius and his four intoxicated bodyguards; and after a vitriolic argument ensued, the punk whippersnapper first beat the shit out of, and then allegedly slaughtered the five wimpy, drunken adults with his bronze sword. The young thug-murderer happened to be Oedipus, and by slaying his father, he had fulfilled Apollo's pathetic prophecy that had been forecast by the lesbian *Oracle at Delphi*.

A rumor circulated around Thebes that an army from the city of Athens had slaughtered Laius, along with his loyal bodyguards. The heavy gossip thus glorified the former despicable, feckless Theban king as a warrior, and as a martyr. However, one of the bodyguards had not died in the melee, and had only been critically wounded. A traveling fruit and vegetable huckster had stopped his oxcart at the intersection where the altercation had occurred; picked-up the sole survivor, and transported the lucky asshole to the crowded marketplace in Thebes.

Now, no one in Thebes (not even *his* wife/cousin Jocastra) gave a flying shit about Laius's cruel death, because the city was then being besieged by a very great threat. A monster that was known as "the Sphinx" had been terrorizing and killing any Thebans who dared venture outside the city's southern gates. The Sphinx had a lion's body; eagle wings; a woman's face; a female elephant's tits and ass, and a fantastically gigantic clitoris, even bigger than the one that the *Oracle at Delphi* had.

The venomous creature clandestinely hid in waiting, and halted any traveler it confronted on his or her way to Thebes. The Sphinx presented the apprehended trekker with a ridiculous riddle, and when the unfortunate traveler could not give the correct response under great duress, in a one-minute time period, the horrible creature ferociously devoured man after man alive, first sucking, and then eating their tender dicks, and then chewing-up and swallowing the remainder of their predestined, doomed bodies; flesh, blood, sweat, tears, piss, shit, and all.

After Laius's funeral, attended by three people, the seven great gates that allowed entrance into and exiting Thebes were permanently closed, and within a month, the citizens began suffering from severe famine and pestilence. Worse yet, the horrid Sphinx had devoured most of the Theban men, and consequently Jocastra and the other promiscuous ladies of the accursed city became even bigger lesbians, in the absence of eligible males, than the fucked-up *Oracle at Delphi* ever was.

Soon, a total stranger with exaggerated physical features similar to those of the deceased King Laius arrived at Thebes. The brawny newcomer knocked-down one of the gates, and egotistically entered the city. The intruder was intelligent, intrepid, obnoxious, arrogant, and audacious. He introduced himself' to the usually apathetic Theban citizens as Oedipus the Fifteenth, from Corinth, and the son of entrepreneurial King Polybus, who owned a fleet of chariot and oxcart taxi cabs.

"I am in self-exile," Oedipus told his new acquaintance Jocastra outside the regal palace. "The *Oracle at Delphi* had told me that I was destined to kill my father, which oftentimes is not a bad idea for wise-ass, acne-faced teenagers to consider."

"So, why have you come to Thebes, stranger?" Jocastra asked her itinerant son, Oedipus, whom she never recognized. "Aren't you afraid that the Sphinx will consume you? She has a fuckin' *edible complex* about men, ya' know!"

"I didn't want to kill my father, Polybus," Oedipus lied to his biological mother, "because I am a strict practicing heterosexual, and it is a myth in Corinth that Polybus eats from a magical cunt tree, out in the country. If I was to savagely kill my father Polybus, then I could not learn where this magical cunt tree out in the country actually is located!"

"I have planted a similar tree in the center of my palace bedroom," Jocastra confided and informed Oedipus, presuming that her son had been dead for many years atop the distant mountain peak. "But only my lady friends and I are allowed to eat the delicious fruit of the womb from my bedroom cunt tree, which is not out in the country!"

Oedipus set-out on foot to walk from Thebes to Corinth to locate King Polybus's famed mythical cunt tree out in the country. On his ramble, the tragic hero encountered the wicked, detestable Sphinx, who then presented her singular riddle for the guilty wanderer to solve in one minute's time.

"What creature walks on four legs in the morning, two at noon, and three appendages in the evening?" the contemptible monster nefariously asked the hero.

"That's easy, Bitch!" Oedipus confidently replied. "The answer obviously is 'a man'. As an infant, the child creeps and crawls on all fours all over the fuckin' place; in manhood, he walks erect, with or without an erection, and in old age, a man walks with his staff, and if he doesn't have any goddamned secretaries, the jerk-off walks alone with his fuckin' cane, without his fuckin' staff. What do ya' *Sphinx* about that incredible bull-shit, you dumb fuckin', cocksuckin', riddling man-eater!"

Oedipus had amazingly delivered the correct response to the monster's cryptic conundrum. The Sphinx was so pissed-off that she killed herself by first biting her gigantic swollen clitoris off, and subsequently, bleeding to death, and finally, dramatically plunging-off of her high cliff.

Thanks to Oedipus's mental dynamics, the Thebans had been miraculously saved from their wretched nemesis. The jubilant numbskulls transported their new-found champion into the city, and gave Oedipus a terrific hero's welcome. The happy revelers merrily roasted the disgusting dead creature in *ancient grease,* carved-up the Sphinx's corpse, and ate fresh meat at a splendid barbecue and *hot wings* feast.

At the jubilant All-Meat Banquet Buffet, the grateful citizens quickly elected Oedipus as their new king, and Jocastra was pissed-off that she had to marry a young stud with a big dick, because it violated her avowed lesbianism, and also, because his thrusting pecker would naturally force the concrete in her vagina all the way up to her windpipe, whenever she would have to engage in *straight* sex with her royal son.

It seemed to Jocastra that Apollo's prophecy, delivered by the *Oracle at Delphi,* had been false, since Oedipus the Fifteenth was believed to be the son of King Polybus of Corinth, who claimed that he had secretly gotten a vasectomy at the age of four.

Jocastra reluctantly allowed Oedipus to screw her, and that's exactly how Oedipus became the biggest ball-breaking (and vagina breaking) mother-fucker in all history. That sinful incest behavior inadvertently brought a terrible plague, administered by Zeus, to Thebes. Men died from venereal diseases all over the place, and it didn't matter whether the horny assholes were screwing their wives, their girlfriends, or sodomizing sheep, or ramming rams during that fucked-up, toxic time of lethal peril.

Herds of animals, and orchards of fruit, also inexplicably died. It was even rumored that King Polybus of Corinth's, and Thebes' Queen Jocastra's cunt trees had both dried-up; had shriveled, and then had regrettably expired. And those unlucky mortals that didn't die from sex diseases, or who were eliminated in the next locust invasion, were then also plagued by an atrocious famine. Oedipus felt guilty for living on the damned Earth, and possibly having caused the devastating 'damnations' all over his damned nation.

Oedipus was developing a complex about all of the disasters that were occurring in and around Thebes. He dispatched his Uncle Creon (Jocastra's older brother who still liked coloring books) to the notoriously gay *Oracle at Delphi* for the purpose of learning how the abominable plague, and the formidable famine, could be eliminated.

Creon returned with meritorious news. The *Oracle* (whose heart, as you already know, had only one auricle) revealed that Apollo would lift the wicked curses, only on one outstanding stipulation. "Whoever had killed King Laius at the crossroads must be severely punished," Creon wrote with his favorite coal crayon, for all to see on a scroll of papyrus, and then being read as distasteful graffiti all over the city's walls.

"I'm relieved, and I haven't even taken a decent shit!" Oedipus told Creon. "Surely, by virtue of the Oracle's definite words, the men, or the individual, that had killed King Laius must still be alive, and can be captured and brought to justice. Then, Oedipus spoke to his disgruntled, pissed-off subjects from the palace balcony:

Citizens and Assholes of Thebes: Let none of you *harbor* the killer of Laius, since Thebes is not located anywhere near an ocean, or anywhere near the sea. Don't give the anonymous murderer of Laius any shelter, including tax annuity shelters, animal shelters, or fuckin' fallout shelters. You are hereby officially directed to bar the obnoxious, anonymous shit-head from your homes and businesses. You must bar the unknown asshole from your taverns. And most importantly, you must bar him from your bars, and also from all your asshole bar *ass*ociations.

Laius's unidentified murderer is a villain that must be condemned, mocked, scorned, tortured, and perpetually whipped and punished. And I sincerely pray that the gutless, cut-throat bastard-assassin's dick rots-off, and that his balls also should become polluted, infected, and contaminated, requiring immediate castration.

Oedipus then sent for Teresias, the hoary blind prophet, and the most-revered of the three remaining Theban men. The soothsayer had once *blind*sided Oedipus, while the prophet was trying to drive a runaway chariot along a narrow alley-way. Teresias's Theban mom was the famous, Mother Teresias.

"Hey Teresias, you' old dumb blind fuck," Oedipus began his greeting. "Use your gift of prophecy to tell me the identity of the men, or man, that had evilly killed King Laius."

"If I told you'," the shrewd, old blind fool cautioned, "you'd be mighty pissed-off. You might first be inclined to beat the shit out of me, or maybe even go into a blind rage! They don't call you Oedipus *wrecks* for nothin', ya' know!"

"For the love and mercy of vindictive, emotionally unstable Zeus," Oedipus continued his stern interrogation, "who the fuck killed Laius? Tell me or I'll dig up Mother Teresias, and have you screw her, you' old blind, limp-dicked mother-fucker!"

"Fools!" Teresias cleverly and enigmatically answered. "Idiotic fools disposed of the former king. Only Laius's smelly asshole has remained

206

from the scene of massacre, and as *you* know, his preserved anus has been on display at the *Theban Proctological Colon Museum.*"

"I suspect that *you* were one of Laius's murderers," Oedipus accused the sightless prophet. "And I believe that you, old man, were having an affair with Jocastra, and that *you* had violated the sacred moral precepts of your Mother Teresias by teaching Jocastra the secret formula for making cement."

Those words angered the aged soothsayer, who then communicated a certain ugly truth to the King. "How's this for some concrete thinking? Oedipus; it is *you* that are the murderer whom you seek! It takes a no-good-bastard to murder a no-good-bastard!"

Oedipus thought that the elderly prophet had gone bizarrely insane, so the new king ordered the mentally-deranged old fart out of the palace. "Disappear, old man," the aggravated King screamed. "And never *come* inside this palace again, until you get your next hard-on, which will be fuckin' never!"

Jocastra had eavesdropped on the whole conversation from behind a curtain, and the former widow had heard the old man's startling testimony to her new husband, and regarded it as being absolute bull-shit. "Prophets and oracles have limited knowledge, just like *we* other mortals do," Jocastra ineffectively argued to her despondent husband/son/king, "and *they* are mere mortals, just the same as we are, and twice as fucked-up, too!"

"Stop speaking in preposterous, asinine riddles, Jocastra," the young king warned. "You're beginning to sound like the insane Sphinx. I made her commit suicide, and I'll make you do the same thing if you persist in bustin' my goddamned balls!"

"Oedipus; there's something salient I must disclose," Jocastra articulated. "The stupid priestess at Delphi prophesied that Laius would die at the hands of his son, so my deceased husband and I saw to it that *you,* our remaining son should be left alone on a distant mountain peak to peacefully die with a yo-yo, while playing rock the cradle. Then, Laius later was murdered near the very busy Bizarre Bazaar Convenience Store at 'Three Points', where the triple dirt roads intersect."

"When the fuck did *that* tragedy happen?" the young king asked his matronly-looking wife.

"Just months before you had arrived in Thebes!" Jocastra instantly answered.

"How many assassins had performed the vile deed?" Oedipus interrogated his demented mother/wife/queen.

"Rumor has it that there were four felons in all," Jocastra replied. "All were killed, but one. The surviving highway thief was picked-up by a traveling hawker, tossed onto the back of the huckster's fruit and vegetable oxcart, and then conveyed into the city."

"I must see and question that lone survivor, for only *he* knows the truth as to what had really transpired that day," Oedipus forcefully demanded. "Send for the dirty old prick right now!"

"I shall summon the suspected survivor," Jocastra promised her impulsive husband/son/king. "But what is the truth from *your* perspective? I mean, I'm your damned wife, and I hardly know a freakin' thing about your past, prior to your coming to Thebes. What do *you* think is your real friggin' ancestry?"

"I shall tell you all that I know about my past history," Oedipus contritely stated. "I had traveled to Delphi to consult Apollo's Oracle. A nobleman back in Corinth had divulged to me that I was not the biological son of King Polybus. I was totally pissed-off, because I thought that I would never inherit *his* fleet of chariot and oxcart taxis, and would never possess his mythical cunt tree, located somewhere out in the country. Anyway," the newly-elected Theban King pontificated. "I was not about to apologize to Apollo for anything. The psychotic priestess at Delphi then told me a most horrible thing."

"That you had herpes, syphilis and gonorrhea?" Jocastra sarcastically asked.

"The fucked-up Oracle foretold that I would kill my father, marry my mother, and would have children uglier than someone named Octopus, and even uglier than the lousy Sphinx. I didn't want to kill Polybus, so I left Corinth and journeyed here to Thebes."

"But you could've been a pillar of the community back in that other city," Jocastra theorized and then communicated. "You could have been a Corinthian column in that other city!"

"Anyway, you dumb, lesbian slut," Oedipus elaborated. "On my way from Delphi to Thebes, I came upon a man and his bodyguards at a crossroads."

"Near the busy Bizarre Bazaar Convenience Store at Three Points?" his middle-aged wife asked in amazement.

"Yes," Oedipus reluctantly verified. "We got into an intense argument as to which one of us had the right of way. There was no 'Yield' or 'Stop' sign at the congested Three Points dirt trail crossroads."

"So, you got cross at the crossroads!" Jocastra nastily criticized. "Like biological father, like biological son, is a very true moral axiom! Some punk delinquent teen vandals must've stolen the damned traffic sign," Jocastra hypothesized and related.

"Anyway," Oedipus interrupted his mother/wife/queen. "The short-tempered man riding on the chariot's platform struck me with his whip, and being a young whippersnapper myself', I swiftly killed the dumb cock-sucker, along with his goddamned weak attendants."

"Holy shit, Oedipus! The one man that had survived the ordeal returned critically wounded to the city on the back of a huckster's oxcart," Jocastra informed her astonished, attentive son. "He reported that Laius had been assassinated by a bandit attempting to get-away with highway robbery. And I then wept for another five-minutes, because my remaining son had died upon a distant mountain peak, and now my bull-headed husband was also dead."

"Did the fear of you' possibly killing your father drive you from leaving Corinth?" Jocastra asked.

"No; it was my black horses and my chariot that drove me from Corinth, and then to Delphi, and then to Three Points near the busy Bizarre Bazaar Convenience Store," Oedipus stupidly divulged.

At that moment, an anxious courier from Corinth coincidentally arrived at the Theban palace to deliver an important message. "King Polybus has died," the messenger solemnly informed Jocastra and her husband/son Oedipus. "He died of a parched tongue, mouth, and throat while eating some dried-up fruit of the womb, growing on his remarkable cunt tree out in the Corinthian country."

"I'm relieved that Polypus died a peculiar natural death rather than being killed by me!" Oedipus vociferously exclaimed. "My false guilt has been satisfactorily eradicated. I'm now vindicated from being accused of committing the alleged vile sin of murdering my father!"

"Polybus was not *your* biological father," the Corinthian King's loyal, secret-keeping servant attested. "The king had raised you from childhood, as if you shared his fucked-up genetics, but you were definitely not the son of King Polybus, and his wife Queen Omnibus."

"Well then, exactly how did I get into the King's hands?" Oedipus insisted on knowing. "Where and how did *you,* or anyone else, get to deliver me to the King of Corinth?"

"I know nothing of your true biological parents," the messenger from Corinth acknowledged. "But a wandering shepherd had found you freezing to death on a mountainside while toying with a yo-yo in your rocking cradle, and then the pleasant peasant presented you to me. I donated you as an orphan to King Polybus and Queen Omnibus," the loyal servant indicated. "Dear Oedipus; I am afraid to disclose that *you* are a mere, red-blooded commoner, presumably the son of impoverished mountain indigents, and a definite impostor to blue-blooded royalty."

"What kind of fuckin' bull-shit is this story you have just told?" Oedipus yelled in a fit of rage. "You' say and assert that I have been discarded by mountain low-life, scumbag parents? I'll have you slain right this minute!"

Jocastra's countenance turned whiter than a lily. Absolute horror radiated from her face. "Oedipus; don't pay any attention to this old, senile Corinthian fuck. He's even more fucked-up than Teresias and *his* dead Mother Teresias. Everything this moron from Corinth has told us has been imaginatively fabricated, except possibly the fact that King Polybus is dead!"

"Jocastra, you are claiming that *my birth* origin doesn't fuckin' matter?" Oedipus impetuously yelled. "You're a bigger bitch than the Sphinx ever was!"

"Say no more, you' pathetic ignoramus," Jocastra admonished her son/husband/king. "My agony and my misery are now complete! I must replenish myself at my cunt tree, situated in the center of my private bedroom garden!"

Teresias then accidentally stumbled into the palace's throne chamber, thinking that he had entered a public restroom to take a three-hour leak. The messenger from Corinth instantly recognized the chief Theban prophet.

"Oh, noble King Oedipus; that's the old fuck shepherd that gave *you* to me," the courier recollected and stated. "He was a blind young fuck shepherd, though, at the time!"

"Hold your tongue!" Teresias balked as the revered soothsayer recognized the voice of his past acquaintance and distant cousin from far-away Corinth.

"Teresias, did you bring me from Thebes to Corinth and place me on top of the mountain?" the shocked Oedipus asked his chief counselor.

"I must confess the truth, and get the whole fuckin' mess off my conscience," the old blind prophet explained. "Your wife Jocastra is also your mother. She and Laius gave you to me for disposal. I didn't have the heart to leave you abandoned up on the foreign mountain, so I presented you to my distant cousin, who then orphaned you to King Polybus and

Queen Omnibus. Quite apparently, my shepherd cousin soon became King Polybus's loyal messenger."

"I made my father into dead meat. I made him into road kill!" Oedipus sobbed. "And today, I am also most grieved upon learning of King Polybus's passing. But worst of all," Oedipus concluded, "the people of Thebes have been right on the money every time the gossipers call me a dirty mother-fucker! Indeed, I have been accursed by that son-of-a-bitchin' Apollo and his lesbian Priestess at Delphi, who had maliciously collaborated, slyly tricking me into marrying my dyke mother!"

"The priestess's prophecy has been fully confirmed," Teresias verified. "You have murdered your biological father at the crossroads; and you have also married your biological mother, who has turned from an active bisexual into a practicing lesbian with a concrete love tunnel. You, dear Oedipus, have been drastically cursed by Phoebus Apollo, and as a result, have been completely fucked-up your whole damned life!"

Oedipus left the Theban throne chamber in a wild, raging state of mind. The youthful king searched the entire palace until he eventually found his mother/wife/queen lying dead inside her private bedroom garden. "She's choked to death eating fruit of the womb from her cunt tree! Her throat is fuckin' clogged with black, brown, blonde and red pubic hair!" the Theban monarch sorrowfully realized and muttered.

Then, Oedipus evaluated th sequence of his entire, fucked-up life. 'I hate viewing and reviewing what fate has presented me,' the King of Thebes regretted in despair. 'I'm going to blind myself and become a disciple of eminent Teresias. It is better to live life blind to its myriad evils, rather than see reprehensible events happening before my very eyes, every fuckin' day. What a lot of stenchy bull-shit both eyesight and human life really are!" Oedipus mourned to his mirror-reflection, inside Jocastra's private garden water-pond, situated next to her now-lethal cunt tree.

"Jason and the Golden Fleecers"

Aeson was the dethroned King of Iolcus, whose infant son Jason was escorted out of the city to safety by a loyal royal adviser to the deposed ruler, during a swift and successful insurrection. The soon-to-be toddler was taken to Chiron, a stern Centaur, who operated the queerest of schools in a remote cave for prospective effeminate boys, who probably would eventually grow-up into full-fledged, gay faggots and transvestites.

Chiron the Centaur was both a quadruped and a bi-penal, meaning that the odd tutor had the legs and body of a white horse, the head and shoulders of a man, and the renowned 'medical healer' possessed two very long independent dicks that always remained erect. Despite his weird physical appearance, Chiron was a superb teacher and scholar, who on occasion, demonstrated a nasty disposition, and some of the Centaur's more famous students had been: Philoctetes, who later killed Paris, and a few other important cities; Asclepius, who became a notorious sex-therapy doctor; Hercules, a legendary hero strongman; and also "that heel Achilles", who gradually matured into a prominent Greek hero during the *Trojan War,* also known to more serious historians as "the prophylactic conflict".

The erudite Centaur taught his distinguished pupils how to play the harp, and how to kill harpies; how to cure diseases; how to cure smoked ham, and how to heal smoked tobacco, all at the same time. Chiron also taught his pupils how to use the sword, and also the shield, in order to lethally kick ass; how to read and write, and finally, how to jerk-off using only horse's hooves.

When Jason was six-years-old, the lad asked Chiron a very intelligent question. "I'd rather see women take-off their clothes at the local strip mall, than engage in all of this homosexual behavior you've been teaching me," the precocious boy tersely stated. "Why can't we simply learn some basic moral heterosexuality at this damned cave school? Do you want us to evolve into culturally retarded cavemen or what? How is the human race going to survive if we're all practicing homos?"

"Shut the hell up and keep sucking my two long flaccid dicks until they get harder!" Chiron bellowed in a very perturbed tone of voice. "When you become my age, Jason, you can teach your own kids anything you fuckin' want; you little snot-nosed cock-sucker!"

And so, Jason had to suck-up to Chiron from when the recalcitrant kid was a little tyke, up to the time that the son of Aeson was a fully-grown teeny-bopper. Upon reaching his eighteenth birthday, Jason was now ready to go-out into the fucked-up world and seek his already-prescribed fame and fortune.

"Is it true Chiron that I am a prince, and that my shameful Uncle Pelias had stolen my father's throne away from him?" Jason asked Chiron right before receiving his graduation sheepskin, which the arrogant knucklehead proudly wore over his athletic body, along with his leopard skin, which made the inquisitive Prince easy to spot from a distance.

"No, Jason. Pelias sits on the same throne your father Aeson had sat his ass upon," the famous Centaur humorously replied. "So, your father's throne was not taken in any grand larceny, felony scheme. But your criminal Uncle Pelias is a real mother-fucker because the bastard has been porking your mother all these past eighteen years. Now if demented Pelias and your mother were totally gay like I am, that sort of adulterous bull-shit would've never happened between your promiscuous mommy, and your uncle in the *hamlet* of Iolcus."

"I'll punish my immoral Uncle Pelias for being such a cad like legendary Cadmus was," Jason promised his mentor Chiron. "I'm not gonna' fuckin' *horse around* in a cave the rest of my life like you've stupidly elected to do!"

Chiron had given Jason two spears (that incidentally were not from Brittany), and a new pair of sandals as graduation presents, and soon the proud, young adolescent left "the Cave Academy" and proceeded on his merry way towards Iolcus. A half-hour later, the young fellow came to a river-rapids, and instead of walking downstream and crossing where the water was less turbulent and shallow, the punk idiot began fording the fast-flowing current right at its most difficult crossing. The eddying, roaring stream soon caught Jason off-guard in his haste, for it was springtime, and the river was much broader than it was during the non-rainy season, and the melting snow complicated matters by rushing down from distant *Mt. Olympus*.

The young adventurer paused in the middle of the current to consider his options, and other important stock exchange strategies. 'I must be careful. There are many jagged rocks here in the middle,' Jason analyzed and evaluated. And when the carcasses of several drowned sheep, cows, horses, elephants, and hippopotamus' families floated by the stationary youth, the haughty-naughty teenager finally realized and interpreted correctly that he was in the midst of a dangerous situation-in-progress.

'I can't swim against such a damned strong current,' the callow fellow considered. 'And worst of all, I can't even fuckin' swim.' Then, Jason reflected some more. 'My mentor and tormentor Chiron had no wild river flowing through his smelly cave to teach me that particular skill. Oh shit! I've lodged my right foot between two goddamned jagged rocks! What a fuckin' bummer this perilous predicament is! It's a good thing that my fuckin' dick and balls are still safely attached!'

"Are you experiencing a degree of difficulty?" a curious female voice asked the troubled neophyte from the riverbank. "You must not have had a decent education, since apparently, you have not been prepared to cross such a cascading stream as this sucker happens to be. Heed my sage words, you juvenile delinquent!"

Jason was more embarrassed than offended, even though the river-crosser was quite aware that his life was at least temporarily in jeopardy. And being directly chided by an old, wrinkle-faced woman was perhaps the ultimate of insults for a conceited young man to have to suffer and endure.

"Perhaps you ought to yell for Chiron the Centaur to arrive and rescue you from your uncomfortable dilemma," the old hag further admonished her humiliated listener. "But *that* egotistical, dumb bastard doesn't know how to swim worth a damned rat's ass, either! If you get to the opposite shore, and then successfully return to this bank I'm standing on, then you'll go down in mythology as being the best double-crosser ever!"

The encumbered lad studied the old lady's appearance, and noticed that the hoary whore wore a grimy, old, drab shawl over her unkempt mediocre tunic; held a crooked old staff in her left hand with a wooden cuckoo carved on top, and furthermore, carried a half-rotten pomegranate (an out of season fruit) in her left palm. And Jason also noticed that a tame dependent peacock stood by the old bitch's side, looking rather comatose.

"If I didn't have dual bad cases of arthritis and rheumatism right now," the old hag commented, "and if I were a mere hundred-years younger, then I would salvage you from your *rapid current* problem. Where are you heading Jason?"

The son of Aeson was startled that the decrepit, gray-haired woman knew his name; knew his former teacher's identity; knew *his* general background, and knew his present, uncomfortable problem stuck in the middle of the narrow river. "Oh, psychic, hideous-looking bag woman," Jason pleaded. "I'm heading to Iolcus to challenge King Pelias to make him abdicate his throne and relinquish it to me, the rightful heir. The throne originally and legitimately belonged to my father, Aeson," the naïve and idealistic lad thoroughly explained. "But right now, I'm experiencing a rather upsetting obstacle that is severely hindering my necessary progress."

"Well then, Jason. I happen to know what you're up to. You're *up to* your waist in the roaring river, ha, ha, ha," the old woman humorously giggled. "And when you're through giving me a lot of irrelevant bull-shit, I request that you take me on your back, so that I may cross the river with minimum danger. Since there aren't any goddamned *Boy Scouts* around yet, please forgive the inane anachronism, your awkward services will just have to suffice. My peacock and I have some important business to conduct on the *other side,* and I don't mean down in Hades. But first Jason; you must empty the urine from *your pee-cock* into the swirling stream. Ha, ha, ha, ha! And please don't fuckin' *double-cross* me, ya' hear, ha, ha, ha! I only wanna' go one damned way, and I'm not requesting round-trip service from you, ha, ha, ha!"

"Good old hag bag woman," Jason too sincerely answered. "Your business cannot possibly rival my pursuit of removing a most evil illegitimate king from my father's throne. And if I should stumble transporting you to the other side, we'll both drown, and soon be really going to the other side on Charon's barge across the *River-Styx.* In the final analysis, I doubt whether I'm strong enough to convey you across, going against such wild and forceful-flowing rapids. For you see, old hag," the youth eloquently clarified. "I am blue-blooded, and was not born into damned mainstream society."

"Look, Asshole. If you aren't strong enough to carry my butt to the other side," the elderly wench rankled, "then you certainly aren't strong enough to remove King Pelias from his goddamned toilet throne. You don't seem to have the testicles, or the required sperm count, to lead a coup d' etat, whatever the fuck that is! Now either carry me across the stream, or else live in humility and defeat for the remainder of your already fucked-up life!"

"Okay, you' old hoary dirt bag, you win," the brawny youth conceded. "If you can leap upon my back, I'll gladly conduct you to the other side without even desiring a toll, a fee, or a raunchy, lousy, rotten piece of smelly ass. I'd rather have us drown together than to witness you drowning in these rapids, while my damned foot is caught between two close rocks. We might as well fuckin' drown together old woman. That way, your certain demise will not be on my conscience, for it will have happened at *your* suspect volition."

Much to Jason's astonishment, the old bitch carefully placed her peacock upon her right shoulder, took twenty paces backwards, and then possibly believing that she was Archimedes, the old dame let out a shout of "Eureka!" as she fiercely sprinted to the river's edge. The seemingly-demented bitch then used her staff with the cuckoo on its end, and acting very cuckoo herself, she planted the long stick into the ground as she hustled forward and then athletically pole-vaulted onto Jason's back. The jolt from the impact momentarily sent Jason underwater, and when the choking kid violently arose with the old woman still desperately clinging to his back, the formerly encumbered asshole had accidentally turned his right foot, and amazingly, freed his aching ankle from its snare.

The young man courageously staggered through the surging currents to the opposite bank, using both of his spears as supports, and also as improvised wading sticks. "Oh shit!" Jason exclaimed. "I have lost my right sandal in the underwater river crevice. Now, I'll be the fuckin' laughing stock of King Pelias's court, appearing in front of him with only one golden-stringed sandal. What a sandal scandal that shit-eatin' event will be!"

Upon reaching the other side of the raging river, the depressed-but-aspiring Prince stooped-down to allow his passenger to drop from his posterior onto the pebble-laden riverbank. And after then standing erect, the old hag had some truly consoling words to deliver.

"Don't take your sandal loss to heart," the old lady pleasantly lectured. "Now, I am certain that you are indeed the lad that the garrulous Speaking Oak had been describing to me. That tree could out-predict the much-praised *Oracle of Delphi,* and also the equally gifted *Augur of Philadelphia."*

"But what of my missing sandal?" Jason muttered and complained. "Malicious Uncle King Pelias is liable to think that I'm Shoeless Joe Jacksonocles and not his feared nephew Jason, the rightful heir to *his* father's throne. I guess I won't be vacationing at any fictional *Sandals* resort in the fuckin' near future."

"I assure you that a new pair of sandals will be forthcoming in due time," the old bag stated with arcane certainty and conviction. "And when Pelias takes a gander at your bare right foot, his face will turn as pallid as my white smelly ass. Now, follow your path to Iolcus with my humble blessing, kind Jason. And after you are triumphant in your aspirations, and finally ascend to your high throne, please remember this wretched, handicapped, old bitch that you had carried across this fucked-up river."

The old dame with the curved back and hunched shoulders then hobbled-off, giving the youth a broad smile, and winking her large brown eyes as if she were flirting with, or favoring him. And Jason received the fanciful impression that there was something wonderfully majestic about the feeble woman's general demeanor, despite her apparent aging appearance; her arthritis, and her unsteady gait. And the old hag's peacock then fluttered-down off the woman's shoulder, spread its feathers, and exposed its tiny attractive ass specifically for Jason's attention, admiration and approval.

When the old woman and her handsome bird were out of sight (neither of them was actually blind), Jason proceeded on his vital trek to Iolcus. 'My father would be generous and considerate enough to have a bridge built over that wild river,' the boy contemplated. 'But cheap, parsimonious old Uncle Pelias doesn't even own a goddamned unabridged dictionary. What a waste of protoplasm that miserable son-of-a-bitch is! Wait a minute! I don't want to dishonor my damned anonymous, paternal grandmother!"

In another hour, the on-a-mission wanderer arrived at the outskirts of a seashore city situated at the base of a rugged mountain. In the distance, a huge puff of smoke was wafting skyward, and so Jason felt compelled to inquire of a stranger what large object was being burned in the distance.

"That over yonder is the city of Iolcus," a blind man answered. "And we people are the subjects and predicates of our ruler King Pelias, who is presently in the process of sacrificing a bull to Poseidon, Lord of the Oceans, along with being the official monarch of all roosters, and also of all the chickens of the sea. That dark smoke your eyes perceive is rising from the city's centrally located sacred public altar. Everything in the bull's body is being incinerated, even all the bulls-eyes, and all the bull-shit, too."

Another more curious stranger in the crowd, who had been eavesdropping on the hollow bull-shit conversation, observed that Jason had a missing sandal, and the nosy chatterbox also perceptively noticed that the lad's general dress featuring a leopard's skin, and *that* primitive garb was quite unlike the more-modest fashion trends prevalent in Iolcus. Soon, the new arrival became quite embarrassed at all the natural public scrutiny.

"Look at him! Stare your eyeballs upon him, will ya'!" everyone began jabbering. "Do you see that he wears only one sandal? He's the dreaded man with one sandal. What does he plan to do? What pithy remarks will King Pelias say to this pathetic, alien upstart?"

'These assholes must be very ill-bred to act like complete obnoxious jerk-offs, behaving and gossiping so indiscreetly in public,' Jason thought as the new-arrival hurried through the gathered throng, and soon wound-up near the sacrificial bull and bull-shit altar. 'Shit! The smell of that smoking bull is making me damned hungry for barbecued meat Where's the beef?'

The crowd's noise suddenly distracted King Pelias from his official ceremonial capacity, and the monarch turned around with a frown upon his crater-face countenance, and focused his beady pupils upon Jason. But the assembled multitude was so densely crammed around the visitor that the perturbed King was presently unaware of the young man's missing sandal.

"How dare you interrupt my sacred bull being solemnly sacrificed to Lord Poseidon!" the King blatantly chastised. "Who the fuck are you that violates my time-honored ritual? What written right do you have to disturb my unwritten rite? Speak now, or forever hold your peace, and also your vulnerable testicles."

"Your majesty; you must blame your rude and detestable subjects for making such a disruptive ruckus, rudely interrupting your irrelevant bull session," Jason ineffectively argued. "The idiots are bickering and gossiping very loudly, just because my damned right foot happens to be bare. Is a trivial, accidental, non-intentional, minor matter such as my missing sandal a fuckin' egregious crime, or even an unforgivable, indecent immorality around here? Are your subjects and predicates a bunch of mini-minded pinheads, or what?"

The insulted king glanced-down at Jason's walking appendages, and then predictably gasped in alarm. "Ha! You are indeed a one sandaled, insolent asshole! What the fuck should I do with you?" the crimson-faced Pelias stammered, as the tyrant firmly and angrily held the bloodstained sacrificial knife in his right hand.

A murmur arose from the restless witnesses to the unexpected confrontation, and then one wise, blind, old fuck in the crowd gleefully screamed-out, "The one-sandaled man has finally come. The remainder of the fuckin' prophecy must be fulfilled. The son of King Aeson has…." And then quite unfortunately, the old, blind prophet clutched his chest and fell dead to the ground.

Now, seventeen years prior, the very revered Speaking Oak of Dodona had informed King Pelias that a young man wearing only one sandal would show-up in Iolcus to remove the illegitimate monarch from dominion over the exploited citizens, subjects, and predicates. And Pelias had issued an edict stating that no one with only one sandal should ever appear in his midst. The royal treasury had financed thousands of pairs of sandals, so that Pelias would be free to wander about his capital without dread of being assassinated by some athlete with athlete's feet wearing insufficient footgear. And now, because of the controversial sandal incident, and Jason's defiant attitude, the wicked King Pelias had been publicly agitated, and exceedingly humiliated to the point of madness.

"My good young fellow," the pernicious king feigned in a much calmer voice. "You are indeed welcome to tarry in Iolcus. However, we are civilized people and not prehistoric hunters, and we do not wear primitive garb such as leopard skins in this tranquil, peace-loving, homosexual city. Just because my chatty subjects live in an urban area, that fact doesn't fuckin' necessarily have to mean that the city residents must act urbane. Pray tell young pecker-head," the King chastised. "Who in their right mind educated you? Where did you ever receive your stinking, controlled bravado that is quite demonstrative and observable?"

"The profound saying is true that a leopard skin and its wearer doesn't change its, and his spots," the proud juvenile guest stoutly stated. "I am Jason, and I have been faithfully instructed by the very noble Chiron the Centaur, who has taught and educated me about medicine, music, horsemanship, battle combat, and how to immediately recognize dangerous jerk-offs when I encounter them!"

"I have heard of this peculiar individual Chiron, although he is definitely no pal-o-mino," Pelias answered with a lame pun. "And you, young man, had to put-up with *his* fundamentalist horse-shit for a number of years, I suppose," the malicious King further chided. "Anyway, young Jason, since you are obviously very scholarly, I have a specific philosophical question to advance. Are you willing to respond to my interrogatory?"

"I don't pretend to have totally mastered the art of wisdom," Jason modestly replied. "In fact, I have yet to possess adequate knowledge in the more-simple, mundane school subjects, like gym and cafeteria."

The diabolical king's true intentions were to trick and then trap the gullible youth into an uncompromising situation, which would ultimately cause extensive suffering and destruction to Pelias's inexperienced "wet-behind-the-ears" rival. The monarch formed a smile upon his now-florid, ruddy face, and then asked his tormentor a rather poignant question.

"Intrepid Jason; what would you do if a man were out to ruin your reputation, and had a mind bent on slaying you? If you were a king, Jason, what would you do within the jurisdiction of your power to fuckin' counteract and stifle the no-good bastard?"

Jason considered and analyzed the evil and the malice that was being expressed upon King Pelias's sourpuss. 'I cannot tell a lie, and I must exhibit good public decorum, even though I despise my mother-fuckin' uncle with an angry passion that defies description or explanation!' Jason thought. 'The greedy son-of-a-bitch knows who the fuck I am, and is now contemplating having me publicly mortified, and then officially slain in cold blood. But I must keep my word, and earnestly answer the no-good, gutless piss-head!'

"If such a persistent man bothered the hell out of me," Jason proudly-but-imprudently declared, "I would most-certainly send that annoying tormentor in an adventurous quest of the legendary Golden Fleece. That almost-impossible enterprise should keep my wick-dicked adversary fully occupied, and most likely, would eventually terminate in getting the dirty, conniving prick either seriously maimed, or killed!"

King Pelias's eyes sparkled with vengeance and great satisfaction. "Well then, brash Asshole with the singular sandal; go and bring me back the magical Golden Fleece, since you've been so damned impetuous and outrageously *ram*bunctious."

"I shall gladly embark like a stubborn bloodhound on this dangerous exploit," Jason answered with evident dignity. "And if I fail, that means, you, cruel Pelias, will retain your stolen crown. But if I succeed, and come back to Iolcus with the grand prize, then craven King Pelias, you must surrender your unearned throne; your unearned wealth; your unearned scepter, and all of your unearned runs, too."

"That I will gladly and voluntarily do," the ruler sneered and vowed before all of his appalled and resentful subjects. "I shall meanwhile keep my extensive properties and gold coins safely in my custody, until you have satisfactorily completed your silly, impossible escapade."

Jason left the center of the jeering crowd and sought-out the services of the world's greatest boat builder, a craftsman named Argus, who was very happy to accommodate the youth for promise of a cut of the profits in obtaining the remarkable Golden Fleece, and for one percent of Iolcus's annual taxation revenues upon Pelias's abdication of power.

"No ship of such colossal dimensions has ever been constructed," Jason marveled and admitted to Argus. "Many timbers must be hewed, and at least six months of time devoted to completing the massive project. But we can't sail all the way to Colchis in a chariot, ya' know."

"If the crew you fuckin' assemble is as fine as this boat will be," Argus remarked, "then thanks to you, Jason; *my ship* will have finally come in."

Messengers were dispatched to every Greek city to recruit warriors to journey on the fabulous "Golden Fleece Expedition". Only forty-nine of the bravest soldiers would be chosen for the quasi-military campaign venturing to the other side of the Black Sea in "the *Argo*", and the crew would be logically called "the Argonauts", named after the historic ship, which obviously had been named after the famous, fucked-up shipbuilder, who regrettably was named after the extremely fucked-up city of Argos.

"I'll be the fiftieth asshole Argonaut aboard the *Argo*," Jason told Argus from Argos. "I say that we have a fifty-fifty chance of succeeding," the son of Aeson foolishly joked. "That is, if the son-of-a-bitchin' Golden Fleece really exists, and isn't just a wild, fanciful myth circulating all over the goddamned known, ancient world."

"That's what makes mythology interesting," Argus blithely agreed with a wink of his right eye. "And anyway Jason; it's really great being a character in this new myth that's being developed. I mean, who the fuck needs history when we can all fuckin' argue and debate all day long about bull-shit mythology?"

Daring, enthusiastic, aspiring champions from all over Greece were immediately attracted to the Golden Fleece challenge, and then drawn to Iolcus, bearing bronze helmets, swords and shields. The forty-nine best candidates were selected after competing in numerous athletic contests, and among them were the best boxers; wrestlers; mud wrestlers; javelin throwers; swimmers; pussy lappers, and masturbators in all of the totally bizarre, Ancient Greek World. The qualifiers all eagerly clambered-up the *Argo's* gang-bang-plank, many of whom had been educated by the faggot quadruped Chiron the Centaur, who always desired being the undisputed 'Centaur' of attention in his dirty, stenchy, unkempt, cave classroom.

Some of the Centaur's former students that were also mariners on the *Argo Expedition* were the mighty Hercules; twin brothers Castor and Pollux, and the legendary Theseus, who had just recently slaughtered the savage Minotaur. Other famous heroes participating in the daring mission were keen-eyed Lynceus, and the noble musician Orpheus, and to appease the influential woman's rights' liberals, Jason had selected Atalanta, who had been weaned by a mountain bear, but who screwed like a mink. And so, the Argonauts would have a wonderful piece of ass, along with daily great blowjobs, to keep themselves happy and motivated while sailing on their extended, perfidious, all-encompassing quest of the renowned, legendary Golden Fleece.

The young captain appointed Tiphys to be the *Argo's* helmsman and navigator, because *he* was an amateur astronomer (well, actually a dumb-ass astrologer) who understood how zodiac constellations and certain prominent stars (except any from a distant place called *Hollywood)* could guide the ship through even the most perilous of waters. And Lynceus had been delegated chief lookout, and was stationed at the *Argo's* prow, where he could spot various prowlers and potential enemies a full day ahead. "I have twenty-twenty vision," Lynceus amiably informed Jason. "But I have difficulty seeing more than forty fuckin' objects at a time."

The *Argo* finally embarked out to sea amidst total apathy from the pedestrian population of somnolent Iolcus, but with apparent extreme joy on the part of the avaricious King Pelias. The rowers assiduously stirred their oars into the harbor's deep water in precise unison, and the *Argo* gently glided in the direction of the northern horizon. Pelias watched the colorful spectacle occurring from a high promontory overlooking his dumpy metropolis.

'Thank Zeus that those stupid-ass fools will never return,' the vindictive monarch reckoned. 'The *Argo's* destiny is nothing but doom and gloom. And with the vivacious broad Atalanta aboard, throw in a little womb and tomb, too! Ha, ha, ha!'

After passing through the Hellespont, the enthusiastic sailors began discussing the origin of the Golden Fleece, which was a Boeotian ram that had transported two endangered children (way before there were any endangered species) over land and sea to Colchis. The female rider, Helle, fell-off of the flying ram's back, and plummeted into the sea, and as a result, the point where the uncoordinated girl landed became known upon all ancient maps as the Hellespont. The young boy Phrixus was then transported safely ashore, but the incomparable flying ram became so fatigued that it died as soon as it eventually landed.

Phrixus attempted giving the ram artificial respiration, but by accident, vomited his guts down the benign animal's throat, thus making the poor gasping creature choke to death. The ram's fleece immediately, miraculously, and mysteriously turned to gold, and was hung over the branch of a huge oak tree in a secret meadow. Many attempted forays were made to confiscate the priceless fleece, but all of the sieges were in vain. No pirates or plunderers were ever capable of fleecing the Golden Fleece from Colchis.

One evening, the Argonauts were resting in their vessel near a certain anonymous island, when the crew spotted another much smaller boat heading in their direction. The two sailors aboard turned-out to be exuberant princes that were then returning from Colchis back to their native Greece.

"The tree on which the Golden Fleece is hung is guarded by a terrible dragon that especially feasts on hunters, sailors, soldiers and bodyguards," the first out-of-breath, thrilled-at-being-rescued prince related. "And the dragon eats men raw, and especially savors the taste of blood and uncooked flesh."

"You cannot intimidate us with such fanciful bull-shit!" Jason indignantly answered his salvaged guests. "My 'comrades' and I will not turn back, even though none of us are card-carrying ancient communists. And anyway, dear suave princes, voluptuous Atalanta nightly eats me raw, and the gorgeous chick swallows too, all done down in the *Argo's* exclusive galley lounge, all the fuckin' time. She must think my friggin' dick is a goddamned sperm bank!" Jason ejaculated to his thoroughly-amused, and extremely effervescent rescued listeners.

"If there's a blow-job or two waiting for me on this magnificent ship," the second Greek prince attested, "then I say fuck the fierce dragon, and put the son-of-a-bitch on hold! Who the hell wants to live a long, dull, boring life and then die in a fuckin' rocking chair devoid of erections? On second thought, now exactly where's this horny, slutty-bitch Atalanta you've been fuckin' bragging so much about? Down in the galley you say?"

Two days later, King Aeetes of Colchis learned of the Argonauts arrival in his mostly gay and lesbian community, where many promiscuous gays had sex on tree limbs, and when the boughs broke, the whimsical faggots would fall. Aeetes sent for Jason, and the lad, upon initial examination, did not like the King's pocked stern face, which immediately reminded him of his mean uncle, the deranged King Pelias of Iolcus.

"Welcome to Colchis brave Jason," the sly king falsely flattered. "Are you on a random pleasure cruise, looking for loose women? Are you working for a map company, and casually exploring the local geography? What personal pursuit has brought your ass to my peaceful court?"

"Your Benign Excellency," Jason began with an exaggerated bow. "I beg you to endorse my noble purpose in coming to Colchis. And do not worry. The Argonauts are not here to round-up faggot homos' and lesbians that abound in your insane land, in order to take them back to Greece to be our fuckin' sex slaves."

"Then, what exactly brings your fantastic, well-equipped fighting ship here besides the fuckin' wind and currents?" Aeetes demanded knowing.

"Kind King," Jason politely replied, before clearing his slightly hoarse throat. "My deceitful uncle, King Pelias of Iolcus, has promised to relinquish his throne to me, only if I am successful in retrieving the illustrious Golden Fleece, and then taking it back to Greece and presenting the fabulous trophy to him. I humbly solicit your permission in repossessing the world-famous fleece, which as you know, had originated from Greece, my native land."

Now, the avaricious King Aeetes valued the Golden Fleece even more than he liked kinky gay sex, and even more than the greedy fuck appreciated four-hour-long erections. The ruler had trouble disguising the intense scowl seemingly welded upon his already-ugly visage. "Jason, you conspiring, distrustful fleecer; are you aware of the dreadful conditions you must complete before successfully acquiring the Golden Fleece, which incidentally, possesses magical curing powers?"

"I am cognizant that a carnivorous dragon guards the Golden Fleece in a remote garden, or dell, of sorts," the callow youth answered. "And I most certainly run the risk of being viciously mauled and devoured."

"I see that you have more than adequately studied our culture and our customs," Aeetes falsely praised. "But before you can earn the privilege of being consumed by my pet dragon, you must first tame my ferocious, fire-breathing, mechanical bulls that Hephaestus, lame god of *Olympus,* had personally manufactured for me in his laboratory workshop. The blacksmith god has placed an eternal furnace inside each of their enormous stomachs," Aeetes comprehensively explained, "and anyone who approaches either of the snorters will automatically be incinerated by the fuckin' flames that spout-out of their mouths, whenever the bulls belch; and then also shoot fire out of their big fat asses whenever the lethal animals continuously fart. Do you consider my most compelling, true story bull-shit?" Aeetes requested knowing.

"The danger of your fire-breathing bulls does indeed sound like a lot of exaggerated bull-shit, but their challenge stands in the way of my next objective, which is to kill the savage dragon that guards the wonderful fleece," Jason valiantly and eloquently stated. "Therefore, King Aeetes, I must satisfactorily complete my significant purpose in coming to Colchis."

"Well Jason," the devious king nonchalantly continued in an effort to scare the living and dead shit out of his persistent tormentor. "After you have tamed my erratic bulls, you then are required to yoke the critters to a plow, and make thirteen deep furrows in the sacred grove of Ares, *our* mutual god of war. After eliminating the bulls, you next must sow the dragon's teeth from the nearby field, and fight to-the-death the armed warriors of the ancient cad Cadmus. Those foes will be soldiers that shall spring-up from the sacred soil. They are immortal, and will ultimately defeat you and your determined Argonauts in battle," King Aeetes stated and snidely snickered. "Have you ever had your ass kicked before by a fuckin' crew of immortal, armed, red skeletons?"

"The acclaimed pedagogue Chiron the Centaur had taught me how to fight and defend myself against even the most formidable and aggressive enemies," Jason arrogantly boasted. "And we weren't exactly engaged in fuckin' horseplay at his academic cave, either. These immortal, non-comical, red skeletons, with limitless energy, absolutely sound like worthy opponents to my well-trained and well-prepared rowdy, doughty, crew of ass-kickers."

"Well, sanctimonious Prince Jason. I hope that you aren't too complaisant in rushing to judgment," Aeetes sternly warned. "Now, you and your dumb-fuck crew of frivolous misfits should make yourselves comfortable and merry in my banquet room, for tomorrow will probably be your last stinking day on this stinkin', fucked-up planet!"

While King Aeetes was bull-shitting with Jason, and accurately sizing-up the ambitious lad, a gorgeous young female was standing in a corner of the throne room and sizing-up the cute bulge between the handsome Greek representative's hairy legs. The knockout girl (the only heterosexual in all of Colchis) was assessing the prospective hero's personal equipment, and a warm, wonderful, scintillating tingle began quivering away inside her furry crotch area. And when Jason finally departed from the hard-spirited king's presence, the lonely, neglected young maiden, who totally despised her cold-fish father, discreetly followed the motivated hero out of the royal chamber, and immediately initiated a conversation.

"I am the King's daughter, Medea," the princess shyly introduced herself. "But you don't have to worry, because I don't belong to the Colchis mass media," Medea pathetically jested. "I am omniscient in some respects, and as long as I remain a virgin, I will know plenty more about future events than the average deflowered lady does, that's for damned sure. I don't write the damned mythological laws. I only heed and obey the ludicrous, nonsensical traditions that my culture portends."

"Indeed Medea; if you can deftly assist me in obtaining the Golden Fleece, then you can be independent of your cold-hearted, fucked-up father, and come and live with me in beautiful, downtown, metropolitan Iolcus," Jason maintained. "And I have a fantastic female friend named Atalanta, who will teach you how to properly screw, and how to administer good head in the most correct manner. It'll be worth losing your special virgin powers that you have just alluded to."

"Jason, I know exactly how you can tame the fire-breathing bulls, and then plant the dead dragon's teeth in order to obtain possession of the Golden Fleece," Medea intimated to her first genuine heterosexual boyfriend. "And I can't wait to have my hot honey-well explored by your eager fingers. I'm already tingling all over, and can feel my squiggly clit' button throbbing and pulsating, and its absolutely begging to be fondled and massaged by you, dear Jason, and by you alone."

'This strange princess, if not handled properly and delicately, could amount to a very grave threat, even more formidable than the awesome, fire-breathing bulls, and possibly even more dangerous than the sowed dragon's molars and incisors,' the invading military expedition's captain realized and concluded. 'Perhaps this attractive, vivacious bitch Medea is also a damned malevolent witch.'

A moment's pause was broken with Jason advancing the relevant question that was playing havoc upon his unsettled mind. "Medea, are you an enchantress? You appear to have an unusual, other-dimension quality about you."

"Indeed, my dear Prince Jason," Aeetes's daughter hesitantly confessed. "And the famous sorceress Circe happens to be my deranged father's deranged sister. I can tell the future, but I don't know exactly what to tell it! I don't know what the future looks like, or specify precisely what I should say to it. But I can easily identify the old bitch with the obnoxious peacock, the cuckoo staff, and the pomegranate that you had conducted across the raging river, that was devoid of white-water rafters. And my dear Jason," Medea added. "I also know all about the damned sex games you used to play with that faggot pedophile Centaur Chiron, who had more than sufficiently corrupted your already emotionally scarred childhood through many perverted and unwarranted pedophile molestations," the beautiful witch disclosed. "So, in essence jerk-weed, be careful, because I know what the hell you're thinking before you ever say it, and I also know what you may attempt speaking otherwise, in order to conceal your secret thoughts and motives."

"Look Medea, the dragon's threat presently doesn't perplex me," Jason honestly admitted. "I'm now more concerned about the fire-breathing bulls that might singe my pubic hairs, and start a roaring inferno inside my lower pelvis area, which might even ignite the vital hair follicles in and around my tender asshole."

"When you encounter the brazen fire-bulls, your heart will hold the appropriate solution to their savagery," Medea nebulously predicted. "But first and foremost, Jason, you must be insulated from *their* terrible fire-breathing bad breath. Both pyromaniac specimens have severely bad cases of halitosis. In *this* case I am holding is a most-advantageous ointment that will prevent you from being charred and scorched to embers. But be sure to rub extra amounts of the formula over your dick, balls and ass, because if those precious organs become burned-off your cute, firm, taut body, I might then lose interest in your upcoming marriage proposal. Do you read me?"

"Like a book of *Aesop's Fables,*" Jason intelligently and creatively answered. "Now please hand me the box, and I'll generously apply the lotion, in private, to my privates. If I allow you to do it Medea," the abashed hero said while abundantly blushing, "then I might squirt several pounds of sperm juice all over the damned place, and soon lose my strength, because I won't have the necessary balls to tame the lousy fire-shooting, flame-shitting bulls."

"Here you are, my special champion," Medea said as the princess handed her box to Jason. "I only wish that my callous, sinister father were half as kind-hearted, courteous, considerate, polite, sentimental, romantic, affectionate, sincere, truthful, innocent, and well-endowed as you are."

"My heart shall not fail me in this monumental endeavor, except if I suddenly have a massive coronary attack," Jason cleverly conveyed to his lady admirer. "And so, Medea, just give me the appropriate time and the place where I might domesticate those ferocious fire-bulls. In the meantime, I'll practice some shadowboxing, and pretend I'm hitting the two snorters right in the center of their bulls-eyes. Maybe it would be safer if I actually hit them in the bulls-eyes with fuckin' arrows from my bow, rather than with my very vulnerable, mortal, clenched fists."

At midnight, steadfast Jason met and embraced Medea outside the impeccable palace botanical garden. Then, the horny love-blinded princess betrayed her father, and presented her new-found companion with a small wicker basket.

"Here Jason; the essential dragon's teeth, that were pulled and removed by that cad Cadmus a hundred years ago, are inside this wicked wicker container," Medea confidentially communicated. "And don't worry one iota about the damned bulls. Their taming will be no more difficult than pulling teeth."

Medea then led her companion to the particular pasture where the fire-breathing bulls were kept, and where the natives and the steers did all of their foul bull-shitting. The constellations were glistening in the warm summer night sky, and the moon was showing ample reflected sunlight for the two rare heterosexuals to accurately survey their immediate environment.

"The deadly creatures are preoccupied crapping-out their hot intestines over there," Medea indicated while pointing to her right. "Allow them to see you Jason, just to make your contest a fair, death-struggle competition. The damned element of surprise is only for weak and wimpy cowards to employ."

"Are you crazy?" Jason shrieked while accidentally disturbing the yonder bull-shitting bulls. "The behemoths have a tremendous size advantage over me, and are very experienced at instantaneously turning young men into mini-infernos! I think the scientific process is called spontaneous combustion. How many unfortunate men have perished attempting to tame those wild beasts?"

"Only several thousand or so," Medea nonchalantly replied. "But none of the idiots had the special magic ointment smeared all over their bodies like you now do. I mean, Prince Jason; I'm getting hot and tingly all over, just thinking about smearing your marvelous body and not your reputation!"

"Your father probably declares it a holiday whenever someone gets killed trying to settle the brutes' unruly temperaments," the captain of the Argonauts discussed, and conveyed to Medea, a certain behavioral propensity of her father, Aeetes, that *he* had heard about. "I think I once read it in a *bull*etin pinned on the public *bull*etin board in the marketplace, back in downtown Iolcus."

"Whatever you do, Jason, don't allow doubt to engender fear in your heart," Medea wisely advised her new gallant defender. "Now exhibit courage and audacity, or else you'll ultimately experience defeat and certain death."

'Maybe I should've stayed in Chiron's secluded cave and enjoyed a safe, happy lifestyle molesting the new crop of kindergarten kids,' the hero meditated. 'It's now time to either show fortitude and dedication, or be converted into a human-sized cinder-fella'.'

Jason suavely kissed Medea upon her cheek, and then boldly approached the fire-breathing animals. Four foul streams of hot vapor were simultaneously being released into the atmosphere, as if the jets had been expelled from blast furnaces, indicating that the apathetic bulls cared nothing about air pollution, or about bullshit environmental propaganda advanced by ancient, radical, left-wing liberals. Then, the hot spurts diminished and vanished, but several seconds later, the flames reappeared with even more intensity. The moment of truth, and of survival, were now at hand.

"Wow, Medea! Something just occurred to me!" Jason exclaimed while turning-around and speaking to his stationary love. "If those two monsters were sleeping, I'd be slaying a couple of dozing bulls! And whoever heard of anyone, hero or otherwise, killing two bulldozers?"

As Jason approached the temporarily unwary bulls, the beasts were grazing-away, knee deep in bullshit. Then, each of Jason's opponents began sniffing the air, as a distant foreign scent became perceptible to their olfactory senses. And when the intrepid interloper came to within a hundred feet of *their* presence, red hot vapors again shot-out of the creatures' nostrils, and lit-up the whole damned vicinity. And when the brave hero came to within twenty-feet of the animal arsonists, sparks were flying everywhere, and four white-hot jets went zipping across the pasture, and setting fire to trees, fences, grass, weeds, groundhogs, and fleeing rodents.

'Thank goodness I'm smeared like a buttered pig in Medea's secret-formula, enchanted ointment,' Jason evaluated. 'Or otherwise, the white-hot flames would've already made my highly cherished sausage into a barbecued weiner, and my ass and asshole into smoked baked ham. I must now cautiously wait for the bull's ferocious attack, and be patient until their atrocious nostrils finally run out of flames and fuel.'

Just as the snorting aggressors were about to gore Jason's buttocks all over the now-fire-illuminated pasture, the dauntless champion grabbed one of the attackers by the horns with his vice-like grip, lifted the surprised animal into the air, and then flung the heavy beast directly into its wholly-delirious mate, with the two astonished predators incidentally goring each other with their huge, ultra-sharp horns.

'That's how to really shoot the bull!' Jason mused. And ever since that memorable day in Colchis, and as a matter of fact, everywhere else in the whole-wide-world, the catchy phrase "taking the bull by the horns" means to abandon fear, and to overcome immediate peril, despite the accompanying adversities and dangers that are presented by the prospective struggle.

It was no elementary task (but a real *harrowing* experience) harnessing the dazed, wounded bulls, and then yoking them to the rusty plow, but like a determined entrepreneur, Jason plowed right into the project. And a half hour later, the entire fallow field had been converted to furrowed black earth. Jason then effectively used the dragon's teeth from the wicker basket Medea had so helpfully provided, and then randomly scattered the objects all around the plowed pasture.

'I wonder what the fuck's gonna' happen now?' Jason imagined. 'Certainly, Medea's protective ointment cannot help me against my next unknown obstacle.' Then, the apprehensive Prince decided to again consult with his new-found love. "Medea, how long will it take until harvest season for these amazing teeth-seeds? Is there sufficient time to have some kinky safe sex before the nasty warriors from the past appear?"

"A crop of tenacious soldiers will spring-up from the tilled soil very shortly; way before you can ever have time to achieve a full erection," Medea related in a rather disappointed and depressed tone of voice. "And I must caution you. The red skeleton warriors once killed by that cad Cadmus are violently relentless. Perhaps if you wear my heavy chastity belt, your personals will be spared from brutally being maligned and castrated."

Soon, shiny bronze spear tips wormed their way above the ground under the full moon, and a moment later, brass helmets, swords and shields sporadically penetrated-up through the fertile soil. And then, thirteen gruesome red skeletons simultaneously shot-up above the surface, all having defiant, grim expressions on their very contoured and prominent facial bones. The deceased warriors moved in exact precision and formed a military phalanx, first raising-up their shields to chest level, lifting their swords above their skulls, and then all shouting in unison "Die Asshole!" in a frightening attempt at intimidating Jason.

And next, the unearthly, macabre militia slowly advanced forward in very deliberate, rhythmic steps, with their grotesque bones clattering in what amounted to sensational, shocking unison. "Come on Jason! Conquer us or die!" the uncanny ten red skeletons eerily chanted. "You can't keep your privates private from our persistent thrashing swords much longer!"

Jason held his ground with his trembling right hand brandishing his sword, such as the thespian Shake-*speare* must have dramatized on the *Globe Theater's* stage. The stressed-out lad stood there in overwhelming terror, with streams of piss and diarrhea trickling down his sweating legs.

"Guard the Golden Fleece! Don't let this ambitious prick fleece the Golden Fleece from Colchis!" the advancing vanguard all chorused together, while still moving forward in their weird, morbid, highly-animated choreography.

The trespassing Prince was horrified at the satanic spectacle his eyes now perceived. 'I cannot fight this vindictive, superior platoon all by myself,' the young intruder logically assessed. 'I must reunite with the valorous, stout-hearted Argonauts to make this a more even battle!'

"Quick Jason!" Medea implored. "Pick-up a rock and waste no time hurling it into the center of the advancing vanguard. It is your only available chance of salvation from this fucked-up, supernatural dilemma!"

Jason heeded Medea's intelligent recommendation with little time to spare. The champion heaved a rock into the approaching, unified aggregation, and the solid object collided with a tall red skeleton's bronze helmet. The projectile bounced-off of the helmet, hit another shorter red skeleton in the face, and then ricocheted-off, and next impacted with a third ancient red-boned warrior's elbow. The unexpected attack made the red skeletons lose focus of their prime enemy, and instantaneously, the assaulting idiots began frantically quarrelling, whacking, hacking, punching, stabbing, and decapitating one another. Arms, legs, heads, torsos, pelvises, and boners were soon scattered all over the damned weird combat zone.

'I suppose the best way to get ahead in this world is to become a goddamned headhunter!' Jason mused as the Greek hero generally examined a decapitated skull. 'Oh well; savage see, savage do! Just look at those hilarious assholes feverishly punishing and re-killing each other, as a result of a simple rock incident that I had instigated!'

"Is that all you can think about after employing such a brilliant stratagem?" Medea lambasted. "I mean, asshole; give me my due credit. If it weren't for me, Jason, you'd definitely be Hades-bound right now!"

"Look Medea!" Jason exclaimed. "I gratefully acknowledge your very desirable alliance. Thanks to your unparalleled genius, all of the antagonistic skeleton-warriors have frenetically self-destructed, and have efficiently eliminated each other from being my avowed adversaries."

"Brains, when used cleverly, always triumph over non-intelligence brawn!" Medea philosophically answered her stunned partner. "My father's bodyguards will loyally re-bury their ancestors' remains with full honors tomorrow morning. Such is the fate of simple-minded, non-thinking, compliant soldiers, who without question, obey orders that defy both reason and logic. There's more to life, Jason, than enjoying being a stupid, pathetic, ignoramus fuck-head! Now, go to my father early in the morning," the pretty princess directed, "and inform him of your success with the fire-breathing bulls, and with the red skeleton fanatics. Then, King Aeetes will more-than-likely provide you with additional fucked-up instructions to follow."

At morning's light, it finally dawned on Jason that he should leave the drunken Argonauts in the *Argo's* galley, and again visit paranoid King Aeetes in his opulent palace. After entering the official greeting room, the youthful captain from afar was swiftly led to the "presence room", to present himself to the Pelias facsimile.

"Your eyes look weary, Jason," the cynical king somberly began. "And you must've spent a sleepless night jerking-off, and fondly dreaming of screwing my nightmare daughter. You're probably very concerned about my fire-breathing bulls, not to mention the fearless red skeleton soldiers from antiquity. And I warn you, young brazen impostor, that if you dare screw Medea, and she loses her singular virgin powers of sorcery, then I guarantee you that the least of your hardships will be when I have the Argonauts and *your* wangolas and scrotums sliced-off, and subsequently fed to the hungry fire-snorting bulls. If you' and your demented asshole crew came here to sack Colchis," Aeetes vehemently maintained, "then I'll see to it that *your* dangling scrotum sacs will be severed from your abdomens, as a just and rightful retribution."

"I hate to inform you, Your Majesty, but the tasks you have just described have already been fuckin' performed," Jason indicated with a firm voice to match his firm erection. "The infernal inferno' bulls have been easily tamed and yoked, and your bull-shit pasture has been painstakingly plowed. Also, the dragon's teeth have been sowed, and I've seen to it that the fierce red skeleton warriors have been soundly trounced, vanquished, and destroyed. And now King Aeetes," Jason confidently continued, "I hereby request your imperial permission to terminate the vicious dragon under the sacred oak tree, acquire the Golden Fleece from the overhead tree limb, and abscond from Colchis with both it, and your beautiful daughter."

"And you expect me to accede to those very unacceptable and intolerable conditions!" Aeetes hollered with great disdain. "I only make grandiose promises so that they can be broken. That spectacular Golden Fleece possesses the extraordinary ability to cure every known malady, sickness, and infirmity. And Jason," the king intimated. "I desperately need the fuckin' thing, so that I never ever die from venereal diseases, which for your confidential information, I acquire quite frequently from sodomizing every asshole in sight. And so, I advise you, ambitious charlatan, to abandon your clownish pursuit of the fleece, or risk surrendering your life to my whim."

"But you have vowed that you would surrender the Golden Fleece, if and when I completed the arduous labors you had unscrupulously assigned me!" Jason vociferously protested. "Don't you keep your word? Isn't your word your bond and seal?"

"Look, you idealistic, quixotic imbecile!" Aeetes vociferously argued and reprimanded. "Only suckers, dreamers, and stupid-shit losers keep their' fuckin' promises. And I'm knowledgeable that Medea has meticulously assisted you in accomplishing your prodigious enterprises with her treasonous counsel; with her bizarre enchantments, and with her exceptional soothsaying ability. Without her consultations with you, I would now be addressing an inanimate cinder right before my eyes, and speaking to an insolent, callow, shallow, egotistic, gullible blockhead."

Jason became livid at being denied his most-desired claim. The Greek prince indignantly left the deceitful King's presence and decided to trek to the *Argo* and awaken the forty-nine drunken Argonauts, who always, for some inexplicable reason, fought better when having hangovers, and consequently hanging-over the ship's gunwales and vomiting their healthy guts out. 'We'll raid the Grove of Ares en masse; slay the maniacal dragon; pilfer the glorious Golden Fleece; kidnap Medea, and finally sail the fuck out of here, heading for Iolcus as soon as possible,' the inspired prince methodically plotted and thought on the long trek to his ship.

As Jason was sprinting in full battle array towards the *Argo,* the famed champion, by chance, encountered Medea, who also had had a sleepless night thinking about betraying her rich father, and jeopardizing a lucrative inheritance for the preposterous sake of eloping with a facetious, fanciful fellow with an impressive firm body, featuring an impressive, throbbing, uncircumcised manhood.

"What has my father told you?" Medea anxiously inquired. "I already know from my gift of prophecy, but I desire to hear the truth from your soft, innocent lips."

"Your superficial, selfish, contrarian father will not, under any circumstances, surrender the Golden Fleece, even after I have fully satisfied all of his demanding requirements," the visiting Greek Prince confirmed with regret. "King Aeetes absolutely refuses to allow me to exterminate the gruesome dragon that guards the tree in the Grove of Ares. This Golden Fleece operation is proving to be a really *tree*-mendous challenge."

"And Jason, that's the least of your worries," Medea cried-out while embracing her hero and feeling his semi-erect pecker rubbing against her crotch's slit', leading to the entrance of her hungry, wet pink, love tunnel.

"Be sure to set sail on the *Argo* by sunrise tomorrow morning, or else my repugnant Daddy intends to burn your splendid ship to a crisp, and then castrate and decapitate you and your inebriated crew of rowdies. Now, show patience and fortitude, dear Jason, and wait for me right here at midnight. I shall again utilize my enchantments to help you in your honorable and deserving quest. And furthermore," the concerned princess austerely stipulated. "Let's for now forget all about fuckin' sexual intercourse, or else you won't have any genitals to perform sex, or any mind, or body, to even fuckin' think about it, come tomorrow morning!"

After hiding-out in a gay and lesbian community brothel for the next seventeen hours, Jason sauntered back to the *Argo* to inform his intoxicated mariners that the foray into the consecrated Grove of Ares was imminent. And after the benevolent and rebellious Medea joined the merry party of revelers outside the 'Sacred Grove', the bevy (upon Jason's stubborn insistence), silently proceeded toward the aforementioned garden where the Golden Fleece sparkled and gleamed, while the treasured object remained suspended, in the distance, from a sturdy oak tree limb.

The excited, half-inebriated Argonauts quietly passed the pasture of the now-dead fire-snorting bulls, where two young offspring were busy licking each other's balls and peckers, while trying to establish a new pecking order, or in this case, a new *peckering* order as the offspring singed and scorched each other's reproductive organs, while desperately attempting to establish territorial dominance.

The invading Greek pirates and Medea surreptitiously entered the foreboding Holy Grove of Ares, and helpful Medea guided and escorted the entourage to the great oak tree, that for centuries, represented the home base for the miraculous Golden Fleece.

"Look over on that second, very strong limb," Medea directed Jason's attention. "See that unique ram's coat glistening in the pale moonlight. That resplendent glittering article constitutes your noble quest. That priceless gift is the inimitable, timeless Golden Fleece. Now, all *you* must do to possess it is to vanquish the vile, diabolical dragon guarding its presence."

Jason gingerly stepped-closer to the pulsating, magnificent golden phenomenon, and gazed at, and admired, its resplendent grandeur. 'So many have perished and lost their lives, dicks, and balls in quest of this very magnificent *sheepskin,* that should actually be conferred to me by the reluctant *University of Colchis,'* Jason creatively imagined. 'Now it is time to purloin this treasure, in order to finally accomplish my most essential mission.'

"Stay still, and staunchly guard your family jewels," Medea warned her all-too-impetuous lover. "Over yonder is the venomous dragon with its devastating, scaly tail coiled around the legendary oak tree. Perceptively, just watch that innocent antelope aimlessly bounding through the Grove of Ares, so that you Jason could completely fathom the palpable danger that presently imperils you."

The unaware antelope hastened and hopped towards the alluring Golden Fleece, but then the head of the viperous protector lashed-out like a whip, and its toxic fangs seized the unsuspecting creature, and in another minute, the formerly spry, brimming-with-life speedster was crunched in the predator's jaws, and then mercilessly devoured in one detestable swallow.

Then, the wary dragon's eyes instinctively perceived that many other enemy trespassers had stealthily invaded its off-limits territory. The monster stretched-out its long muscular neck with its evil mouth wide open, featuring sharp and lethal dagger-like fangs. Soon, the dragon's head came to within ten feet of where Jason, Medea, and the accompanying band of drunken, petrified Argonauts were stationed, frozen-still as statues. The viper's undulating head then came wriggling and waving in proximity of the encroachers, and soon managed to reach within a yard of everyone. Jason signaled to his warriors to retreat back several feet to avoid being selected and snatched into the loathsome beast's maw.

"Well, Jason," Medea austerely remarked. "Before you shit yourself and stink-up the whole Holy Grove of Ares, I want to know exactly what you think of your chances of escaping with the Golden Fleece right this very second."

Jason instinctively drew his sword and raised his shield, feigning the external courage necessary to audaciously engage in mortal combat with the indomitable viper. The vernal captain's quick impulsiveness was immediately criticized.

"Don't be absurd!" Medea sarcastically reproached her chosen hero. "Without my vital intercession and scholarly advice, you'll soon be dead meat, and your wonderful penis will cease pulsating and throbbing forever. In this tiny magic metal box is a secret potion that'll prove to be just as potent and wonderful as the hairy pink magic box between my legs."

As the dragon's curious head came to within a foot of Jason and Medea, the Princess neurotically and accidentally dropped the small container onto the ground, and just as Jason was about to be plucked-up and voraciously chewed to tiny bits and morsels, Castor (Pollux's twin brother and certainly one of the more fucked-up Argonauts) came rushing forward, and risking his life, tossed a gallon of his home-made Castor Oil into the throat of the repulsive hissing monster. The foul-tasting, extremely-sticky substance initially tranquilized, and then moments later, incapacitated the villainous dragon, which in a matter of thirty additional seconds, collapsed to the ground with a loud thud. But luckily for Castor, the part-time oil merchant had not strained-out the poisonous seeds from the castor plant, while producing that batch of Castor Oil, and so, the doomed dragon soon died from an overdose of food toxicity.

"That was great strategic thinking!" Jason complimented Castor in the midst of boisterous jeering from the still-drunken, but very impressed, hallucinating Argonauts. "And it's a good thing neither I nor my crew ever sampled any of your fucked-up liquid formula. I'd rather drink twenty-gallons of smelly cat piss than a single ounce of that fucked- up Castor Oil."

"My next project, Jason, will entail designing four sets of very sturdy Castor Wheels to serve as rollers to drag or pull a gigantic wooden horse I've been often dreaming nightly about," the imaginative Argonaut revealed. "You never know when an enormous wooden horse needs to be moved to a city's gates in a fuckin' hurry! I think I'll tell Odysseus about my novel idea!"

Now, as to why Jason is credited for the heroic deed of killing the terrible dragon is to this day incomprehensible, for most certainly, the great achievement ought to be rightfully attributed to the drunken imbecile Castor, who is incidentally discriminated against and despised by every biased chronicler, and by every prejudiced historian that absolutely and positively abhors the lousy, sticky, pungent taste of Castor Oil.

Everyone in the marauding contingent indulgently laughed at Castor's zany description of his next impractical objective. Then, Jason attempted bringing all his crew back to reality by stating something quite rational and plausible. "Men; let us now possess the Golden Fleece, and hightail it the fuck outa' here. King Aeetes plans to burn the *Argo* with or without us in it. Then, the dirty bastard has mendacious designs of severing our balls and our peckers, too, without even giving us any fuckin' severance pay. So, without any further-adieu, let's exhibit alert dispatch, and swiftly sprint our white, sweaty asses back to the *Argo*."

Jason stood on Castor's broad shoulders, and gently removed the coveted Golden Fleece from its traditional tree-limb perch. And when the outstanding hero jumped-down to ground level, avariciously clutching his grand prize, some sensation compelled the doughty Prince to turn his head to the right, where he beheld an old, wretched hag holding a cuckoo-headed brown staff, and sporting a peacock sitting motionless atop her right shoulder.

Then, the old bag yelled for Jason to immediately return to Iolcus, clapped her hands, and impressively transforming into the beautiful goddess Hera. And in an instant, Zeus's fickle wife gleefully vanished into the clear atmosphere that had enveloped her temporary, majestic presence.

The fifty-one jubilant participants dashed the full mile back to the *Argo*, and without wasting any additional valuable time, the ship's anchor was swiftly lifted, and soon the sleek, state-of-the-art vessel was sailing out of Colchis's narrow harbor. In another five minutes, the *Argo* was out of harm's way, and was safely being maneuvered by the intoxicated mariners back and forth across the Black Sea, until the cheerful crew all finally sobered-up, twenty-four hours later, and then finally navigated a straight course towards Iolcus.

"Uncle Pelias will shit himself when he sees me returning with the coveted Golden Fleece," Jason told Medea. "I have, with your illustrious aid, miraculously performed the impossible!"

"Just like my ruthless father, King Aeetes has already done," the astute prophetess Medea obtusely verified. "As everybody presently knows, 'Birds of a feather, often shit together'; or more specifically, the dual vile scoundrels simply often bombard their droppings at the same time in different places, as is the remarkable case of sullen King Pelias of Ioclus, and the equal dastardly bastard, King Aeetes of Colchus."

"Beowulf"

Around fifteen-hundred years ago, the Anglo-Saxon language (the forerunner of modern English) began evolving into the fucked-up vernacular it is today. Stories transformed from oral tradition into an oral sex tradition, where eventually, drab written words would transform from nebulous horseshit, into more sophisticated bull-shit. One of those ass-backwards, dip-shit stories was that of the hero Beowulf, a warrior of *Scandinavian* descent (guys that liked staring intensively at women's sexy, lint-filled bellybuttons).

The Beowulf legends have as their principal settings Denmark and Sweden, two of the most primitive and barbaric un-civilizations in the mythical-mystical Norse *Dark Ages,* which everyone knows was the time before candles or daylight were invented. Most of Beowulf's life had been spent searching pre-medieval Europe for large Italian meatballs, because the champion was tired of being born with, and having to live with, small Swedish testicles.

Hygelac was king of the Geats, a tribe of Viking-like idiots that lived in southern Sweden. The weirdos drank mead from large ram horns. The mixture of fermented water and honey made them drunk, horny, gay, and more fucked-up than the craziest of "you're a peon" insane asylum residents.

Hygelac loved sailing, and the moron loved sailors, so in his youth, he had formed a male exotic gay men's ballet group that danced throughout Denmark's 'meadows', searching for beehives to make mead. The traveling troupe of homosexual male go-go dancers was known throughout that fucked-up area of the maniacal world as the *Ship and Dales.*

"Listen Angelm," King Hygelac commanded his stupid-looking, genetically inferior dwarf-bard. "Fetch thy dissonant harp, and sing for my men and me some marvelous songs about distant whores, sluts, harlots and ancient, ball-breaking jerk-offs! Seafarers have come to us from Denmark, and the traders, or should I say traitors, ought to be royally entertained before I steal their trading products, and then execute each of their asses by sacrificing some of them to Woden on Wednesday, and the remaining dumb-dicks to Thor on Thursday!"

The recently-arrived Sea Captain realized that he had to think quickly in order to discourage Hygelac from eliminating him and his seafaring crew from the distinction of certain extinction, so the clever fellow contrived a fantastic story, in an attempt to earn King Hygelac's sympathy and clemency.

"Great King Hygelac; Hrothgar was a brave warrior king of my retarded ancestors," the worried Sea Captain began his fictional narrative. "And the doltish shit-head built a fabulous mead hall where he and his trusted guards could entertain any itinerant assholes, like me, and my mooching men, that arrived at his great house's door!"

"Are you tryin' to insult me and my thanes?" King Hygelac asked the panicky Sea Captain. "Do you mean that Hrothgar's mead hall was even fuckin' bigger than mine?"

"At least seven times as large and seven times as magnificent," the worm-brain Sea Captain brazenly and honestly maintained. "And Hrothgar's dick was also three times as long, and at least twice as thick, as yours, too. And Hrothgar had golden antlers hanging all over the extraordinary mead hall, and named the place Heorot the Hart, after a very sacred deer that the Danish king had laboriously taught to give oral sex to all his special guests."

"Quit the goddamned bull-shit Captain, and get to your story!" King Hygelac insisted. "Or else, I'll command Angelm to stick your Norse testicles between the strings of his out-of-tune harp, and then wildly rotate his annoying musical instrument, until you're totally castrated and bleeding all over the fuckin' place!"

"Okay, okay," the illustrious-but-alarmed Sea Captain readily agreed. "But Hrothgar would've been better-off if he had choked on a pound of straw stuffed down his throat, rather than have to suffer humiliation and defeat as was his ultimate fate!"

The sly-but-apprehensive Sea Captain then patiently waited for a curious response from the shrewd-but-egotistical ruler of *his* somewhat captivated audience.

"Well then," King Hygelac finally replied. "What the fuck really had made Hrothgar so paranoid and depressed? And why is the Danish king so dissatisfied with his gargantuan, incomparable mead hall? Has it been turned into a public toilet, or converted into some sort of communal outhouse for chronic diarrhea sufferers? Ha, ha, ha."

All of King Hygelac's thanes seated inside the splendid mead hall mimicked their ruler by indulgently mimicking and laughing in unison, "Ha, ha, ha!"

"On the contrary," the experienced-and-coy Sea Captain answered. "Even a king making merry with his chief warriors should perceive who might be eavesdropping and stalking outside *his* cherished mead hall. Even I can't get a decent hard-on inside a nudist colony of beautiful maidens, whenever I think about the looming disaster that perpetually awaited King Hrothgar outside his most-majestic drinking hall!"

"What imbecilic nonsense!" King Hygelac exclaimed, as the insane monarch massaged his young son Heardred's thigh, and then the toddler's hairless, pre-pubescent crotch. "Who was prowling around poor old King Hrothgar's mead hall to cause such unwarranted anxiety? His harem of kinky dykes and transsexual cross-dressers?"

The insulted Sea Captain angrily grabbed Angelm's harp, stuck the midget's head through several of the taut strings, and then strenuously rotated the instrument four times, until the minstrel's face and noggin separated from, and then fell, off his neck. "The evil eavesdropper, dear king, was Grendel the Night Stalker!" the livid Sea Captain disclosed, as Angelm's head rolled-down the slanted floor, and knocked-down ten small miniature totem poles that had conveniently served as bowling pins. "Grendel is known as the Man Wolf; yes, the Shadowy Death that maintains lairs all along the Danish shores, and now also along *your* Swedish coasts and salt marshes. Grendel had heard King Hrothgar's raucous merriments, and the formidable beast absolutely despises laughing and revelry," the Sea Captain warned Hygelac and his very amused and now-captivated thanes. "No thick, heavy, barred door can keep the monster out of even the most colossal and secure of mead halls!"

The warriors seated at the feast table again became silent, and then the arrogant King Hygelac felt compelled to sternly address the Sea Captain. "Do you expect me to put credence in this adult fairy tale you are awkwardly weaving?" the king asked the very serious and worried Sea Captain. "I'm more likely to receive a good blowjob from a neighborhood woodland Troll than to be visited by this patrolling, obnoxious, imaginary nemesis Grendel, if you will. Ha, ha, ha!"

And then the king's strongest warriors mocked the visiting Sea Captain, along with his jerked-off crew, by imitating the crude example of their brutal ruler, Hygelac. "Ha, ha, ha!" the seated thanes impolitely insulted their less-bellicose merchant guests.

The Sea Captain waited for the men's celebrating and loud criticism and jeers to finally settle-down. Then, the storyteller proceeded with resuming his most-abused dissertation. "As I had stated to you pea-brains, Grendel hates all joy and festivity," the worried captain continued, very deliberately. "And the beast lusts for human blood; human death, and human souls. The demonic monster quickly knocked-down a wall to Hrothgar's mead hall and attacked, killed, and dismembered thirty of the shocked king's most valiant thanes, in what constituted a very bloody battle. After the hideous brute completed his dastardly, heinous deed," the emphatic captain proceeded, "the mutilation was so thorough that not a single finger, bone, or dick could be identified in the whole fuckin' place. The Danish king sat petrified like a stone statue upon his ebony throne. In fact, the monarch was too frightened and petrified to even scratch his balls," the merchant ship captain revealed and emphasized. "Finally, leaving just one survivor, Grendel winked at the terrified King Hrothgar, and left the royal premises, which then looked like a total disaster area!"

"This is an evil, obscene story you tell," King Hygelac declared to the visiting Sea Captain. "But King Hrothgar should've been happy seeing potential enemies, his own traitorous thanes, eliminated before *his* very eyes!"

All of King Hygelac's assembled warriors laughed incessantly in response to their leader's astute and sage observation. The thane audience eventually toned-down their excessive levity ten-minutes later, wanting to listen to more verbal horse-shit.

"But you must understand, noble King Hygelac," the garrulous Sea Captain elaborated. "Once Grendel is aroused, the beast lusts for more-and-more human death, and the despicable creature does not sleep or rest after it performs its diabolical massacres. And from that day on, King Hrothgar's mead hall has been wickedly cursed," the seafaring news-bringer related. "And the poor Danish ruler must now sit in a lousy outhouse all day long, even when his asshole doesn't have to take a healthy shit, or else Grendel will destroy the king, and use *his* miniature balls in a custom-made slingshot."

"Indeed, Heorot sounds like an extinct mead hall," King Hygelac observed and orally concluded. "But can't King Hrothgar find any hero in all of Denmark to combat and defeat this wretched Grendel? I mean, can't some ambitious young champion with a hard-on shove a porcupine and a sea urchin up the vile creature's asshole, and make the fucker bleed to death from the inside out?"

The Sea Captain shook his head from side to side, not only because he disagreed with King Hrothgar's suggestion, but also because he had a very stiff neck. "At first, dear thanes, the noble king's thirty audacious warriors that had been tanked-up on mead challenged the vicious beast's might, but after the Danish thanes had been decapitated, castrated, and literally had their balls broken and then pulverized, one by one, by the vicious attacking monster," the Sea Captain described, "no one ever since has had the courage to wander about or near the accursed mead hall."

"And this scourge you call Grendel, does he or it still haunt King Hrothgar's empty mead hall?" Hygelac asked. "Does that monster have a low mental capacity or what? Is the creature mentally challenged? How many large brain tumors does the dumb-shit have? Ha, ha, ha!"

"Ha, ha, ha!" the Swedish king's thanes all roared, mimicking their leader in what was, and is still today known by illiterate psychologists as the "Chameleon Behavioral Effect".

When all of the noise and clamor settled-down, the merchant ship captain continued his intriguing tale. "Grendel stalks and prowls what is now the deserted Heorot Hart Memorial Mead Hall every night in quest of brave men's blood, but since only cowards reside in the area ever since the atrocious thane massacre, poor King Hrothgar has no alternative but to shit, worry, and jerk-off in his tiny wooden outhouse," the Sea Captain explained to his now-mesmerized, drunken audience. "The putrid, foul smell of the monster's scaly body, its urine, and its stench-laden feces is evident all over the fuckin' empty hall, and believe me when I tell you dim-wit knuckleheads that it is no *hall*ucination I'm presently depicting. One day *Weird Wyrd,* who determines men's ultimate fate, will provide Hrothgar with 'weird word' of a courageous hero, both dauntless and strong, to rid Denmark of the insidious, stalking Death-Shadow!"

"If this Grendel ever swims from Denmark to mainland Sweden and starts bustin' my balls," King Hygelac asserted in a very concerned voice, "I'll have to then become a pussy, just like King Hrothgar is over there in Denmark across the sea! I smell something rotten in Copenhagen, yes, I do! And I don't even have a fuckin' small wooden outhouse to stay confined in, either!"

"I assure you, King Hygelac, that Grendel also has several lairs along your coast," the Sea Captain informed.

A certain handsome, gray-eyed thane, who sat near the now-alarmed King Hygelac, astutely watched the monarch fondle and masturbate Prince Heardred's one-inch-long dingle. Then, the alert listener's eyes focused upon the distraught Sea Captain's countenance, and the sea-rover's incredulous story seemed to register, and finally resurrect, a certain memory that had been buried deep inside the gray-eyed thane's subconscious mind.

'I owe King Hrothgar a big favor!' the muscular hero realized. 'If I don't travel to Denmark and slaughter this repulsive Grendel menace,' Beowulf stupidly thought, 'then my beloved native Sweden will become just as fucked-up as fucked-up Denmark is right now!'

Beowulf, King Hygelac's sister's 'delusions of grandeur' son, recognized that it was *his* destiny to establish a noble warrior reputation by soundly thrashing and killing the insidious Grendel. 'Then, I shall return to Sweden, butcher young Heardred, blame it on Grendel's vindictive grandmother, and subsequently, ascend to the throne of Sweden, after I next dispose of that craven asshole, Uncle Hygelac!' Beowulf cunningly contemplated. 'But first, I must repay my family's debt to good King Hrothgar, who must be freezing his ass off over in Denmark, sitting the whole winter upon his tiny outhouse's inferior wooden throne!'

Beowulf's father was Ecgtheow, a member of the famed Wylfing (ancient name meaning "Wild Things") tribe, noted for its insanity and its senility. When the incest-oriented Wylfings became involved in a wicked family feud, Ecgtheow had amazingly escaped the crisis and took to the sea; became a rover (pirate); and spent the rest of his life looking for a Norse paradise on a distant fantasy-continent called Pittsburgh.

Beowulf's father and mother had eventually arrived in Denmark, and the Swedish couple were cordially welcomed into King Hrothgar's regal court. Ecgtheow had died from complications caused by eight different types of venereal disease, but Beowulf had already been born at the Danish court, which existed many centuries before the hilarious founding of the Hague Tribunal.

'I shall hop into my long battle boat, select some staunch yeomen rowers from King Hygelac's motley mead hall, and get the hell out of Sweden before the Dumb Ass monarch realizes that I've stolen his men, and planned to assassinate that little gay faggot Heardred; and next his fucked-up, cowardly, homosexual Daddy!' Beowulf imagined. 'Uncle Hygelac must never know that my mother (his sister) had been a hooker back in Denmark, and that I am not *his* legitimate nephew!' Beowulf intelligently speculated.

The following morning, Beowulf organized a loyal crew that included his kinsmen Waegmund, Prince of Wigland; and also, Hondscio of Honcho, and Myassisgrass of Myassisgrassland. 'If I can only recruit the hero Eurdikisshown, then my crew shall be complete,' Hygelac's illegitimate nephew imagined.

The following historic night at the Swedish mead feast, Beowulf rose to his feet and approached the faggot King Hygelac, who was preoccupied fondling Prince Heardred's one-inch-long miniature boner. "My Lord Hygelac," Beowulf firmly said to the perverted pedophile. "I beg a leave of absence from your fucked-up court in order to have a spectacular adventure in Denmark, and successfully eradicate Grendel for your favorite trading toilet-mouthed buddy, King Hrothgar of Hopper."

"Do you require anyone besides your normal crew of worthless, despicable assholes?" King Hygelac asked the ambitious-and-greedy young warrior.

"Yes, I'd like to recruit Eurdikissshown!" Beowulf requested.

"What the fuck's wrong with you!" King Hygelac admonished. "My dick is not showing! Only Prince Heardred's tiny one-inch-long tassel is presently observable!"

"No, your High-ass," Beowulf quickly corrected. "I meant that I would especially like to have the renowned jerk-off Eurdikisshown to accompany my crew and me on our daring voyage to Denmark to get laid; to get blown by beautiful nymphs, and to finally eliminate Grendel from the hearts and minds of cowardly, craven, feckless kings like Hrothgar and you!"

Hygelac stopped fondling young Prince Heardred, and then perceptively peered into Beowulf's gray eyes. "Tell me why you wish to risk your life and foolishly make a preposterous journey to Denmark, simply to get laid; to get blown, and to futilely battle this imaginary Grendel!" Hygelac screamed at his illegitimate nephew. "Don't we have enough good-looking cunts for you and your kinky crew to screw and lick right here in Sweden? What the hell's wrong with Swedish whores?"

"When my seafaring father needed a friend to provide him with food, shelter, welfare, porn' and social security," Beowulf admirably testified, "he found such an idiot in King Hrothgar of Denmark. My first memories after being born were being wrapped in a soft wolf skin blanket, and being held next to a warm fire, and intensively sucking on my mother's firm tits and their rubbery nipples. Even at a young age, I was pretending to be a contented calf sucking away on one of my mama's delicious udders!"

"But I already know all the phony bull-shit about your harebrained father, Ecgtheow," King Hygelac indignantly related. "Why do *you*, quixotic Beowulf, feel indebted to this fucked-up King Hrothgar?"

"Hrothgar paid a Wergild, which in Denmark is a ransom-fine to the Wylfings for the man my father had murdered after finding my unfaithful daddy in bed with *your* promiscuous, incestuous sister," Beowulf truthfully articulated to the already pissed-off Swedish king. "I remember that I was but six-years-old, but I still had a dick three times as long as Prince Heardred's tiny penis, even though I hadn't had my first hard-on yet. Anyway," Beowulf continued. "King Hrothgar gave me shelter, money and his daughter and wife to screw, so as you can plainly see, I am somewhat indebted to the stupid fuck-head, and now I need to reinstate him as the eminent ruler of Denmark."

"I suspected as much; I suspected as much," Hygelac woefully answered. "Beowulf, my whoring sister's son; I'm aware that you are foremost among my intrepid thanes. Next to young Heardred here, you are perhaps my closest kinsman. I grieve to witness you embarking on such a treacherous, international mission. I shall be watching for your return from the cliffs overlooking my castle's fiord. And when you return to Sweden," Hygelac predicted, "Prince Heardred will have finally experienced his first authentic hard-on and successful ejaculation. I guarantee it with all of the dozens of sperm in my shriveled-up balls!"

"Thank you, King!" Beowulf exclaimed with his right hand over his heart, and with his left palm firmly gripping his balls and pecker, which was the official Geats' geeks way of saying "Goodbye and fuck you".

"Be sure to sail with Waegmund, Prince of Wigland; Hondscio of Honcho; Myassisgrass of Myassisgrassland, and finally, Nephew Beowulf, don't forget to stow-away Eurdikisshown," the king reminded the gallant warrior.

Beowulf and his merry crew finally made it from Sweden to Denmark, after enjoying wild *Ball*-tic orgies in Norway, Finland, Russia, France, and England. The hero and his crew removed King Hrothgar from self-exile inside his stenchy *wooden* outhouse (dedicated to Woden), and the men then daringly entered Heorot, the King's deserted Hart Memorial Mead Hall, where *Danish* (thanes) without coffee had been served to Grendel.

"Beowulf, soon it will be dark," Hrothgar nervously declared after being successfully liberated from his outhouse. "And I fear the wretched monster will again plunder the hall, and mutilate all of your brave men right before my sorrowful eyes. Are you certain you and your asshole thanes wish to fight Grendel?"

"My ongoing venture shall be a glorious adventure," Beowulf affirmatively and redundantly articulated. "And I'm not one to flee from a formidable challenge, or retreat from a dangerous opponent. I came here to Denmark to kick ass, and then to celebrate my victory by injecting sperm juice into every decent-looking whore's snatcheroo I can find!"

"I always knew you were a great Geat!" Hrothgar praised his remarkable visitor. "Beowulf, I shall reward you with all of the pink, hairy crotcholas you want from all over my vast kingdom, starting with my ugly fat wife, and my sex-crazed daughter. You'll never get bored in one of my bordellos, I assure you. Now tell me honestly Beowulf," Hrothgar continued his weird inquiry. "What valiant, crusading men have you brought with you?"

"Waegmund of Wigland; Hondscio of Honcho; Myassisgrass of Myassisgrassland, and Eurdikisshown!" Beowulf proudly and haughtily announced.

"I agree that my ass is grass if my dick is showing," King Hrothgar readily admitted, "and I also concur that someday Waegmund of Wigland will become the Head Honcho replacing Hondscio."

"You're actually more fucked-up than King Hygelac is, or ever was!" Beowulf confided to the woebegone Danish King Hrothgar. "I never knew that there were so many perverted, gay, faggot rulers all over the goddamned known blown world! Your fuckin' kingdom seems more like a low-budget gay and lesbian community."

"The great, abandoned, mostly-destroyed mead hall is yours until morning arrives," Hrothgar verbally conveyed to Beowulf. "Now young fellow, I leave you and your noble yeomen to perform your duty, while I cowardly retire to my bed and smell my wife's raunchy, dried-up, atrophied slit-hole, while my kiss-up cousin Lord Eatitall sucks my mediocre, royal fadorkenbender!"

All throughout the great Heorot Hart Memorial Mead-Drinking-Hall, Beowulf's audacious soldiers found sleeping areas where the assigned sentinels were to nervously await Grendel's stealthy appearance amongst them. Hrothgar's obedient thralls (slaves and servants) laid-down comfortable wolf-skin mats for the paranoid fifteen Swedish warriors to rest upon. The guest warriors anxiously listened for Grendel's furtive approach, and the night shadows slowly descended into the totally-silent, now-sinister, partially-destroyed mead hall.

"Bar the doors," Beowulf imperatively commanded, "so that way, we can hear the monster poaching, encroaching and approaching. I pledge to all present hearing my words that whoever cuts Grendel's dick-off gets a free month's vacation licking all kinds of succulent pussy up in Lapland!"

"Hooray! We'll have to go north before we can go south!" yelled one of the fifteen ecstatic Swedish combatants named Kaytee, who was helping to bar the door. "Hooray! Hooray!" the fourteen other morons chanted rather vigorously.

Myassisgrass and Eurdikisshown then assisted Kaytee by lifting a huge wooden bar from the bloodstained mead hall floor, and then inserted the heavy board securely into the socket slots.

"Shit; I got three splinters in my right forearm!" Myassisgrass exclaimed to his temporary partners.

"That's incredible!" Eurdikisshown replied. "Your right forearm looked like a fuckin' splinter before you ever got three additional splinters in it! But now your friggin' right forearm looks like a goddamned toothpick!"

"Suck my wet dick all the way to Lapland!" Myassisgrass shouted at Eurdikisshown. "May your mother's left wooden peg-leg get fully infested with a fuckin' hungry termite colony."

The contingent of brave soldiers sat along the inside perimeter of vast Heorot Hall, picking their noses; scratching their asses, and smelling each other's sweat, stenchy farts, armpits, and crotches. The fatigued commandos finally retired beside their swords and suits of armor, while Beowulf handed Waegmund of Wigland *his* charmed crested helmet; his charmed sword, and his charmed sweaty jockstrap.

"Mortal weapons are quite useless against supernatural creatures such as Grendel," Beowulf told Waegmund of Wigland.

"Why do we even bother with stupid-assed spears and swords?" the loyal disciple asked.

"Because my sword works like a charm!" the hero ingeniously answered. "And so does my helmet, and my stenchy jockstrap, too. And I must tell you Waegmund of Wigland; if it wasn't for enterprising assholes like us," Beowulf indicated to his somewhat-appreciative subordinate, "then the world would be without fucked-up legends, and would also be devoid of fucked-up myths to tell! How about that for fascinating bull-shit?"

"Aren't you afraid of dying?" Waegmund of Wigland wanted to know.

"Once I die, I'll finally achieve happiness in Valhalla," Beowulf calmly and irrationally replied. "Then, my dear Waegmund of Wigland, I'll be able to fight each day; get killed in battle; become gloriously reincarnated into myself; enjoy a great feast, and then have the pleasure of again getting killed in combat, and so on, and so on! What a fuckin' fabulous existence, with me doing and repeating the things I love most, over and over again, for all eternity!"

"You have a lot of *Nirvana* talking about Valhalla like that!" Beowulf's only listener joked. "I'm content simply dealing with the trivial chicken-shit of this friggin' world, without ever having to think about, or contend with, the heavy-duty bull-shit associated with the afterworld!" Waegmund of Wigland smartly concluded and shared. "I mean," said Beowulf's rather dull-headed apprentice, "supernatural bull-shit, to me, seems rather incomprehensible and insignificant when compared to the natural bull-shit I can't even fuckin' understand in *this* hellhole, forsaken life!"

In the darkest hour of that late April night, Grendel exited its concealed lair under the sea, and crawled its way to accursed Heorot Memorial Mead Hall to snack on some recently arrived Swedish human meatballs. The mammoth creature slinked its way to the hall's porch, and sniffed all around, looking for newly-arrived warrior feces to merely whet *his* disgusting appetite. The monster soon discovered that the formerly unbolted door had been defiantly fastened shut. The hideous, grotesque creature used his sharp talons as sharp claws, and then easily thrust its massive anatomy through the door's thick timbers.

The internal darkness camouflaged Grendel's form as the awesome behemoth slinked and slithered around Heorot Memorial Mead Hall, searching for human flesh to consume, and human blood to drink. In a second's span, Grendel leaped-out to the right side of Hrothgar's once-splendid mead hall, and grabbed onto the surprised Hondscio of Honcho, and in ten-seconds-flat, the fearsome monster had voraciously shoved the screaming warrior down its horrible, cavernous throat.

The creature's sharp teeth could be heard crunching and severing Hondscio's brittle bones between its unearthly jaws. The monster then latched onto Eurdikisshown, but before the despicable dragon-like predator could even inspect his victim's exposed pecker, or swallow any of the seaman's semen, Grendel suddenly felt a strong grip seize his scaly right claw. The abominable creature felt fear enter its heart for the very first time.

"You have met your match if not your master," Beowulf yelled in vain, because the illiterate Grendel knew few words in Geat, Swedish, Danish or Monster. "Do you know Eurdikisshown?"

Grendel immediately dropped Eurdikisshown, because those words' meanings *he had* remarkably completely fathomed. The hostile monster glanced-down to see if *his dick was showing*. In one swift swing of his mighty, enchanted iron sword, Beowulf cut-off the creature's two-foot-long, limp, genital-sperm-injector.

'How am I ever gonna' be able to piss now?' Grendel thought, as the horrid-looking creature looked-down and saw green blood gushing-out of his former reproductive and urine-excretory organ. 'Holy shit! I'm still a fuckin' virgin, and *now* I'm fuckin' dick-less!' the creature angrily and frightfully realized.

Then, Grendel tossed, turned, howled, and screamed all over the floor, attempting to liberate his four-ton-body from Beowulf's steel-like grip. The pair rolled over and over again, while the relieved Eurdikisshown took a healthy crap in one corner of the mead hall, as the other drunken warriors, still obliviously slept upon the hard floor, while dreaming of comfortable hammocks, soft haystacks, and hairy pussies galore.

During the tremendous, four-hour-long, marathon tussle, Grendel shrieked and squealed, while Beowulf hardly breathed deeply, as the duo rolled all over the memorial mead hall, crashing and banging into walls, and careening off of myriad tables and benches. All during the lengthy fracas, Eurdikisshown kept shitting on the wooden floor, and his thane companions kept sleeping and dreaming of screwing horny old hags in hammocks and haystacks (while snoring inside the four-feces-infested corners of Heorot Hall).

Hrothgar and his Danish court anxiously stood outside the vast memorial mead hall, and earnestly listened to the intense, violent struggle going-on inside. The craven king and his feckless advisers were too weak and too cowardly to dare enter the gigantic chamber. The Swedish warriors inside finally awoke from their deep slumbers, and each immediately grabbed his sword. However, the visiting entourage was fearful of accidentally slaying Beowulf, while attempting to assassinate the very mobile Grendel.

Myassisgrass tried penetrating Grendel's scaly exoskeleton with his flimsy sword, but the monster's covering was sheathed in a magical surface, and the blows merely glanced off the creature after each impact. Then, Myassisgrass came-up with a very clever idea. The shrewd swordsman grabbed some wet turds recently shit-out by Eurdikisshown, and deftly shoved them into the rolling creature's mouth. Grendel began choking relentlessly, as he and Beowulf caromed off of walls, furniture, benches, chairs, tables and Eurdikisshown, who was frantically trying to maintain his balance while still vulnerably stooping-down to take the most-wicked dump of his entire life, and of recorded history, also.

When all of the dense walls of Heorot Hall had been knocked-down, and the roof had partially caved-in, Grendel attempted one last-ditch effort to liberate himself from Beowulf's almost-superhuman clutches. The two figures finally separated, and Grendel desperately departed the devastated mead hall without his fearsome right arm and shoulder, which were still in the astonished Beowulf's bloody hands.

"Oh, vile wretched creature!" Beowulf yelled at the fleeing monster. "You have met my *'arm-a-gettin'!'*"

"And it's not even *Disarm*ament Day!" a grateful Myassisgrass gasped. "Wow Beowulf; you really ripped-off Grendel! You should go into business as a fuckin' con-artist!"

"That Grendel scared the shit out of me!" Eurdikisshown panted as the slow-learner raised his fighting kilt exposing his massive penis and dirty smelly ass. "Please tell me, guys, if I had shitted my stomach onto the floor! Hey, what happened to the goddamned roof and to the freakin' walls?"

"Your dick is showin'!" Myassisgrass pointed-out.

"I'm glad I still have it!" Eurdikisshown exclaimed, as the dumb-ass idiot flaunted his genitalia for everyone present to see and inspect. "If my dick had been devoured by Grendel, then I would think that *my ass is grass!*"

Beowulf finally realized the magnitude and meaning of the marathon grappling demonstration that he had just participated-in with Grendel. The Swedish hero dropped to the planked floor of what remained of Heorot Memorial Hart Hall, and began whimpering like a baby. The visiting warriors all gathered-around their invincible leader, and next closely examined the ripped-off, scaly, bloody remnants of the totally vanquished Night-Stalker.

"Not even the Troll-creatures could survive such a savagely administered lethal wound!" Waegmund of Wigland joyfully exclaimed. "Grendel will surely die alone in his lair, if he has been lucky enough to make it to that secret hideout location."

"Lucky Hondscio of Honcho successfully make it out of this miserable life, and has happily advanced to Valhalla!" Myassisgrass theorized and shared with his close companions. "His name should've been Myassisgrass!"

"Thank Thor that my testicles, pecker, and asshole are still attached to my lower abdomen!" Eurdikisshown shouted as the cretin again exposed to everyone his enviable apparatus.

The men celebrated Beowulf's unprecedented victory over Grendel by nailing the monster's huge, scaly arm and shoulder (using foot-long spikes) onto a still-standing, semi-vertical beam, situated above Hrothgar's memorial mead hall throne.

When dawn appeared upon the eastern horizon, Beowulf and his vanguard of primitive warriors stood upon a chilly Danish shore, and dreamed of heading back north in their seaworthy boat toward Sweden. The exhausted combatants then observed tremendous waves turbulently churning and soaring in the distance.

"That must be Grendel's lair," Myassisgrass noted. "The monster must be drowning under the sea!"

"It's probably just a school of giant sperm whales farting their' way south, and enjoying immense multiple orgasms under the damned ocean!" Eurdikisshown insisted. "I've seen that same bull-shit phenomenon many times before over near Wales!"

All over that area of Denmark, merriment was occurring, as news of Beowulf's fantastic triumph circulated around Hrothgar's one-mile-square kingdom. The king's royal bard paraded through the revelers, and organized an appropriate song of praise commending the Swedish champion's extraordinary accomplishment.

Hrothgar and his Queen arrived at Heorot Memorial Hart Hall, and ordered that the almost-demolished structure be immediately rebuilt on time, with its future magnificence to even exceed its past glory, in order to celebrate the planned evening's festivities in tribute to Beowulf. All the while, everyone gazed in astonishment at the great claw trophy that had been nailed above the king's splintery, ebony throne.

"Hrothgar, I originally intended to wrestle the creature down on the floor, and choke the son-of-a-bitch to death," Beowulf recollected and sincerely stated. "But despite all of my stamina and endurance, Grendel was able to frenetically grapple with me for many hours, as we rolled all over your damned ramshackle memorial mead hall."

"I knew I should've purchased a more comprehensive insurance policy on the mead hall building!" King Hrothgar lamented. "Now I have to sell my prized human midget and dwarf collection to defray the expenses for the massive hall's reconstruction."

"No insurance company will ever cover the destruction of a building because of a death-struggle fight between a grotesque monster and a handsome hero!" the Danish Queen logically interrupted. "Forget insurance. Honesty is the best policy!"

"The creature's scales are like a sheath of thick armor," Eurdikisshown uttered, completely off subject. "Beowulf; you have indeed performed a most-excellent, superhuman deed of epic proportions, truly worthy of our honor!"

252

"I have now repaid the favor *you* had done for Ecgtheow," Beowulf disclosed to the cheerful Danish king.

"Who the fuck is Ecgtheow?" Hrothgar wonderingly asked. "Is he a traveling salesman, or a local fruit and vegetable huckster? A notorious pimp, perhaps?"

"He was my father," Beowulf solemnly replied. "Ecgtheow was servicing your wife while you were cavorting all over Denmark, having freaky, perverted sex with faggots, lesbians, and other assorted queer homos'!"

"That means that all of my heirs are illegitimate bastards!" Hrothgar realized and lividly yelled. "Kill all the covetous, greedy, leeching, parasitic, genetically-inferior bastards and bitches right now!" the king commanded his military leader.

"My father Ecgtheow has finally been joined in Valhalla by dear Hondscio of Honcho," Beowulf ecstatically related. "Now the lucky men can battle, die, feast, and get drunk and laid, for all eternity."

Hrothgar placed his right arm around Beowulf's still bleeding shoulder and divulged, "After my guards kill-off all of my direct male descendants and potential heirs," the king whispered into the hero's ear, "then you, Beowulf, shall be my adopted son, because you have also always been my biological son," the naughty ruler confidentially disclosed. "My most coveted secret I have now shared!"

"But I always had thought that *you* were a gay, fucked-up, son-of-a-bitch?" Beowulf returned in a bewildered, low, disbelieving voice.

"When I was a young man, I happened to be a bisexual," King Hrothgar informed the dumbfounded, stunned hero. "I had been a carefree, practicing bisexual, until one fine day, I finally wised-up and realized my true sexual identity."

"The Fourth Voyage of Sindbad"

The Voyages of Sindbad are part of a body of literature known as *The Arabian Knights*. A big-crotched queen had betrayed her little-dicked husband by being unfaithful. The monarch was not a good lover in bed, but had keenly, economically screwed everyone in his sleazy realm, especially ruining the horny queen's family's wealth. According to oral (sex) tradition, the angry, small-peckered ruler murdered his wife because of her gross infidelity, and the rich, mentally-warped monarch then vowed never to keep another marriage partner longer than a day, who might publicly gossip about his miniature penis.

So, every morning the paranoid, self-conscious king married a new woman, porked her with his minuscule beef injector in the afternoon, and then killed her the following dawn before randomly marrying another promiscuous female. Then, a courageous lady named Shahrazad married the crazy king with the incredible inferiority complex, and to prevent herself' from being killed, the new wife would tell the insecure monarch a wonderful story each night, so that the dumb-ass did not execute her, and wanted to hear the next tale in the amazing bull-shit saga.

After a thousand and one thrilling nights, the loony king decided to keep Shahrazad as a wife, especially when the garrulous woman told the neurotic emperor that she was really married to the notorious Sindbad the Sailor, and that her jealous husband would castrate and systematically dismember the wimpy king should *he* dare lay a hand on her in an uncouth manner, in one of his uncouth manors. Here is one of the spectacular tales about *her* alleged spouse Sindbad that had captured the maniacal king's imagination, and had also intensified his fear. Shahrazad narrated the story in the first person, while pretending to be her very famous fake husband, Sindbad, telling the tale.

Being stranded in a foreign land really sucks. The territory and its alien inhabitants seemed more fucked-up than I was, and I persistently cursed and muttered, as I trekked onward toward a faint glimmer in the distance, which I suspected to be a 'mirage', even though I knew that I wasn't anywhere near *Caesar's Palace*. My illusion turned-out to be a dozen men gathering pepper from plants that were growing wildly along the rugged coastline. The simpleton bastards were sneezing all over the damned place, every time the ninnies tried talking, and the twelve nutcases were covered from head to toe in hideous snot and mucus globs.

As soon as the pepper gatherers noticed me approaching, the imbeciles instinctively hastened in my direction, while discharging an abundance of mucus all over the goddamned place. "Who are you, and where the fuck do you come from?" the snotnoses all amazingly chanted simultaneously.

'Either these sneezing and spitting jerk-offs have a limited vocabulary, or the dolts all think the exact same thoughts!' I naturally imagined. "I'm a poor stranger to this extraordinary fucked-up land, and I'm allergic to pepper, so I want to warn you erratic assholes to keep your damned distance, or else I'll have to surgically cut your balls off with my scimitar," I sternly answered.

"That's nothing to sneeze about!" the twelve idiots all stated in unison. "We don't want to have our testicles tested like that!"

"But I want you nasal dunces to know that I'm simply a poor unfortunate, wandering, shipwrecked sailor, stranded in this very desolate land," I articulated. And then I felt compelled to relate my sensational adventures to the *nosy,* gasping pepper gatherers, and the dipshits listened intently to my intriguing stories, while disgustingly wiping their sticky nostrils onto each other's clothing. The hunched-over pepper pickers were astounded by my incredible revelations, and almost sneezed their tracheas and lungs out at the climax, instead of jerking-off' at the climax, as normal men would surely do.

"By Allah's grace; your tales are absolutely marvelous!" the stupid-fucks all chanted, while coincidentally sending wet green boogers spraying in all directions. But apparently, one of the allergic morons had a mind of his' own.

"But Sindbad, how did you manage to escape the cannibals on the far side of this island, who devour anyone that trespasses into their off-limits territory?" the curious snot-nose nicknamed "Sergeant Pepper" asked, before spitting-out a large green lunger onto the hot beach sand to watch it sizzle like an egg being fried. "No one ever escapes the savages' *clutches,* or eludes their automatic thought transmissions."

I told the sloppy sneezers about the other ship survivors' unlucky fate. My sailor colleagues had come under the cannibals' witchdoctor's peculiar spell. The pepper gatherers felt sorry for *my* cruel plight, and provided me with adequate food (two pepper sandwiches), which I immediately washed in a nearby stream, even though at the time, I knew nothing about such harmful things as germs and bacteria. I noticed some blackbirds flying and cawing overhead, scavenging for food morsels, so I rather *raven*ously ate the lousy pepper berries, sandwiched between bread slices, which I had been given.

The pepper gatherers then escorted me to their small ship, lifted anchor, and skillfully sailed toward their nearby island home. The nosy men with large, grotesque, gorilla-type nostrils led me to their round-bellied king, who looked somewhat like a hamburger, and whom the natives humorously called Burger King, because he was the chief authority in their burg. The corpulent Burger King asked me about my history, without me ever learning anything about *his* geography, science, mathematics or sociology.

I described to the obese ruler all that had happened to me on my various voyages since leaving Baghdad, my home city of mystery and enchantment. The fat king's emaciated advisers also listened to my profound recollections. One person in my audience was the emperor's wife, who had big tits, and had grown-up on a prosperous milk farm, so I mentally dubbed Her Majesty 'the Dairy Queen'.

I dined with Burger King and Dairy Queen, and ate their delicious foods, as if I was the main guest at a Boston market. Then, we all gave thanks to Almighty Allah for all His glorious gifts and favors, none of which I could think of, or remember, at the damned time. After the sumptuous meal had been consumed, I left the Burger King and the Dairy Queen's strange company, and strolled-around the avenues of *their* rich, populous city. The marketplaces were well-stocked with food and utilitarian items, and female whores and male-prostitute slaves were being aggressively and openly bartered for coins and paper currency.

'Ah, this is indeed a very pleasant city, just like the Baghdad I remember!' I thought. 'I shall make friends with the people, and perhaps the inhabitants will provide me with a beautiful slut that I could screw and sodomize, until *we* could forget all about the mundane screwing part.'

All of the citizens of this weird land rode exotic thoroughbred horses that had no saddles and bridles. I was curious about that particular weird fact, so I inquired about my perceptive observation, sharing my introspective concerns with the vociferous Burger King. "Oh, your High Ass, er I mean Highness," I began. "How come your riders' horses do not have saddles or any 'saddle lights'. A saddle definitely increases the rider's control and ease; it loosens-up constipation, especially when one vigorously bounces up and down, and a saddle also gets a woman's pussy wet and juicy when her crotch continuously rubs and bumps against it."

"What is a saddle?" the dumbfounded king incredulously asked. "I never saw or used one ever in my restricted, aristocratic life, but since I always have trouble taking daily shits, and since my wife's crack is as dry as the Arabian Desert in the height of summer," the King confided, "I think I could've used one of those saddles you're alluding to, forty or fifty years ago."

"Your Highness; I'll make you a splendid saddle, so that all the imbeciles in your asinine kingdom can accurately and proudly call you Your High Ass just like I do," I jokingly replied. "And after you try it out sitting upon a real horse, you'll undoubtedly say that *it* is definitely much better than having sex."

"Anything is better than sex with my wife's juiceless-useless pussy," the Burger King admittedly regretted. "And if this saddle can alleviate my chronic constipation, I'll be able to sit on the hopper every day like an ordinary commoner, and not just once a week like a suffering monarch, while excreting little hard turds that are more than a *little hard*."

After His Excellency furnished me with some needed wood, the King introduced me to an imaginative carpenter that had colonies of carpenter ants meandering-about inside his pants. I sketched a basic saddle design out onto the wood for the carpenter, who was wiggling around all over the damned workshop, and after the nutcase noticed the drawn stirrups, the itchy asshole told me, "I think I made similar objects for the local gynecologist, and also for Madame Saddam de Sade, who owns the popular local *S and M* parlor."

I sheared some wool from a bleating sheep, and then crafted it into felt that even felt like felt. I next covered the saddle with a rich leather exterior, which I vigorously polished even better than I ever polished my sandals with my feet inside them. Next, I attached the belt, the buckle, and the stirrups, as five-hundred horny women gathered around, asking me embarrassing questions about getting laid with their open legs placed in the stirrups, so that their husbands and lovers could be back in the saddle again.

"You're absolutely right," I chuckled to my female audience. "These splendid, helpful stirrups can be best used when something goes into your pussies, and also when something like a crying baby comes out! Ha, ha, ha!"

Next, I commissioned a non-union blacksmith, at the king's expense, to manufacture bridle bits to my exact specifications, which naturally would complete the prototype saddle's general properties. And so, the highly-versatile, cordial *blacksmith* (whose name was Mohammed Afro-Jones) forged the metal stirrups, buckles and bits that were eventually incorporated into the kingdom's first official saddle and bridle combination.

I asked the King for one of his finest royal Arabian stallions, and after I attached the saddle to the marvelous beast, I led the good-tempered animal over to the 'Royal Pain-in-the-Ass'. The Ruler thanked me for my special ingenuity, and the nincompoop rode the beautiful white creature all around his capital city, erratically bouncing up and down, and happily taking royal diarrhea shits all over the formerly immaculate metropolis. "All systems are go!" the ignoramus kept screaming like an obsessed maniac. "Especially my fuckin' hyperactive, digestive system!" the insane bronco rider kept deliriously repeating like a retarded parrot having dementia.

The king finally had flushed-out his colon along with his semi-colon, while farting most of his hemorrhoids right off his now-hyperactive rectum ring, and the royal fool was so thrilled with his fecal discharges that he rewarded me handsomely for my illustrious contribution to his backwards civilization.

And then, the king's chief adviser examined the marvelous saddle, and the object reminded him of his paramour's fat ass, so the low I.Q. counselor wanted me to make a special one for him, too. And when the other nobles in the court inspected the monarch's impeccable saddle, which resembled a pregnant butterfly, it also reminded them of Dairy Queen's massive ass (which *they* had been frequently porking), so I immediately had more customers that paid me rather prodigious prices for their custom-made "fuck saddles".

So, then I hired both the blacksmith and the carpenter, and *we* were merrily busy, day and night, assembling saddles for all of the brothels and maternity delivery rooms in the whole damned land. Soon, the commoners gave me their life savings, so that they could screw their lovers and their wives more satisfactorily, and I even gained three-hundred-woman (most of them dykes) customers too, who preferred being on top of their mates during their perverted brand of sexual intercourse. After a month of our assiduous labor, little was accomplished, or had been produced, in the fucked-up kingdom, because everyone in the population was always fucking around, but no one, including me, really cared or gave a shit about anything else except getting laid, blown, or sodomized.

Then, one day, I was reading an illustrated pornographic book to the illiterate Burger King when the regal shit-head said to me, "Sindbad; you really know how to sin bad, ha, ha, ha," the faggot cretin profusely and repulsively laughed. "I hold you in great affection. Now you can either receive a wife from me, or be my personal lover!" the Gay Lord exclaimed. "I demand your obedience in this regard, or else you'll be swiftly and promptly executed at dawn."

You can imagine the great consternation, along with the tremendous pressure, I had felt at that unique moment, when I had to immediately make a serious decision. "Oh, my great Gay Lord," I nervously prefaced. "By Allah's invincible will, I owe you much praise and kindness. Indeed, I am one of your humble servants that prefers screwing and sodomizing women rather than to sodomize, or be sodomized, by portly bald men," I reminded the doltish emperor. "Therefore, I would prefer to marry a gorgeous woman, and take her as my sex-starved wife, rather than to have my ass dilated ten times a day by *your* very mediocre salami, that quite honestly, looks more like an abbreviated hot dog."

"Oh, Sindbad; I will see to it that you marry a lovely, intelligent, stunning woman. And next, I'll decree that you'll automatically become a noble citizen of my fabulous land," the Burger King explained. "Then, you can be in the saddle, so to speak, for the rest of your adult*ery* life, residing in my magnificent kingdom that has only a few major laws, the most prominent edict being 'freedom of sex with anyone'."

"Is this woman I have been selected to marry very wealthy, and does she bring me a fantastic dowry?" I innocently asked. "I don't wish to wed a pedestrian, street-walker pauper."

"She's my wife's fucked-up sister, and the whore likes straight sex, even more than I enjoy perverted sex!" the bullshitting king indicated. "And my screwed-up sister-in-law is not a virgin, and she already has had her maidenhead broken on a maiden voyage to Baghdad," the birdbrain emperor roared as the delusional jester gestured, slapping his knees in glee. "You, dear Sindbad, being a sailor, you must really appreciate that fucked-up *naughty*-cal joke! Ha, ha, ha! And after you and she marry, then you both can live with us here in *The Palace,* which as you know, at night is converted into a terrific, spectacular burlesque and vaudeville orgy theater."

I was so flabbergasted that I could not speak. I nodded my head in tacit approval of the dunce-like king's inane proposition, even though that was the first time I had ever been propositioned by a demented Gay Lord' ruler. Finally, I carefully answered, "Oh great Faggot King; your great wish is my command!"

So, the fickle Gay Emperor summoned a Kazi and a Kamikaze, and instructed the two judges to marry me to a charming woman that had already been tested for venereal diseases, and who had been found to have only two types of those nasty maladies. The woman, like her sister, the Queen, owned many dairy farms, estates and very profitable whorehouses throughout the peculiar kingdom, all of which were exempted from paying taxes and tribute to the Imperial Gay Emperor. As a result, all competing houses of prostitution had been economically forced out of business, because the myriad brothels had to pay the hedonistic Burger King ninety percent of their profits in the form of taxes.

I really enjoyed humping and pumping my lovely prearranged spouse, whom I must admit, also gave me fabulous blow-jobs and misogynistic massages, too. I soon forgot about all of the numerous hardships and travails I had experienced as a struggling merchant-mariner, sailing on my many voyages. The Gay King was so grateful sodomizing his faggot advisers in the saddle, which I had diligently manufactured for *his* white Arabian horse that the horny fellow had provided me with my own miniature palace, accompanied by a loyal staff of eunuch slaves and bisexual regal officers, whom I was allowed to discriminately screw economically, physically, and intellectually.

I promised myself, 'When I finally return to Baghdad on the majestic Tigris, I'll *bag* a few whores for my *dad* from this land. Also,' I whimsically thought. 'I'll take my pretty wife to Baghdad to live with me, so that I won't be between Iraq and a hard place for the remainder of my goddamned existence on this totally insane, cryptic planet."

But destiny eventually governs cruelly over every itinerant sailor, and unfortunately, my fate was no exception. One morning, I learned that Almighty Allah had taken the wife of my nearest neighbor. However, the information I had found-out next really scared the shit out of me! I visited next door to comfort and mourn with my tri-sexual neighbor, who naturally was grieving, and very despondent and disconsolate.

"Your wife is presently with Allah," I sympathetically noted to the inconsolable husband. "And now she is enjoying His benevolent mercy, while enjoying eternal sex and suave kindness with others among the deceased. Allah will surely in time grant you another wife with a luscious, wet, pink, juicy pussy," I assured the saddened fellow, "so you should now be rejoicing rather than weeping, you sentimental, asinine asshole!"

But then, my sobbing neighbor revealed something rather extraordinary that almost made my swollen balls pop right off of my body. "Oh, my dear friend," the dimwit sadly answered. "How can I ever enjoy another wife, when I only have one more day left to live? That's not even enough time to jerk-off six times, and be luckily ejaculating five delightful loads!"

261

"What the fuck's the matter with you!" I loudly criticized, quite out-of-character. "You're as healthy as a bull, or as potent as a stud-horse in heat. You are strong, rich, powerful and tri-sexual!" I elaborated. "Surely you can acquire another attractive wife in a jiffy, and then give her many terrific jiffy lubes!"

"My dear straight friend," the sorrowful tri-sexual aristocrat continued his grief. "I swear to you that tomorrow, I will be sentenced to die, and that you will not again see me until *Judgment Day,* when we will both be presented with our virgin harems at that great promised bordello in the sky!" the mental case stated as my upset neighbor pointed to the heavens, which just at that moment happened to be his bedroom ceiling.

"Stop speaking in idiotic and ludicrous riddles, you fucked-up, hysterical buffoon!" I boisterously yelled. "Explain yourself more precisely."

"It is a custom in this Gay Faggot King's land that when a married person dies, his or her spouse will also be buried the next day, so that neither husband nor wife may enjoy life after losing his or her mate," my thoroughly-distraught, fucked-up neighbor divulged. "Only the royal Faggot Burger King is exempt from this heinous law, so that's why the fat prick allows all of his advisers, and every other *burger* with *ham* smeared on his dick-meat, to screw to death *his* wife, the kinky Dairy Queen."

"By Allah!" I shrieked. "This wretched tradition that you've just described is a most horrible law that borders on being bizarrely grotesque. Not one of the Gay King's insubordinate subjects should ever be subjected to it!"

Soon, other mourners arrived at my neighbor's opulent residence; even the pregnant women that were suffering from *mourning sickness.* Some of the sympathizers were skilled morticians that prepared the woman's limp body for proper burial. After setting her perfumed corpse upon the funeral bier, everyone in attendance drank three funeral beers each, and then *we* carried her body outside the city to "the Metropolitan Cemetery'. At a mountainside near the island's end, we pallbearers stopped, dropped the funeral bier onto the ground, and heartily imbibed three more funeral beers each, while bull-shitting and listening to the eternal sea beat its relentless surf upon the jagged rocks.

Then, I was directed to help roll a huge stone, which was specifically designed to secretly conceal a deep, pitiful pit. I peered-down into the dark hollow, and the shaft reminded me of a vertical death tunnel. My perverted mind immediately imagined the perpendicular tunnel to be a giant birth canal in reverse. On the count of three, and with the absence of any ritualistic ceremony, the pallbearers tossed the woman's corpse into the deep pit, and we all heard her body smash against the rocky floor of the cave below.

"We save more funeral bier, casket and cemetery plot expenses that way," one of the more parsimonious funeral attendees confidentially told me. "One must be frugal nowadays, so that one can save his money for good, highly-skilled prostitutes, because nowadays, decent whores that want to do it for free are really fuckin' hard to find."

Next, the zany entourage tethered a rope around the fearful, hysterical husband's waist, and soon lowered the weeping knucklehead down into the oddball subterranean graveyard to be eternally reunited with his dead wife. As was *their* ridiculous custom, the mourners afforded the sentenced husband a jug of fresh water, and seven biscuits, to sustain him until the saddened jerk-off finally reached the outskirts of Heaven.

When the crying fool reached the bottom of the un-scale-able pit, the cavern prisoner obediently untied his loose manacles. The mourners drew back the rope, sealed-up the mouth of the burial grounds with the mammoth stone, drank three more quarts of beers each, and then the drunken fools returned to the sprawling, decadent city. I stayed behind to pray for my dear neighbor's soul, and to study reality, and wish-upon the awesome, eternal sea.

"By Allah," I cried and sobbed. "This certainly is a terrible way to die." 'Holy tits!' I thought and realized. 'If my wife the Dairy Queen's sister dies, this same insane bullshit is gonna' fuckin' happen to me!'

I ambled back into the king's exotic, erotic city and sought-out His Majesty, whom I found sitting upon his palace bathroom throne, taking his standard royal dump. I was quite disenchanted with the marriage/death law that *his* imperial government had been requiring and enforcing. Finally, I broke his serious concentration and asked the pecker-head a germane question.

"Oh, my Faggot Imperial Lord; why do you bury the living with the dead?" I asked.

"It's a lot cheaper that way," the sanctimonious Gay King glumly remarked. "We obviously don't have to maintain two separate cemeteries; one for the dead and one for the living. I must balance my friggin' fiscal budget every damned year, ya' know! I need more budgetary revenues for expenditures that are especially earmarked for royal pleasure, and for regal entertainment!"

"No, Your Highness," I attempted to clarify. "Why does an implausible law exist in your land where the living spouse must be buried with his or her deceased marriage partner? The law seems to defy all morality!"

"Sindbad," the Gay Monarch very deliberately replied. "You're now referring to an ancient custom handed-down from my island's sacred *dead* ancestors. When a husband or wife dies, the spouse must die too, leaving the entire estate to the king. How the fuck do ya' think I can stay so rich and maintain such an opulent and decadent lifestyle?" the incensed emperor lividly maintained. "And besides, Asshole; the husband and wife can be reunited in the afterlife. It works-out well for them too, but most of all, it works-out well for me!"

"Oh, noble Faggot King; if the wife of a foreigner such as I Sindbad should fall ill and perish," I hypothesized and lucidly stated, "would I then predictably be buried the same day with my wife, even though I had come from another land?"

"It's sure as hell, you would," the king abruptly indicated. "And why not? Why should a dumb ass like *you* inherit my sister-in-law's great wealth, when you weren't even fuckin' born anywhere near my wondrous kingdom? Sindbad; are you some kind of ambitious, parasitic gigolo or what?"

When I heard the Queer King's verification of my worst-case scenario, my nuts shriveled-up to the size of raisins, and my dick nearly turned inside-out. My mind became dizzy and dazed, and I giddily felt trapped inside the horrid massive jail cell, commonly known as my Gay Emperor's kingdom. I frenetically rushed-out of the opulent palace with my mind in a complete stupor, wishing that I had never dreamed of owning a chain of fucked-up hamburger taverns in the fucked-up Burger King's shitty-assed country.

'I don't want my wife to die, and then me having to be buried alive next to her,' I feared. 'Who the hell wants to have sex with his dead wife? It's bad enough to have it when she's fuckin' alive. Maybe I'll get my dick and balls caught in some kind of jerking-off machine having moving parts,' I speculated, 'and I'll luckily and gladly die first, before my wife gives-up the ghost! Oh Allah, please show me such a splendid, God-sent, masturbation machine when I am ninety-nine years old, and will be an elderly fuck, too old and weak to ever fuck again!'

I then intentionally distracted my already-confused mind from further contemplating the uncivilized marriage/death law by occupying myself', essentially performing certain mundane daily tasks and chores. But a month later, my native-born wife became ill while losing four pints of blood having her daily period, and then she unexpectedly died two days later.

Now, I was scared anxious, paranoid, neurotic and pissed-off beyond belief, all at the same time. The Burger King and his wife, the Dairy Queen, came to my small palace to console me in regard to the death of my spouse, and in regard to reminding me of my awaiting fate. I felt like cutting all of their balls, dicks and tits off with my trusty scimitar, but there were two-dozen distressed mourners present to successfully kill everyone, without eventually sacrificing my already-doomed life, too. 'I want to feed the king's puny nuts to the local squirrels and have the creatures violently fight-over their inadequate meal!' I vengefully imagined.

The women then cleansed and perfumed my wife's body, which remarkably was still having its period even after her untimely death. She was lavishly dressed in a white gown, and expensive golden necklaces and bracelets adorned her neck and arms. Then, the contrite trite mourners all drank myriad beers, lifted-up her bier, and transported my dead spouse to the distant mountain having the aforementioned macabre cave cemetery. The funeral procession halted, dropped the bier upon the ground, and the participants drank three more beers each, but I wasn't the least bit thirsty. I felt like I had to condemn the assholes for wanting to lower and deposit my valued ass into the morbid death pit.

"Almighty Allah had never instituted such a despicable law as the one you evilly practice and adhere to," I futilely protested. "And I absolutely hate your wicked custom. Had I known about its practice, I would've remained single, and would've been perfectly content screwing the poop out of the Dairy Queen's rich sister, along with ten thousand other horny whores who practice humping-and-pumping their asses off on this damned remote, Allah-forsaken-peninsula!"

"Ha, ha, ha!" the thoroughly-amused Burger King indulgently laughed, inspiring his entire funeral procession-entourage to imitate his inane zaniness in a 'Chameleon Behavior Effect'. "Only stupid men find-out too late that marriage is always a death trap, no matter who the fuck dies first!" the egocentric ruler cruelly ridiculed.

After dumping my wife's body into the deep pit, the muscular funeral bier carriers then grabbed my arms, tied me up against my will (I didn't actually need *a will* because the Burger King would automatically acquire my small palace and savings, anyway), and then the robotic assholes slowly lowered me into the dark hollow, along with a jug of fresh water and seven dry biscuits. When I finally had been descended to the bottom of the hundred-foot-deep cave, the attendees yelled for me to untie myself', so that my parsimonious 'executioners by default' could pull-up the rope to use it again.

"Fuck you, you cheap, niggardly bastards!" I screamed-up. "The fuckin' rope stays down here with me!" my voice echoed.

"Up your peasant-class, lowlife yazoo, Sindbad!" the cowardly Burger King hollered-down. "You're at the end of your rope anyway, you dumb, misguided, idealistic jerk-off!"

The heavy rope was tossed-down, and it nearly knocked me unconscious when its mass, in the dark, landed directly onto my head. Next, the cruel sadists rolled the enormous stone in front of the pit, sealing me inside the macabre graveyard without a damned hint or clue as how to escape.

Sufficient dim light existed for me to peruse my immediate surroundings, which were very unpleasant to see and to smell. The stenchy cavern was full of decayed and rotting bodies, with many male skeletons situated on top of female anatomies. Apparently, the husbands had endeavored screwing their deceased wives, or former girlfriends outside of marriage, one final time. The underground cavern's air was full of a putrid odor emanating from the numerous stench-laden corpses, and I heard the groans and moans of the dying off in the distance, instinctively electing to enjoy sex with new-found partners, one final time before predictably expiring into the opaque afterworld.

'By Allah,' I thought. 'I deserve such an ignoble death, since I've been a complete fucked-up asshole my entire life!' I penitently concluded. 'I'm so depressed that I don't even feel like penetrating my wife's cold, perfumed, cleansed pussy, still having its period. And to think of how totally fucked-up I've been all my damned errant life, before ever arriving at this entirely fucked-up burial place! It's the absolute pits!'

I sorrowfully meditated and wept about my unbearable misfortune for a long time. 'Oh Allah, the Glorious; Oh Allah, the Great!' I solemnly prayed. 'You have allowed me to escape one catastrophe after another, and I now beseech You, to permit me to survive this inhuman tribulation, so that I may escape this fucked-up land and screw normal women with hairy pink pussies back in wonderful Baghdad! Please spare me of this impending, miserable, demoralizing, uncivilized, and humiliating death!'

I cursed the Devil and praised Allah, hoping for either a miracle or for instant salvation. I threw myself onto a heap of bones, rubbed my crotch against them, and could not even get a boner. I prayed for Death to envelop me, but even the formidable Fiend appeared to be on vacation. I was besieged with hunger and thirst, so I felt around for the biscuits, ate one of them that happened to be covered with insects, and surprisingly, the damned bugs tasted much better than the small cake I had swallowed. I quenched my dire thirst by avariciously gulping-down several mouthfuls of stagnant water from the jug I had been provided.

I stood, and then in the shadowy recesses, explored the extensive cavern, discovering many small side caves, but none leading anywhere, except to Death. Hideous corpses, skeletons and raunchy-smelling, decaying flesh were everywhere. Many now-brittle bones from ancient times had broken-off from their owners' anatomies. I finally crawled into a small, secluded cave, where I gingerly curled- up into the classic fetal position, and soundly slept from exhaustion.

Three days later, after my food supply had become depleted, I searched-around, and avariciously pilfered several stale cakes from other more-feeble, defenseless, dying victims that had also been doomed to be buried with their wives. 'I hope my meager supplies don't run-out before I expire,' I prayed. 'I don't want to die from starvation. Perhaps Allah will mercifully rescue me from this horrid, relentless, Devil's environment!'

After I had consumed my final cake, a startling thing happened. The stone was again rolled back, and another deceased man was thrown-down to his grave. Then a gorgeous woman was lowered with fresh biscuits, and a new water jug. I carefully watched her weeping from my secluded corner of the cave, and the beautiful lady did not suspect my presence while enduring her burdensome grief. Soon, the enormous stone was rolled back, and the cursed cave was dark once more. 'This part of the King's burg is the absolute pits!' I despairingly reckoned. 'Maybe its original name was Pittsburgh.'

Then, I inexplicably turned into a wanton madman. I rapturously raped the frightened woman, and pumped her pussy dry before irrigating her hot receptive honey-well with warm semen from this lustful seaman. Then, when she asked me for more sex to comfort her overwhelming grief, I reached for and lifted a huge utilitarian thighbone, and banged her over the head three consecutive times with the solid femur. The demanding wife moaned, groaned and then went unconscious.

I found a nearby corpse buried inside a sack. I removed the covering, and then greedily gathered-up all of the necklaces, bracelets, rings, gems, trinkets, and jewelry that the deceased had been wearing when she had been conveniently buried. I conveyed my new food supply, and my pilfered acquisitions, to the remote side cave, where I greedily ate and covetously felt my booty sack, and alternately rubbed my scrotum sac. 'I must survive, escape, and live, so that I can be a rich, nasty bastard just like the bastard Burger King,' I pondered. 'Then I could tell the damned Devil to go fuck himself' up the ass with his ugly red dick!'

Every time a live spouse had been lowered into the abominable mass tomb, I killed him or her, and confiscated the jewelry, the biscuits, and the damned putrid water. I was going insane from greed, murder, and an obsessive lust for life and sex. I benevolently rescued the first beautiful woman I had knocked unconscious, and shared my biscuits, dick and water (and she shared her biscuits, buns, pussy and tits) in exchange for standard, straight, subterranean sex. I promised the still-dazed, disheveled, and beleaguered wife that I would find and kill the scumbag bastard that had knocked her silly with the solid femur bone.

"How do you know that someone hit me over the head and knocked me silly with a solid femur bone?" the buried-alive wife boldly and surprisingly asked.

"I saw in the dim shadows the nefarious scumbag-bastard do the brutal deed to you," I lied. "But at the time, I was too damned weak and disabled to stand upright, let alone fight him to the death."

"Okay, show me that nifty sixty-nine position again!" the woman pleaded, entirely forgetting about her dead husband; his dead dick, and the phantom molester wielding the solid femur bone.

One night, I was awakened from my slumber by something mysteriously scratching and digging inside the cavern. I raised my trusty femur bone, left my snoring female companion, who was sleeping soundly, and cautiously advanced toward the noise's origin. I perceived a wild beast, similar to a wolf' in its habitual mannerisms, and my fatigued legs pursued the wild animal to an extremity of the cavern. Suddenly, my pupils perceived points of light coming from the night sky, and I immediately recognized the sparkles as being twinkling stars in the *Orion* constellation, which I knew would be, at *that* particular position, in the night firmament. There were crevices formed in the cave's rocks, and never before had I enjoyed a mere hole in the Earth more than I cherished a woman's hairy slit tunnel.

The cavern's crack was indeed better than a woman's furry pussy, and the hungry wolf-like creature had penetrated through the narrow opening with its entire body. I strenuously labored, making the newly-discovered aperture wider, and soon, it was big enough to allow a human of my muscular size to crawl through. Then, I proceeded back to my secret hiding place, caressed the sleeping woman's tits, but regrettably, squirted a semen discharge all over her already-white face in a premature ejaculation, when she (in her rapturous sleep) thereafter, sucked on my stiff wet pulsating erection. The woman instantly awakened, and next I carried my booty sack, and roughly led the buried-alive wife to the newly-located and expanded cavern tunnel, which we each individually, and easily, squeezed through.

My lady companion and I rested upon the mountain's grassy slope, overlooking the inviting salty sea. We were exhausted from our arduous ordeal, but overjoyed at our escape from the morose pit.

"Look," I stated to the attractive female, whose comely face I could then see. "There's enough jewelry in this sack to buy a chain of hamburger joints, or barbecue beef' greasy spoons, in any other country!"

"You've sinfully stolen from the dead?" my wonderful, new female associate asked in a shocked-but-sanctimonious tone of voice. "Are you an accomplished thief?"

"Why should I not? These gems and expensive golden items would only go to waste and rust underground back there in that hideous mass cemetery!" I convincingly and sternly argued. "If you're smart and practical, you'll permit me to share them with you in our happy future life."

"You're smarter than the average wolf or bear, I must say," the knockout lady complimented with a facial blush. "Just give me back the articles that originally belonged to me, and I'll verify your complete story, whatever your crazy tale may be, to anyone in authority that challenges or disbelieves it."

"We'll camp-out on this campy mountain underneath the celestial stars," I suggested to my new woman friend. "Perhaps a passing ship will spot us before the smallpox will spot us."

I had in my travels committed numerous other ungodly atrocities, short of cannibalism, just to stay alive. Each week, I re-entered the cave and used my trusty femur weapon to club a recently buried-alive victim. Then, I would eagerly steal his or her biscuits and water for sustenance, and his or her jewelry for prospective wealth, for both me and my grateful lady friend to later sell or barter.

One late spring day, I observed a merchant ship sailing upon the eastern horizon. I removed my woman companion's dirty white tunic and wildly waved it in the air, realizing that the sailors would come in response to a naked woman's body first, and to my animated distress signal second. The mariners quickly noticed us perched upon the steep mountain slope, and sent-out a salvage boat to investigate.

"Who are you?" the bewildered crewmen's leader bellowed. "We have never before seen any adventurous human standing on this treacherous slope!"

"I am the famous Sindbad of Baghdad," I proudly answered. "And this is my humble wife. We were stranded here by ruthless road bandits, but then I killed them all with my bare hands; cut their testicles off with my scimitar, and tossed their scumbag bodies into the eternal sea."

"Holy shit!" one of the impressed rowers hollered-up to us. "Sindbad the Sailor! You're very acclaimed all over the world! Your fabulous reputation and exploits indeed precede you! You're even more famous in these remote parts than fuckin' Popeye the Sailor Man! You even make Popeye seem wimpy! Do you stick your sore dick in olive oil?"

My new wife and I hopped-down into the sturdy rowboat, and we were speedily transported to the mariner's merchant ship. Once the captain found-out my identity, the head-honcho warmly shook my hands, and immediately forgot all about his diabolical intentions of fondling, molesting, porking, and sodomizing my newly-acquired, subterranean cemetery wife.

"Could I offer you some pearls and diamonds in exchange for safely being conducted to Baghdad?" I inquired as I jiggled my sack containing valuable rings, necklaces, trinkets, and bracelets into the thoroughly-amused captain's face.

The captain admirably rose above the strong temptation I had offered. "Sindbad; I would never fuck with anyone who possesses your famed international repute," the sea boss laughed. "And if we are attacked by pirates near a dangerous place known as Pittsburgh, I am sure that even their hemorrhoids would shrink back, once the lawless buccaneers learned of *your* noble, renowned name."

"Thank you, my lord, for safely rescuing us from the gruesome mountain overlooking the sea," I gratefully acknowledged. "And if you please, show my wife and me to a comfortable cabin where we can get washed-up, and have some decent food and sex in privacy."

"It is our fucked-up custom that whenever we find a shipwrecked man, it is our duty to feed and clothe' him, and then take the lucky prick to his native port," the captain disclosed. "But quite truthfully, Sindbad, this is the first time I've ever picked-up together a stranded man and a stranded woman! I must pray to Allah for some new instructional guidance!"

My new wife and I again graciously thanked the addled captain for his assistance, and also for his benign generosity. We entered our designated cabin; ate a decent meal; had fantastic sex, and when I exited to fetch a pitcher of fresh water, I witnessed eight sailors eavesdropping with their left ears pressed against inverted glasses on the side of our ship's quarters, while intensively jerking-off with their right hands. When I returned to the room with the fresh water, my new mistress and I prayed to Allah on behalf of the merciful captain and his jerk-off crew, and then we got it on again.

As we passed by the Burger King's coastal metropolis, my new mistress and I both gave the pompous Gay Emperor of the land, and his arrogant Dairy Queen wife, the royal double fingers. The ship voyaged to the Island of Bell, and next it sailed onward to Kala near the land of Hind, where *hind*sight was always better than foresight. Hind was famous for its *rattan* and camphor marketplace, which incidentally had been constructed out of those rare materials, because dishonest furniture salesmen had *bamboo*zled the city's gullible dwellers. The next destination stop on our journey was Al Basrah, and finally, the ancient ship sailed up the Tigris and next, docked and anchored at Baghdad.

"What are you going to do with your magnificent treasure trove?" my very curious mistress asked.

"I'll give a ten percent donation to all of the Fakirs, and to all of the mangy Mother-Fakirs in Baghdad," I facetiously informed my impostor spouse. "And some of my fantastic fortune I'll use to establish a viable hamburger restaurant chain, just to spite the deplorable Gay Burger King, whose dominion we had just escaped. And when I've exhausted the remainder of my diminishing fortune, buying extravagant and lavish gifts for both you and me, Shahrazad," I continued my sacred and somber pledge, "I shall sell you into slavery to a tiny-dicked king, and soon return to the sea for more superb adventures, wild sex, and valuable plunder."

About the Author

Jay Dubya is author John Wiessner's initials (J.W.) and also his pen name. John is a retired New Jersey public school English teacher and he has taught the subject for thirty-four years. John lives in southern New Jersey with wife Joanne, and the couple has three grown sons.

Jay Dubya has written other adult literature besides *Mauled Maimed Mangled Mutilated Mythology*. *Black Leather and Blue Denim, A '50s Novel* and its sequel, *The Great Teen Fruit War, A 1960' Novel* are humorous literary endeavors. *Frat Brats', A 60s Novel* completes Jay Dubya's action/adventure trilogy.

Pieces of Eight, *Pieces of Eight, Part II, Pieces of Eight Part III and Pieces of Eight, Part IV* are' short story/novella collections featuring science fiction, paranormal and humorous plots and themes. *Nine New Novellas* is the companion book to *Nine New Novellas, Part II, Nine New Novellas, Part III and Nine New Novellas, Part IV*, and the four story-collections are written in the same style as the four *Pieces of Eight* books. And, *So Ya' Wanna' Be A Teacher* is a satirical autobiography describing the author's thirty-four-year educational career in American public schools.

Ron Coyote, Man of La Mangia is adult humor and the work is an imaginative satire/parody on Miguel Cervantes' *Don Quixote*, published in 1605. *The Wholly Book of Genesis* and *The Wholly Book of Exodus* are also adult satirical humor. *Thirteen Sick Tasteless Classics*, *Thirteen Sick Tasteless Classics, Part II*, *Thirteen Sick Tasteless Classics, Part III and Thirteen Sick Tasteless Classics, Part IV* are adult satirical rewrites of famous short fiction.

John has also authored a trilogy of young adult fantasy novels, *Enchanta*, *Pot of Gold* and *Space Bugs, Earth Invasion*. *The Eighteen' Story Gingerbread House* is a new collection of eighteen diverse and creative children's stories.

Jay Dubya likes '50s rock and roll music, and he also enjoys pop' songs by the Beach Boys, Beatles, Fleetwood Mac, the Eagles, the Rolling Stones, *ELO,* John Mellencamp and by John Fogerty. When not writing stories or listening to music Jay Dubya likes watching *76ers* basketball and *Phillies* and *Yankees* television baseball games.

Author Biography

Born in Hammonton, NJ in 1942, John Wiessner had attended St. Joseph School up to and including Grade 5. After his family moved from Hammonton to Levittown, Pa in 1954, John attended St. Mark School in Bristol, Pa. for Grade 6, St. Michael the Archangel School in Levittown for Grades 7 and 8 and then Immaculate Conception School, Levittown, Pa. for Grade 9. Bishop Egan High School, Levittown Pa was John's educational base for Grades 10 and 11, and later in 1960, the aspiring author graduated from Edgewood Regional High, Tansboro, NJ. John then next attended Glassboro State College, where the future author was an announcer for the school's baseball games and also read the nightly news and sports over WGLS, GSC's radio station.

John Wiessner had been primarily an English teacher in the Hammonton Public School System for 34 years, specializing in the instruction of middle school language arts. Mr. Wiessner was quite active in the Hammonton Education Association, serving in the capacities of Vice-President, building representative and finally, teachers' head negotiator for 7 years. During his lengthy teaching career, John had been nominated into "Who's Who Among American Teachers" three times. He also was quite active giving professional workshops at schools around South Jersey on the subjects of creative writing and the use of movie videos to motivate students to organize their classroom theme compositions.

John Wiessner was very active in community service, being a past President of the Hammonton Lions Club, where he also functioned for many years as the club's Tail-Twister, Vice-President and also Liontamer. John had been named Hammonton Lion of the Year in 1979, and in 2009, the community helper earned the prestigious Melvin Jones Fellow Award, which is the highest honor that a Lion can receive from Lions International.

John also was a successful businessman, starting with being a Philadelphia Bulletin newspaper delivery boy for two years in the late 1950s in Levittown, Pennsylvania. After his family moved back to New Jersey in 1959, John worked at his grandparents and his parents' farm markets, Square Deal Farm (now Ron's Gardens in Hammonton) and Pete's Farm Market in Elm, respectively. He later managed his wife's parents' farm market, White Horse Farms in Elm for three summers.

Also, in a business capacity, for 16 summers starting in 1967 John Wiessner had co-owned Dealers Choice Amusement Arcade on the Ocean City, Maryland boardwalk and also co-owned the New Horizon Tee-Shirt

Store for eight summers (1973-'81) on the Rehoboth Beach, Delaware boardwalk. In addition, "Jay Dubya" was a co-owner of Wheel and Deal Amusement Arcade, Missouri Avenue and Boardwalk, Atlantic City. And then, for 18 summers beginning in 1986, John had been the Field Manager in charge of crew-leaders for Atlantic Blueberry Company (the world's largest cultivated blueberry farm), both the Weymouth and Mays Landing Divisions.

After retiring from teaching in 1999, writing under the pen name Jay Dubya (his initials), John Wiessner became the author of 59 books in the genre Action/Adventure Novels, Sci-Fi/Paranormal Story Collections, Adult Satire, Young Adult Fantasy Novels and Non-Fiction Books. His books exist in hardcover, in paperback and in popular Kindle and Nook e-book formats.

Most recently, John Wiessner (Jay Dubya) has been recognized by Marquis Who's Who in America for outstanding community service, book writing, public school teaching, and business activity, and Who's Who has chosen John as being one of nine national recipients to be honored with "Lifetime Achievement Awards", and then featured in a major Wall Street Journal article.

Google: Jay Dubya books

www.ingramcontent.com/pod-product-compliance
Lightning Source LLC
Chambersburg PA
CBHW060249100726
47907CB00003B/821